THE DOOLITTLE IRONY

THE DOOLITTLE IRONY

Jim Kelly

Columbus, Ohio

This book is a work of fiction. The names, characters and events in this book are the products of the author's imagination or are used fictitiously. Any similarity to real persons living or dead is coincidental and not intended by the author.

The Doolittle Irony

Published by Gatekeeper Press
2167 Stringtown Rd, Suite 109
Columbus, OH 43123-2989
www.GatekeeperPress.com

Copyright © 2019 by Jim Kelly

All rights reserved. Neither this book, nor any parts within it may be sold or reproduced in any form or by any electronic or mechanical means, including information storage and retrieval systems without permission in writing from the author. The only exception is by a reviewer, who may quote short excerpts in a review.

ISBN (paperback): 9781642376142
eISBN: 9781642376135

Printed in the United States of America

In the spring of 1942 the US Government imprisoned 120,000 Japanese-Americans because it said they could not be trusted to defend America. Wouldn't it have been ironic had the famous Doolittle Raid on Tokyo succeeded only because of the heroism of one of those Japanese-Americans? In fact, that just <u>might</u> have been the case!

Disclaimer

This book is a meld of fact and imagination, a "could-have-happened" tale spun against the social and political backdrop of the early World War II period. The author has attempted to keep the story authentic and the accounts of Pearl Harbor, Doolittle's Raid, the Battle of Midway, and the internment of Japanese-Americans are basically factual. The roles of the major political and military figures portrayed—FDR, Admiral King, Admiral Halsey, etc.—are also in keeping with the historical record, but their specific actions and conversations are imagined as a literary device to tell the story. Similarly, lesser known figures—Commander Rochefort, Captain Buckmaster, and General DeWitt, etc.—are real and their roles in this story, though imagined, are modeled on their characters as portrayed in biographies and other reference material. Other story characters—Hiro, his family, Captain High, Lieutenant Russo, Kathleen, Imhoff, Stanley, Mama-san, and the various lesser characters—are wholly imagined.

Acknowledgements

Many people helped me write this book. Principal among them is my elder daughter, Beth, who offered excellent criticism, produced numerous copies of drafts for others to read, and pushed me along to publication. I am likewise indebted to Lela Gilbert, a professional writer and Fellow at the Hudson Institute, who read my manuscript, liked it, and offered counsel on making it better. I also thank my classmates at the Osher Life-Long Learning Institute who encouraged my writing and pressed me to put my ideas into the form of a novel. Thanks also to my many friends and relatives who kindly read various drafts and offered far-too-kindly critiques.

Dedication

This book, as well as most of the good things in my life, I owe to Donna, my wife of nearly 60 years. She never complained about the excessive time I took to write this book. She read draft after draft with never a negative comment, and she delivered innumerable sandwiches to the family den where I holed up to write. She is the kindest person I have ever met.

On a different level, I dedicate this book to the Japanese-American men and women who were unjustly interned during World War II, but who rose above their tormentors and remained true to the United States, their adopted country.

About the Author

Jim Kelly spent a career as an intelligence officer for the Navy, the Defense Intelligence Agency, the CIA, and as a private consultant. He has lived in and traveled through the Western Pacific and West Coast of America, the settings for this book. He has a BA from the University of Pittsburgh, a Masters from American University, and is a graduate of the National Defense University.

CONTENTS

Introduction 13
Prelude 15

Chapter 1   The Beginnings 19
Chapter 2   War Clouds 37
Chapter 3   All Because of Mama-San 46
Chapter 4   Pearl Harbor Plans 56
Chapter 5   The Voyage to Tokyo: Off and On 65
Chapter 6   Japanese Intentions 74
Chapter 7   The Voyage to Japan 87
Chapter 8   Yoshikawa and the Hikawa Maru 98
Chapter 9   Hiro Aboard the Hikawa Maru 109
Chapter 10   Leading up to Pearl Habor 125
Chapter 11   Yoshikawa Acts Again 131
Chapter 12   Back Home 139
Chapter 13   Yoshikawa Detained 145
Chapter 14   In Japan 153
Chapter 15   Back Home 167
Chapter 16   Ogawa's Pitch 171
Chapter 17   Tension in Crawford 182
Chapter 18   Turning the Prisoner 188
Chapter 19   Pearl Harbor 194
Chapter 20   Reaction 201
Chapter 21   Following the Attack 207
Chapter 22   Looking for Revenge 217
Chapter 23   War Hysteria 224

Chapter 24	At Sea aboard Picket Ship #23	228
Chapter 25	The Tokyo Raid Takes Shape	232
Chapter 26	Internment	237
Chapter 27	Bound for Tokyo	245
Chapter 28	The Raid	255
Chapter 29	Internment Hits Home	274
Chapter 30	Good Luck and God Bless	281
Chapter 31	Internment Begins	288
Chapter 32	Escape to China	293
Chapter 33	Escape to Hawaii	298
Chapter 34	Camp Harmony	305
Chapter 35	Damage Control	311
Chapter 36	On the Homefront	322
Chapter 37	Incentivizing Hiro	325
Chapter 38	In the U.S. Navy	342
Chapter 39	Dawning Reality	359
Chapter 40	Cards on the Table	363
Chapter 41	Midway Looms	368
Chapter 42	Good News	370
Chapter 43	Kathleen Arrives	375
Chapter 44	Disappointment Back Home	380
Chapter 45	Midway Takes Shape	386
Chapter 46	The Engagement Party	393
Chapter 47	Midway: The Most Significant Naval Battle of WWII	405
Chapter 48	The Aftermath	421
Chapter 49	75 Years Later	443

| Epilogue | 471 |
| Bibliography | 473 |

Patriotism is supporting your country all the time,
and your government when it deserves it.

—Mark Twain

INTRODUCTION

In the spring of 1942, America's morale was at low ebb. The Japanese had rolled up a series of dramatic military victories at Pearl Harbor, Guam, Wake, the Philippines, and elsewhere. Reeling in defeat, America feared that an invasion of Hawaii or perhaps even the West Coast may be next. A U.S. victory was sorely needed to boost national morale.

To provide that boost, President Roosevelt authorized the Pacific Fleet to conduct a daring raid on the Japanese homeland. Vice Admiral William "Bull" Halsey was directed to lead a naval task force secretly to the ocean area just east of Japan, launch a surprise air strike on Tokyo, and then quickly withdraw before the Imperial Japanese Navy could retaliate. Jimmy Doolittle, a popular American aviator, was assigned to organize and lead the air strikes. He would achieve surprise by employing a risky tactic never before used—and he would succeed.

The raid was executed with daring, courage, and a lot of luck. Halsey's Task Force crossed the Pacific undetected to about 650 miles west of Tokyo. There, however, a Japanese picket boat sighted Halsey's carriers and radioed a contact report to its headquarters. Realizing his task force had been discovered, Halsey directed Doolittle to launch his attack aircraft immediately, despite being well short of the planned launch point. The bombers caught Tokyo's air defenses by surprise. Without loss of a single plane, they bombed Tokyo and escaped toward their planned recovery airfields in China, while the carrier task force from which they had launched escaped unharmed

INTRODUCTION

back to Hawaii. America had its dramatic victory. It had retaliated in kind for Pearl Harbor.

But it might have been different. The daring victory might have become just another cruel defeat had it not been for simple good luck and, possibly, the actions of one young Nisei (a second generation Japanese-American). He claimed that while visiting Japan before the war began, he had been unwillingly drafted into the Imperial Japanese Navy, despite being an American citizen. Due to the most unusual of circumstances, he was on the scene as the raid unfolded and saw an opportunity to aid the American force. His actions may well have saved the day for Doolittle.

The young Nisei's story was never made public, perhaps because it was so unlikely or perhaps because, in the context of 1942, it would have been politically embarrassing to admit that a young man of Japanese descent saved the American attack on Tokyo. The young man's actions did not reach print until many years later when it appeared as a fragmentary remembrance in a WWII battle memoir.[1] It's probably now too late to verify the story. Time has passed, memories faded, and many of those with firsthand knowledge of the matter have died. Nevertheless, just the possibility that this young Nisei MIGHT have told the truth was enough to inspire this book.

---

[1] *HUMBLE HEROES, How the USS Nashville CL43 Fought WWII*, Steven George Bustin, Copyright 2007, ISBN: 1-4196-5884-0, E-Book ISBN: 978-1-4392-8904-4

PRELUDE

AT SEA, FAR FROM HOME

The little ship lifted its prow sharply skyward and climbed the mountain of dark green water rushing beneath it. At the top it slowed, briefly held there by the icy 30-knot wind blowing against its bow, then tipped precariously forward and plunged down into the icy Pacific darkness on the back side of the wave.

Hiro tried to catch his crypto pad as it slid past him off the desk of the radio shack and onto the deck where other papers sloshed about. But just as he thought he had it, the *Nitto Maru #23* smashed its prow into the trough of water at the base of the wave. Hiro was thrown roughly against the radio equipment and the ship shuddered along its entire length, rivets strained and deck plates creaked. Then the little ship began laboriously to raise its prow from beneath the tons of water under which it had just been buried. As the prow righted, tons of green water rushed down the *Nitto Maru's* length, shearing off anything not battened down. For a few brief seconds the ship leveled and only the roar of the gale force winds could be heard. Then the next 30-foot wave arrived and the tumultuous cycle began all over. The weather had raged like this for several days, and Hiro wondered how much more of this pounding the little ship could take.

The *Nitto Maru* had originally been a fishing boat, designed with the expectation that its master would seek shelter during weather like this. But that was before the Imperial Japanese Navy

PRELUDE

attacked Pearl Harbor, and before Japan chose to employ the Nitto Maru to guard against the threat of American retaliation. Admiral Isoroku Yamamoto, the naval officer thought of as the "father" of the attack on Pearl Harbor, had spent several tours as a naval attaché in the United States. He had studied at Harvard, learned to play an astute hand of poker, and was convinced that America's frontier spirit would not allow it to accept defeat easily. He was convinced it would retaliate for Pearl Harbor, possibly in kind. Considering that Tokyo sat along Japan's East Coast, it seemed a likely target for a surprise aerial attack launched from American aircraft carriers. Indeed, America would consider a surprise attack on Tokyo as tit-for-tat ironic justice.

Yamamoto issued an order to prepare for such a strike. It began with the Japanese proverb, "After victory, tighten your helmet strap." Air raid drills were instituted. Japanese aircraft patrolled the Pacific waters east of Japan looking for American warships, and 170 small ships like the *Nitto Maru* were impressed into service from Japan's fishing and coastal fleets. The Japanese Navy dubbed them picket boats and gave each a number–the Nitto Maru was #23—then outfitted each with a few small guns and radios. The boats were deployed to form a cordon strung along the country's East Coast 600—700 nautical miles out to sea. Their mission was to provide warning of approaching American warships, so they stayed on station regardless of the gale force winds. From the standpoint of the Imperial Japanese Navy, if a few sank they could be easily replaced. As for the crews, their deaths would be ennobled by the tradition of *Bushido*, Japan's warrior code that glorified dying for the Emperor.

Hiro knew little of *Bushido* and certainly did not intend to die for the Japanese Emperor. Why would he? He was an American! True, he was an American of Japanese descent, but nevertheless a true red-white-and-blue American. He had been raised in a small town near Seattle, attended American public schools, loudly sang the American National Anthem before baseball games (to the embarrassment of his Caucasian friends), and had registered proudly for the draft. How could a man with that background possibly have come to be a crewman aboard a ship of the Imperial Japanese Navy?

THE DOOLITTLE IRONY

The situation was certainly not of Hiro's choosing. His presence aboard *Picket Boat #23* was the product of a misadventure so incredible that it was painful for him to recall. Worse, it had come about because of his naiveté. If only he had exercised simple common sense, he might be home now with his family, near the girl he loved. Instead, he was a hostage crewman aboard an enemy ship, soaking wet, bone cold, physically exhausted, emotionally drained, woefully homesick, and in fear of his life. His situation was desperate—and would only get worse.

CHAPTER 1

THE BEGINNINGS

It was the spring of 1941 when Hiro and his family came to the fateful decision that set all of this in motion. Hiro Yamada was a "Nisei," the son of Japanese immigrants. He was 22 and about to graduate from an engineering program at the University of Washington. The family—Hiro, his parents and two younger sisters—had just sat down for the evening meal at the table in the center of their house. The food was Japanese, but the table was typically American with conventional kitchen chairs. Like most of the family's life, meals were an amalgam of East and West.

After polite exchanges in Japanese about each other's day, Hiro's mother turned to him and asked in broken English with exaggerated nonchalance, "Why you stay late at college so much?"

Hiro winced inwardly. Mama use of English was a bad omen. She spoke only Japanese at home so her children would develop fluency in her native tongue. After all, they spoke English outside the home all day. They even signed their names in the western fashion, with the given one appearing first and the surname last. That was the opposite of the way Mama had learned, and a regrettable concession to American custom in her estimate.

"Mama-san," Hiro replied deliberately, "As you know, I have finals coming up. I've joined a study group and it meets after class. So I can't come home at the usual time," His tone took on an edge,

CHAPTER 1

"Finals will be hard. I have to study." He paused for effect then added, "I know you want me to do well." Hiro like to stress the need to "do well" when talking with Mama-san. It appealed to her work ethic.

She seemed to relent a bit but, after reflection, commented dourly, "Books same at home as college."

Mama-san loved that elementary and high schools here in America were free for her children, and she was quite proud that Hiro had done so well in them and was able to go on to college. Indeed there was much about America that was good, but there was also much that was frivolous. She worried that "study groups"—whatever they were—were frivolous. Her given name was Hanaco, meaning rose, and like any rose, she included a few thorns. Mama-san was small, wiry, less than five feet in height, 98 lbs. in weight, and tough as nails.

Hiro knew Mama-san would not end the conversation there. She had her own agenda, and it stemmed from the fact that he was the only son in a society that practiced primogeniture, the custom of the oldest son inheriting the family property and with it responsibility for overseeing family affairs. Papa-san was now in his sixties and, if he followed the practice men his age observed back in Japan, he would soon retire, leaving his elder son to become the family patriarch. That meant Hiro would need a "proper" wife. Mama-san defined "proper" to mean a Japanese girl from a traditional Japanese family, who would be submissive to Hiro's parents—especially Mama-san! Unfortunately, there were few such prospects in the area. That worried Mama-san. She worried even more that Hiro had shown no interest in marriage—or the prospect of becoming the family patriarch. Mama-san had been patient but recently decided this matter had languished too long. She must take a more direct role and move things along a bit.

She had begun by dropping the names of local Japanese girls during the evening meals. "I saw Sushiko in town today. Very nice girl," Mama-san said trying to be casual.

Hiro knew what was behind the remark and went directly to counterpoint. "I know Sushiko is a very nice girl, Mama-san, but I don't really like her and she certainly doesn't like me." Then, venturing into a topic that he and his mother had argued many times before

THE DOOLITTLE IRONY

he added, "Besides, Japanese girls are not much fun. Why don't you like Kathleen? She's always a lot of fun."

Hiro had met Kathleen Kelly, a pretty White girl, at Crawford High School. They were seen together frequently. Local matrons, both White and Yellow, had raised their eyebrows. Romance between a White girl and a Japanese boy was not socially acceptable. Local White and Japanese adults were willing to accept one another on an occasional social or business basis, but certainly would not countenance intermarriage of their offspring. Hiro and Kathleen were both very aware of the taboo. If a romantic attachment existed, they had been careful to keep it *sub rosa*. He was enrolled in an engineering program, and she in nursing, both at the nearby University of Washington. No one had yet reported seeing them in a romantic situation. Nevertheless, they both lived at home in Crawford and their commuting patterns aboard the local bus were oddly congruent. Mama-san was suspicious.

At the mention of Kathleen's name Mama's brow furrowed. Like most Japanese, her vocabulary depended heavily on the unspoken gesture. Sensing that he was treading on dangerous territory, Hiro gathered his courage and plunged ahead. "Kathleen is really a very nice girl, Okasan," he said using the formal term for "mother" to placate her. "You would like her. I don't know why you object to me even mentioning her. After all, this is 1941."

Mama-san smiled sadly, thinking Hiro naïve to consider 1941 a time when White Americans and Japanese immigrants had grown amicable. As she saw it, White Americans treated Japanese as foreigners in their land. She didn't realize that her son's generation, the Nisei and their White contemporaries, had already broken many of the barriers. They played together, went to school together, and—left on their own—eyed one another romantically. But the elder generation remained nearby to enforce the old boundaries. Mama had brought Hiro into this world and, as any mother, would do her best to assure that he conducted himself in a fashion that would assure his future.

Mama-san wondered how she should handle her stubborn son. Having expended most of her options with respect to local Japanese girls, she decided on a bold move. "If you no like Japanese girls here, I tell my sister send girl from Japan." Mama-san's sister had been left behind in Japan when Mama-san's parents immigrated to the

CHAPTER 1

U.S. The sister had married well and, although she and Mama-san were not close, Mama-san was confident she would help. "My sister choose very nice girl."

There was a long pause, and then Hiro replied firmly, "Mama-san, we have discussed that before. This is America. Men here choose their own wives. Elders do not do that. I will choose my own wife!"

It was unlike Hiro to speak to Mama-san so forcefully. She wondered if perhaps she had unknowingly lost control of him. Raising a son in a frivolous society like America, anything could happen. Mama-san decided to play the trump card she had been holding in reserve. "OK," Mama-san countered, "if no Japanese girl here OK for you, and you no allow my sister send Japanese girl here, then you must go there. Find girl in Japan."

Hiro had not expected that. "What?" he asked, somewhat startled. "Me? Go back to Japan? Why would I do that? You know that going to Japan is not smart for 'Nikkie,'" he said using the term that referred to all Japanese immigrants. "Japan and America are not friends. Our neighbors would think we want to be Japanese, not American. The Tagano family sent Kenzo to Tokyo for schooling and now he's back here spouting how glorious Japan is. People here don't like that. Kathleen told him he should go live there."

Mama was stunned at Kathleen's boldness. A proper Japanese girl would never do that. Kathleen was certainly not a girl for Hiro, so right then Mama resolved to bring the issue to a head. Summoning her most imperative manner, she stated boldly, "It time for you to marry, Hiro. If you no like Japanese girls here, and you no want my sister send girl from Japan, then you go Japan, find wife yourself."

The family stopped eating. Hiro's two sisters were motionless. Papa said nothing. Although he was the family patriarch, Mama was the ultimate authority in matters involving the children. She would decide and later, to save face, Papa would add his imprimatur. In turn, Mama would pay lip service to his authority, prefacing any allusion to the decision with, "Papa-san says." Of course, the children knew better.

Hiro seemed to understand the *gravitas* of the moment. He gazed quietly at the chop sticks in his hand, expressionless. The family could not tell if he was angry or resigned. The silence lengthened.

THE DOOLITTLE IRONY

Finally, without looking up, Hiro replied in a steady voice, "OK, Mama-san, I'll go to Japan," he paused for emphasis, "But only on the condition that I can pick out my own bride. Don't get your sister involved. If I don't find a suitable wife on my own, I'll just come home without one." He paused, looking at Mama directly. "Do you agree, Mama-san ?"

Mama hadn't anticipated the part about not finding a wife, but no matter. "Yes," she replied tersely. She had not scored a strategic victory, but she was willing to settle for a tactical one—at least for now.

The family relaxed and went back to dinner. Hiro, always the dutiful son, had acquiesced to his mother's request. Sometime after graduation he would go to Japan, ostensibly to seek a bride. The fateful decision had been made.

Well, not really. In fact, the agreement was only one of temporary convenience. Hiro saw it as just a charade to placate Mama. He reasoned that if he made this trip to Japan and returned with no bride, she would concede that her son's nuptial decisions were hopelessly beyond her control. Perhaps then she would release him from his presumed responsibility to take over the farm and become the family patriarch. He would be free to marry Kathleen.

Mama's agreement was also disingenuous. She thought that once Hiro reached Japan, he would meet a traditional Japanese girl and see that Mama was right. But Mama had left Japan 40 years earlier as a young girl, and her personal memories of Japan were vague. Her parents had filled her with their own remembrances of a courteous, well ordered society. But Japan had changed. With its victories in the Russo-Japanese War and World War I, it had developed a new self-image as a modern nation. In the 1920s and 30s, it had sought to have the world recognize it as being on par with England and the United States. Its militarist government had pressed jingoist policies. It had sought to create and lead a Greater East Asia Co-Prosperity Sphere, and came to regard the U.S. as a principal obstacle to its ambition. Mama's fond image of a gentile, pastoral Japan had become an anachronism.

⊕ ⊕ ⊕

CHAPTER 1

It was the next day in class that Hiro began to realize his promise to go to Japan may have been badly timed. In the spring of 1941, a war raged in Europe. Matters in the Pacific were tense, and at the University of Washington the tension intruded on academics. Students and instructors were both prone to take class time to discuss international issues.

During Hiro's Physics 412 class the instructor commented, "The political situations in Germany and Italy has prompted some of their foremost physicists to flee. We all know about how Einstein came to this country. Enrico Fermi, a Nobel Laureate, is a more recent example. He fled Italy because of Mussolini's racial laws. He now heads a team of physicists at the University of Chicago."

That led to discussion of German-American relations and the America First Committee, the American movement that supported isolationism. Just the night before, Charles Lindbergh had addressed the America First convention in New York and called for "Peace Now," seen by many Americans as a euphemism for urging England to surrender to Germany. One of the students commented bitterly that, "Lindbergh is a traitor." Another disagreed, saying, "Lindbergh is just being realistic. The Wehrmacht has conquered the Continent. England cannot possibly prevail against it. Churchill would do well to follow Lindbergh's advice while England still has some bargaining power."

Somehow the discussion then turned to the Tripartite Pact, an alliance concluded just the previous fall by Germany, Italy, and Japan aimed at deterring the U.S. from entering the war. Mention of Japan added to the tension in the room. Racial or ethnic differences rarely played a significant role in the student's interpersonal relations, but in the context of international relations Japan seemed to pose a more immediate threat than either Germany or Italy.

One student offered: "Washington seems focused on Europe. I worry more about Asia. Japan is a militaristic nation. It took Manchuria, invaded China, and set itself up as the champion of a so-called East Asia Co-Prosperity Sphere. Now it has occupied Indo-China and seems bent on driving the U.S. out of the Western Pacific. That worries me because this college sits on the shores of that same ocean as does Japan. I know we are many miles distant but," and then he gave voice to the elephant that usually sat silently amid such

THE DOOLITTLE IRONY

conversations, "We already have a large number of Japanese in our community. They comprise the largest minority here on campus. That makes some people uncomfortable."

The four students of Japanese descent in the class visibly bristled at the implication. Hiro spoke up heatedly, "Hey, wait a minute. I see several Germans and Italians in this class. Why doesn't 'some people' feel uncomfortable about them? They're children of immigrants just like Nisei. They probably still speak their parents' native language at home just like I do. But being German or Italian doesn't seem to matter because they're White. Japanese are Yellow so you think we are different, that we are not 'American.' Well, I registered for the draft and will fight if called. I am an American, just as much as you!"

Hiro's outburst brought a look of contrition to the face of the young man who had raised the matter. "I didn't mean you, Harry." That was the name Hiro was known by on campus, Harry, an Anglicization of Hiro. Many Nisei used names that were easier for their White American friends to remember. Everybody called Hiro Harry except for his closest friends and, of course, Kathleen.

In fact, the White American classmate who had spoke up about the Japanese community was not a bigot. Anti-Japanese sentiment was largely absent from campus life. True, there was bigotry of a style evident in society at large during that period. Students of Japanese and other Asian ancestries were denied membership in traditional fraternities and sororities, but then again so were Jews, Negroes, and even Roman Catholics. There may have been private resentment about that, but it was not publically discussed. Minority groups simply turned the tables and developed their own social organizations and excluded White Anglo-Saxon Protestants! For example, the 400-plus Nisei on campus had formed a Japanese Student Club for men and a counterpart for women called Fuyo Kai (Hibiscus Club). Students seemed to accept this mutual segregation without much question. It wasn't personal. Japanese students were frequent visitors to White fraternities and vice versa. And their similarities seemed to dwarf their differences. Japanese and Caucasian students dressed the same, they ate the same cafeteria food, and their academic performance was on a par. Both majored in "practical" areas that seemed to offer job prospects.

CHAPTER 1

The apologetic student continued: "We all know you and we all know you are one of us. But we read in the newspaper stories that many Japanese immigrants do strange things. It's hard for us to know what's really true."

The young man's reference to media reports of "strange things" was correct. West Coast radios, magazines, and newspapers had for several years printed hysterical rumors about spies and saboteurs. A recent series alleged that Japanese-Americans were moving to surround ports, U.S. naval bases, Army Air Force installations and defense plants! Others had told about alleged offshoots of the Black Dragon Society, a Japanese group that had spied on Russia before the Russo-Japanese War. None of these reports ever stood up to scrutiny, but federal and state law enforcement agencies had launched investigations. Some had even speculated in reports back to Washington that Japanese-Americans might collaborate with Japan if it were to invade the West Coast.

Of course, Hiro was sensitive to White suspicions. Indeed, all Japanese-Americans were. But this was the first time in Hiro's experience the issue had been discussed openly in a University of Washington classroom. The school prided itself on being a place of tolerance. The discussion struck him as ominous and he wondered if traveling to Japan amid such growing tension was a sound idea. He had never traveled more than a few score miles from his home, and now he was proposing to embark on a 6,000 mile trip across the Pacific Ocean. Moreover, he would be doing so amid deteriorating relations between Imperial Japan and the U.S. Violence could erupt without notice. A trip to Japan could be quite dangerous for Hiro.

The instructor did not like the turn the discussion had taken. "Gentlemen," he said lifting the class text above his head, "Let's turn our attention back to the real reason we're here today: Newton's Second Law of Motion."

Hiro's willingness to undertake a risky venture such as a trip to Japan was quite in keeping with parents' characters. Like most Asian emigrants, they had come to America seeking economic opportunity.

THE DOOLITTLE IRONY

Papa-san—whose given name was Taiske—was the second son of a small farmer in Western Honshu. His father retired in his early sixties, leaving Taiske's and his older brother to operate the farm and care for their aging parents. When his father died, Taiske knew it was time for him to leave. The small farm could not be broken in two. It was simply not large enough to support two families. It was because of that harsh reality that Japanese farmers had adopted the practice of primogeniture: the eldest son inherited the farm and the other children left the homestead to find employment elsewhere.

But, search as he may, Taiske could not find other employment in Japan. So when he learned that men were being recruited to work the sugar and pineapple fields of Hawaii, he signed on as a contract laborer. In return for his transportation to Hawaii, Taiske agreed to work five years on a pineapple plantation belonging to the Hawaiian Pineapple Company, founded a few years previously by James Dole. Taiske was transported by train to Osaka and put aboard a small steamer with about a hundred other Japanese men, bound for an island he had never heard of before called Oahu. He slept in a hammock in the ship's hold. It was filthy and stank of human excrement. The voyage was long, the seas were rough, and Taiske became very sick. Worse, when he arrived on Oahu he found working conditions there to be horrible. He was paid $18 for working 26 days per month, 10-hours per day. Although he was used to the rigors of farm work back in Japan, on Oahu the sun was very hot, the barracks dirty, the water tainted, and sanitary conditions unhealthy. The prospect of working five years in those conditions was daunting.

Oddly, it was those very conditions that indirectly led to an early release from his indenture. A number of his fellow Japanese laborers who had endured such conditions for years, finally could tolerate no more and did a very un-Japanese-like thing. They went on strike. They simply walked off the job and, when asked why, complained that Philippine and Puerto Rican laborers were being paid more than they. They wanted their living conditions improved and their hours reduced. The plantation owners were shocked at such audacity. They refused to even consider the Japanese demands and resolved to rid themselves of such troublemakers. They dismissed the Japanese, even

CHAPTER 1

those who had not participated in the strike, and thereafter would hire only Philippine labor.

So, hardly a year after he arrived on the island, Taiske was set free of his contract and told to leave the plantation. He did so gladly, even though he had little money on which to survive. That's when he learned that men were being hired to work in the fish canneries in a place called Seattle. "You should go," a friend advised him. "The work is indoors and Seattle is much cooler, a lot like Japan." Again, Taiske signed on, and again was put aboard a small steamer. This time he did not get sick, and as bad as they were, he found the fish canneries a significant improvement over the pineapple fields.

Hanaco had immigrated to America as a young child with her mother and father. She attended a small school that taught only in Japanese, and so never learned to speak or read proper English. By 1918, both of her parents had died and Hanaco lived with a Japanese family friend, supporting herself by working in a cannery processing fish. Her friend was aware of Japanese society's marital expectations, and on occasion would remind Hanaco of them. "Hanaco, you are 22. It is soon time you find a man." But Hanaco was a girl of serious purpose and regarded the business of courtship to be frivolous. Nevertheless she recognized that a man was necessary if she was to have her own family. She began to assess the male prospects around her. It was then she noticed Taiske. He worked at the same cannery as she and was well thought of by his fellow employees. After observing him for a month or so, Hanaco assessed him to be pleasant, gentle, and even a bit handsome. Without ever having been introduced to Taiske, Hanaco decided to marry him.

Of course, Japanese-American marriages of that day were "arranged." Any concept of spontaneous, romantic love would have been dismissed as frivolous or even immoral. *Those who come together in passion stay together in tears.* Nuptial arrangements were usually made by the couples' parents, and neither bride nor groom was ever consulted. But Hanaco did not feel bound by social restrictions and so decided to move things along on her own. Considering that both she and Taiske's parents were dead, friends would have to stand in.

THE DOOLITTLE IRONY

In keeping with her usual straightforward manner, Hanaco pointedly asked one of her older friends, "Michiko, is Taiske married?" That was all it took. Understanding Hanaco's tacit message, her friend approached one of Taiske's friends. "No," came the reply, "he is not married—but should be." An agreement was quickly reached. There was a 15-year age difference but that was fairly common with such matches. It was agreed. Details were planned. The couple met only once, briefly, before the marriage, but even then did not speak to one another.

The wedding rite was Shinto. Only a few friends attended. They sat cross-legged around a low table while the couple stood and exchanged vows. The groom wore a simple business suit borrowed from a friend, and the bride wore a White kimono, though not of the traditional silk brocade. That would have been too expensive. Nor did she wear a *Tsuno Kakushi*, the traditional bridal hood. That also would have been too expensive. The wedding vows were abbreviated. Hanaco pledged to be humble and courteous toward her husband and submissive to his family—merely a gesture since he had no family. Taiske vowed to be responsible toward Hanaco and never stray from the true path of matrimony. Then the two sipped sake from the three traditional nuptial cups representing the unity of bride, groom, and the families. When the ceremony was finished, all stood and clapped twice to call the *Kamis'*—Shinto deities—attention to the marriage and seek their blessing on it. The ceremony was not as elaborate as it might have been had the wedding taken place in Japan. But this was America. Things were different.

The marriage was successful. As Hanaco had anticipated, Taisko proved to be a gentle mate. She remembered fondly how he helped when the children were born. "You stay in house today. I work in field." Initially, the bond between the two was based on practicality, but as they lived and toiled together, especially after the children came, a warm bond grew between them and, during the ensuing two decades of shared striving, it developed into mature love. The two lived meagerly, saved their wages, and in time leased 10 acres of land across Lake Washington in an area that now hosts some of America's high tech industry. They would have preferred to own the land but legal ownership of land was prohibited to Japanese-American

CHAPTER 1

immigrants. That restriction had emerged during the years following World War I when the U.S. reverted to its pre-war isolationism. Immigration quotas were enacted and restrictions imposed on all "aliens," oriental and occidental alike. On the West Coast, Whites became increasingly suspicious of all Asians, especially Japanese. Washington State passed laws prohibiting them from owning lands, and many were forced to sell their property.

But the Japanese immigrants were not so easily defeated. They circumvented the laws by putting their land in the names of their children, who were citizens by dent of having been born in America. Court cases went back and forth, and more legislation was enacted; but through sheer tenacity the Japanese seemed to prevail. By the early 30s there were more Japanese farms in Washington State than there had been before the ban on alien ownership.

It was then that the Yamada family leased its farmland. It was a long term lease and the couple hoped that before it ended the restriction against Japanese ownership would be lifted and they could buy the land. Besides, ten acres of land was more than they could have dreamed of farming back in Japan.

The farm was near Crawford, a small town east of Seattle. It was not a highly ethnic enclave like the "Japan Town" in Seattle. There were too few Japanese for that. They had to live with the Whites, buy from them, sell to them, and go to school with them.

When the Yamadas leased the farm, it was dry and infertile. Indeed, that was why the White owner had agreed to lease it. But Papa-san remembered the agricultural practices he had learned from his father, and put them to good use. He spread compost and dug irrigation ditches. He planted crops in rotation. It took years of toil, but the Yamadas turned the 10 arid acres into a prosperous farm. It had livestock, a large garden, and lots of poultry. It met most of the family's food needs and generated enough extra cash to send Hiro to college. It even had a small shed with a wooden tub the family used for hot baths.

Mama-san and Papa-san raised three children on the farm: Hiro, the eldest; a daughter, Avaron, four years Hiro's junior; and Natsuko, two years Avaron's junior. The elder Yamadas sought to imbue their offspring with the values they had brought from Japan: respect for elders, the centrality of family, the importance of saving, the need for hard work, and the value of education. In a land where, as Hanaco saw it, children of the majority White race were raised permissively, instilling those values was not easy. Mama-san knew she had to be vigilant, lest her children lose their way.

⊕ ⊕ ⊕

Hiro and Kathleen Kelly had been classmates at Crawford High School's class of 1937. They seemed to get along well right from their freshman year. Though never together on a "date," they were often together in a crowd. They seemed to seek one another out, sit together, talk, and laugh. Kathleen was bright, vivacious, and talkative. Hiro was bright, quiet, and reserved. Their personalities worked well together, but in high school a romance never quite developed. Social taboos against a White girl and a Yellow boy being romantically involved were quite strong, and the two maintained a proper distance.

The fall following their high school graduation both matriculated at nearby University of Washington, she as a prospective nurse and he as an engineering student. On campus their "chance" meetings resumed. They had talks on the quad, sometimes shared lunch, and occasionally had serious discussions about international affairs. "My father hopes we stay out of Europe," Kathleen once told Hiro over a meatloaf sandwich. "He had to serve there during the last war and doesn't want my brother to do the same. He never says so, but I think he favors the Germans. He certainly hates the British. Calls them 'Johnny Bulls' and blames them for the Irish Diaspora and potato famine. Likewise, he thinks that some of Germany's grievances are legitimate—he even says the Austrians will be better off with Hitler. But he doesn't like the Nazi's militarism, and worries that they will get us into another war."

Hiro had little background in European matters. Japanese-American families discussed more immediate matters at their dinner tables: crops, weather, family, etc. Mama-san and Papa-san, being Issei—first generation immigrants—had little interest in politics, having been legally denied American citizenship and the right to vote. But Hiro was Nisei, second generation. As such, he was a cit-

CHAPTER 1

izen by birth, entitled to vote, and had recently reached voting age. He was fascinated by Kathleen's reports of her family's discussions and frequently probed to know more about them.

"Did your parents vote for FDR?" he inquired. "Oh, sure," Kathleen replied. "They voted for FDR because he's helped working people and he's getting the U.S. out of the Depression. But Dad says he doesn't know who he'll vote for in this coming election. FDR probably can't run because it would be his third term."

⊕ ⊕ ⊕

Kathleen and Hiro's relationship progressed entirely on a Platonic level until that night in 1940 when *Gone with the Wind* came to town. The movie's arrival had created a bit of a controversy in the area, and the college crowd wanted to see for themselves what the fuss was all about. Kathleen's father had objected when he learned of her plans. "Kathleen you should know that some of our local citizens wanted to ban the movie from being shown here." He was the chief of police in Crawford and so knew such things. Her mother jumped in, "I heard on the radio that the movie uses filthy language!" and then scolded, "I don't see why any good Catholic girl would want to see it."

But Kathleen was not easily deterred. "Mom, Dad, we talked about this in my class on government. The First Amendment guarantees freedom of speech. Censoring the arts—and that includes Hollywood—is socially unhealthy and unconstitutional." Then she added with youthful righteousness, "Besides, this is 1940, not the Middle Ages!" Sensing that her parents were weakening, she used an arrow from her quiver that had proven effective in previous such encounters, "After all, I am a responsible college sophomore, with good grades, brought up in a good Catholic home. You should know you can trust me. So don't flip your wigs."

Her parents exchanged quizzical glances. Flip your wigs? Apparently campus slang, not worth inquiring about. In fact, they tacitly agreed that carrying on this whole movie debate was probably not worth the trouble. Dad went back to his newspaper and Mom to the kitchen. As with most arguments that Kathleen entered, she had won.

THE DOOLITTLE IRONY

That evening Kathleen arrived at the local movie theater, located her group of college friends, and quickly found Hiro. They each bought tickets and filed into the movie. As usual, the two sat side by side, but this time they happened to end up seated a row behind the others, in a fashion that allowed them some unaccustomed privacy. They chatted about their school subjects. "I really like Government 101," Kathleen offered, "It really provides a lot of useful information," and smiled slyly remembering the earlier conversation with her parents. Hiro inquired about her family. "Is your father still mad at the British?" She smiled and speculated that would likely never change.

The theater darkened, a newsreel provided images of the Nazi expansion into Austria, and then the feature movie began. Up on the silver screen happy slaves worked in the fields of Tara while Hattie McDaniels cheerfully trussed up Vivian Leigh's corset. In the darkness of the theater, Kathleen's arm touched Hiro's. After a bit he casually placed his hand over hers, and a few moments passed. Slowly, it dawned on them both that they were holding hands. A few more moments passed and Kathleen turned slightly toward Hiro and looked up at him. That's when the social barriers collapsed, leaving bare all the biological tension that had built up over the years. Looking into one another's eyes in the dim glow of the movie screen, they became oblivious to their surroundings. Without thinking he bent and kissed her. On the lips! And she kissed him back! He was stunned, unable to think. He had never kissed any girl before–much less Kathleen. Now it was happening, and it was wonderful!

But propriety was not so easily set aside. As quickly as their passion surfaced, the spell broke. Kathleen drew away and sat stiffly upright. Hiro feared he had overstepped his bounds and Kathleen would never talk to him again. He waited, stunned, half expecting her to storm out of the theater. But she stayed in her seat, and he did too, both unmoving, right through the intermission. Their friends glanced back from the row in front and asked if they wanted popcorn. Hiro just shook his head numbly. The movie continued. Rhett Butler delivered his scurrilous line, "Frankly Scarlett, I don't give a damn," and the movie ended. There was a smattering of applause from the audience. Hiro and Kathleen left without another word

CHAPTER 1

between them. Neither would remember much about the movie, but they would never forget that first kiss.

◈ ◈ ◈

There was a lull in Hiro and Kathleen's relationship following that kiss. The two seemed to do self-imposed penance for their social transgression. They exchanged pleasantries when passing one another on campus, but always with an undertone of embarrassment. Months passed, then in the fall semester of their senior year, 1940-41, their class schedules coincided and they began riding the morning bus together.

Once, when the bus was crowded, they had to sit next to one another. After acknowledging one another politely, Hiro chose to test the waters. "Tell me, Kathleen," Hiro asked lightly, "Does your father cheer when he sees the Johnny Bulls being bombed in London?" Kathleen thought for a moment, recognizing the underlying intent of Hiro's question, then replied wryly, "Not out loud—but every once in a while I catch him smirking a bit when he reads the newspaper headlines." They both smiled, and the tension lessened. Both seemed to realize that their self-imposed period of contrition was over. Each morning's bus ride seemed to draw them closer.

Of course, the adult bus riders were not entirely insensitive to what was happening between the two young people. At first their looks reflected disapproval of this glaring breach of the established social divide. But as the mornings continued, it became apparent to them that the two young people bore a touching affection for one another. So the bus passengers were patient, possibly remembering their own youthful indiscretions. They would allow Hiro and Kathleen their flirtation—at least for the time being. If signs that the social code was being breached in a more serious way, well, something would have to be done, perhaps an oblique mention of the matter to their parents.

Indeed, the relationship did develop into something more. In the following months, Kathleen was increasingly on Hiro's mind. Now, late in his senior year, Hiro practically ran to the bus stop each morning to get the seat where he knew she would join him two stops away. And when she did the two would feign elaborate casualness, smile hello, and perhaps open a book. When they thought no one was noticing, Kathleen would look over at him with that smile that seemed to brighten Hiro's entire world, then reach for his hand.

Kathleen was quite pretty, in the fashion of the-girl-next-door. She was Irish, 21 years old, 5'3" tall, with auburn hair that fell loosely in natural curls. Her complexion was fair, with just a sprinkle of freckles across her cheeks. She did not consider the freckles becoming, so Hiro never mentioned them—although he thought them marvelous. Kathleen was given to wearing print dresses with puffy sleeves that had been sewn by her mother from a Simplicity pattern. Hiro thought Kathleen was the most beautiful thing he had ever seen, and his heart raced when she was near.

Kathleen was equally smitten with Hiro. He was 22, well muscled as men become who have been raised on a farm. He had thick, jet black hair and heavy eyebrows that gave him a serious look. His facial features were almost Western, his skin tone light, and at 5'7" he was tall for a Japanese. There was something in his composure that set him apart. He sat erect and viewed the world before him confidently, with none of the timidity exhibited by first generation immigrant Japanese. This was his world. He was not Japanese: he was American of Japanese descent.

In another age, Kathleen and Hiro would have made a handsome young couple whose families would have viewed them with pride. But this was 1940 in Crawford, Washington. The White and Yellow adults here maintained only a reluctant *modus vivendi*. They would co-exist in the same community; do business with one another; even exchange pleasantries when passing on the street. But that did not extend to allowing interracial romances among their offspring.

Hiro and Kathleen knew that. They understood full well that their relationship was unacceptable to the world in which they had grown up. That did not stop them. It just forced them to keep their relationship *sub rosa*. "Will I see you this weekend" Kathleen asked? "Sure," Hiro replied sardonically, "I'll come by

CHAPTER 1

your house. Maybe your Dad and I can talk about the Johnny Bulls—that is, if he doesn't throw me out first."

"Oh, Hiro, my Dad would really like you if he just got to know you. He's really not prejudiced against Japanese. He admires them in many ways," Kathleen opined, then added ruefully, "I wish I could say the same about my mother!"

Hiro nodded. "Yes, I know about mothers!" he replied with exasperation, "Mama-san's feathers ruffle whenever I even mention your name. She said you are an American and probably don't even know how to cook rice." Kathleen's eyebrows arched and she acknowledged that matter with a smile, "She's right, I don't!"

Such exchanges were common between the two. While violating the racial taboo, the two seemed to accept its existence. Topics that would have been common had they been of the same race were never broached. Marriage, children, and domesticity were out of bounds. Nevertheless, there developed between Kathleen and Hiro a tacit understanding that somehow they would be a part of one another's future. Neither had any idea how that might develop, but youthful naiveté prevailed. Both believed that somehow the stars would align in their favor.

CHAPTER 2

WAR CLOUDS

Yokosuka Naval Base, Japan, February 1940

Captain Kanji Ogawa was a senior official in the Imperial General Staff's 3rd Section, the Intelligence Bureau. His position description read that he was responsible for intelligence aspects of the planning and execution of national defense strategy as it involved America. He sat at his imposing desk. Behind him a large window overlooked the Yokosuka Naval Base at the head of Tokyo Bay. Ogawa was a somber man, which he thought to be in keeping with his lofty position. His countenance was unsmiling as he looked up from his papers, finally acknowledging the presence of a dozen or so officers that had assembled quietly around the large conference table in his office. He spoke in the aloof manner that most senior officers of the Imperial Japanese Navy seemed to cultivate. "What I am about to tell you is very sensitive," he cautioned, " You are to repeat it to no one, and you are not to discuss it even among yourselves outside these walls." The room became very silent, "I have just met with Admiral Yamamoto." Again, he paused for effect. Marshal Admiral Isoroku Yamamoto was Commander-in-Chief of the Combined Fleet and Japan's foremost naval strategist. His name struck awe in Japanese naval circles.

CHAPTER 2

Captain Ogawa resumed, "He spoke of the international political situation in the Pacific. He said that he anticipates Japan's relations with the Western powers will continue to deteriorate, and that war is ultimately inevitable." Again, Captain Ogawa paused to assure he had his staff's complete attention. "The Admiral is already preparing wartime options so as to have them ready when our national leadership calls for them. One such option would be a surprise attack. He believes that if we strike without warning, we might be able to neutralize the U.S. Pacific Fleet, and if we do that, then we will have time to establish a strong defensive perimeter around the Western Pacific. If it is strong enough, the U.S. may conclude that defeating it is not worth the cost. Admiral Yamamoto sees this as perhaps the only way we can nullify the West's industrial advantage. He says its success will depend on a strong first strike, and in that regard he has given this staff a special role." The staff officers seemed to lean forward.

"The Admiral believes that the focus of our surprise attack should be the U.S. military complex on Oahu in the Hawaiian Islands. The American Pacific Fleet has just moved its headquarters there from the Mainland, and Naval Station Pearl Harbor now serves as home port for the Pacific Fleet. In addition, there is hundreds of U.S. Army aircraft stationed at Hickam Air Base, and vast quantities of fuel stored nearby. We must destroy all of it."

The Captain continued, "Admiral Yamamoto said he can only guess about when we might have to launch such an attack, but at the rate relations are deteriorating, it could well be within a year or so. That's not much time to collect and prepare all the intelligence our forces will need. So he has ordered us to start now. I want you to return to your desks, drop what you've been doing, and get busy on three things: (1) a recap of intelligence we now hold on military installations on Oahu; (2) a list of what intelligence we lack; and, (3) a plan to collect that intelligence. I want your report early next week."

Commander Nokimura, the senior officer of Ogawa's staff, responded smartly: "Sir, we will give you full particulars next week, but for now let me say briefly that we have little solid information about Hawaii in our files, and little capability to collect more. We have only one officer under cover in the Honolulu consulate, and only limited access to a German agent that the *Abwehr* runs. So far they have produced little of value, mostly just press clippings and road maps. We desperately need a qualified observer on the scene to collect technical information, fleet movements, order of battle information, weather data, and other such."

Captain Ogawa nodded. "What about recruiting new agents on the Island? There is a large colony of Japanese emigrants there."

"True," Commander Nokimura said, "But they are mostly farm and plantation workers. We had thought about using them previously, so we asked our Foreign Ministry colleagues at the consulate in Honolulu whether they knew of any we could recruit. They said we should not trust the Japanese on the Island. Their loyalty has been eroded since leaving the homeland. They see themselves less as Japanese and more as American. Incidentally, we also checked with our consulate in San Francisco and got the same reading about Japanese there."

Captain Ogawa pondered a bit. "That's disappointing," he observed, "One would hope that our citizens would have longer memories. But keep trying. Americans have not welcomed Japanese immigrants. They have been cruel to them in many respects. Surely we can find a way to exploit that."

⊕ ⊕ ⊕

U.S. NAVAL HEADQUARTERS, WASHINGTON, D.C., SUMMER 1940

Lieutenant Bill Russo, USN, age 28, was the son of a Chief Petty Officer who had loved the Navy, served in the Asiatic Fleet, and wanted nothing so much as for his son to become a commissioned U.S. Naval Officer. Bill had bought into that ambition. He was bright, athletic, a Navy brat, and had no difficulty getting into the Naval Academy. As a cadet, he did well academically but became known as something of a maverick about conventional naval wisdom. Consequently when, as an upper classman it came time for him to select his career specialty, Bill chose neither of the two paths normally selected by ambitious young ensigns: flying air-

CHAPTER 2

planes or driving ships. Instead, he elected to become an intelligence officer. That was not a good "career move." Intelligence was simply not a skill that the Navy valued highly, so choosing it meant forfeiting practically any chance of becoming an admiral. But Bill didn't really consider that much of a sacrifice. He thought the Navy was stodgy—resistant to new ideas, new technology and new tactics. He had resolved to push its boundaries and make it deal with problems it would not otherwise undertake. Today's meeting was his latest effort in that direction.

"Thanks for seeing me today, Captain," Bill started, "I asked to talk to you rather than running this up my own chain because it is more operations than intelligence." Bill was referring to the division of labor that exists in most military organizations wherein "Intelligence" develops information about the enemy and "Operations" uses it. For example, "Intel" might learn that an enemy is developing a dangerous new weapon within a particular building. It provides that information to "Ops," who then sends bombers to destroy the site.

"This is a not a standard Navy problem," Bill continued, "But it does affect the Navy. It's more a social thing and it may have to be addressed at the policy level. I know you can elevate this to the CNO, and that's the reason I brought it to you." Bill was referring to the Chief of Naval Operations, the most senior officer in the Navy. "It's about the Japanese-Americans out on the West Coast."

Captain Robert High raised his eyebrows, wondering how the Navy might possibly be concerned about some ethnic group in California.

"Some of the White citizens out there worry about Japanese immigrants. They think that if we ever went to war with Tokyo, they might support Japan rather than America and so they want to take measures to suppress them. I think they're wrong, and I think that alienating the Japanese immigrants could actually work to the detriment of the Navy."

Captain High listened more closely.

"The FBI is compiling names of so-called 'Suspected Aliens,' and has sorted them into A, B, and C lists," Bill went on.

"Well, isn't that what the FBI is supposed to do?" the Captain interrupted.

THE DOOLITTLE IRONY

"Not necessarily, sir" Bill responded, "As you know, I've specialized in Japan. I learned the language, spent two years in Tokyo as an Assistant Naval Attaché, and visited the West Coast with Lieutenant Commander Rangle examining Japanese-American communities. We looked for signs of disloyalty. Yes, we found some sympathizers—*Kibbie* mostly, Japanese born in America but educated in Japan. They spout a lot of the same ideas we hear from Tokyo, calling us colonial oppressors. But it's all just talk. We found no evidence that any of them ever took any concrete action to harm the U.S. I'll bet the FBI hasn't found any real evidence either. The Japanese immigrants are just peaceful, hard working folks, somewhat stand-offish because of cultural and racial differences, but that's true of most immigrants."

Bill paused to allow that to register then continued, "But that hasn't stopped the FBI from compiling these lists. It has put together some 2,000 names: community leaders, doctors, lawyers, fishermen with boats, ham radio operators, even a few farmers."

"Wait," Captain High interrupted a bit impatiently. "Are you accusing the FBI of malfeasance? Of concocting evidence? Why in god's name would they do that?"

"Valid question," Bill acknowledged, "I think the FBI is reacting to political pressure. Whites on the West Coast are prejudiced toward the Japanese. They've passed laws restricting Japanese immigrants from becoming citizens and from owning land. Frankly, they are afraid of them. They think the Japanese are going to ruin their businesses, push them out of their markets, and take over their jobs. So they go to the FBI with lies about Japanese-American loyalties. When the FBI tries to check out the claims, the local cops confirm them because they're White bigots too."

"To make matters worse," Bill went on, "the WMD is generally incompetent." He was referring to the Western Military Defense Command, the Army element responsible for security on the West Coast. "I don't trust its judgment. I've visited the intelligence element there and it looked like amateur hour to me."

Captain High raised his hand as if to call time out and said, "OK, maybe the FBI has been too zealous, and maybe the Western Command is a bunch of morons, but why tell me about it?"

CHAPTER 2

Bill raised his index finger. "Sir, you are close to the boss." Bill meant Admiral "Betty" Stark, then Chief of Naval Operations. "If we go to war with Japan, and the Army or the Department of Justice comes forward with some plan to 'manage' the Japanese immigrants, I think Admiral Stark will be asked to chop on it." That was Navy jargon meaning he would be asked to approve it from the Navy's perspective.

"At that point, I think the CNO needs to be told about the work that Ken Rangle and I have done out there. He needs to know that the Japanese-Americans are not treacherous slant-eyes. They are trustworthy Americans and we should be using them now in our cryptanalytic efforts to break Japanese codes. And if we go to war, the Navy and Marines will need people with Japanese language skills to interrogate prisoners, create propaganda documents, listen to enemy radio nets, and other stuff. We'll need those Japanese-Americans, so let's not alienate them."

Captain High stared out his office window in Main Navy, the 'temp' building that had been erected on the Washington Mall more than two decades before as an expedient to house WWI naval offices. Bill's information coincided with other reports the Captain had heard about incompetence in the Army's Western Defense Command. Moreover, Bill's concerns about needing the Japanese-Americans were well founded. If we entered the European War, it would be an Army effort mostly, fought on the continent. But if a war with Japan developed, it would be a Navy war, fought across vast expanses of the Pacific Ocean. As Bill warned, the Navy would need lots of people that speak Japanese and have knowledge of the country. Where better to get them than from among America's own immigrants, especially the bright young ones who had grown up here.

The Captain looked back at Bill. "I take your point, Lieutenant. I'll bring this to the boss's attention. He may find it useful. You can never tell what the Army will come up with next," he said sarcastically, reflecting the bitter rivalry between the two services.

✦ ✦ ✦

THE DOOLITTLE IRONY

It was just five days later that Bill Russo received a summons from Captain High's office. This time it was the Captain who had news to share. "Thanks for coming by, Bill. Cup of coffee? You might need it after I tell you about this."

"Thanks, Captain, black and bitter," Bill replied, a Navy phrase used to mean no sugar, no cream. Captain High poured coffee for Bill and himself from an urn that his secretary kept full for him, and placed both cups on the coffee table. The Captain was of a rank that warranted certain perks such as an office with a coffee table and overstuffed furniture. The prestige that such furniture was meant to convey was, in this instance, somewhat diminished. The furniture—like the rest of the Main Navy building—had not aged well.

The Captain had not sat behind his desk as he normally would have in a meeting with an officer as junior as Bill. Instead he sat in the overstuffed chair opposite the sofa where Bill had settled—a move that Bill interpreted to be ominous.

"As I promised, Bill, I passed your information about the Japanese-Americans on the West Coast to Admiral Stark. He was not surprised. There seems to be concern in some Washington circles about a so-called "fifth column" in this country composed of alien immigrants. The word among senior leadership is that if war with Japan develops, the Army will propose to relocate a large number of Japanese immigrants away from the West Coast—send them inland somewhere where they cannot collect information about our defenses and pass it to the Japanese."

Bill was shocked. "Relocate? What does that mean, sir? There are over 100,000 of those people up and down the Coast. You can't just "relocate" them. Where would you put that many people?

The Captain nodded understanding. "Yes, I agree Bill; there are a lot of questions. Even more than the logistic problems there are serious questions of legality. A lot of these people are U.S. citizens, born right here in the U.S. They can't be handled like aliens. They have rights."

Bill shifted uneasily. "Sir, where is Admiral Stark on this? Is he going to fight it?"

"Well," the Captain replied, "he's certainly not going to endorse it. He will speak out and voice the Navy's concern that this would

CHAPTER 2

be an overreaction we may one day regret. But he's not optimistic that anyone will listen. Official Washington is in no mood to consider civil rights arguments. Today national security trumps constitutional niceties. Hell, the Army is already drafting relocation plans. Moreover, State may soon freeze all German and Italian assets in the U.S. Japanese assets may not be far behind."

The Captain paused a moment, considering whether he should go on because the next bit of information was very sensitive, "That's not all that Admiral Stark is worried about. As you know Bill, about a year ago the Navy moved the Pacific Fleet's home base from San Diego to Pearl Harbor. That wasn't the Navy's idea. It was a White House political decision. The Administration wanted to underline just how seriously it viewed Japan's move into China and thought that beating a few war drums might make their point."

"But from the Navy's point of view," the Captain added sardonically, "Pearl Harbor was not a smart choice. The Base is just not defensible, especially against a surprise attack. It's out in the middle of the Pacific where Japanese carriers can get to it. The advantage lies with the attacker. He gets to choose the time and the direction from which he'll attack. By contrast, we have to remain on alert 24-hours a day, seven days a week. Maintaining surveillance of the ocean area 360 degrees around Oahu is grueling, expensive, and prone to failure. Moreover, we know that a surprise attack is part of Japanese military doctrine. They used it successfully in the Russo-Japanese War, and they never heard of the Marquis of Queensbury Rules. Bill, we've conducted exercises at Pearl simulating a surprise attack and you know what? They worked."

"So why did we do it? Why did the Navy move the Fleet from San Diego to Honolulu?" The Captain asked rhetorically. "Simply stated, we did it because we were ordered to. ADM Richardson, who was Chief of the Pacific Fleet tried to stop it, but the White House was in no mood for arguments. Admiral Richardson was unceremoniously relieved and now Admiral Kimmel is out there trying to get Pearl Harbor on a war time footing. He's got his job cut out for him."

Bill winced, "So I guess the upshot is that Admiral Stark has seen what happens to naval officers that cross swords with the White House. He's probably not willing to stick his neck out too far on the Japanese-American issue."

THE DOOLITTLE IRONY

"Don't be too hard on the guy," the Captain countered. "He knows he has to deal with this White House for some time to come. FDR has decided to run for a third term. Wilkie doesn't stand a chance. So the Admiral has to pick his fights carefully. If he's going to fall on his sword—probably not a very good metaphor these days—it can only be for something absolutely crucial to the Navy. The Japanese-American situation is not that."

"OK, Captain , I read you," Bill replied, "I'll keep quiet. But let's hope we don't regret this someday."

CHAPTER 3

ALL BECAUSE OF MAMA-SAN

Traveling back to Japan was a problem for Hiro in many respects, but the most immediate was that he simply could not afford a steam ship ticket for the 6,000 mile voyage. It occurred to him that perhaps he could work his passage, and that Mr. Tanaka might be able to help in that regard. Mr. Tanaka was a leader in the Japanese community. Though he held no title, he was the *de facto* Japanese mayor. He was well connected in both Yellow and White communities, and likely able to help Hiro if anyone could.

"Mr. Tanaka, how are you? It's been a long time," Hiro said to the smiling, fiftyish Issei who answered the door.

"Hiro! Oh my! It is good to see you!" Mr. Tanaka exclaimed. "Please come in. Sit down. May I get you tea?" Hiro politely refused the tea but did take a chair. Mr. Tanaka's house was Western in character, much like the rest of Mr. Tanaka's life style.

"Since you've gone to college it seems I never see you. How are you? And how are your mother and father?" With that Mr. Tanaka paused and his smile changed to a look of concern. "I hope it's not bad news that brings you here." Mr. Tanaka's concern stemmed from the fact that he owned long range Ham radio equipment which he used occasionally to convey important personal news from the local Japanese immigrants back to Japan. All too often the news involved the death of a family member.

THE DOOLITTLE IRONY

"No, Mr. Tanaka, Mama-san and Papa-san are just fine," Hiro replied. "In fact, they asked me to say hello"–a small White lie. Then he launched into a small speech he had rehearsed on his way. "Mr. Tanaka, I came by to ask for your help in something that's very important to me. I need to go to Japan, but I don't have enough money to buy passage. I remembered that you once told me you had been a radio operator aboard a steam ship. As you know, I was a member of our high school Ham Radio Club and have a Ham operator certificate. Do you think I could get a position like you had? Maybe aboard a ship going to Japan?"

Mr. Tanaka reflected a bit. "Well, you certainly have the technical qualifications, Hiro. I remember you were quite skillful with the equipment here, but getting hired as a crew member requires more than technical skills. You have to cope with union rules, company regulations, ships' schedules, and lots of other things. So there is no simple answer to your question, but," he added with some satisfaction, "I know an agent for a Japanese shipping firm right here in Seattle. Let me raise this matter with him. No promises, but if anyone can help, he can."

As Hiro was expressing his gratitude Mrs. Tanaka joined them. Hiro greeted her and, as a matter of courtesy, explained why he had come. Unlike most Japanese women, Mrs. Tanaka was inquisitive about matters beyond the home. After listening to Hiro's explanation, she asked the obvious question, one that her husband had been too polite to pose: "Hiro, why do you want to go to Japan? You are about to graduate from college. Won't you be looking for a job here in Seattle?"

"Oh, you don't understand, Mrs. Tanaka," Hiro answered. "I don't want to live in Japan. I'm going to look for a bride." Immediately he regretted making such an impetuous statement. He thought of trying to explain, but the matter was just so complex that he decided to not even try. Besides, he had yet to explain all of this to Kathleen, and he did not want anyone else to tell her first.

Hiro noticed that Mrs. Tanaka looked a bit puzzled, as though his answer did not fit the facts as Mrs. Tanaka knew them, but he dismissed that as just his imagination. After all, no one knew about him and Kathleen so why would they be puzzled about him finding

CHAPTER 3

a Japanese bride? He again thanked Mr. and Mrs. Tanaka and, as he left, told Mr. Tanaka he would stay in touch with them regarding the shipping agent in Seattle.

"A Japanese bride?" Mrs. Tanaka asked of her husband after he closed the door, "Very odd!"

"Odd?" Mr. Tanaka repeated, "Why odd?"

"Because I see Hiro and the Kelly girl looking at one another with big goo-goo eyes. So why would he be going to Japan to find a bride? Something's fishy!"

Hiro had gone straight to see Kathy, concerned that somehow she would hear the information he had just shared with the Tanakas and misinterpret it. She was leaving class and looked surprised to see Hiro. When he said, "Kathleen, I have something to tell you," she became immediately concerned. They found an empty classroom in which to talk and Hiro began his story. He could sense that Kathleen was probably not going to take this well. Just a few sentences into his explanation his pessimism proved well founded, "You're going to do what?" Kathleen exploded. "You want to go to Japan to find a bride?" She sat down suddenly as though someone had pulled her legs from under her.

"No, no, Kathleen, not to find a bride. I'm only going there so my mother thinks I am–I mean looking for a bride." This was not going well. He was groping for words and not finding the right ones. "I will stay only long enough to make it look good!"

Kathleen heard nothing that Hiro said other than "looking for a bride."

"Oh, Hiro, I don't know what to say. Somehow I thought that you and I …" She could not finish the sentence.

"No, no Kathleen. You were right. I thought the same thing," still not daring to use the word "marriage." "I still think that. But my mother is very old fashioned. So is your mother. So if we go thru with this charade…"

"We?" Kathleen interrupted, her tone taking on an edge, "WE are not doing this, Hiro. You are!" She paused, trying to make sense of Hiro's sudden announcement. "How could you agree to such a thing without even talking to me about it? What will I say to our friends?"

"Our friends? What do our friends know about us? Did you tell them?"

"Oh, don't be ridiculous, Hiro. Of course our friends know about us, and no, I didn't tell them. They just see us together all the time and they figure things out. I can tell from their comments and questions about you that they know we are in love."

Love. The word struck Hiro like a hammer. He had always been afraid to say it. He knew he was in love with Kathleen but wasn't sure she felt that way toward him—not at least knowing how her mother felt about Japanese-Americans. Now she was using the word herself. She was admitting that she was in love with him. Hiro was stunned. He was beginning to realize what a bad idea this trip to Japan was.

"Kathleen," he blurted, unable to contain his emotion, "Is that true? Do you really love me? I mean, I certainly love you, but we've never talked like this before." He tried to embrace her but she shoved him away.

"I THOUGHT I loved you, Hiro. But how could I love anyone who could be so cruel. You just walk in here and tell me you're going to Japan—TO FIND A BRIDE! My god, Hiro, you must think I'm just a rug you can walk on." Kathleen's voice rose in volume. "You SHOULD find a Japanese bride, somebody who will bow and scrape, who will walk six feet behind you, and do just everything you tell her." By now she was in such a rage that Hiro chose to step back a few paces. The phrase "Irish temper" occurred to him. "That's not me Hiro. I'll never be that way." Now she was shouting. "So go to Japan and find your bride. My mother was right, after all."

"No, no, Kathleen, please listen ..." But it was too late. She ran out the door, sobbing, and became lost among the welter of students in the corridor. What had happened? Hiro was dumbfounded. How could he have been so stupid? How could he have agreed to go to Japan? And how could he not have foreseen Kathleen's reaction? He thought she would understand and go along with his little scheme, maybe even express admiration for his guile. That had been really dumb! He sat at a desk in the vacant classroom and tried to recover his composure. He

CHAPTER 3

couldn't catch her now, and even if he did she would not listen. He told himself he would see her again when she calmed down.

◈ ◈ ◈

But she apparently did not calm down. In the next few days Hiro looked for her at school, in town, and on the bus. He even phoned her home, something he had never done before. A female voice said simply that she was not there and muttered an abrupt good bye. He asked one of her girl friends. The girl stared at Hiro icily. "Kathleen has gone to visit relatives, Hiro. She's out of town."

The friend's attitude conveyed an unmistakable message: she knew what was going on and despised Hiro for it. He persisted nevertheless. "How can I contact her? Do you have a phone number or address? I really need to talk to her."

The reply was curt. "No, Hiro, I can't help you." The girl strode away with a look of satisfaction for having inflicted pain on the man who had jilted her friend.

The next few weeks were hardly bearable for Hiro. It seemed the whole campus knew what had happened and chosen to shun him. He thought the girls saw him a pathetic cad and the men as a weakling who had knuckled under to his mother.

Hiro had looked forward to his graduation for four years, but now that it was here he found no joy in the ceremony. He looked frantically for Kathleen, but the School of Nursing held its graduation separately from the School of Engineering. Her name appeared on the list of graduates, but he was not able to determine whether she actually attended to receive her diploma. It made him doubly sad to think that he might have spoiled her graduation.

To make things worse, Hiro's mother and father did not attend his graduation ceremony. They considered such matters too "white"– not really an appropriate place for Issei. They were proud that Hiro had earned a college degree, but thought it would be overreaching were he to expect to benefit from it in this White world. It was his place to return to the farm.

His sisters did attend his graduation ceremony but seemed unenthused. They didn't even congratulate him for having gradu-

THE DOOLITTLE IRONY

ated with honors. He assumed—mistakenly, as it turned out—that they were just reflecting their parent's attitude.

His classmates held graduation parties, but did not invite Hiro. He was *persona non grata*.

⊕ ⊕ ⊕

The 4th of July fell on a Friday in 1941, making it a three-day weekend for people employed in banks, stores, and other occupations not ruled by the imperatives of weather and season. Most White Americans held family picnics, attended band concerts in the park, and watched the fireworks display that night. Hiro's parents did not. As Issei, they never thought of themselves as "real" Americans and so did not participate in patriotic activities. But Hiro was a Nisei, and saw himself as a patriot, so he made sure to finish his farm chores early and walk by himself into town for the festivities. He had always enjoyed them, but this time his real agenda was to find Kathleen. It had been several weeks since she stormed out of the University classroom where he had told her of his charade to appease his mother by going to Japan to find a bride. "What a dumb stunt that was," he thought to himself for the thousandth time!

The holiday festivities that year were held on the grounds of the Crawford High School, just as they had been each year since 1938 when the Works Progress Administration had finished constructing the school. Hiro had just rounded the corner of the building and was entering the football field when a familiar voice called out. "Hiro, over here!"

It was Mr. Tanaka. "I was hoping to see you. I have news about traveling to Japan."

"Oh, no," Hiro thought to himself, "That's the last thing I want to talk about." But being a deferential young man, he stopped, waved, and walked over to Mr. Tanaka to hear his news.

"Hiro, I haven't much time." Mr. Tanaka began. "I'm at these festivities because someone appointed me to represent the Japanese community. In just a few minutes I'm supposed to go up on the stage with the mayor and some others, so I must be quick. There is a Japanese passenger ship that will be here soon, and it might be

CHAPTER 3

the answer you're looking for. You may have heard of it: the *Hikawa Maru*." Indeed, Hiro knew of it. It was a liner that plied the waters between Yokohama and the ports of Seattle and Vancouver. The more affluent members of the Japanese-American community used it occasionally to visit Japan, or send their children there for education.

Mr. Tanaka continued, "You probably read that the ship delivered about 80 Jewish war refugees here. They escaped Germany, fled east across Russia to Vladivostok, and then into Japan. Can you imagine such a trip, Hiro? Thousands of miles! They must have truly feared for their lives. In Yokohama they boarded the *Hikawa Maru* and sailed here. You probably remember their arrival. It caused quite a stir. Some people thought other Jews might follow, but now the Nazi have invaded Russia so even that escape route is cut off."

Mr. Tanaka paused to see Hiro's reaction. He knew Hiro was an aspiring engineer, and engineers were rarely interested in international developments. Hiro was apparently an exception because his face registered understanding. Mr. Tanaka raised his hand, as though waiving someone to stop. "But all of that is just background. The real news is that the *Hikawa Maru* is en route to Seattle. She left Yokohama on 5 June, arrived in Vancouver on the 17th, and is due here in Seattle soon."

Mr. Tanaka paused again, preparing to deliver his bottom line. "If you want to go to Japan, Hiro, this may be your best option. It provides a safe, reliable crossing, and the cost is not that high–a third class ticket costs $187. Perhaps even more important," Mr. Tanaka continued, "it may be your last chance. The U.S. Government has embargoed trade with Germany and Italy. I think we can expect to see the same thing happen to Japan very soon. And when it does, shipping between here and there will stop. So decide quickly. My friend who gave me this information can reserve a passage for you, but I must let him know soon."

Hiro cringed. "How do I get out of this?" he asked himself. He was too embarrassed to tell Mr. Tanaka the truth, so he reluctantly chose to be a bit disingenuous. "Thanks for the information, Mr. Tanaka. You've been very helpful, but the cost may be more than my family can afford. I was hoping to be able to work on the ship for my passage. Let me talk to my parents and I'll get back to you."

THE DOOLITTLE IRONY

Now he really had to sort things out. Mr. Tanaka's information had forced the issue. Hiro would have to make some major decisions in the next few weeks.

✢   ✢   ✢

It was just two days later that Hiro received the note from Professor Johnston. "Hiro, Remember the paper you did on the Tacoma Narrows Bridge? I need to talk to you about it."

He remembered the paper well. His class had made a trip to see the remains of the Tacoma Narrows Bridge. It was a suspension span—one of the longest in the country—that crossed Puget Sound connecting the Tacoma area with the Kitsap Peninsula. It had been open only a few months when high winds caught it, twisted it like a snake, and sent it crashing into the Sound below. It had been a national scandal, in part because its collapse was captured by motion picture cameras. The footage was spectacular and was shown on practically every newsreel screen in America. Hiro had subsequently written a term paper for an engineering class on the subject that he entitled, *Resonance and Damping*. It had earned him a high mark and his professor actually forwarded a copy to the team at Scott Engineering, a large, well respected civil engineering firm in Seattle that was doing the post mortem on the bridge's failure.

When Hiro arrived at Professor Johnston's office, the Professor greeted him excitedly. "Your bridge paper caught the attention of one of the design engineers at Scott's," the Professor blurted out. "He brought it up at a staff meeting and the group liked some of your ideas. They asked if they could talk to you about it. I must say, Hiro, I was impressed. Being invited to talk with Scott engineers is quite an accolade for a young engineer just out of college. It would be a good experience and, who knows, it could even lead to a job. If you agree, I'll set it up."

"Agree?" Hiro repeated dumbfounded. "Of course I agree!"

✢   ✢   ✢

CHAPTER 3

Mama-san was not thrlled with Hiro's news about Scott Engineering. She began again in her stilted English, "You Japanese, not American. Only American get fancy job. You take care of family, run farm. That what Japanese do."

Mama-san was right, in so far as her generation was concerned. For Mama-san's contemporaries, some land to cultivate, or maybe a small store to tend, and an education for their children was quite enough. In gratitude they docilely accepted their subordinate status, avoided confrontations with their White neighbors, and took refuge in the values they had brought from Japan. But what was right for Mama-san's generation was not right for Hiro's.

"Mama-san, I'm not sure I want to run the farm. I think I want to live in the city. It's more interesting. There are people to talk to, places to go." He paused, and then with unaccustomed candor blurted out, "Besides, living in the city is not as much work as living here on the farm."

Mama-san listened and then, speaking in Japanese to be more fluent, asked rhetorically, "And what about me and Papa-san and your sisters? Who will take care of us? Papa-san is already old. He could die soon. If you are not here to step into his shoes, who will take care of the family?"

Having played the guilt card, Mama-san followed up with a dose of brutal reality. "Do you really think you can be American, Hiro? Do you really think you can find a bride here? I don't. American girls don't marry Japanese men, and if they did it would not turn out well. They don't speak the Japanese language. They don't eat Japanese food. Their children would be funny looking, welcomed by neither Japanese nor Western. Not to mention that Americans hate Japanese. No American father would let his daughter marry one."

Hiro shriveled a bit under Mama-san's attack. Certainly hers was the conventional wisdom. He had heard older Japanese-Americans say the same things many times. It worried him. Mama-san was a wise woman. Could she be right?

⟡ ⟡ ⟡

THE DOOLITTLE IRONY

He decided it might be useful to discuss the issue with his 18-year-old sister, Avaron. Normally, he would have just dismissed her opinion as irrelevant–after all, she was hardly out of high school–but Avaron was of the younger generation. Perhaps she saw things differently than Mama-san. As it turned out, Avaron saw things *considerably* different than Mama-san.

"Hiro, how can you be so stupid?" Avaron demanded. Like many younger sisters, Avaron was not especially zealous of her older brother's self esteem. "You tell Kathleen that you're going to Japan to find a bride and you expect her to just *understand*?"

Hiro had hoped for a more sympathetic reaction and maybe some advice on dealing with females, a subject on which he was beginning to understand just how woefully deficient he was.

"And you even thought that your relationship with Kathleen was a secret? Hiro, everyone in my school knows about you two, and I'll bet everyone in your school does too. I wouldn't be surprised if Mama-san knew also. Maybe that's the reason she wants you to go to Japan so bad, just to get you away from marrying an American girl."

Avaron went on, pontifically. "You need to decide who you are, Hiro. Are you Japanese or are you American? You can't be both. As for me, I have made my decision. I am an American. I don't like Japanese customs. Why should I let my parents choose a husband for me? Walk six feet behind him? Work in the fields? Not for me! I want to pick my own husband and I don't care whether he's White, Yellow or green! She paused in mid-rant to collect her thoughts. "So don't expect me and my future husband to take over the farm in your place. Whoever I marry will want to live in a city where people don't hate Japanese, maybe on the East Coast, or maybe even somewhere overseas–but not here. Crawford is a small town populated by small people with small ideas. I'm leaving just as soon as I can!"

Hiro's hopes of shifting the burden of the farm to his sisters were obviously ill founded. He would have to think of something else.

CHAPTER 4

PEARL HARBOR PLANS

IJN Intelligence Headquarters, Yokosuka, June 1941

Captain Kanji Ogawa looked over the naval officers assembled in the room. His staff had grown significantly since Admiral Yamamoto had assigned him the task of preparing intelligence for a strike on Pearl Harbor. "Gentlemen," he began, "I have received the news you've been waiting for. I have been authorized to tell you–and this is NOT to leave this room–the Imperial Japanese Navy has been authorized to train for a surprise attack on Pearl Harbor. Our hard work of the last 18 months is going to be put to good use."

The group erupted with clenched fists in the air and shouts of *Banzai*. The Captain smiled with satisfaction, held his hands up to command silence, and shifted to the business at hand: "We have more work before us. This past week America has closed all German and Italian Consulates within its borders. Ours remain open, but that may change on short notice. My question to you is: does the loss of these German and Italian political posts hurt our collection effort against Pearl Harbor?"

He looked toward Commander Nokimura, his chief of staff, and was pleased to see he had a ready answer: "Sir, it is true that we

THE DOOLITTLE IRONY

have in the past used some Italian and German intelligence reporting, but it has never been very significant. Losing it will have little consequence, especially considering that our own assets are now reporting quite effectively. Ensign Takeo Yoshikawa has been especially productive since his arrival there last spring."

The Captain nodded, knowing all about Ensign Yoshikawa.

"You may recall that he is the flyer sent there under cover as a minor diplomatic officer." Ogawa had, in fact, selected Takeo himself but had not shared that information with Commander Nokimura. "Compartmentation" it was called in the intelligence business. One was told only what one needed to know, and Nokimura had not needed to know about the selection. Besides, keeping that information close to his vest enabled Ogawa to check up on the rest of the staff. In the internal politics of the intelligence bureaucracy, as elsewhere, knowledge is power.

"He has been very aggressive collecting the information we need," the Commander continued, "He motors around the island in a car, flew over it in a small plane, and has taken many pictures. From a hill overlooking Pearl Harbor he has sketched the port, the position of the ships, and even determined that Sunday is consistently the day when most ships are in port. He has done similar work on aircraft movements. Once he even took a cab into Hickam Airfield and recorded the numbers and types of aircraft on the flight line. No one even challenged him"

The Captain nodded, "Yes, I've been impressed by the ensign's ingenuity. But we need many eyes and ears. In particular, we need to be able to report the number of ships in Pearl Harbor just before the attack is to be launched. What of the Japanese emigrants. Have we recruited any?"

"Not really, sir," Nokimura replied, "A few have aided in minor ways, but mostly it is as we discussed previously. Japanese emigrants to America, whether on Oahu or the West Coast of the Mainland, seem only to be interested in making money. Our consulates in both Honolulu and San Francisco tell us that Japanese-Americans are unreliable. They recommend against recruiting them as intelligence assets."

"Really?" the Captain mused, "Our expatriates have apparently forgotten the proverb we learned as children: *Making money is like*

CHAPTER 4

digging with a needle. Being loyal to the Emperor is far more important." As he walked back to his desk, he asked himself silently, "I wonder what the expatriates really think of America? Perhaps they are as indifferent to it as they are to Japan."

⊕ ⊕ ⊕

MAIN NAVY, WASHINGTON D.C., JULY 1941

"Come in, Bill," Captain High said cheerfully, "and shut the door behind you. I've got some things to talk about." LT Bill Russo smiled and pulled one of the office chairs alongside the Captain's desk.

"Bill, there are important decisions being made right now," the Captain began. "ADM Stark has given me a few tasks relative to those, and has asked me to work on them with someone from intelligence. I'd like that to be you, but before you decide let me tell you a little more about it."

"First, let's note for the record that you and I are on separate elements of this staff. I'm in operations, you're in intelligence. Normally we don't work side-by-side because of the so-called 'need to know' principal. You tell me only what I need to know about intelligence and I tell you only what you need to know about operations. That way there's less risk of compromise."

He looked a bit sardonic. "Sounds good, but sometimes it doesn't work very well. For example, if you provide me intelligence that the enemy is producing weapons in a particular building and I bomb it, that's good, right? But what if the agent that gave you that information is in the building and gets killed? That's bad, because I've just shut off a source of future information. We could have avoided that had I known more about your source and you had known more about my operation. We could have bombed the place when he wasn't there. Well, ADM Stark agrees. He thinks there are times when ops and intel need to exchange information more fully. So he told me to pick an intelligence guy who I trust and can work with. I took the liberty of naming you, and the ADM said OK. Your boss wasn't happy about the matter when I told him and muttered some stuff about chain of command. He also insisted that you must agree to the assignment. That's only fair, so now it's up to you. "

A few phrases occurred to Bill about how he had frequently wondered what people in operations did with intelligence and how this would give him a chance to learn. He also knew that the Captain was a pretty capable guy and this would give provide a chance for Bill to learn from him personally. But this was the Navy. Elaborate explanation was not part of the culture. Terse answers were. So Bill simply responded, "Yes sir, I'd like that."

Captain High grunted an acknowledgement. "Great.' He said. "Then we're partners, and 'need to know' doesn't exist between us. We lay it all out on the table. But remember, that's just you and me. When we deal with others, it's still strictly 'need to know.'"

The Captain motioned with his hand as though to clear the air. "OK. Let's get started." He reached across his desk for some hand written notes. "Our first item has to do with some economic moves against Japan that the White House and State Department are mulling over. As you know, we have been pressuring Japan to end its expansion into China. In 1939 we stopped selling them airplane parts, but it was a voluntary thing. The newspapers called it as a 'moral embargo.' Then last July Congress put some teeth into the matter with the Export Control Act. It authorized the President to embargo the export of just about anything in the name of national security. Well, the White House wants to use that authority now. It wants to stop exports of all oil and scrap metal to Japan."

Bill registered surprise. "Wow! That's pretty strong stuff, Captain. Japan is heavily dependent on us for both of those."

"Yes, State and the War Department know that. What they don't know is how an embargo would affect the Imperial Japanese Navy. Our part will be to give ADM Stark some idea about that. The Admiral will also be getting advice thru normal staff channels, but he thinks that will be pretty canned. He says he already knows what the Navy's conventional view is. He'll be looking to us for an independent view."

The Captain looked optimistic. "Bill, I think we could do this. You've been to Tokyo as an assistant attaché. I've sailed throughout the Pacific and think I have some sense of the naval problems the

CHAPTER 4

Japs face. Together maybe we can put together something worth the Admiral's time. So let's get started on this immediately. Remember, you also have *carte blanche* access to any information that bears on this issue. If you get the impression that information is being withheld, just start throwing Admiral Stark's name around."

Bill's brow furrowed. What if his own intel people would not cooperate? Threatening your own organization was usually not a good career move. He would have to finesse that somehow.

The Captain concluded, "Let's get to work on some initial ideas and meet again tomorrow, say 1300, right here in my office."

Bill knew exactly where his next stop would be: the N-2, the Chief of Naval Intelligence, the same officer that had muttered objections to Captain High about assigning Bill to him. The N-2 had a look of astonishment on his face. "You want to WHAT?"

Bill had anticipated the reaction and confronted it directly, "Sir, I want permission to share both Naval and Diplomatic COMINT with Captain High." COMINT is an acronym for Communications Intelligence, intercepts of an adversary's internal communications. COMINT could be extraordinarily valuable. It could enable U.S. officials to read Japanese political and military directives almost as quickly as their intended Japanese recipients. Of course, it was rarely that easy. The Japanese had taken great pains to encrypt their communications and breaking that was extremely difficult.

"You know, Lieutenant," he said stressing Bill's rank to emphasize just how junior he was, "I don't get to read the PURPLE stuff myself." The N-2 was referring to the name U.S. intelligence had given to the Japanese diplomatic encryption system. It employed an Enigma Code Machine that Tokyo had acquired from the Germans. The Japanese had done a few things to improve it and thought they now had a code system that was unbreakable. In fact, it nearly was. It took significant time and effort to decrypt even fragments of Japanese messages. Those fragments were considered very valuable–and very sensitive. If the Japanese even suspected that we were reading their diplomatic traffic, they would immediately change their

THE DOOLITTLE IRONY

encryption system thus depriving the U.S. of an invaluable source. Consequently decryptions of PURPLE were shown to only a very few top Washington officials: the President, a few of his top aides, and perhaps the Secretary of War or Secretary of State. Moreover, any such intelligence report was hand delivered by a special courier personally to the official. The courier waited while the official read it, and then took it directly back to lock it up.

"Yes, Sir," Bill responded, "I understand I'll have to deal with State regarding diplomatic intelligence. I thought we could restrict our review to JN-25 and OP-20-G stuff." JN-25 was the designation the Navy had given to the encryption system the Imperial Japanese used. OP-20-G was the Navy element that collected it. "That's just Navy information."

The N-2 did not look comforted. "For god's sake Lieutenant, we're talking here about the family jewels. And you refer to it as 'just Navy information!'" He stared accusingly at Bill to emphasize his concern.

Bill shifted uncomfortably and chose not to defend himself.

After a pause, the N-2 resumed, "OK, I know the CNO said 'need to know' be damned, but I don't think he really meant it." Again a pause, "Maybe we can reach a compromise, Lieutenant. I'll allow you to review the COM-14 Daily Reports with our friend Captain High, but only if you do it in behind the Green Door, and he signs a non-disclosure agreement."

Bill smiled. Success! He had his information and, perhaps, had even managed to salvage his career.

Captain High was a bit surprised when Bill asked him to move their 1300 meeting from his own office in Main Navy over to Bill's in the Munitions Building, another temp on the Mall. In the Navy, Lieutenants come to Captains, not the other way around. But Bill was a good officer and probably had a good reason, so the Captain was not surprised when he found Bill waiting for him outside the entrance to the Munitions Building. Bill saluted and the two exchanged pleasantries. Bill showed the Marine guard behind the

CHAPTER 4

desk a piece of paper, and then asked Captain High to follow him. They came to a dead end corridor, at the end of which was a door with a large combination lock and a buzzer.

The Captain smiled. "Now I get it. I'm going to be admitted to the *Inner Sanctum*. Good! I've seen these doors before and always wanted to know what you guys were hiding."

"We call it the 'Green Door,'" Bill said, "Even though they're rarely green. And you'll probably be disappointed by what's behind them."

Bill spun three numbers into the combination lock on the door and they entered what appeared to be a standard office with the usual government-issue desks, chairs, and bookcases. There were filing cabinets along one wall and yet another door secured with a combination lock. Bill again spun the dial on that door and invited the Captain inside. It was a conference room with a long mahogany table in the middle and eight chairs situated around it. At one end was a projection screen, maps covered the walls, and carpets covered the floor giving the room a hushed tone. A number of manila folders were stacked in the center of the table.

"This is our briefing room. It's specially built—sound proofed, no windows, that sort of thing—so we can handle the most sensitive information here.

Bill asked the Captain to take a chair and then sat opposite him. "Sir," Bill began, "the information you're to see here today is classified "Top Secret/Codeword." If it were compromised it would cause grave national harm. Normally only people who have been specially cleared have access to it. But the CNO has asked that you personally review this intelligence, so we are sharing it without the usual precautions; however, we ask that you sign this paper. It's an oath that you will never divulge any of this."

"Sure," the Captain said, picking up the pen, "I can do that. I just hope all this mystery is worth it. Anyway, I picked up a few secrets of my own over at State that I can share with you. Maybe we can make some sense of it all."

With that, Bill pushed a thick folder over to the Captain and the two began.

THE DOOLITTLE IRONY

◈ ◈ ◈

Twelve hours and at least a gallon of coffee later, the Captain pushed back from the table, folded his hands thoughtfully, and tried to summarize the matter.

"OK, these appear to be the underlying facts: (1) Japan has only miniscule amounts of oil in its Home Islands, and so must import virtually all the oil it uses. (2) Currently, almost all of that oil it imports is from the U.S. (3) Its Navy has about a two-year reserve of bunker oil, calculated at its present rate of usage. (4) If the Imperial Navy were to accelerate operations to a wartime level, it would quickly deplete Japan's national reserves. Without imported oil, the Imperial Fleet would have to severely limit its operations—we estimate as much as 85%. It can't do that. Japanese interests are spread all over the Western Pacific. Unless its Navy can operate effectively throughout that area, Tokyo's influence in the Western Pacific becomes questionable.

"So," the Captain continued, "To the CNO's question, *What effect will a U.S. embargo of oil to Japan have on the Imperial Japanese Navy?* I think our answer can be summed up in one word. Disastrous! Cutting off its oil would effectively sink the Japanese Fleet. That raises the question, *What will Tokyo do to prevent that loss?*"

The Captain paused to gather his thoughts, and then continued, "The Dutch East Indies has oil. Tokyo has tried pressuring the Dutch into selling it, but they have to deal with the Dutch government-in-exile, which refuses to do business because of Japan's connections with Hitler. But Tokyo is not willing to back off. That's not its style. Like Nazi Germany, it will more likely resort to the use of force. So we looked for evidence of that and indeed, we see indications that both Navy and Army units have been moving generally southward. We think Tokyo is deploying ships and infantry to positions that can support a military seizure of petroleum in the Dutch East Indies. Japan's move into Indochina is almost certainly a part of that strategy. It looks to us like Tokyo is preparing to use military action to seize oil facilities."

Bill applauded quietly. "Well said, Captain! If you are ever looking for a job, we could use you over here in intel."

CHAPTER 4

"Thanks, Bill, but I don't know how many 12 hour sessions like this I could take. It's now the wee small hours. Let's try to get a few hours sleep. I think that we should try to get this to the CNO ASAP," the Captain declared. We'll tell him it's an initial report, and we'll update him as necessary."

Bill nodded, and the next day they did just that.

CHAPTER 5

THE VOYAGE TO TOKYO: OFF AND ON

Crawford, Late July 1941

"Mr. Tanaka! How good to see you. What brings you out here?" Hiro had been checking the now-almost-ripe corn rows when he saw Mr. Tanaka walking up the road. He went over to the fence to greet him.

Mr. Tanaka smiled, "Hiro, I'm so glad I caught you. I have news that may affect your plans to go to Japan."

"Uh oh," Hiro thought. He had been procrastinating about that. Mama-san was still pushing for him to go, and he had just about concluded that Kathleen would never again speak to him. "Mr. Tanaka, you should not have walked all the way out here. It is over a mile."

"I thought you should know, Hiro," Mr. Tanaka said, breathing a bit harder than normal, "Yesterday the Japanese marched into Saigon and Washington immediately embargoed the sale of oil and scrap metal to Japan."

Mr. Tanaka waited for a reaction, but Hiro remained silent. Mr. Tanaka shook his head despondently. "That will end any commercial traffic between the two countries. It's too bad. I hate to see relations

CHAPTER 5

come to this state. But the news I really wanted to bring was that it will not end *all* traffic between the countries. There are Americans in Japan who want to return here. There are also Japanese here in America that want to go back there. "

Then, with a note of satisfaction, Mr. Tanaka said, "So Washington has authorized a small exception to the embargo. Do you remember the passenger liner that we talked about in our last conversation, the *Hikawa Maru*? It will continue to operate, shuttling refugees back and forth, Americans from Yokohama to Seattle and Japanese from Seattle to Yokohama. It's due here in just a few days. I asked if I could get you on board, but it is fully booked with Issei and Nisei that believe war is inevitable. They say that if it happens, Japanese immigrants will not be safe here. I think that's ridiculous. After all, what could happen?"

Hiro ignored Mr. Tanaka's rhetorical question, and said simply, "So I guess that puts an end to any consideration of me going to Japan. I can't possibly go now."

"Not necessarily, Hiro, "Mr. Tanaka responded, "I spoke to a booking agent in Seattle and he said there will likely be at least one more trip by the *Hikawa Maru* after this one, but he didn't know when."

"In my case," Hiro replied, "It probably doesn't make any difference. Matters have moved on." Without explaining his remark he thanked Mr. Tanaka for his kindness and cautioned him to walk home slowly in the late July heat. He then decided that he too had had enough heat for one day and began his walk home.

That evening he tried to explain to Mama-san that events had taken the decision about going to Japan out of his hands. "Mama-san, the U.S. Government has cut off all trade with Japan. Even if we had the money for my fare, I could not go. Ships no longer sail there." Mama-san's reaction was stolid. Hiro could not tell if she didn't understand or simply refused to believe his news.

"We will see," she finally replied in Japanese.

Hiro noted Mama-san's expression of doubt, and wondered to himself whether the matter was indeed settled.

⊕ ⊕ ⊕

THE DOOLITTLE IRONY

AUGUST 1941: SEATTLE

Professor Johnston had set up Hiro's session with the engineers from Scott Engineering, LLC at the firm's headquarters in Seattle. Seven engineers were present, all seated around a heavy mahogany conference table. Hiro was asked to sit at the head. He was nervous and it showed. The engineer who seemed to be in charge asked Hiro if he would like coffee. Hiro refused politely, hoping to get this thing over quickly.

"Mr. Yamada," the same engineer–apparently the lead engineer–began, "Thank you very much for coming. You can relax. This is not an oral examination. It's just a friendly meeting among people who share a common interest in determining why the Tacoma Narrows Bridge collapsed. We were taken by your academic paper, and thought some of your explanation was refreshing. We wanted to you to explain it to us without all the elaborate prose and citations that an academic paper involves."

Hiro smiled, "Yes, I can understand that. Actually the engineering calculations that I offered were mostly window dressing, done to impress Professor Johnston. I suspect that you've already concluded that."

He looked a bit guilty and the engineers smiled empathetically, themselves having had to endure the rigors of engineering school. "In fact, my explanation about how it might have occurred was the product of a story my mother told me about a bridge near where she grew up in Japan. She lived on Shikoku Island in Tokushima Prefecture. Her home was in the mountains, and a deep ravine separated her village from the next where her uncle and cousins lived. There was a rope suspension bridge across the ravine that had been in place for many years. The villagers decided to replace it and, in the process, improve it by adding a wooden deck. It was a wonderful bridge but a high wind would cause it to twist and tangle. It was hard to get anyone to go out over that deep gorge and untangle it. Finally someone suggested that they take every other board out of the wooden deck. It worked. The next high wind that came along left the bridge unaffected. It was just that the wind blew ***through*** the bridge, not against it. The wooden deck had acted like a sail or even a wing, causing the bridge to twist. I thought the eight-foot solid girder and deck on the Tacoma Narrows Bridge might have done the same thing. That's why I suggested that the bridge deck be interspersed with steel grates–to let the air through."

CHAPTER 5

"So," the lead engineer asked quizzically, "it was your mother's childhood experience with a primitive rope bridge that led you to this explanation, not any experimentation of your own?"

"Correct," Hiro replied, "I have no independent data to offer. But my mother's description of her childhood bridge's behavior in high wind closely matched what I saw on the newsreel footage of the bridge's collapse."

"Well," the lead engineer observed, "you seem to have come to the same conclusion that many of us have. They offer wind tunnel tests and elaborate engineering calculations to support their conclusions, but maybe that's all just window dressing too." There was a round of laughs at that comment. "Let's talk more about the details of your paper. I want to go around the table and ask each engineer here to pose his own questions."

They did and, to his surprise, Hiro was able to manage most of the technical exchange. A few of his points even brought nods of appreciation. The session was collegial and Hiro relaxed and felt comfortable with these men. The session had gone on for about an hour when the lead engineer stepped in, "Gentlemen, we should probably end this so you all can get back to your desks. Hiro, I want to thank you for coming by. A fresh perspective is always useful. If you have time, we'd like you to stay for lunch."

Hiro did, and chatted amiably with the staff engineers about engineering science, mutual acquaintances at the University, and even how hot it had been that summer. When he left he was convinced that he wanted to live in the city amid this more collegial, more cerebral culture. He was also gratified that not a single person at Scott Engineering had seemed to notice he was Japanese.

LATE SEPTEMBER 1941: CRAWFORD

Fall had arrived in the Puget Sound. The deciduous trees along its shore had begun to turn color, a minor chill was in the air, and the cold, damp winter of coastal Washington State would soon arrive.

THE DOOLITTLE IRONY

Temperatures would dip into the low thirties but rarely below, days would be darkened by near constant cloud cover, raw winds would prevail out of the northwest, and the sun would brighten the area only a few days each month. Another depressing Seattle winter seemed to be in the offing.

On the Yamada farm the yearly crops had been harvested and the family was settling into its winter routine. Hiro had begun repairing the farm's various tools and machinery: replacing broken handles, sharpening blades, oiling rusty parts, and tuning up the small Ford tractor that his father was so proud of. Mama-san worked in the garden caring for her cabbages, beets, radishes, and other cool weather crops. The girls fed the chickens, slopped the pigs, fed the cow and went to school. Papa-san was less and less active. He obviously welcomed Hiro's return to the farm full-time after graduation, and happily relinquished his duties to him.

But Hiro was not happy. He looked about him and wondered if this is the way he would spend the rest of his days. Two months had passed since his meeting with Scott Engineering and the offer of employment he had hoped for had not materialized. Moreover, he had received no news of Kathleen. Many of her friends had drifted away after graduation, and no one admitted to having any knowledge of her whereabouts. He thought about her constantly. He did not sleep. Loneliness gnawed at him. Had he known where she was, he would have gone to her regardless of Mama-san, the farm, or whatever.

Hiro's fortunes made a significant turn-around in mid-October. Dr. Johnston sent a note: "Hiro: The Scott Engineering firm called and asked me to set up another appointment with you. I hear from an 'alum' with the firm that they like you. Maybe a job offer is in the works." Then he added a comment that surprised Hiro, "I told him that if they do hire you, they will never regret it." Hiro was astonished. Dr. Johnston had never before complimented him.

Hiro showed up at the Scott Engineering offices in downtown Seattle at the appointed hour. This time there was only one person he

CHAPTER 5

was to see, not a panel like last time. The outer office was intended to impress: dark walnut, plush carpet, and a primly attired, middle-aged secretary. She took Hiro's name and used the intercom to announce him. Hiro entered a large, expensive office with an excellent view of downtown. The man seated behind the desk arose extended his hand, and introduced himself as Willard Hardman, the firm's Personnel Director. The two exchanged pleasantries, Hiro accepted a cup of coffee and sat in the guest's chair in front of the desk. Mr. Hardman resumed his seat behind the desk, the traditional position of the authority figure, and Hiro felt appropriately intimidated.

Mr. Hardman opened the business part of the meeting: "Hiro, you made a very favorable impression on our engineering staff when you last visited. They believe you have the sort of attitude and talent that this firm needs. They asked that I look into your background a bit with a view toward possibly hiring you. I made inquiries and learned you have an excellent reputation among the UW faculty, your town elders, and your student colleagues."

Hiro was gratified, smiled an acknowledgement, but remained silent.

"In other words, Hiro, I concluded that our engineering staff was right. You are just the type of young person we like to hire."

Hiro smiled again, sensing that Mr. Hardman was leading up to a problem. He was.

"Unfortunately," Mr. Hardman went on, "we don't hire engineers without experience. We generally require at least three years at an appropriate job. But, as I said, we all liked you and so we struggled to come up with a solution. That's why I've asked you here today–to outline our solution to you and get your reaction to it."

Finally Hiro spoke: "Mr. Hardman," he began earnestly, "Thank you for your kind words. If your staff liked me, I'm flattered. I was certainly impressed with them. They are the sort of professionals that I aspire to be, and the work they do is the sort that I've studied hard to prepare for. Frankly, Mr. Hardman, I would very much like to work at Scott Engineering, so no matter what the 'solution' is you have in mind for me, I think I'm going to like it."

Mr. Hardman broke into a broad grin. "Well, Hiro, I have to say with all due respect that you may never make a good labor negotiator. You just gave away all your bargaining leverage. But I do think you'll make one hell of an engineer. So let's talk about what we have in mind."

Hiro edged forward, anxious to hear every word.

"You may not know this, Hiro, but we do not have a single Japanese employee here at Scott Engineering. We never consciously avoided hiring Japanese, it just we had so little contact with them. But we see that changing. There are capable young Nisei like you, who are coming out of our Universities and moving into responsible positions throughout Seattle. They are talented, highly motivated people. They will succeed and move into positions of responsibility. Scott Engineering needs to know about these people. What are they thinking? What values will guide their business decisions? What would they likely expect from our firm? Your duty would be to advise us on such matters.

"But that's only one aspect of the job. Another would be for you to serve as liaison with our Japanese colleagues at Universities in the Tokyo area. We currently exchange ideas with several professors there. We find them especially well informed on techniques for building earthquake resistant structures. As you know, seismic activity is a concern that Tokyo and Seattle share. You speak Japanese and you understand the basics of structural engineering. I think those two qualifications would make you a fine go-between.

"The third aspect of the job would be for you to assist with the actual engineering that your liaison work entails. For example, we would want you to be knowledgeable of the engineering problems involved in designing earthquake-resistant buildings. In fact, we see that as your first area of specialization. I'm talking about actual engineering problems–slide rule stuff. And we want to get you involved before you begin to meet with our Japanese colleague."

Hiro's brow furrowed, "You mean the professor in Tokyo?"

"Yes," Hardman replied, "The job would require that you travel to Tokyo. Personal contact is important to assure Professor Ito–that's his name–understands our ideas, and we understand his."

Hiro's brow remained furrowed. "But what about the embargo?" he asked, "What about all the rumors of war?"

CHAPTER 5

Mr. Hardman nodded, understanding the question. "Hiro, the embargo is on commercial goods, not intellectual property. I assure you that we've consulted with the State Department and it has given us a go-ahead on this. They have even given us permission to use repatriation ships as transport. Those are Japanese passenger ships that will continue to sail between Yokohama and Seattle. They are exempted from the embargo so they can transport Japanese and Americans who had been resident aliens, but who choose to go back to their homeland.

"As for the rumors of war," Mr. Hardman continued, "Well, they're just rumors. Tokyo and Washington are negotiating the issues that separate them, and the State Department is sanguine that diplomacy will produce a peaceful settlement."

With that Mr. Hardman stopped and waited for Hiro to speak.

"Well, Mr. Hardman," Hiro responded, "That's a remarkable job you've outlined. I'm overwhelmed–and very pleased. The answer to whether or not I would accept the job is YES, YES, and YES! I'm really very grateful." He had already begun to think how he might use a trip to Tokyo to placate Mama-san.

"Great!" Mr. Hardman smiled, "Your salary would be about $1,700 per year, about what you would earn as a beginning officer in the military. Plus there are benefits like insurance, the potential for promotion, re-employment rights if you are drafted, and bonuses if the firm does well. I don't think you could do better than that in another firm. So come back tomorrow at 9:00 AM, and I'll have the paperwork ready for you to sign. Oh, and Hiro, be ready to go to work right after that. We need you to hit the ground running. Your engineer colleagues want to get you started on the seismic work."

They shook hands again and Hiro left, hardly able to comprehend what had happened. He walked to the bus stop in a daze, going back over the job offer in his mind. He stood there for a minute, then flung both arms in the air and yelled an unintelligible "YAAH!" It startled the others waiting for the bus. They eyed him warily, but then decided it was just a youthful exuberance. "One middle-aged lady ventured, "It must have been good news!" Hiro smiled with embarrassment and replied, "Yes, it certainly was."

THE DOOLITTLE IRONY

◆ ◆ ◆

Mama-san was dumbfounded when Hiro returned from the interview and told her of his job.

"You get fancy job?" she blurted out. "How you do that?" His attempts to explain were inadequate. She thought he was mistaken.

When he told her what his salary would likely be her eyes showed even more disbelief.

"Mama-san, don't you see?" Hiro exulted, "That means we don't have to depend on the farm anymore. Sure, we can stay on the farm, but we won't have to grow anything if we don't want to. We can live on my salary."

The disbelief in Mama-san's eyes didn't go away. And the idea of abandoning farm work for a life of leisure was not something Mama-san could easily imagine. It was simply not in her DNA.

When Hiro got to the Tokyo trip, Mama-san became convinced her son had lost his senses. "You go Tokyo? And get fancy job?" Mama-san thought that to be nonsense, but then began to wonder if it were not nonsense whether it might lead to a "proper" wife for Hiro. Mama-san's priorities had not changed.

CHAPTER 6

JAPANESE INTENTIONS

WASHINGTON, D.C. FALL, 1941

The more he thought about it, the more Captain High worried that the report he and Bill had given the CNO didn't go far enough. True, it summarized the current situation and concluded that Japan was preparing to seize both the Dutch and British oil facilities on Borneo, but beyond that there was little grist. Questions occurred to the Captain like: is there a way we can deny Tokyo the oil, even if it does seize the fields? How will Japan defend the oil fields after that? Does Japan have the necessary tanker fleet to ship the oil back to Japan? How would it defend those tankers from interdiction by the U.S. Pacific Fleet?

The Captain had contacted Bill Russo and set up a second session to consider such questions. Again, the two met in the conference room "behind the green door." This time Bill brought a guest to join them from the Library of Congress.

"Captain," Bill began. "I want to introduce Walter Snyder. His outfit normally works for members of Congress, but it sometimes help us as well. Walt specializes in naval matters, and he has done projects for us on Japanese naval history. I thought we might be able to use some historical perspective to our discussion this afternoon."

THE DOOLITTLE IRONY

The Captain smiled, "Damned good idea," he observed, "If the Imperial Navy is anything like ours, history and tradition are pretty damned important. What can you give us to get started on, Walt?"

"Actually, the Imperial Japanese Navy doesn't have a whole lot of history," Walt began, "Japan's an island nation and for the two centuries before Admiral Perry's 1853 arrival in Tokyo Bay, it had isolated itself from the Western world, which it saw as corrupt. No visits to Japan by foreigners, no visits by Japanese to foreign lands, construction of ocean-going ships was forbidden. Hell, they wouldn't even allow Japanese sailors who had been stranded in foreign lands to return to Japan."

That brought a wry smile to the Captain's face. "Probably didn't do much for the tourist industry," he remarked.

"But Admiral Perry's visit changed that," Snyder continued, "It made the Japanese realize that foreign contact was no longer something they could control. The military weapons that Perry had would enable the U.S. and other Western nations to establish enclaves in Japan by force, just as they had done in China. So the Japanese leadership reconciled itself to the new reality and began to modernize. By 1868 the old political order had been replaced by the Meiji throne, which was basically just a front for the new leadership. Japanese students were sent abroad to learn Western technologies. Military academies were founded. Japan bought weapons and ships from Western nations, and established the Imperial Japanese Navy."

"So the IJN is really less than 100 years old?" the Captain asked?

"Yes," Snyder confirmed, "But the IJN was the centerpiece of Japanese modernization, and by the early 20th century it had become one of the most capable navies in the world. It demonstrated that prowess when it defeated Russia in the Russo-Japanese War of 1904-05. More to the point of our discussion, however, I think the IJN walked away from that war with two lessons appropriate to our discussion here: (1) surprise attacks are effective. Their 1904 attack on the Russian Navy's Pacific Squadron at Port Arthur demonstrated that. And (2) dealing with a weakened enemy makes success much more likely. That was the case at the Battle of Tsushima Straits. There, Russian warships which had been part of the Baltic Fleet were finishing a grueling 18,000 mile voyage. Their purpose was to reinforce

CHAPTER 6

the Russian Navy there which had been depleted by losses Russia at Port Arthur. But before it could reach Vladivostok, the Japanese Navy intercepted it in the Tsushima Straits. The Japanese decisively defeated the Russians, even forcing some of its units to surrender while at sea. Sure, the victory was because Japan had better ships, more modern weapons, better training and superior tactics. But it was also because the Russians were on the final leg of a punishing 18,000 transit from Northern Europe. They were physically exhausted; their morale was low; and they were thousands of miles from home."

"So," Captain High offered, "You're suggesting that in the current context, Japan might strive to put those lessons to use. In other words, (1) strike without warning, and (2) choose a battle location far removed from our bases, forcing us into a long, punishing voyage."

"Right," Bill chimed in, "A voyage along which we could fall prey to Jap subs, maybe long range bombers, or maybe even typhoons."

"Right," Snyder concluded, "So the question for you two becomes, where and when? Where and when do they conduct a surprise attack, and where and when do they invite engagement? Answer those and I think you'll have a worthy next chapter for your report to the CNO."

The Captain grinned broadly, raised his eyebrows skeptically and replied, "Right, and after that we'll get busy designing a perpetual motion machine."

Snyder grinned, "Or maybe engineering world peace." With that he excused himself, left, and Bill pushed a stack of folders into the middle of the table.

"So much for history, Skipper." Skipper was the nickname that Navy people called their commanding officers. Bill had recently started using it with Captain High, even though High was not his commanding officer. It was a sign of respect, and the Captain was flattered by it.

"I thought we should take a hard look at our own capability to collect intelligence on the IJN," Bill continued, "So with the reluctant blessing of our N-2, I've got some recent evaluations of our electronic intelligence capabilities: HF/DF, traffic analysis, cryptanalysis, that sort of thing. And after that I've got some evaluations of our aerial reconnaissance around Pearl and Subic Bay in the Philippines."

THE DOOLITTLE IRONY

The Captain sighed. Another long session! Bill poured them both a cup of coffee.

◈ ◈ ◈

Yokosuka, October 1941

CAPTAIN Kanji Ogawa sat behind his desk with the look of a man who was bursting with important news. His chief of staff, Commander Nokimura, sat opposite. He sensed his boss's mood and was anxious to learn what the news was.

"Commander Nokimura," Ogawa started formally, "our country is about to embark on an historic venture. Admiral Yamamoto this morning advised the senior staff that the recent Imperial Conference has issued its findings. It concluded that maintaining the international *status quo* in the face of the U.S. oil embargo is intolerable. Japan must have an assured supply of oil. Unless the embargo is soon lifted, we must take action. The Emperor has been consulted and agrees. If the embargo continues, the Army and Navy will move against the Western Powers. Understand this is not a go-ahead, but it's pretty close to that. My guess is that we have only a month or two before we are at war."

CAPTAIN Ogawa paused to let that sink in, and then continued. "I have been allowed to read The Combined Fleet Operations Order No. 1, not yet issued to the Fleet. It is ambitious. It provides for a surprise attack on Pearl Harbor followed by simultaneous advances throughout the Pacific and Southeast Asia. The lynchpin is the attack on Pearl. We must destroy the American Pacific Fleet if we are to succeed elsewhere, and the best place to do that is in its home base at Pearl Harbor. That brings me to the point: where are we on that task? Any last minute problems?"

"I think we're ready, sir," Nokimura replied. "As you know, we've provided aerial and hydrographic maps to our strike forces. We have sketches and diagrams of the harbor and shore facilities ready to distribute to the fleet. We have packets of American money for the pilots and crewmen to carry in case they go down. We can even give

CHAPTER 6

them addresses of friends on the ground who might–I stress the word 'might'–be willing to provide them refuge."

He paused, hoping for a bit of recognition for the good work he had produced. Failing to receive it, Nokimura continued, "But I'm a bit worried about getting reports on the enemy's disposition just before the attack. Ideally we should know what naval units are in port, their alert condition, last minute changes in the order of battle–that sort of thing."

"You mean we can't do that?" Ogawa asked worriedly.

"Well, not with human source reporting," Nokimura said, "As you know sir, we have had no success recruiting local Issei or Nisei. The Germans think they have a reliable agent in place, but I don't trust them. Of course, Ensign Yoshikawa is still in Honolulu but I had hoped to get him out of there soon. He's concerned that Army intelligence has become suspicious of him. He thinks they may have him under surveillance. Besides, he's done pretty much all he can do and we could certainly use his knowledge of that area back here in headquarters."

"If that's the case, Nokimura," Ogawa interrupted, "Get him out of there. We cannot risk having him uncovered as an espionage agent. It would give America a reason to raise an international outcry and maybe call off the peace talks. We want those to continue for the time being!"

"Very well, sir," Nokimura acknowledged, "We'll direct him to return but if he is under suspicion, he would be stopped when he tries to leave the country."

"Then have him come back clandestinely. Do you have an escape plan in place?" Ogawa asked.

"We do sir, but it involves a submarine and I don't think we've come to that yet. There are probably ways to do it without diverting fleet units. Yoshikawa may have to go to a third country–probably Mexico–and then somehow find ocean transport back here. The Trade Ministry has under-the-table contacts in Mexico that buy commodities for us–copper, oil, and other things the embargo has cut off. They send it back here on flag ships from neutral countries. He could probably get on one of those. In any case Yoshikawa has plenty of money and he's an intrepid sort. If there's a way to get back here, he'll find it."

THE DOOLITTLE IRONY

"Good," Ogawa said gruffly, "Now let's get back on the subject at hand. Where are we on preparations for the attack?"

Nokimura resumed his report. "Sir, with respect to information about whether ships in port when we attack, we have high frequency direction finding and radio monitoring to detect their arrival or departure. It won't be as certain as a pair of human eyes reporting on what they see from a nearby hill, but it will probably suffice."

Captain Ogawa again held his hand up to stop Nokimura. "Wait, Commander. There's an important point to be made here. Our focus should not be identifying American ships in Pearl Harbor just before the attack. The fleet can launch scout planes to do that. But by then it will be too late. The attack force will already have been committed. You see, according to our attack plan, the *Kido Butai*, our force of carriers and cruisers that actually conduct the strike, will initially sail to standby positions northwest of Honolulu. There they will await a decision by General Headquarters to GO or NOT GO. Once they get the GO decision, there will be no turning back. They will need three or four days to refuel and steam into launch position. That is why we need three or four days advance knowledge of the carrier's location."

Nokimura was impressed. Why hadn't he thought of that? "Yes, I see. That's a very important point, Captain." This was not Nokimura's day. The Captain had corrected him twice. A third could bring his career to an end and perhaps orders to an oiler at sea.

⊕ ⊕ ⊕

ENSIGN YOSHIKAWA, IMPERIAL JAPANESE NAVY

Yoshikawa opened the radio telegram that had been delivered to his hotel room. It originated in a telegraph office in Tokyo and read, "MOTHER NOT WELL STOP COME HOME STOP." It was from the Imperial Japanese Navy's intelligence Headquarters, sent from an "accommodation address," a commercial telegraph office that had no connection to intelligence. It was an order for him to return home immediately, and he had expected its arrival ever since

CHAPTER 6

he reported that he might be under surveillance. It was welcome. The newspapers daily chronicled how relations between the U.S. and Japan were deteriorating, and in Yoshikawa's opinion, war was imminent. He wanted to be part of it, flying a fighter airplane, not interned in Hawaii–which is where he would end up if he was still in Honolulu when war broke out. He had collected just about all the intelligence he could, given that he was not permitted to recruit Westerners. Too risky! He had sent roadmaps, ground photos, aerial photos, port sketches, etc., back to Tokyo in the diplomatic pouch, and dozens of information reports by coded message.

His return was doubly important because he had come by a document that he knew would have extreme value to the IJN if it attacked Pearl Harbor. The document was a compendium of about 35 legal-sized sheets of paper that showed fleet movements planned for the last quarter of 1941. It had a card stock cover with an official Navy seal and a header and footer that read SECRET in bold red letters. It was entitled, <u>PACFLT MOVEMENT SCHEDULE: Fourth Quarter 1941</u>. Inside there were two pages of introduction and explanation, followed by 31 lined pages, each showing a row of dates across the top and columns for each day of the month aligned below. Along the left side of each page appeared a list of every major combatant then in the Pacific Fleet: three aircraft carriers, nine battle ships, 12 heavy cruisers, and eight light cruisers. In rows across from each ship was its location and activity for each day of the month. For example, the battleship Nevada on the 29th of the month might be shown as, "At Sea, Exercise Sunrise," or "In Port, Pearl," or some other such activity. Hence, for any day of the month one could determine where any given ship in the Pacific Fleet was and what it was doing.

"Wow," was Yoshikawa's only comment as the value of such information dawned on him.

Yoshikawa had acquired the document from a prostitute. She had come to his hotel room and explained that she previously sold such items to one of the Japanese men in the consulate. When the man had to return to Japan, he told the prostitute if she ever had any more information to contact Yoshikawa. She explained further that a drunken young American Naval Officer had left it in her room, and wondered if Yoshikawa would pay her for it. Yoshikawa was suspicious, but after a brief inspection, he decided to take a chance and offered the girl $50. Her eyes lit up and she left his hotel room with the money tucked in her bra. Since then Yoshikawa had examined the document thoroughly and concluded it was very likely an authentic U.S. Navy document. If it been a trap set by Army Security, he reasoned, he would have been arrested by now. He placed the document in an innocent looking business envelop and put it in the lining of his suit coat.

Just then there was a knock on the door and a delivery boy handed him a second telegram. "ASK YOSHIKO TO HELP STOP." Sending a separate telegram from a different telegraph office was a standard security precaution. "Yoshiko" was a codeword meaning that he was to return home IMMEDIATELY via clandestine means. "I wonder if this means they have other information that I am being watched," he mused. If so, he would indeed have to leave as soon as possible, before Army security could put him under arrest.

Choosing to play it safe, he packed a small bag that would not attract attention as he left through the lobby. Then he tried to remember if there was anything in the room he should get rid of. The Embassy was now closed so he could not send the document back to Tokyo in the Diplomatic Pouch. He would have to take it with him. He tossed it into his bag.

Getting transportation back to Japan would not be easy. Ocean traffic there had ended when America imposed the embargo. Sailing to an alternate country would take too much time, and Yoshikawa was determined to get the document back to Tokyo before the war started. There was one possibility that occurred to him, a long shot but maybe the only way he could get back in time.

Yoshikawa left the Japanese-language hotel where he had stayed since his arrival in Honolulu and found his way to the OR&L Train Station. The railroad was a narrow gauge line that had been built to serve the sugarcane plantations, but now also carried mail and passengers. It was the preferred means of travel to Pearl City, because the road there was pot holed and slow. Pearl City contained several immigrant settlements: Chinese, Filipino, and Japanese. Yoshikawa had visited the latter seeking to recruit Issei or Nisei informants–

CHAPTER 6

unsuccessfully, of course. In the process he had met a Japanese immigrant that worked at the Pan American Clipper Terminal. From that vantage point, one had an excellent view of the U.S. Naval Base located on Ford Island. Yoshikawa had sought to recruit him as a port watcher, but the man just ignored his overtures. Yoshikawa hoped this time he could get his attention.

Pan American Clipper flights had begun between San Francisco and Honolulu in 1935, the first commercial passenger service to transit the Pacific. The aircraft used were Boeing 314B seaplanes–Pan Am Clippers–large enough to carry sufficient fuel for the long 19-hour flight to Honolulu. There they would refuel and continue island hopping across the Pacific via Midway, Wake, Guam, Manila, and finally Hong Kong. They carried 76 passengers in luxurious accommodations with formally attired stewards and silver dining service. A round trip from San Francisco to China cost an astronomical $1,368, so only the very wealthy ever flew them. Being seaplanes, the aircraft did not land at Rodgers Field, Honolulu's main airport. They "landed" in the seaway at Middle Loch, the bay along the west shore of Pearl City, and then taxied to the Pan American Pier where the Honolulu-bound passengers would disembark for the eight-mile train ride into the city.

The Issei that Yoshikawa had sought to recruit was a porter. On days there were Clipper flights he would help load or unload baggage, clean the planes, and load food for the next leg of the flight. When there were no flights–which was most of the time because service was only weekly–he would clean the terminal building or perhaps provide personal assistance to one of the Pan American officers. It was in the latter capacity that Yoshikawa had found him potentially useful.

He waited at the tea house for the man to make his usual stop, the same place Yoshikawa had attempted to engage the man in conversation a month earlier. When he entered, Yoshikawa waved, as though seeing an old friend, "Masao, how are you? And how is your daughter's health?" On their previous encounter he had provided the man a small sum of money in response to the man's report that his daughter was sick. Actually Yoshikawa suspected there was no sick daughter and the man was simply trying to scam a little extra income. But that was OK. It had been an opportunity to put the man in Yoshikawa's debt, a standard tactic by intelligence officers seeking to recruit locals. It might now prove to have been money well spent. The Pan American Officer for whom the porter worked was the officer who controlled the sale of Clipper tickets in Honolulu, and thus a man who might now prove useful to Yoshikawa.

Securing Masao's cooperation would require a delicate approach. Yoshikawa would not simply offer a bribe. He would dignify it with a plausible story. "As I told you when we met before," he said to Masao across the table in the tea room, "I came to Honolulu to care for my ailing uncle. But I was too late. My uncle died and then the Americans imposed the embargo. I am stranded here. Can your boss get me aboard a Clipper flight? My uncle left me a substantial amount of money so I can afford the fare. I know that the flights are booked months in advance, but maybe your boss would let me know if any cancellations developed. I would be willing to pay **twice** the standard fare."

Yoshikawa realized that his offer to pay "twice the fare" might be recognized as a thinly veiled bribe. But Masao's boss had likely served in other areas of the Orient where such matters were common business practices and would likely not be offended. And even if he was, well, $1,368 would be difficult to turn down for doing no more than juggling a single reservation.

"Of course," Yoshikawa continued to Masao, "I would insist that you take a sum of money for helping me. I know your daughter's illness is serious and you need help." The porter's eyes lit up greedily. It would take an additional sum to secure his cooperation, but Yoshikawa didn't care. He had plenty of money. His contact at the consulate had passed him $25,000 before leaving to return to Japan. Yoshikawa smiled at the porter, expressed his concerns about the man's daughter, and slid an envelope across the table with $500 in it. Yoshikawa knew it was a huge sum to such a man, and would allay any compunction he might have about risk.

Satisfied with his effort, Yoshikawa found a Japanese hotel and stayed the night.

⊕ ⊕ ⊕

CHAPTER 6

The following afternoon, Yoshikawa again met with Masao who shook his head when he saw Yoshikawa.

"What?" Yoshikawa said in genuine surprise, "There are no possibilities at all?"

Masao shook his head firmly and reported in broken English, "Boss say China flights checked by Army. Worry about spies. No chance to move you onto flight unnoticed."

Yoshikawa sighed.

But the porter wasn't done. "Boss say one flight possible. Maintenance flight. But not go China. Go U.S."

"The U.S.?" Yoshikawa echoed, thinking that was the last place he wanted to go. "Where in U.S.? San Francisco?"

"No," Masao replied, "Tacoma.," he said, mispronouncing the name, "Where plane factory is."

"Tacoma?" Yoshikawa repeated aloud. His knowledge of U.S. cities was limited, but being a pilot he knew that Boeing, the company that manufactured the 314B Clipper aircraft, was located near Seattle. Tacoma must be near Seattle–and Seattle was a maritime port, so perhaps he could get a ship out. He pondered only briefly. Time was becoming critical and this might be his last chance to get off the island. Besides, if it worked out, he might develop a few insights to offer Japanese intelligence when he got home about the American home front.

"OK," Yoshikawa said. "I'll do it. What are the details?"

"Only one detail," The porter replied, "Price the same. Boss say very expensive to fly Clipper, even to Tacoma. Still OK?"

Yoshikawa cringed a bit. He didn't mind the money. It wasn't his. But he didn't like being scammed, and he felt that was just what had happened. Nevertheless, he smiled and said simply, "Sure. Why not?"

✥ ✥ ✥

SEATTLE, 1 NOVEMBER

On 1 November 1941, just 37 days before aircraft of the Imperial Japanese Navy would attack Pearl Harbor, Yoshikawa boarded a

THE DOOLITTLE IRONY

314B Pan American Clipper bound for the Boeing Repair Facility near Tacoma, Washington. There were only three other passengers on board—Tacoma was apparently not a very popular destination. All three were Caucasian and none, Yoshikawa was happy to note, were gregarious, so he did not have to worry about small talk. Getting through customs and immigration controls would not be a problem. Those applied only to international flights, and arrivals from Hawaii were domestic. Nor did he worry about Masao or the Pan American officer raising questions. They would keep very quiet about the whole matter. They had a vested interest in seeing him get to Tacoma successfully.

Yoshikawa's outlook was buoyant as the plane left the pier and taxied out to the seaway. The 314B impressed him with its size. He would have loved to watch the takeoff from the cockpit, but he thought that asking to do so would raise his profile. So he contented himself with enjoying the plush passenger cabin, his oversized seat, and the view of Diamond Head as it drifted by on their port side. He worried that Japan had no long range seaplane like this, even though it was a maritime nation. He mused about what that implied regarding Japan's ability to wage modern war, but then decided to let someone else worry about that. He was just an ensign and his task now was simply to get back home.

He had reason to be optimistic. Tokyo had reported via telegraph that despite the embargo, two Japanese ocean liners would continue to sail between Seattle and Yokohama. The U.S. Government had designated them "repatriation ships," and they would transport Japanese and American citizens that had been living as aliens in one another's countries, back to their homelands. According to headquarters, one of the ships, the *Hikawa Maru*, had left Yokohama on such a voyage 20 October and was due to return there 18 November. Given that the transit required about 12 days, that meant it would leave Seattle on 6 November, less than a week away. He resolved to be on that ship.

Yoshikawa disembarked from the Clipper flight at the Boeing landing pier near Tacoma. As a courtesy, Boeing provided a station wagon and driver to take the three passengers to Seattle. The driver was Japanese and suggested a place in Japantown where Yoshikawa

CHAPTER 6

could stay: the Frye Hotel at Third and Yeser. The desk clerk asked him to sign the register and he penned in Kanji, the Japanese written script, *Matsumoto Ryo*, the alias he traveled under.

It was late and Yoshikawa welcomed the opportunity for a good night's sleep. He had five days to figure out how to get aboard the *Hikawa Maru* for its voyage back to Yokohama. He was confident that he would do so.

CHAPTER 7

THE VOYAGE TO JAPAN

It was Saturday, and Hiro had completed two weeks and one day at his new job. It had proven to be all he had hoped for: the work was challenging, the older engineers treated him with dignity, and the younger engineers accepted him as a peer. In fact one of the younger engineers had invited to meet him for a beer and sandwich today, Saturday. Going into the city was a rather long bus ride just to have lunch, but Hiro did not want to appear unfriendly. So here he was, at a neighborhood bar near this fellow's apartment, engaged in conversation about predictable topics: each other's personal background, their education, expectations about their jobs, office personalities, a *sub rosa* romance between one of the engineers and a pretty secretary, etc. Hiro mostly listened.

Stanley Polasky, Hiro's luncheon mate, was from Pittsburgh. He proudly referred to himself as a "Polack," a term that Hiro correctly assumed was an ethnic slur that Stanley had adopted to reflect perverse pride in the inferior social status of the Polish. He was tall, broad shouldered, fair skinned, and blue eyed. Hiro wondered why a 'Polack," that looked so Caucasian would be considered socially inferior.

Stan's size and athleticism had won him a football scholarship to the University of Pittsburgh. Although he was never good enough to make the first string, the scholarship paid his way to an engineering

CHAPTER 7

degree. Stanley explained that after Pitt he worked as a structural engineering apprentice for US Steel and learned a lot about working with metals. The job promised a comfortable future, but by then his parents had both died and Pittsburgh was too much of what its nickname proclaimed–a Smokey City. Stan left in search of cleaner air and Seattle provided that–though perhaps a bit wet and occasionally raw.

Stanley moved the conversation in a more serious direction. "Mr. Hardman probably told you that the firm looked into your background, Hiro. They do that for all new hires–but they don't hire detectives to do it. They assign regular staff. I was the guy they asked to check you out." He smiled slyly, "So I probably know more about you than you suspect."

That caught Hiro's attention. "Really?" Hiro responded, "Not a very interesting investigation, I imagine. I've led a boring life"

"Well," Bob replied, "Actually I thought it was quite interesting. I saw it as the classical ethnic struggle. Nisei tries to break out of the immigrant mold; goes to University; does quite well, but struggles with divided loyalties: his family or modern America? Old versus new?"

"I hadn't thought of it in quite those terms," Hiro said, "Are you sure you didn't major in sociology?"

"Maybe I should have," Stan laughed, "but I haven't yet mentioned the most difficult part of this struggle: your romance!"

Hiro stared at Stan and wondered if he should take offense at this intrusion in his personal life. But Stan's remarks sounded well intentioned, even sympathetic. He wanted to hear where he was taking this conversation. "You obviously did a thorough investigation, Stan. Have you any conclusions?"

"In fact I do," Stan said, "And I offer them with hopes that you'll accept them as coming from a new friend, one who hopes someday to be an old friend."

Hiro listened closely, a bit afraid of what he might hear.

"I learned that you and Kathleen are a really good pair. If it weren't for this clash between the so-called White Americans around here and you Japanese-Americans, you and Kathleen would probably be talking about a wedding date. Instead you have both been victimized—I don't think that word is too harsh—by your loyalty to your parents. You, Hiro, are trying to placate your mother by conducting a charade to find a Japanese bride, and Kathleen is hiding away because her mother thinks that Japanese boys are Yellow dwarfs."

Hiro was stunned. Stan's investigation had indeed been thorough! But it was the point about Kathleen that caught Hiro's attention most. "What do you mean," Hiro interrupted, "hiding away?"

"Just that, Hiro. When Kathleen's mother found out that she was seriously involved with you, she sent her out of town, where no one was likely to find her. It's an island, highly secluded, no telephone, a long way away." Stan paused.

"The worst part is that she has made Kathleen feel very guilty for having fallen in love with you. That's the reason Kathleen has chosen not to escape her little prison. Filial piety—that's a phrase that I learned in Catholic school—keeps her there. She thinks that if she left, it would cause some terrible fate to befall her mother. "

Again, Stan paused to organize his thoughts. "Look, Hiro, I'm from Pittsburgh and I don't pretend to understand the antipathy many of the Whites have for you Japanese-Americans—and vice-versa! But I am pretty sure that Kathleen loves you and you love her, and the hate that parents carry ought not to interfere with their children's lives. I don't want to see a Shakespearean tragedy played out in Scott Engineering."

Hiro was overwhelmed. "Stan, how do you know all this? How do you know where she is? How do you know she still loves me? How do you know all that?"

"Two ways," Bob replied. "One, I talked to her father, and two, I talked to her."

"You what?" Hiro exploded.

"That's right, I talked to her father. Nice guy, but it seems that even though he's a policeman who's supposed to maintain public order, he has difficulty controlling his own wife. You see, Hiro, like me he conducted his own little investigation. He concluded you're an OK guy. But his wife can't get past your skin color. He finds that especially funny because the two of them had a similar problem. Kathleen's mother is not Irish-Catholic. She's German. Grew up Lutheran. When the two of them decided to marry he told her

CHAPTER 7

that he wanted a Catholic wedding. So, over her parent's strenuous objections she converted and even raised the children in the Catholic Church. You know what they say about the converted: even more devout than those born to the faith! Her Dad thinks that Kathleen still loves you because every time he visits her she pumps him for every little detail about your life. When he told her you were not going to Japan to get a bride, she said, 'Oh, I knew he would never do that.'"

"And you talked to her in person?" Hiro asked incredulously.

"Yes. Had to. No telephone. Her dad told me where she is so I just drove up and knocked on the door. When I explained why I was there she wasn't surprised. She told me that she had always been sure you would get a good job and added that you were a 'genuinely wonderful person'—which I took to be just a bit mushy and didn't include in my report. She also asked that I do everything I could to help you. That's what prompted me to ask you here for lunch. It's probably not the kind of help she had in mind, but it's the kind I think you need."

Hiro smiled ironically, "And I thought this was just a beer and sandwich lunch!"

He waited a moment to see if Stan had anything more to add, and then got directly to the point, "Stan, you know where she is. I want you to tell me. I want to go see her right now!"

Stan smiled, "Then I consider my little intrusion in your life a success. That's exactly what I hoped you would do. She's on Whidbey Island, couple hours drive north. Here's is her address," he said handing Hiro a 3x5 card he pulled from his shirt pocket. "The place is just across Deception Pass."

Hiro's brow furrowed. "Is there a bus?" he asked. "I don't own a car."

"Yes, well, I rather anticipated that," Stan sighed, holding up his own car keys. "Take mine. It's right outside, a 37 Chevy. And be careful. It's four years old, but I just bought it."

Hiro took the keys, then added with embarrassment, "Stan, I hate to ask, but will it need gas? I didn't bring any extra money."

"Oh, for gawd's sake," Stan laughed and brought out his wallet, "Here's three dollars. And if this romance works out, I expect the first boy to be named after me!"

THE DOOLITTLE IRONY

As he ran out of the restaurant, Hiro wondered how that would sound: Stan Yamada. He decided it had a nice ring.

⊕   ⊕   ⊕

WHIDBEY ISLAND, WASHINGTON: THE EVENING OF 1 NOVEMBER

Whidbey is a long, narrow island that meanders up Puget Sound from Seattle for about 50 miles. Deception Pass is located at its northern tip, separated from the Mainland by about a 1,000 foot of scenic water. The bridge across the Pass had been a Depression Era project finished in 1935. Hiro had visited it a few years ago with a buddy that owned a car. He had been struck by the stunning views of Puget Sound 180 feet below, and the steep, pine covered mountains that rise abruptly out of the Pacific.

Getting there was a long drive, up through Everett and Mount Vernon along roads that seemed to transit every small village. It took over two hours, and the sun had begun to decline when he crossed Deception Pass Bridge.

He passed knots of tourists enjoying the views, and stopped at a local general store about a mile down the road to ask directions. "Oh, sure," the lady behind the counter said when she looked at the address on his 3x5 card, "That's Charlotte's place, not far at all."

The woman provided directions. Hiro thanked her and wheeled the Chevy back out onto the highway. A mile later the woman's directions took him down a dirt road to a pleasant cottage with a stunning view of the Pacific. As he stopped the car, a large dog looked out the window of the house, began barking, and exploded through the front door toward the car. The dog was of substantial size, black, and of dubious pedigree. Hiro wasn't sure whether it would greet him or attack him.

"Don't worry," called a middle aged woman who emerged on the porch. "He's all bark and no bite."

She walked down to the car to quiet the dog. "Shush, Shadow." She instructed, "He's a friend."

CHAPTER 7

By then Hiro had got out of the car to explain his presence. "Hello," he said, "Let me introduce myself ..."

But the woman interrupted good naturedly, "Not necessary! I know who you are. Your name is Hiro and you're here to see Kathleen." Hiro was stunned. This seemed to be a day for surprises.

"It's about time you arrived," the woman went on not giving Hiro a chance to respond, "I thought you'd be here days ago." She grasped his hand and said, "I'm Kathleen's Aunt Charlotte."

She was an earthy woman, middle aged but fit, with a no-nonsense air. Hiro thought if Hollywood ever made a movie about her it would star Marjorie Main.

"I am really glad you're here," Aunt Charlotte enthused, "She's been moping around for months and I was beginning to wonder if she'd ever leave."

Hiro tried to break in, but Aunt Charlotte was on a roll.

"You know," she went on, "I just don't understand all this. It's not like Helga–that's Kathleen's mother, my sister–didn't have her own problems when she married. She was German Lutheran, and she wanted to marry an Irish Catholic. Her family thought she was marrying down, just like Helga thinks Kathleen is doing. Anyway, Helga not only married a Catholic, she raised her kids in the Catholic Church too. Now it's Mass on Sunday, no meat on Friday, says the rosary every day, the whole shebang!"

Charlotte wasn't done yet. "And despite all that, she's wrapped around the axle about you being Japanese. I told her it could be worse. You could be a Hereford bull. Or even worse, you could be a Nazi. She got my drift about that but I don't think she liked it. Anyway me and Pat–that's her husband–haven't figured out a way to handle her yet without causing permanent damage. That's why I was hoping you'd come along and do a Prince Charming thing. You know, sweep her off her feet. When Stan Polasky showed up, I was sure he'd go right back and tell you where she was and you'd be here that same day."

She paused long enough in her stream of consciousness for Hiro to break in. "Well, ma'am," Hiro said, reluctant to call her Aunt Charlotte, "It was almost like that. I guess Stan was reluctant to intrude. But he finally told me over lunch less than three hours ago and here I am. I didn't waste any time!"

THE DOOLITTLE IRONY

"Good for you, Prince Charming," Charlotte smiled, "Now I guess you want to see Snow White. She walked down the steps to the dock. Shadow will show you." She said looking down at the black dog. "Shadow loves Kathleen. She throws his stick for him." Charlotte pointed toward the handrail of the steps behind the house and spoke to Shadow as if he were human, "Go get Kathleen, Shadow. Go ahead. That's a good dog. Get Kathleen."

Sure enough, the dog loped toward the steps and plunged down them out of sight. Hiro went after him, but Shadow was far too fast. By the time Hiro reached the bottom, Kathleen was standing on the pier with her back to him, throwing Shadow's stick in the water. The dog plunged after it, and Hiro called out Kathleen's name.

She heard it, turned, saw him, and let out a yelp like a child running out of school on the first day of summer vacation. In that instant he realized why he loved her so much, she was so full of life, so much fun to be with! And she was also a fast runner! Before he knew it, she had closed the distance between them and leapt the last yard to come down with her arms and legs wrapped tightly around him. Hiro tried to catch her but the impact was too much. They both tumbled to the ground, laughing and hanging tightly on to one another, unwilling to let go even to look in one another's face.

Oh, Hiro she blurted out, "I have missed you so much! Hiro, I love you, I love you, I love you!"

Hiro pulled back just enough to see her face. "Kathleen, I was beginning to think I would never see you again. I have missed you too. I am never going to let you go."

But at that very moment he felt something wet fall on his neck. It was a stick. And just above it was Shadow's friendly face, wondering why these two adult human beings were lying on the grass. The grass was his domain, not a human's. Then, having dropped the stick, he shook the water from his shaggy coat in the fashion that dogs do, and sprayed a substantial part of the cold Pacific Ocean all over Hiro and Kathleen.

It broke the moment. They both jumped to their feet laughing uncontrollably, and then looked at one another as though quenching the loneliness of the past months in one another's countenance. They kissed again, with an embrace that began as simple affection but

CHAPTER 7

developed into a passionate, feverish clutching, their bodies pressing desperately close to one another.

"Oh, Hiro," Kathleen breathed heavily in his ear, "I think we'd better stop."

Hiro did not want to stop, but her embrace loosened and she pulled away. All the reasons why they must stop were there. It was 1941. Couples did not have sex before marriage–well, not many anyway. The threat of pregnancy and social opprobrium was too great. And they already had enough problems to deal with being a biracial couple.

Kathleen took Hiro's hand and led him to a White, slatted wooden bench large enough for the two of them. They sat, Hiro's arm around her, and looked out at the water. The setting sun glinted off the water like a thousand diamonds. They were silent for a few minutes, trying to understand what was happening. There was so much to talk about.

"First tell me about your new job, Hiro" Kathleen began. "Are the people nice? Do you enjoy the work?" Then with a mischievous smile Kathleen asked, "And do you enjoy riding the bus without me?"

"No," Hiro responded truthfully, "I find talking to a lot of other men with lunch boxes not much fun!" He grinned at that, and then launched into a long story about his employment interviews, his job, his salary, Mama-san 's reaction, and finally his lunch with Stan Polasky that very same day.

Kathleen listened intently, happy for his good fortune.

"There is one thing I left out," Hiro added with a glint of mischief in his eye, "I'm going to Tokyo after all." He stopped and watched for her reaction.

"You're WHAT?" she exclaimed. "But my Dad said you were NOT going to Tokyo! Oh, Hiro, …" With that Hiro broke out into a laugh and clamped his hand over her mouth.

"Shhhh!" he said, "I'm not going to find some dumb Japanese bride. I'm going for the firm, to meet a Japanese professor and talk about earthquakes."

Kathleen hauled back and hit Hiro on his shoulder with her fist. It hurt. "Don't tease me like that, Hiro," she yelled, "I almost had a heart attack!"

THE DOOLITTLE IRONY

Hiro reflected that a proper Japanese bride would probably not hit so hard. He embraced Kathleen, as much to prevent her from swinging a second time as out of affection for this spirited young woman he had fallen in love with. "Kathleen, I have something important to talk about. I am going on my first trip to Tokyo Thursday, and I have one important question that I want you to answer before I leave."

"Oh," Kathleen looked up slyly and said, "And what might that be, Hiro?"

He thought about getting down on one knee, but decided that she might laugh at him. Kathleen was not the kind of girl that read pulp romance magazines. He went right to the point, "Will you marry me, Kathleen?"

"Oh, Hiro," she burst and put her arms around his neck, "you don't have to wait for Thursday to get an answer to that. Yes, I'll marry you," she effused, "And I'll have your children. And I will love your family. And I may even learn to cook rice!"

Hiro was so happy that tears appeared. He hugged Kathleen tightly so she would not see them and perhaps think him weak. He had never been so happy. Life was wonderful.

He would remember this moment in the months that followed. It would get him through some very difficult times.

Hiro and Kathleen had talked about their future into the wee small hours that morning on Whidbey Island. They had so much to decide, so much to plan. But they agreed the first order of business had to be telling their parents. It was not a task either of them relished. Hiro knew he would have to be firm.

The next evening after coming home from work, he framed his story to Mama-san in candid, factual terms. Mama-san listened patiently and then furrowed her brow. She began in English–not a good sign–and Hiro braced himself.

"So, you now tell me what I already know," she began forcefully, "You think I not know about Kathleen? You think nobody tell me nothing? You think I not see you mope around like sick calf? Why

CHAPTER 7

you not tell me before?" Mama-san paused and changed back to Japanese, "So now you are telling me that Kathleen will make a good wife for you. You are in love. That is dangerous. Japanese have a saying for that: *Those who come together in passion stay together in tears.* You think that life will always be as happy as it is now, but I know better. You listen to Mama-san. When you go to Tokyo, I want you to go see my sister. She will introduce you to lovely Japanese girls …"

"No, Mama-san," Hiro interrupted forcefully, "When I go to Tokyo it will be to talk about earthquakes, not brides. I have made up my mind that Kathleen will be my bride." Hiro knew that Mama-san was pressing the issue because she sincerely thought that a Japanese bride would make him happy. But he also realized that Mama-san was worried about her own future. He had just as much as told her there would be no son running the farm and there would be no dutiful Japanese daughter-in-law to care for Mama-san in her old age. She was understandably distraught, and Hiro tried to reassure her.

"Don't worry, Mama-san, Kathleen and I will always make sure you and Papa-san are well cared for. We probably won't marry for several years. I have to establish myself on my job, and Kathleen wants to pay her family back for her college tuition. So there is plenty of time. And you will love Kathleen, and she will love you."

Mama-san grunted and thought to herself, "Love! It sounds like a Hollywood movie!"

Like Hiro, Kathleen was having little success with her mother.

"You simply don't know what you're getting yourself in for, Kathleen," her mother intoned. "Having a romance on campus is one thing but living in society is quite another. Young people are open to new ideas. Older people are not. They dislike what they don't know. The White community will not accept Hiro, and the Japanese community will not accept you. And while you and Hiro may be willing to live with that, what about your children? Where will they belong?"

Kathleen had had enough. "Mom," she interrupted, "I don't know how you can say all that. You and Dad had the same problems. You managed."

"Religious differences do not run as deep as racial differences, Kathleen."

"Well, that's not what Gramma and Grampa thought when you told them you were converting to Catholicism and marrying in the Catholic Church. They wouldn't go to your wedding. They wouldn't allow Dad in their house. Well, they got over that. Now they love Dad like a son. And I know they love me and my brother. It was just silliness Mom. You know my friends in college say Catholics are just Lutherans who took Latin!"

Kathleen's mom had heard that line before and even thought it had considerable merit, but she was not about to concede that to her daughter. "Really, Kathleen, coarse humor is not helpful. Have you thought about how you will raise your children? As Catholics or Buddhists?"

"Really, Mom, that's far in the future. Hiro and I have not even discussed it." That was a truthful statement. They had not discussed it–but Kathleen had indeed thought about it and made a decision. The children would be raised Catholic. There was no other option. Moreover, she was sure that Hiro would agree.

Kathleen and Hiro regarded their respective discussions as victories. They had made their intentions known. Their parents may not have approved, but neither had they threaten to disown the two. Kathleen and Hiro were confident that over time their parents would come around.

CHAPTER 8

YOSHIKAWA AND THE *HIKAWA MARU*

That morning Yoshikawa ate the hotel's breakfast special—a fried egg over rice with miso soup—and engaged the waiter in conversation. The waiter welcomed the diversion and happily explained that he was Nisei, as were most Japanese-Americans in the area. He spoke English fluently, but his Japanese included much of the antiquated vocabulary that the Issei had brought with them from Japan. He explained that Japantown–*Nihonmachi*–was a relatively small section of Seattle, centered on Pioneer Square and stretching eastward along Yesler and Jackson streets. It was composed of shops, restaurants, groceries, a Japanese theater, and maybe 5,000-10,000 Japanese. Although residents were mostly Japanese, many Whites ate and shopped there. The waiter knew very little about the *Hikawa Maru*, but directed Yoshikawa to the NYK Lines office on Alaskan Way that had been opened specifically to handle this sailing.

Following the waiter's directions, Yoshikawa took the streetcar and along the way observed that the city appeared prosperous. Cars crowded the streets and parked along the curbs. Some even parked in the middle of the streets. The stores were well stocked and customers crowded the sidewalks laden with packages. Yoshikawa had to admit that Seattle looked more affluent and more modern than Yokosuka, where he had been stationed before going to Honolulu.

The clerk in the NYK Office looked puzzled when Yoshikawa asked if he could get a berth on the Hikawa Maru. "No," the clerk replied, "I'm surprised you asked. The ship is entirely booked and has been for a long time. In fact we are overbooked and have a list of people awaiting cancellations. I thought everybody knew that."

Yoshikawa considered how to respond, and then explained. "I am a Japanese citizen. I had been attending a sick uncle in Hawaii, but then he died and the embargo stranded me there. I finally caught a Pan American Clipper flight here, but now I need a way to get back to Japan. People say the *Hikawa Maru* is a repatriation ship, and I need to be repatriated."

The clerk was mildly amused at Yoshikawa's last statement, and said, "Yes, I see the need, and I'd like to help you, but we are sold out," and then added dismissively, "Perhaps you could get a ticket for a later sailing."

Yoshikawa did his best to look forlorn. "But it's important that I get back now. My family needs me. I have children and an aged mother." Then he tried the thinly-veiled-bribe gambit again. "I'd be willing to pay double the usual fare."

The clerk looked up, a little disappointed at Yoshikawa's gauche overture. "No sir, "he said, "I'm afraid there nothing we can do for you. Nothing at all."

"Well," Yoshikawa thought as he left the office, "Now what?" He decided on a different tack.

He boarded a streetcar back to Japantown where he asked the same convivial waiter to recommend a Japanese restaurant. "Maneki's," came the reply, "It's an old Japanese restaurant, and has a pleasant bar with a good selection of sakes." Yoshikawa was most interested in the sake bar. He thanked the waiter, bowed, and set off toward Maneki's.

The restaurant was indeed old, as the waiter had said, but it was also comfortable and, most important, its sake bar was full of men chatting amiably. The room was furnished with low tables, tatami mats on the floor, and shoji screens providing partial separation between the tables. It's only concession to Western comfort were the

CHAPTER 8

legless chairs that rested directly on the floor and provided backs against which customers could lean. Yoshikawa removed his shoes and took a seat near a table with two men. A waiter arrived and he asked for *shinshu* sake. Sake is a kind of rice wine, but with higher percentage of alcohol. Unlike wine, it is best when fresh. It had been a staple of social intercourse in Japan for centuries, and obviously had continued in that role here in America.

The *shinsu* was surprisingly good. Yoshikawa savored it, and then lifted his *sakazuki*–the sake cup–toward two men at a nearby table. '*Kaurai*," he offered the traditional toast. The men smiled and lifted their *sakazukis* also. Yoshikawa took that as permission to join them, and was soon recounting his tale of being stranded here, unable to find passage back. They listened politely but had no solutions to offer. One of them suggested Yoshikawa try to find someone who already had a ticket and offer to buy it.

Yes," Yoshikawa responded, "If I knew of such a person, I certainly would do that."

"Actually," said the man who had made the suggestion, "This might be a place to do just that. The ship sails in just a few days, and I've noticed a few customers in here recently that look like they are going aboard."

"Great," he said, "I can't think of a better place to wait." He smiled inwardly. He would go "fishing" right here in the sake bar. He would bait his hook with sake and a smile, and wait for the right fish to come along.

During the remainder of that day restaurant patrons did show up carrying small valises or suitcases. Yoshikawa guessed they had just dropped off their sea chests and other heavy luggage at the NYK office he had visited earlier, and now were waiting until they could board the ship. He approached them all, went through the niceties of introducing himself, explained his situation, and offered to buy their tickets at a handsome price. None was even remotely interested.

He repeated his performance thru 3 and 4 November, but got not a single nibble. He was getting desperate. The *Hikawa Maru* was now in port. It had disgorged its American repatriates returning from Japan, and tomorrow would begin boarding Japanese repatriates heading for Yokohama. He began to consider outright robbery, but had no idea about how to go about it. He had been in flight training when he got orders to an intelligence school. There he was instructed on the use of cameras, maps, optical devices, identification of ships and aircraft, orienteering, etc. But they taught him nothing about physical violence. He was a combat pilot and could drop bombs from 1,000 feet knowing that they would kill people, but he would never see the corpses up close. Death to him was an abstraction, not something that he could easily visit on another human being.

Unless his duty to the Emperor demanded it!

⊕ ⊕ ⊕

The Day Before the *Hikawa Maru* Sails

It was getting late in the evening of 5 November when the man came into the sake bar. He was young–about Yoshikawa's age–and appeared tired and discouraged. Yoshikawa knew instantly this was the one. Even before the man sat down, Yoshikawa intercepted him with a warm smile. "You look tired," he said to the man, "Come, sit with me and relax," then added casually, "You must be boarding the *Hikawa Maru* also."

The man was guarded at first, but Yoshikawa's friendly bearing disarmed his caution and he sank unto the low chair gratefully. "Yes," he said with exasperation, "I've been traveling all day, only to get here and find there is no place to sleep. Hotels are all full and I can't get aboard the ship until tomorrow. What's more, I've got a terrible headache."

Yoshikawa laughed casually, "I sympathize. I too am waiting to board the ship."

After three days of trying, Yoshikawa had concluded that none of its passengers would ever sell him their ticket, no matter how much he offered. It was now just hours before the Hikawa would sail so he would have to try something else. When he saw this young man enter the sake bar, especially when he learned he had nowhere to sleep, a dark plan came to Yoshikawa's mind.

"Thank goodness I got here a few days ago," Yoshikawa said smiling, "Before the hotels filled up." He paused and then asked, "Did you have to come a long way?"

CHAPTER 8

As Yoshikawa had hoped, the man took that as an invitation to tell his story. "Yes," he explained, "I live in Oregon with my parents. They grow strawberries. They sent me to Tokyo for my last two years of university, and I just got back last summer. Things changed while I was gone. Relations between the U.S. and Japan had gone down the drain. The Whites around our farm had got really nasty. They hated me. *Kibbie*, they said, making the word sound dirty. He's probably a spy. I felt like it was only a matter of time before one of the thugs caught me in a dark alley."

"Really?" Yoshikawa asked with genuine interest. This was something that headquarters might find useful.

"Yeah," he replied. "So I talked about it with my parents and we decided that I should go back to Japan until this blows over. Besides, Japan is not all that bad. Its government has become a bit extreme and I certainly disapprove of its invasion of China, but I think cooler heads will prevail. The people are good hearted."

Yoshikawa grimaced inwardly, and thought, "This guy is living in another world. Japan is a modern nation. It has broken out of its island confines and becoming the dominant power in the Western Pacific. Why doesn't this guy see that? He should rejoice, not stand around and wait for Japan to return to some quiet agricultural preserve like it was in the last century."

Of course, he said none of that aloud. Instead, he smiled and got to the point, "Look, I have a room. There's only one bed, but there is a couch. Why don't you sleep there tonight? Tomorrow you'll be rested and ready to start the long voyage back."

"That's very kind of you," the man replied, "But I couldn't possibly allow you to do that. It would be a terrible imposition."

"Nonsense," Yoshikawa replied, "It's settled. I'm in the Panama. It's not far. We can walk."

The man put on a show of reluctance, but agreed.

"How can I repay you?" he asked.

"Maybe a drink on board ship," Yoshikawa grinned, "But scotch rather than sake! Oh, one other thing. We should probably go through the lobby one at a time, to avoid having the desk clerk ask questions. I'll go first and you can come up about ten minutes later. Room 212. And maybe you should ask the waiter here if you can leave your valise here overnight. Carrying it past the desk might cause the clerk to ask if you're a paying guest."

"Sure," the man replied, "Whatever you think. Incidentally, my name is Akihito Shigemitsu," he said. Yoshikawa noted that he listed his given name first and surname last. It reminded him that this was the Western custom and he should use it in the future.

Yoshiko didn't really want to know the man's name, but acknowledged it politely and added, "And I'm Ryo," he said," using his alias.

◈ ◈ ◈

Yoshikawa used the ten minutes before "the man" (Yoshikawa preferred not to think of him as a person with a name) arrived to prepare for what he reluctantly had to do. He opened his shaving kit and removed the safety razor, fumbled with its handle briefly, and snapped open a hidden compartment. An ordinary looking capsule rolled out. It was cyanide–a "lethal, quick acting" dose Headquarters had told him. It had been issued to him along with the other items he would need to travel under cover: an alias passport, forged documents using his alias, pocket litter such as American book matches, and this concealed "suicide pill." Yoshiko thought it a bit melodramatic at the time, but as a novice spy he was not about to question the authority figures at headquarters. He was glad now that he had it. The pill would make this quick and clean.

"The man" walked past the desk clerk without arousing suspicion and knocked softly on the door of Room 212. Yoshikawa opened the door and welcomed him. He had spread a sheet and blanket from the closet over the sofa and motioned for the man to relax and try to recover from the day's trauma. He was grateful, and sprawled on it with his feet stretched over the sofa arm.

"Still got that headache you complained about earlier?" Yoshikawa asked.

"Nothing too serious," the man replied.

"Well," Yoshikawa countered, "I've got something here that will cure any headache in town. It's a powder that my mother always gave us kids. I don't know what's in it, but I know it works." Yoshikawa

CHAPTER 8

picked it up from the bedside table, got a glass of water, and held them out to the man.

"Well, I guess I can't go wrong with your Mom's medication. Thank you." He said as he looked the pill. "Wow, Mom uses gel capsules. You sure Mom isn't a druggist?"

Yoshikawa had an instant of panic, then recovered, "Well she's not but my brother is. The gel capsules are his contribution. I accused him of intending to sell Mom's concoction as a patent medicine in his drug store."

The man laughed, said, "Maybe he'll get rich," and one swift motion tossed the pill in his mouth and washed it down with the water.

Yoshikawa thought the man would fall off the sofa instantly, possibly dead before he hit the floor. Instead, he leaned back and said that he was very, very tired. He remained still for several minutes. Yoshikawa was getting worried that headquarters had given him a placebo and he would have to use violence to kill the man. He picked up a heavy ashtray, but as he did the man began to breathe hard, and then started noisily gasping for breath. Yoshikawa had to silence him before someone heard. He grabbed a pillow and clamped it over the man's mouth, but the man began to convulse violently and clutched Yoshikawa in a hysterical embrace. They struggled, falling on the floor, rolling over one another, the man agonizing.

The cyanide slowly had its way, stopping the flow of oxygen to the man's blood stream. His writhing began to subside, and Yoshikawa was able to extricate himself from the man's grasp. It must have taken ten minutes for him to die, hardly the "you'll-never-feel-a-thing" death that headquarters had promised.

He went thru the man's pockets and found a passport but no steamship ticket. The man must have put it in the valise that he left back at the restaurant. Yoshikawa examined the passport. His plan was to switch identities with the man, leaving him here in the room with Yoshikawa's alias documentation, and board the ship as Akihito Shigemitsu. The man's passport suited his needs well. His age, build, and height were all close. His facial features were rather different but Yoshikawa did not consider that critical. Caucasians didn't look closely at Japanese people. He remembered two White immigration officials discussing Japanese passports back in Hawaii, "Hell," one had said, "I can't tell one of these damn slants from another." Yoshikawa was confident he would pass as Shigemitsu Akihito.

He pulled the body up on the bed and arranged it in a fetal position, just as it had looked after its death throes on the floor. Then he took the sheet and blanket from the sofa, folded them neatly and placed them back in the closet, and tidied up the room to remove any evidence of a struggle. Then he took most of the money from his own wallet, set it on the table, and put his wallet in the hip pocket of the corpse. He removed the other items from his pockets and carefully placed them in the corresponding pockets of the corpse. He picked up the cash from the table, sat down, and wrote a note in Kanji on hotel stationery. "*I cannot get back to Japan. When war breaks out I will be imprisoned here in enemy country. I will not suffer that shame. My duty is clear. I die for my Emperor. Matsumoto Ryo*"

Yoshikawa had signed the note using his travel alias, the same name shown in the Japanese tourist passport that headquarters had issued him, and that he had used to sign the hotel registry.

He looked down at the corpse. Its skin was bright red and black spittle leaked from the corner of its mouth. The man had died a cruel death, and Yoshikawa was sorry that it had been at his hands. He rationalized that if the man had gone back to Japan he would probably have been drafted into the army and sent to China. Chances are he would have died there, so perhaps this was just as well. Many men would die before the West conceded to Japan its rightful place as leader of the Greater East Asian Co-Prosperity Sphere. The dead man was simply a casualty of war.

Yoshikawa knew that he had to leave the hotel room. He could not take a chance on someone discovering him there with a dead body; besides, he was too squeamish to stay with the corpse overnight. He would have to find someplace else to sleep. The weather was cold and wet, so he bundled up in the overcoat that the man had arrived in, quietly descended the hotel's rear staircase, and strode through the lobby trying to appear casual. Once outside he walked toward the waterfront and, after some searching, found a construction site with a shed that must have been used as an office. It was locked but the hasp was attached quite poorly and came off with one

CHAPTER 8

yank. He entered, found some matches in the dead man's overcoat pocket, lit one, and found a chair. That's where he remained the rest of the night, huddled in the cold, sleeping fitfully.

When the first light of dawn filtered into the shack, Yoshikawa awoke and took a minute to get his bearings. He walked to the door, looked around to see if anyone was watching, and then left the shack being careful to put the door's hasp back in place so no one would notice it had been broken. He walked through the morning mist back to the restaurant where the valise had been left. It was just opening for breakfast and he was grateful to note that the waiters had changed. No one there this morning would have seen him and the dead man together the night before.

"Good morning," he said, smiling at the man near the front door. "I left my valise here last night and I'd like to pick it up."

The man at the door was busy arranging chairs and just pointed down the hallway. "It's probably in the cloak room," he said.

Yoshikawa stepped to the half-door of the cloak room expecting to simply enter, find the valise and leave. Instead a girl appeared and asked if she might help. "My valise," Yoshikawa said pointing, "I think that's it over there on the floor. I'd like to pick it up."

"Oh," the girl said, "Do you have a claim check?" she asked in very good English.

Yoshikawa wasn't prepared for this. "A claim check?" he echoed. Now where would the dead man have put a ticket? He fumbled through his pockets and found nothing. "Oh, my," Yoshikawa feigned embarrassment, "I must have lost it. But I can prove the valise is mine. There's a steamship ticket inside for the *Hikawa Maru*. It sails today."

The girl looked at him oddly. "You are going to Japan? Don't you like America?"

Yoshikawa did not want to get into a discussion about such matters so he simply said, "Look. Here's my passport. My name is Shigemitsu Akihito. You can check the name on the steamship ticket. It's really my valise."

THE DOOLITTLE IRONY

The girl looked at his passport, then back at him. He instantly regretted that he had offered it. She was a young Japanese girl, accustomed to looking at Japanese men. She might realize the photo was not his.

"Not a very good photo," she said flatly, but then picked up the valise and handed it to him without bothering to check for the steamship ticket. "Going to Japan is going backwards." She said with disdain. "The future is here in America."

"Another damned Nisei," he thought silently, "They will soon learn that the future is in Japan. They will be begging to come back."

Yoshikawa picked up the valise, checked to make sure the ticket was inside, heaved a sigh of relief when he found it, and then turned back toward the waterfront. As he approached the pier he noticed a knot of White men standing opposite the boarding ramp where a tent had been set up for an official to check passports. There must have been a dozen or more shoddy looking White men who acted like they had already begun drinking even though it was early in the day. Two of them carried signs reading, *Good Riddance Japs*, and *Slants Go Home*. Yoshikawa skirted the rowdies, ignored their threats, and got in the passport line. As he expected, the official gave his passport only a cursory glance, stamped and returned it to Yoshikawa, and waved him aboard.

At the top of the gangway the Ships Purser welcomed him. He looked at Yoshikawa's ticket and apologized that he had not been able to accommodate his request for first class accommodations. "We are just overwhelmed with requests for passage, Shigamatsu-san." The Purser explained, and directed a nearby cabin attendant to take Yoshikawa to the third class cabin he had been assigned. Yoshikawa cautioned himself to listen carefully for his newly acquired name, Shigamatsu. Failing to respond to it could lead to questions he would rather not have to answer.

The cabin he had been assigned was small, had no porthole, and two beds. That meant he would have a roommate for the next 13 days. He dropped his overcoat on the bed closest to the bathroom, picked up the valise and went topside to view the activity on the pier. The rowdies were still there, and Yoshikawa noticed them passing around a bottle in a paper bag. He was disgusted by their per-

CHAPTER 8

formance and thought smugly that this was a display of why Japan would win any confrontation with America. Japan was clearly its moral superior.

He found a deck chair and sunk into it, exhausted because of the trauma of the previous night and because he had had such little sleep. As he sat in the chill fall air he examined the contents of the valise. There were some letters, a few Japanese magazines, and some pictures, probably of the man's family. Yoshikawa skimmed several of the letters. They were mostly from his friends in Japan, young people from good families. Shigemitsu had apparently attended school with the scions of Japanese officialdom. As he drifted off to sleep, he mused about how that might play out in the future. He would find out soon enough.

CHAPTER 9

HIRO ABOARD THE *HIKAWA MARU*

Hiro checked his pocket to make sure he had his passport, checked his brief case to be certain the firm's papers that he was to deliver to Professor Enjo were all there, picked up the suitcase he had borrowed from Stan, and left to catch the bus to Seattle. He had met Kathleen the evening before–she was again living at home in Seattle–and they had had dinner together at a cafeteria.

Kathleen was worried about his safety. "President Roosevelt just transferred the Coast Guard to the Navy," she reported, "And that usually happens only in wartime. Plus the Germans are closing in on Moscow. Who knows what might happen next, Hiro?"

He tried to reassure her. The firm had discussed his trip to Tokyo with the State Department. State had approved his passage saying that dealing with earthquakes was not something that should be interrupted by an embargo. They thought it was safe. "What's more," he added, "The *Hikawa Maru* has already announced its return schedule. I'll be gone only a month: 13 days over, five days there, and 13 days back. If you need anything while I'm gone that your parents can't provide, call Stan. You can get him at the office. He's been a swell friend, and he's already agreed to help with whatever you need. You can trust him completely."

Hiro made the long bus ride into Seattle, and then transferred to a streetcar to get to the pier where the *Hikawa Maru* was tied

CHAPTER 9

up. By then it was about 9:00 AM, just three hours before the ship was scheduled to sail. A short line of passengers were waiting at the boarding ramp to go through immigration and a group of hecklers were stationed across the pier being obnoxious. A few other people of Japanese descent were scattered about, wishing *bon voyage* to a few of the departing passengers. Then Hiro spotted Mr. Tanaka.

"Mr. Tanaka," he shouted, "It's me, Hiro, over here."

"Mr. Tanaka recognized Hiro, smiled broadly, and walked over to join him as he waited in line. "I'm here to see one of the crew. I was hoping I would see you too, Hiro," he said, "I heard about your trip."

"Yes, I'm excited about it. I feel quite lucky."

"Indeed, you are lucky, Hiro, not many Nisei of your generation will get to see Japan. Will you have a chance to travel about while you're there?"

"No, Mr. Tanaka," Hiro replied, "I'll have only five days there, and I expect they will be very busy. Then I'll have to leave because that's when the *Hikawa Maru* is scheduled to return here."

"Well, Hiro, it's probably well that you do return soon. The international situation is unstable. I fear war is not far off."

"I hope you're wrong, Mr. Tanaka," Hiro said, "My firm has talked to its contact in the State Department. He seemed to think negotiations were going to tamp down this current tension."

And then Hiro abruptly changed the subject. "Do you see those drunks over there? Why do they hate the Japanese? We've never did anything to harm them."

"The answer is very complicated, Hiro," Mr. Tanaka offered, "Partly it's because humans are territorial creatures. We like to think we have a legitimate claim to the land where we were born and raised. We call it 'home' and we defend it against any intruders." Mr. Tanaka paused to judge from the movement of the line how much time he would have for his little thesis. "An intruder can be lots of things, but usually it's an alien, someone who doesn't speak the same language, pray to the same god, eat the same food, or look the same as we do. In the eyes of those drunks, we fit all those conditions. They would be happy if every Japanese person in Seattle were put aboard this ship and sent home. And it's not as if we Japanese weren't guilty of the same behavior. Are there any Whites in Japan? Or blacks? Or

THE DOOLITTLE IRONY

browns? No. It's because we keep them out. There is practically no immigration to Japan, even from other Asian countries. Visitors to Japan are labeled 'gaijin'–foreigners–and the label is usually meant in a mean way. Until Admiral Perry, we wouldn't even carry on trade with another country. And when we immigrate to other countries, we usually build our own communities and stay to ourselves."

But then his tone lightened and he smiled broadly at Hiro. "But I hear that doesn't apply to you Hiro. My wife told me about you and Kathleen, and we are very happy for you both!" Mr. Tanaka's smile was radiant.

"Oh," Hiro said with surprise, "I didn't think you would know."

"Crawford is a small town, Hiro. You are big news."

"I guess I'm also bad news, at least to some," Hiro speculated.

"Of course, Hiro, it's the times we live in. But matters are changing. We Issei are old and will die soon. You Nisei will make things better. And when you die, your children, the Sansei, will have forgotten all about such silliness."

"Thanks, Mr. Tanaka, that's a very hopeful note," Hiro said, and then quickly added as the line moved forward, "Uh oh, it looks like my turn. Tell everyone I said goodbye."

Mr. Tanaka said "Sayonara, Hiro," the two shook hands, and Hiro disappeared into the immigration tent. As he did he thought Mr. Tanaka was indeed a wise man. He should be mayor someday.

"Passport, please" the immigration official intoned, and Hiro handed him his document with the State Department's Seal embossed on the green, cardboard front. The official took it, flipped through the 28 pages that were provided for entry and exit stamps, and noticed they were all blank. He glanced again at the photo and identifying information, and then looked up quizzically. "You're an American citizen, Mr. Yamada. Why are you boarding this ship?"

"Sir," Hiro responded, "I am a member of the Scott Engineering Firm here in Seattle. I am going to see a professor at the Tokyo Imperial University to exchange information with him about seismic activity. I'll be coming back aboard this same ship when it departs Yokohama on 23 November."

"Oh yeah," the official commented, "You're the earthquake guy they told us about," without explaining who "they" were. "OK," he

CHAPTER 9

said, "Good luck. I hope I see when the ship gets back." With that he waived Hiro up the gangway to the ship.

The Purser checked Hiro's ticket and told a cabin attendant standing by to show Hiro to his cabin. He led Hiro down two ladders to a deck labeled "Third Class." Hiro noticed that its furnishing were not up to the same smart standards evident on the main deck. He also noticed that he would have a cabin mate. In fact, the man had apparently already arrived because his overcoat was thrown over one of the bunks. There was no porthole to look out, so Hiro went back up to the main deck to watch the activity. This was all new to him and, like any tourist, he was intensely interested.

Mr. Tanaka returned from Seattle aboard the late morning bus. He had met his brother, wished *bon voyage* to several Japanese friends, and then ran into Hiro Yamada as he was boarding the ship. He knew that Hiro's mother would be worried about him and while Mr. Tanaka could do little to allay her overall concern, at least he could tell her that Hiro was safely aboard.

He walked out the dirt road to the Yamada house, through a chilly afternoon with low hanging clouds blocking the sun. As Mr. Tanaka entered the Yamada garden, Mama-san was pulling out the roots of bean vines that had grown up a wooden trellis. She was pleased to see him, "Konichiwa, Tanaka-san," she greeted him. "You have walked a long way." They always spoke to one another in Japanese.

"I was just in Seattle to see my brother and met Hiro as he was boarding the ship, Hanaco," Mr. Tanaka said using Mama-san's given name, "So I thought I'd tell you that he boarded safely."

"Oh, that is so nice of you. Please come in." Mama-san was flattered that Mr. Tanaka had thought of her, "Mr. Yamada has gone into town," she said, glad to be using Japanese in which she was more comfortable, "but we can have tea–but not *ocha*," she said, alluding to the traditional Japanese tea ceremony, "I have forgotten how to perform such graces. But we can have tea at our table."

THE DOOLITTLE IRONY

Mr. Tanaka smiled, noting that America had eroded even Mama-san's Japanese ways. "I was disturbed that there were White hooligans on the pier heckling the Japanese passengers as they boarded. It was very rude."

Mama-san commented, "Rude? Yes. Unusual? No. Americans do not like us. We are intruders. They feel like we are robbing them of their birth right." She paused, "You know, of course, about Hiro and his White girl friend."

"Yes, I know they are a couple" Mr. Tanaka allowed, "And I know they are both very nice young people."

"But there is much that separates them, Mr. Tanaka," Mama-san asserted while pouring hot water into a cup in which she had placed a round tea bag. "The girl cannot even cook Japanese food."

"Well, Hanaco," Mr. Tanaka commented while looking conspicuously into his cup of tea, "We all seem to adjust to new ways."

Mama-san understood Mr. Tanaka's point immediately, "Yes, tea bags!" She laughed softly, "My mother would never have approved. It's not even green tea, its black. And worse, it's Liptons!" They both had to laugh aloud at that.

"That's my point, Hanaco," Mr. Tanaka said, "If we are patient with one another and try to see the other's point of view, we can live together despite our differences."

"You are a patient, understanding man, Mr. Tanaka," Mama-san said, "I wish there were more like you, but there aren't. In fact, I think things have got worse since the embargo began. In the past few months my daughters have told me of fights in the high school between White and Yellow boys. And rude White men make me move off the sidewalk in town as they pass by. When we took our vegetables to the market, many of the Whites would not buy from us even though buying the same item from a White farmer was more expensive. I don't think patience and understanding will soften their hearts."

There followed a rather lengthy silence–not considered awkward in Japanese conversation–while each thought of the deteriorating situation in Crawford. "You may be right, Hanaco," Mr. Tanaka resumed, "Like you I have noticed more tension in the community recently, and I suppose it's because of the embargo. But we can't do

CHAPTER 9

anything about that, can we. We are Issei. We can't even vote!" He paused, and then added, "But our sons and daughters are citizens and soon they will be voting. And when they do, things will get better. Politicians will court the 'Japanese vote.' We may even get some of our own people in local offices."

"I hope you are right, Mr. Tanaka." Mama-san said, "But for now I just want to tend my garden and raise my family. I don't care about politics or war. I just want to be left alone"

Unfortunately, that was not to be.

Hiro had watched from the main deck as the ship got underway and steamed north some 60 miles through the Puget Sound, then turned west at Port Townsend to head into the Strait of Juan de Fuca. It was there that the ship was just about abreast of Aunt Charlotte's cabin on Whidbey Island. Hiro thought of the day he had found Kathleen there after several months of thinking that he may never see her again. By now the light had faded, there was nothing to see except an occasional flash from a channel buoy. He decided to go below.

When Hiro opened the cabin door Yoshikawa was unpacking his suitcase. Yoshikawa turned and introduced himself as Akihito Shigemitsu, using the name of the man he had murdered and whose identity he had assumed. Hiro introduced himself and the two shook hands, each bowing slightly. They were about the same age. Hiro was an inch or two taller, better muscled, and perhaps a bit more confident in his bearing. After exchanging pleasantries, neither man volunteered anything about his background, as would normally be the case. Yoshikawa wanted to avoid small talk. The background story Headquarters had given him to use with his alias identity was no longer useful. Now he had another identity—Shigemitsu–and the only thing Yoshikawa knew about him was that he was from a family that grew strawberries in Oregon and was prosperous enough to send him back to Japan to finish his education. What if someone in the course of casual conversation asked him how to grow strawberries, or which university he had attended in Japan. He had no rehearsed answers. If he stumbled, that could lead to other questions. His solution was

THE DOOLITTLE IRONY

to avoid any conversation, at least until he had time to concoct a reasonable cover story.

Hiro had his own reasons for avoiding conversation. He was on a ship full of Japanese people who, having lived in America, had chosen to repatriate and return to Japan. They had apparently not bought the American Dream, or perhaps had concluded the American Dream could never include them.

Hiro's cabin mate was a curious sort. He was of an age to be Nisei, but few Nisei would go back to Japan under these circumstances. Like Hiro, their ultimate loyalties would lie with the U.S. Moreover, the few sentences that the cabin mate had used were obviously modern Japanese, not the antiquated sort that most Nisei learn from their parents. That meant he was *Kibbie*, and had probably been influenced by the jingoism that had infected all of Japan. Whatever the case, he was probably not well disposed toward Americans. If he knew Hiro was returning to America just five days after arriving in Japan, he would have questions, and that could lead to rancorous arguments. Personal confrontation was not something that Hiro needed at this point.

He decided to look around the ship. The *Hikawa Maru* was well known for its luxurious style of travel and Art Deco furnishings. Celebrities like Charlie Chaplin had sailed on her. Hiro left his cabin on Deck C and walked up the stairwell past the First Class Dining Saloon on Deck B to Deck A. There the First Class lounge and smoking areas were normally off limits to third class passengers, but such distinctions had been abandoned on this voyage. The ship normally carried about 325 passengers but had been rearranged to handle 400 on this crossing.

By now he was hungry, and he noticed it was time for meal service to begin in the First Class Dining Salon. As he entered, the hostess who greeted him asked for his name, and then checked a list at the lectern-like stand that held the menus. "Oh, Mr. Yamada, the Captain has asked that you be seated at his table."

"Really?" Hiro asked with surprise, "Are you sure?"

"Yamada Hiro is your full name?" responded the hostess. When Hiro nodded yes, she led him off toward a table alongside a large glass window at which was seated three of the ship's officers in uniform.

CHAPTER 9

The older of them stopped eating, stood, and extended his hand.

"I'm Captain Tanaka," he said, "And you must be Yamada. Won't you be seated?" He signaled a waiter to bring the menu.

"Thank you," Hiro replied with a bow, and took a seat opposite the Captain. "I'm not an experienced traveler, but I do know that sitting at the Captain's table is considered a privilege. I can't imagine what I did to deserve it."

The Captain laughed and looked at Hiro, "I will tell you why I've invited you, but first let's eat. I recommend the prawn tempura. We have a chef aboard who was trained in Europe and I think you will find the food delicious!"

It was. But Hiro would have enjoyed it more had he not been so nervous about what the Captain had in store for him. During the meal there was polite conversation among the three ship's officers at the table, and an occasional comment to Hiro to make him feel he was not being ignored. Finally the Captain turned to Hiro with a friendly look and said, "Hiro, I apologize if I have kept you waiting, but I wanted you in a good frame of mind when I asked my question. A full stomach will often help in that regard. I hope you will forgive my little ploy."

If the Captain meant to set Hiro at ease with those remarks, he failed. Hiro suppressed an urge to blurt out, "Just get on with it Captain," and merely replied, "Oh, yes sir."

"As you know, Hiro," the Captain began, apparently understanding that Hiro was accustomed to hearing his given name in familiar speech, "These are tense times. We are in the middle of a trade embargo. We have 400 Japanese passengers aboard who are fleeing the U.S. in fear of their safety. We have just delivered 400 American passengers who were fleeing Japan in fear of their safety. A war is raging in Europe. Ships are being sunk in the Atlantic. Just last week the American destroyer Kearney was torpedoed by a German submarine."

He paused briefly for effect, and then continued, "Now against that backdrop, consider that we are going to be at sea for two weeks, and in that length of time a lot can happen. Before we reach Yokohama there may be incidents in the Pacific just as there have been in the Atlantic. Our route is a lonely one, northerly, away from shipping lanes and ports of refuge. If an incident occurs, we are on our own. So we should know about such incidents immediately, then we can take whatever action is necessary." Again, the Captain paused for effect, then finally voiced his question, "Which gets me to my point: Hiro, I want you to stand watch in our radio shack and monitor whatever news broadcasts you can receive for news of anything you think I should know about."

"Oh, I see, Captain," replied Hiro, "Of course I will be happy to help, but I'm surprised that you don't have your own wireless operators aboard."

"We do, Hiro," the Captain said, "But they are radio telegraphers. They deal with CW–Morse code. They don't do well picking up spoken newscasts. They don't really even speak English, and that's the language of most international news reporting. You have been a ham operator. You know that receiving long range transmissions requires patience and an adroit tuning hand. I hear you're quite good at it."

"You do?" asked Hiro, "How do you know so much about me?" And then he realized, "Oh, wait. Your name is Tanaka. You are related to Mr. Tanaka!"

"My brother!" the Captain replied proudly, "He's how you got on board. Yes, your firm paid for a ticket, and your State Department gave permission for you to sail, but it was my brother that made it happen. He contacted me, asked for my help, and I added your name to the passenger manifest. The ship was packed and you would never have made it otherwise–State Department or not. Don't worry. It's one of the little perks of being ship's Captain."

"Well, thank you, Captain," Hiro said gratefully, "I have great respect for Mr. Tanaka, and I truly appreciate your help. And I'm happy to help you in return. Besides, thirteen days at sea is a long time, even aboard a beautiful ship like this. Monitoring the news will be a pleasant diversion."

"Great," the Captain said smiling, "I'm looking forward to your reports already."

⊕ ⊕ ⊕

CHAPTER 9

When Hiro returned to the cabin, Yoshikawa was fiddling with his valise.

"Have you eaten?" Hiro asked?

"No," came the reply, "I'm not very hungry. Besides, I don't know if I'll get seasick, so I thought I should avoid food for the time being."

"Oh, sorry," Hiro replied trying to be sympathetic," I hope you can eat soon. The food is delicious."

"Maybe tomorrow, for breakfast," Yoshikawa offered, "Maybe by then I'll know if I'm going to get sick."

Trying not to be conspicuous by his silence, Yoshikawa asked, "Do you get seasick Yamada?"

"I don't know, frankly. Maybe I should be avoiding food, just like you. But I heard we probably will not hit any really rough weather until later in the voyage. Someone said we are following a 'great circle route' and will get very far north. I'm not sure what a great circle route is."

As an aviator, Yoshikawa knew much about great circle routes. Impulsively he offered, "It's really quite simple. As you know, Seattle and Yokohama are on roughly the same latitude, so it might seem logical that the shortest route between the two would be just to sail due west. But that's not the case. If you had a globe of the earth and you stretched a piece of string between the two ports, you would see that the string curves up through the northern Pacific and then back down to Yokohama. They call that a 'great circle' and it's always the shortest distance between two points on a globe."

"I see," Hiro said admiringly, "That's an excellent explanation. You must use maps in your profession."

Immediately Yoshikawa regretted his helpfulness, thinking this is just what he wanted to avoid–any opening that might raise questions about who I am.

But all he said was, "No, just something I picked up in geography class."

"Really?" Hiro asked, "It must have been a very interesting class. Where did you go to school?"

"Oh, me and my big mouth," Yoshikawa thought. He had never attended a University.

THE DOOLITTLE IRONY

"I attended Tokyo Imperial University," he replied to Hiro. It was the first University that popped into his mind.

"What a coincidence," Hiro exclaimed, "I'm on my way to Tokyo Imperial University. I'm going to see a Professor Ito. Do you know him?"

"No, I don't," Yoshikawa replied, "It's a big school." Then before Hiro could ask any more questions, he added, "You know, I think I'm going up to the main deck to get a breath of fresh air. I'm feeling a bit ill. Maybe I am getting seasick."

With that he opened the cabin door but before he could exit, Hiro exclaimed, "Wait, you've left your valise out. Do you want me to put it out of the way?"

"Damn!" Yoshikawa thought to himself, "I don't want anyone near that valise."

What he said was, "Oh, thank you, no. Let me take care of it," and he carefully closed and slid the valise beneath his bed. Tomorrow, when Hiro was elsewhere, Yoshikawa would finish hiding his purloined copy of the "PACFLT Movement Schedule" in the lining.

Hiro rose early the next day and found his way to the radio shack. He introduced himself to the radioman on duty, a young man about the same age as Hiro. They exchanged pleasantries and the radioman explained that he had been told that Hiro would be monitoring the commercial broadcast bands for international news that might affect the *Hikawa Maru*. The radioman expressed gratitude for Hiro's assistance, admitting that he had been unable to do that himself. "Our normal operation keeps us pretty busy. We must monitor the emergency frequencies and coast stations along our route, pass point-to-point traffic, and transmit our own traffic. Of course, that's all CW so we have to use both Morse and Wabun, even Kana." Hiro nodded sympathetically. The radioman was telling him that radio telephony was all CW–continuous wave–transmission, popularly referred to as *dit-dah* radio. Moreover, he had to be able to transmit and receive Morse code plus Wabun and Kana, the Japanese counterparts to

CHAPTER 9

Morse. That was complicated, required attention to detail, and left little time for operators to be listening to International news reports.

Hiro said he was happy to help and spun his chair to the spare HF receiver. He was gratified to see that it was manufactured by RCA. The metal tag on the front identified it as a *Model AR-60R, Manufactured for Nippon Yusen Kabushiki Kaisha*, which Hiro recognized as the NYK Line that owned the *Hikawa Maru*. Hiro mused that American radio equipment being used aboard a Japanese ocean liner was certainly incongruous. Apparently the NYK had little confidence in Japanese technology. He mentally shrugged and put on the earphones.

The *Hikawa Maru* was at this point little more than 150 miles out of Seattle. Hiro was able to receive broadcasts from several radio stations there and chose KOMO on 1000 KC. News of the European War dominated: the German Army's drive to take Moscow had stalled but the city remained in grave danger; Britain was having difficulties protecting its sea lanes against German U-Boats; Finland had rejected U.S. advice to make peace with Russia; plus there was one item of local interest in Seattle that Captain Tanaka might want to hear about.

Hiro made it a point to catch the Captain's attention as he entered the dining area and, as Hiro had hoped, the Captain again asked him to sit at his table. As before, pleasantries were exchanged and menu choices were made. Only after these preliminaries did the Captain look at Hiro and ask, "Well, anything to report on the world's activities Hiro?"

"Very briefly, Sir," Hiro began, "Russia is holding on by a thread against the *Wehrmacht* and Britain is being strangled by German U-Boats. In the Pacific negotiations between the U.S. and Japan seem to be at a standstill."

"Humph," the Captain grunted, "Sounds like the same news we heard yesterday. Anything new?"

"Well, there was one report that involves this ship, Sir. It seems that a Japanese citizen who had been unable to get passage aboard the *Hikawa Maru* committed suicide. He was reportedly a Japanese tourist who had been stranded in Hawaii by the embargo, found his way to Seattle somehow, but could not find transportation back to

THE DOOLITTLE IRONY

Japan. He left a note indicating that taking his own life was preferable to being imprisoned in the United States, so he swallowed some poison."

The Captain's face did not change, but his eyes sharpened with interest. "Really?" he commented. "Did the news report mention his name?"

Yes, sir" Hiro replied, "It was Matsumoto Ryo."

The Captain turned to one of the officers at the table and directed, "Ask the Purser if he knows anything about this man. Any records of a request from him for passage? Any information from our port agent about him?" He paused, reflected, and added, "This is quite curious. Why would a civilian commit suicide rather than fall into the hands of another country? Sounds more like *Bushido*." With that he turned to Hiro and thanked him for the information. "Keep your ears open for any more details. And plan on having lunch here at my table every day. It will give you a chance to bring me all the latest."

"Yes sir, I'll be here," Hiro replied, suppressing his disappointment that the Captain had not extended the invitation for dinner instead of lunch. He was sure that the Captain's table would be served only the best food, and dinner was the best meal. Oh, well.

By the next day the *Hikawa Maru* had sailed out of range of the Seattle radio's daytime ground wave transmissions and Hiro had to rely on night time sky waves. It was actually the same stations he had been listening to, but at night the broadcast signals bounced off the ionosphere, then back to earth, then to bounce again, etc. That meant broadcasts would fade in and out and hearing a complete newscast was difficult. Nevertheless, Hiro showed up at the Captain's lunch table the next day armed with a few new nuggets on the suicide. After recapping the news from Berlin, London, and Washington–nothing really new–Hiro offered his tidbits on the Yoshikawa incident. "Sir, the police have determined that Matsumoto died of cyanide poisoning. Moreover, there's some confusion about his identity. The age shown in the passport was about the same as that of the corpse, but the photo was not a good match. Plus, a hat check girl in a local restaurant reported there was a guy there whose passport photo didn't look at all like the man carrying it. The police are trying to sort it out."

CHAPTER 9

"Hmmm," the Captain mused aloud, "That is strange. Where would he have got cyanide? You can't just buy that stuff anywhere. I wonder how the police determined what poison was used."

The ship's physician was also sitting at the table. He spoke up, "Captain, there are signs in such situations: the smell of almonds, the face of the corpse may be bright red, and sometimes discolored spittle around the mouth. I used to be a physician in a factory that used potassium cyanide for electroplating. I saw one of our workers die after he somehow ingested some of it. Not pretty. It's an agonizing death."

The Captain turned to the officer he had asked yesterday to contact the ship's purser about Yoshikawa. "Anything from the purser?"

"Nothing significant, sir," the man replied, "He said there were lots of requests and he had to turn down a lot of people, but he has no record of a request from a Matsumoto Ryo, and there is no one aboard by that name."

Then one of the young officers spoke up. "Sir, I have something you should know about. Yesterday I was talking to a lady on the promenade deck and mentioned the suicide. She was curious. She remembers being approached by a man in a restaurant a few days before she boarded. He wanted to buy her ticket. When I asked if the man's name was Matsumoto Ryo, she wondered a bit and then seemed to remember that was indeed his name." He paused, and then added, "But then she said there must be some mistake because she has seen that same man aboard this ship."

"Really? Very strange, Sato," the Captain said addressing the officer who had volunteered the information, "Did the woman seem responsible? Could she have been simply seeking your attention?"

"Well, Captain," Sato said, wincing a bit, "She was elderly, so I doubt that was her motive. No, she seemed sincere. If you like I can find her and try to follow up. Perhaps she can alert us if she sees the man again."

"Yes, good idea," the Captain observed, "This is probably all simple coincidence, but we should try to resolve it nevertheless."

⊕ ⊕ ⊕

THE DOOLITTLE IRONY

That evening Hiro returned to his cabin after dinner to catch a nap before resuming his night time radio watch. When he entered the cabin he found his roommate lying on his bed. "Oh, Shigamatsu, I hope I did not wake you."

"Not at all," Shigamatsu replied, "I was just relaxing." Shigamatsu grimaced inwardly, remembering his various names: Yoshikawa, his true name; Matsumoto, the alias that he used to travel; and Shigamatsu, the name of the man he killed, whose name he was now using. He would have to be careful.

"Where have you been?" he asked Hiro, "I haven't seen much of you."

"No," Hiro conceded as he sat down on his own bunk, "I have been monitoring commercial radio broadcasts for the ship's Captain. He heard that I was a ham radio operator and asked if I could help out. It seemed a reasonable thing to do, considering all the problems in the world these days. Wars are underway in Europe, Africa, and Asia. Who knows how it might affect this ship. If hostilities broke out American warships could intercept us. We could be ordered to return to Seattle or divert into a neutral port."

"Yes," Shigamatsu agreed, "There's reason to be worried. Have you heard anything interesting?"

"Not really. The war news seems to be pretty much a continuation of what we knew before leaving Seattle. It looks like Germany will capture Moscow, London is being squeezed by German submarines, and U.S.–Japan negotiations are going nowhere."

"I never had much hope for the talks," Shigamatsu commented, "The U.S. will not be satisfied until Japan pulls out of China, and I just don't see that happening. I think the oil embargo will continue and Japan will have to develop new sources. Washington has left us no alternative." Not wishing to argue the point further, he changed the subject somewhat: "Anything else new from the radio?"

"There is one report from Seattle that our Captain found interesting. A Japanese tourist committed suicide in a hotel room near the pier where we boarded. He left a note saying he was unable to get passage on this ship to get back home, and rather than risk being held as a prisoner by the U.S. he took cyanide. The Captain thought that

CHAPTER 9

was strange behavior for a civilian. He thought it sounded more like an act of *Bushido*."

"Pretty gutsy thing to do," Yoshikawa said.

"Perhaps," Hiro allowed, but then added, "Assuming the report is accurate. But there's a lady aboard who thinks she encountered that guy in a restaurant a day or two before boarding. He wanted to buy her ticket. Of course, she said no. Anyway, she went on to say that couldn't be the same guy who committed suicide because she had seen him on this ship since boarding. You have to admit that's a little weird! So the Captain wants to look into the matter and figure out what's what."

Yoshikawa felt a surge of acid in his stomach. Somebody had recognized him. If she pointed him out to the ship's officers there would be difficult questions. What if the Captain contacted the authorities back in Seattle to confirm his identity? They would contact the dead man's parents and the truth would come out. That would blow his mission. He might be taken into custody, and possibly lose the PACFLT Movement Schedule he had carefully hidden in the lining of his valise. That was a risk he could not take. He hated the idea of taking a second life but it might be unavoidable.

"That's interesting," he said, trying to sound nonchalant, "How do you plan to figure it out?"

"I guess we'll try to contact the woman again," Hiro replied, "The ship's officer that spoke to the woman did not get her name, so he plans to just walk around the ship until he sees her again. He spoke to her on the promenade deck back near the fantail, so I guess he'll be getting a lot of fresh air."

Yoshikawa pondered that a bit then, rising from his bed, stretched elaborately and said, "That fresh air sounds pretty good. I think I'll go get some. See you later." With that he walked up to the promenade deck and found a lounge chair back by the fantail. It was getting progressively colder as the ship headed northwest, but lounging on the fantail would still not be considered unusual. His plan was to stay there in hopes that the same woman would wonder by, recognize him and ask if he were the man she had encountered earlier. He would deny it, and if she believed him, nothing more need be done. If she persisted, he would have to take other action. He eased back in his chair, wondering if his little scheme would work.

CHAPTER 10

LEADING UP TO PEARL HABOR

The CNO had given Lieutenant Bill Russo and Captain High *carte blanche* access to any information the Navy had, and charged them with producing wholly independent views of U.S.-Japanese tensions. It wasn't as though the normal staff was not doing its job, but like many leaders of large, complex organizations, the CNO thought it prudent to get a "second opinion." Too often conventional staffs develop biases because they want to stay consistent with their previous estimates, or they want to protect their budgets, or highlight their favored sources, etc. Two men operating apart from the staff would presumably not have those biases–or at least fewer of them. They could be more objective.

Bill and Captain High had now been a team for over three months. They had previously reported fragments of their assessment to Admiral, but not the whole thing. It seemed appropriate now that they summarize, so they got on the CNO's calendar for that Friday, 7 November 1941.

"OK, Guys,' Admiral Stark began, "Just the highlights, please. I got a thousand things to do today and a full weekend of work ahead. Whatchagot?"

Without preliminaries, Captain High made these major points to the CNO:

CHAPTER 10

Tokyo <u>will</u> resort to military action. It is convinced that negotiations with the U.S. will not achieve its ends. Considering that its oil reserves are adequate for less than two years, Tokyo will take military action <u>sooner</u> rather than later.

Tokyo will seize the British and Dutch oil fields on Borneo. Those are Japan's closest alternate source of oil, they are not well defended, and neither the British nor Dutch Government-in-exile is in a position to retaliate.

Once having seized the oil fields in Borneo, Japan would have to defend the 3,000 nautical mile shipping route from there to its home islands. U.S. Naval and Air Forces in the Philippines would threaten that shipping route so Japan will have to neutralize them. A <u>surprise attack on U.S. air and naval facilities in the Philippines is likely</u>.

An additional–but less likely–possibility is a <u>surprise attack on the U.S. Fleet</u> while it is in port, akin to the British Navy's attack on the Italian fleet in Taranto. <u>Pearl Harbor is the obvious target</u> and previous exercises have demonstrated that Pearl is vulnerable. On the other hand, it would be uncharacteristic of the IJN to conduct an attack so far from its home waters. It has traditionally been a regional force, operating only in the Western Pacific.

The IJN will seek to <u>draw the U.S. Fleet into battle at sea</u>. It is confident it would win that engagement.

Japan will establish defensive positions on islands through the Central and Southern Pacific to prevent our return.

THE DOOLITTLE IRONY

The CNO listened attentively then mused, "Thank you gents. Actually that seems to be the conventional view of the matter around town, but I'm reassured hearing it from two smart guys like you who have no irons in the fire. It begs the question, what can we do about it? I guess we could move fleet units to Subic Bay in the Philippines. That would put it just about athwart the Japanese line of supply that you talk about, but in turn it would make OUR line of supply long and vulnerable. Or we could just keep our fleet dispersed, or perhaps keep a certain percentage of it at sea all the time. Or we could move its homeport back to San Diego–but the White House would never buy that."

He added as an afterthought, "I guess we should also check with the Brits and the Dutch to see whether they are ready to destroy the oil facilities before the Japs can capture them."

"Already checked, sir," Captain High responded. "They're on top of it."

The CNO lapsed into momentary silence, and then observed, "Whatever we do, we seem to be reacting. We have ceded the initiative to Japan. Maybe that's what the White House wants–to force Tokyo to make the first move. Sure looks that way." Again, a pensive pause, followed by his conclusion, "That may be politically smart, but it leaves the U.S. Navy in the hot seat. What if the Japs do something really big–and they're successful? Guess who's left holding the bag!"

He turned to look directly at Captain High. Bill had noticed previously that the Admiral rarely looked directly at him. He wondered if there was a Navy rule somewhere that an officer as lofty as the CNO was not allowed to acknowledge the existence of one so lowly as a lieutenant.

"Tom," the CNO said to Captain High, "Thanks for helping with this. Noodling these ideas around helps a lot. I'll probably have more for you in the future."

Back in Captain High's office, he and Bill discussed their meeting. "Sir," Bill began, "One aspect of this problem that we may not have addressed fully, is the "long term." Sure, either of the two options we offered–decisive battle or surprise attack–would likely achieve a quick victory for Japan. But what about a year or two down the line

CHAPTER 10

when the U.S. industrial advantage begins to take effect, when we start turning out twice as many planes and warships as they do? Most economic experts believe Japan cannot win a prolonged war."

Captain High smiled wryly and said, "Yeah, well maybe Japan hasn't talked to those experts. Or maybe they think we don't have the balls to conduct a prolonged war. Or maybe they're just so full of themselves that they think they really are a modern Western nation that can handle the U.S. Whatever the case, it's like the CNO said; the ball is now in their court. We'll have to wait and see what they do with it."

⊕ ⊕ ⊕

Yokosuka, 9 November 1941

Captain Kanji Ogawa had assembled his immediate staff around the table in his office and now made eye contact with each briefly, as though to assure their complete attention. "Gentlemen," he began, "As you know, several days ago Admiral Yamamoto issued to the Combined Fleet the directive we had all been anticipating: Top Secret Combined Fleet Operation Order No. 1. It provided details for the attack on Pearl Harbor, but not the timing. Yesterday he filled in that blank. The attack is to occur on 8 December, just a month away." Heads nodded around the table, conveying the serious nature with which they regarded the news. "That is of interest primarily to the Fleet, which will carry out the order. From the standpoint of this staff, we have already done most of what we can do. We have provided our Fleet with information about Pearl Harbor's defenses, operational patterns, hydrographic conditions, orders of battle, weather concerns—just about everything it needs to conduct a successful attack. But we still lack one important aspect of information: what ships will be in port when we attack?"

Commander Nokimura spoke up, "But sir, we know that Sundays are the one day of the week that most of the American fleet is in port, and the attack is scheduled for a Sunday."

"Yes," Ogawa admitted, "But knowing that MOST of the fleet will be there is not the same as knowing exactly which units will be

THE DOOLITTLE IRONY

there and which will be absent. Once we have struck, the element of surprise is gone. We will never again be able to catch the Americans in such a vulnerable position. So if we knew that significant capital ships—especially the American carriers—were to be absent, Admiral Yamamoto might choose to delay the strike for a more opportune time." Then, turning to Nokimura, he asked, "Have you managed to recruit a port watcher? Will the watcher be able to communicate his information in time for us to use it? And what is the situation with Ensign Yoshikawa? Has he been able to find his way home and does he have anything to contribute?"

Nokimura noted nervously the change in Captain Ogawa's language from use of the impersonal "we" to the highly personal "you." He suspected that meant he would make Nokimura the fall guy if the lack of information about the location of American combatant ships became an issue. "Sir," Nokimura responded, "On that score I have only bad news. Ensign Yoshikawa failed to report any success recruiting a port watcher on Oahu. It's the same old problem. Our nationals there show no interest in any endeavor that risks their status as immigrants, even if we offer to pay them. They seem to have forgotten their loyalty to the Emperor."

Ogawa nodded his head sadly, and Nokimura went on, "As for Ensign Yoshikawa, we have a disturbing report about him picked up from one of our overseas listening posts. It seems a radio station in Seattle reported that a man committed suicide in a hotel room near the port area. He had been trying to secure passage on the *Hikawa Maru*, but was unsuccessful, and left a note saying he had chosen to take his own life rather than be imprisoned by the Americans if war broke out. The man was identified as Matsumoto Ryo, the alias that Yoshikawa was traveling under."

"Really? How did he die?" Ogawa asked.

"Sir," Nokimura responded, "The news report said he had poisoned himself, and we know that Yoshikawa had been supplied with a cyanide capsule before he left here."

"Really," Ogawa grunted, "Still that does not sound like something Yoshikawa would do. He was smart, intrepid—and as you told me earlier—he had been supplied with plenty of money. I would have guessed he'd have continued looking for another way home, at least

CHAPTER 10

until war actually broke out. Taking his life at this point seems premature. Let's see if we can pick up anything more on this matter."

Then Ogawa added ominously, "I have to report to Admiral Yamamoto's staff whether we can provide up-to-the-minute information on which American Fleet units will be in Pearl Harbor the morning we attack. Admiral Yamamoto intends to preserve the option of delaying or even canceling the strike right up to the last minute. His "go-or-no-go" decision will be based on many factors, not the least which will be the very latest information we have on American ships actually in port. We need to give this our very best effort."

CHAPTER 11

YOSHIKAWA ACTS AGAIN

It was lunch time again, and Hiro was at Captain Tanaka's table to report the latest news from the radio broadcasts the night before.

"Captain," he began, "The German Army continues to pile up victory after victory on the Russian Front. Yalta has fallen so I guess that means the entire Crimean Peninsula will soon be in German hands. There are also a number of developments at sea that you might want to know about: a British naval squadron attacked and sunk an Italian convoy in the Mediterranean en route to Libya carrying supplies for the German and Italian troops there. A German submarine sunk a British cargo ship in the Atlantic. And the U.S. Senate passed an amendment to the Neutrality Act allowing U.S. merchant ships to be armed and to enter combat zones."

The Captain knitted his brow briefly and commented, "It looks like Washington has chosen to support Britain regardless of the risks involved." He paused, and then added, "Maybe they're attempting to engineer another incident like the *Lusitania*. Anyway, that's in the Atlantic and we're in the Pacific. Anything going on here? Anything new on the suicide in Seattle?"

No, sir," Hiro responded, "We're four days out so picking up a newscast from Seattle is technically difficult. Plus an incident like that is of only brief interest to the public. I doubt the media would even bother reporting it."

CHAPTER 11

The Captain turned to Sato, the officer who spoke to the woman who claimed that the man identified as the suicide victim was actually aboard this ship. "Have you found your mysterious woman yet Sato?"

"No sir, I have not," Sato replied, "even though I have looked for her all over the ship."

"Well," the Captain commented, "It's a big ship and there's lots of people on board. Keep looking."

Hiro returned to his cabin and found it empty. His cabin mate was apparently off somewhere, so Hiro took advantage of the quiet to fall fast asleep. He did not awake until after 7:00 PM. His cabin mate was still absent, but Hiro reasoned that he might well have come and gone several times during Hiro's sleep. Not feeling very hungry, Hiro decided to skip dinner and go straight to the radio shack.

News that night contained nothing that would likely prove very interesting to Captain Tanaka. Mostly it was about German Army's advances on the Eastern Front. Sevastopol was under attack in the south, Tikhvin near Leningrad in the north, and Moscow in the center. Russia's future seemed in serious doubt. It was just as Hiro was getting ready to hang up his headphones for the night that a young seaman arrived with a request. Could he please join the Captain immediately? Puzzled, Hiro followed the messenger to find the Captain sitting at a small desk in his cabin.

"Thank you for coming by, Hiro," the Captain said in a business-like voice. "I have a rather disturbing situation to deal with, and I might need your help."

Still puzzled, Hiro simply replied, "Yes sir," and awaited the Captain's explanation.

"Do you remember our conversations about the suicide in Seattle? And Ensign Sato's information about a woman who claimed she had seen the reported victim aboard this ship?"

"Yes sir, Ensign Sato today reported he had not been able to locate the woman again but would keep on looking." Hiro replied.

THE DOOLITTLE IRONY

"Correct," the Captain said, "And today the Medical Officer came to me with information about an elderly woman who seems to be missing. Her husband had come to him saying that she had gone out on the deck last night to get some fresh air, and was gone a very long time. He was afraid she had been taken ill and so had sought out the doctor. When the doctor reported he had not seen her, the man became concerned that she had fallen overboard. They organized a small search party and asked a number of people on deck if they had seen an elderly woman."

The Captain paused to take a breath, "One had, and was able to identify her as the man's wife based on a picture he had. She said the woman had been talking to a young man back near the fantail, and that she had just seen the same man in the smoking lounge. The doctor found him and asked if he knew the whereabouts of the missing woman. The man said he had no idea of her whereabouts. They had talked only of how cold the weather had become. The doctor called me and I spoke to the man also. He seemed OK until I checked his passport. The photo was NOT his. It was of a man whose appearance was similar, but certainly not identical. The hair line and facial features were definitely different."

"You mean the man is an imposter?" Hiro asked in disbelief.

"Yes, I think he well may be," the Captain replied, "which makes me very suspicious. He was seen talking to the lady who is now missing, the same lady who claims she had seen the alleged suicide victim in Seattle aboard this ship. What if that suicide victim is the one shown in the passport photo? I may be imagining things, but what if he poisoned the man in Seattle, made it look like a suicide, and then threw this woman overboard when she recognized him on deck and asked for an explanation?"

"Holy smokes, Captain," Hiro exclaimed reflexively in English, then recovering his Japanese asked, "Why would he do all of that? Do you think he's stolen money? Or trying to escape the law?"

"That's where you might be able to help, Hiro," the Captain began, "We've learned that this man is actually your cabin mate."

"What?" Hiro cried out, "My cabin mate? Wow. I can't even remember the guy's name."

CHAPTER 11

"It's Shigamatsu," the Captain said, "Or at least that's the name on his passport. Do you know anything about him?"

"Not really," Hiro replied, "We hardly talked and he never volunteered anything about himself. The only real exchange we had was when I told him I would be away from the cabin at night because I was monitoring newscasts for you. He asked what news I had picked up."

Hiro paused, and then recalled a bit more, "Yes, I remember. He showed interest in the suicide report. Said it was a 'gutsy' thing to do. I thought that was an odd comment."

"Did he ask about the woman who made the claim," the Captain asked.

"I think I told him that we didn't know," Hiro replied, "But the officer she spoke to would try to find her among the passengers. That's really all I remember about it."

The Captain paused to collect his thoughts, "There's reason to be suspicious about your room mate, Hiro. He's very likely not the man shown on his passport picture, so he's traveling illegally. He was seen in the company of a woman that had identified him as a man who had tried to buy her ticket to this ship–a woman who has now gone missing so she is not here to confirm her earlier identification. If indeed he was that man, then how did he get the ticket? If he simply bought it, then why did he not board using his own passport? Perhaps he stole it, but wouldn't the person he stole it from come forward to the purser to state that it had been stolen and thereby prevent the thief from using it? And then of course there is the reported suicide in Seattle. What if your cabin mate had stolen that man's ticket, and the staged the suicide to cover up the theft? Sounds farfetched, but it's the only scenario I can think of to explain this situation."

"It does sound plausible, Captain," Hiro said after a pause, "Do you plan to turn him over to the authorities when we reach Yokohama?"

"I think we have to act before then," Captain Tanaka observed, "A woman is already missing–possibly thrown overboard by this man. What if there are other passengers who also saw him back in Seattle? What if they stop him and ask how he got a ticket? Does another

THE DOOLITTLE IRONY

passenger go over the rail?" The Captain looked directly at Hiro and asked, "Hiro, are you willing to help me with this?"

"Of course, sir," Hiro said, "Just tell me how."

"OK," replied the Captain, "It might require a bit of acting. Here's what I want you to do."

⊕ ⊕ ⊕

Hiro returned to his cabin and found his cabin mate lying on his bed with his arms folded behind his back. "Shigamatsu, I haven't seen you for awhile," Hiro commented.

"I've been busy," Shigamatsu replied tersely.

As Captain Tanaka had counseled, Hiro did not press for information. "Well, we are now almost halfway through our voyage so I hope you can relax soon," Hiro responded and lay down on his own bed.

There was an extended silence, during which Hiro wondered if the Captain's strategy of waiting for Shigamatsu to make a move would work.

"You said you're going to Tokyo Imperial University, Yamada," Shigamatsu said using Hiro's surname, "Are you going to study there?"

"No, I'm going to meet Professor Ito and deliver some data he wants on earthquakes in Seattle. I was supposed to take some other data back to the U.S. but I'm not going to do that," Hiro offered without further explanation.

Again, a long silence before Shigamatsu asked, "You mean you're going to stay in Japan?"

Hiro rolled over as though trying to sleep, "Yes," he said, "Japanese are not welcome in the U.S. We never were, so I'm returning to my homeland."

"Strange," Shigamatsu thought to himself, "This young man has a quite different attitude than the Nisei in Honolulu. They had no loyalty to Japan. They saw their future with the U.S. But this man has decided otherwise. What would account for that?" He decided to probe a bit further.

CHAPTER 11

"I think I understand,' he said to Hiro," I saw a group of American drunks on the pier taunting our passengers. I can understand why you want to get away from them. Americans are mongrelized–black, White, all variety of European nationals. What can you expect? But in Japan we have retained our racial purity. We are one. The sort of thing that happened on the pier in Seattle never happens in Japan" Shigamatsu paused, then lifted himself onto one elbow and looked over at Hiro in the next bunk, and offered his test question, "Of course, you know you are of draft age. If you stay in Japan you may well have to serve in the military."

"No different than the U.S," Hiro replied, "I've already had to register for the draft in America. If there is a war, I'll have to fight for a country that treats me like dirt." Then, with rising volume he declared acidly, " I worked hard to be accepted. I got an engineering degree from the University of Washington and was hired by an engineering firm in Seattle. I thought maybe I had broken through, but when I began work I realized the only reason the firm had hired me was to have a front man who could introduce them to prospective Japanese clients. Instead of making use of my engineering skills, they made me a glorified courier, carrying mail back and forth to Tokyo. It's demeaning and I will not accept such treatment. So I am rejecting America and throwing my lot in with my homeland."

Shigamatsu tried to sift through what he had just heard. Hiro sounded sincere and his story sounded authentic. Perhaps this was someone Shigamatsu could trust. He may soon need such a person. The Captain's questions today suggested he already suspected there was a link between him and the missing woman. Shigamatsu regretted that he had thrown her overboard, but she was a nasty old crone and had threatened to go to the authorities with her story. He could not allow that. But what if he was detained him for questioning in Yokohama? The civil police there were an independent lot. They would resist attempts by Naval Intelligence to have him released. By the time the matter got sorted out, the attack on Pearl Harbor might already have been launched. He had to get his purloined CINCPAC Deployment Schedule back to his headquarters just as soon as possible. It clearly showed the days when all three aircraft carriers assigned to the Pacific Fleet would be in Pearl Harbor together. One of those days would have to be the date of the attack. As a naval aviator, Shigamatsu knew that aircraft carriers had replaced battleships as the capital ship of modern fleets. He understood that the American aircraft carriers would have to be destroyed if the Imperial Japanese Navy was to prevail in the Pacific.

Shigamatsu sensed that Hiro's alienation with America was authentic. "Hiro," Shigamatsu began, "I am impressed by your expectations of your homeland, and I am confident you will find Japan to be all that you are looking for. But you're obviously a man of intelligence and should not be subjected to the draft. Your talents can be made better use of. As it happens, I have connections in the Imperial Japanese Navy. I might be able to help you."

"Well," Hiro thought, "Captain Tanaka might well be right. Given enough rope, this guy might hang himself." But what Hiro said was, "Thanks, I'm a new guy in what to me is a new country. I could use all the help I can get."

Shigamatsu then angled the conversation to his own purpose. "Perhaps we can help one another Hiro. I find myself in a bit of a quandary. You may have noticed that the ship's Captain regards me with suspicion. He has asked me about a suicide that occurred in Seattle the day we left. I don't know why he asked me. I certainly know nothing of any suicide. Then just today he asked about a woman who is apparently missing. He must have meant the older woman I talked to yesterday. I don't know where she is. If she's missing it's probably because she became sick, maybe a heart attack or a stroke. At that age such matters must be expected. Anyway I'm worried that the Captain thinks that I'm somehow involved. He even mentioned some connection with the suicide. It worries me."

With that, Shigamatsu paused to gauge Hiro's reaction. Did he seem to be buying it? Hiro seemed indifferent to the story–an understandable reaction.

Hiro broke the silence. "So, you want me to tell the Captain you're not involved in either of these matters?"

"No, no." Shigamatsu corrected, "I doubt he would listen to you, just as he does not seem to be listening to me. No, I want you deliver something for me, in the event that I am delayed beyond our arrival in Yokohama."

CHAPTER 11

"Sure," Hiro replied, "Like a package?"

"Something like that, it's my valise. If I am detained for any reason, I want you to get it out from under my bunk and take it to the naval base at Yokosuka. Give it to Captain Kanji Ogawa. I've written his name and address on a slip of paper inside the valise. Tell him you got it from Yoshikawa–that's the name he knows me by–and tell them about how I was detained. The Captain will know what to do. I told you I have friends who might be able to help you with your draft problems. I'm confident that after you deliver the valise Captain Ogawa will be especially appreciative. He will help you."

Hiro feigned appreciation. "Thank you," he said, "Captain Ogawa must be an important man. Tell me, is Yokosuka Naval Base far from where we will go ashore?"

"No, Yokosuka is only about 10 miles from Yokohama. I will put money in the valise so you can hire a taxi. But you must do it just as soon as you get off the ship." Shigamatsu reviewed the timing in his mind. The ship arrives in Yokohama on 21 November. He did not know exactly when the attack would be launched, but he was confident it was near at hand and knowing when the carriers would be in Pearl Harbor was essential to the plan.

The significance of their conversation began to dawn on Hiro. Shigamatsu's denials about being involved in both the reported suicide in Seattle and the missing woman aboard the ship had a hollow ring. Moreover, it appeared that Shigamatsu was involved in some mission for the Imperial Japanese Navy and had information for it that was so time-sensitive he was willing to risk asking Hiro, a total stranger, to be his courier. Hiro wondered uneasily whether he might have got himself involved in something truly dangerous. He would seek out Captain Tanaka's counsel as soon as possible, but for now he determined to play out his hand. "Sure," he said to Shigamatsu, "I'll be happy to deliver your valise. And I thank you for helping me out with my draft obligations. I will admit that the prospect of serving in Mongolia is not very attractive." With that Hiro rolled over and feigned drowsiness. He would get up and go the Captain Tanaka as soon as Shigamatsu left the cabin.

CHAPTER 12

BACK HOME

The secretary poked her head through the doorway of the large, spartanly furnished work space where the young professionals of Scott Engineering worked. It looked much like a factory with workers on stools in front of tall drawing boards, and had been dubbed "The Mill" by the young men who worked there.

"Mr. Polasky," the secretary spoke with a note of tolerance, "You have a call on line seven–a Miss Kathleen Kelly." The mention of a female caller raised eyebrows among the mostly bachelor engineers within hearing distance. They leered with locker room smirks as Stanley Polasky slid off his stool and walked to the outer office where line seven was located. Individual phones were not provided young employees. Several years of life in "The Mill" were necessary before they earned that perk. Until then it was line seven in the outer office.

"Hello," Stanley said sternly into the phone, trying to give the impression that this was a work-related call, "This is Mr. Polasky."

"Stanley, this is Kathleen, Hiro's girl friend. Do you remember me? I'm calling to ask if you have any news on Hiro's arrival in Japan."

Stanley relaxed a bit knowing that this was indeed a work-related call–at least in a way. "Of course I remember you Kathleen," he replied and then for all to hear, "I understand your concern about Hiro, but we have no new information on his status." That should allay the busybodies worried about another employee violating com-

CHAPTER 12

pany policy about personal calls on company time. Then, in a lower voice he added, "Kathleen, where are you now? Have you returned to Seattle? Perhaps we can meet. We should talk about a few things."

"Oh," Kathleen responded with a note of surprise in her voice, "Anything serious?"

"Not at all," Stanley said, "I'm just a bit concerned about developments in the area, and I want to make sure that you and Hiro's family are safe. Is there a restaurant near you where we can have lunch Saturday?"

The two met in Grimm's Drugstore which, as its name indicates, was a pharmacy. But more important to the town were its social amenities: a soda fountain, a few booths, and a grill to prepare short orders. Along with a gas station, movie, bank, post office, general store, and a few small businesses, it composed Crawford's "downtown." Stanley and Cathy sat in a booth. A few White teenagers occupied stools at the fountain and cast curious toward this large stranger in town.

"Stanley, I am so glad to meet you in person," Kathleen gushed. "Hiro has told me so much about you, and we both owe you so much. If you hadn't talked to my Dad and loaned Hiro your car, we probably would not have gotten back together. We are indebted."

'Well", Stanley smiled, "Being a Polack from Pittsburgh, I understand a bit about the problems that immigrants face. Of course, in Pittsburgh we Polacks settled our problems in a different way–which explains the scar over my left eye."

"Considering your size," Kathleen observed, "I'll bet the other guys has several scars!"

Stanley smiled, and then turned serious. "I asked to talk to you in person, Kathleen, because I'm worried about some of the garbage I've been hearing from local rabble rousers. For example, I heard a guy on the radio the other day who said he was from someplace near here. His name was Imhoff. I didn't quite catch the first name, but he was on a rant about the local Japanese. Said they're a threat to America's safety and would side with Japan if we ever got into a war."

"Yes," Kathleen replied, "His name is Fritz Imhoff and he's agitated about the local Japanese immigrants for years. He's a small farmer, and complains that Japanese farmers use night soil to fertilize their crops and that's why they grow more than he does. He says the Japanese should all be sent back to Japan. My Dad, who's the police chief here, says Imhoff is all talk. He's never gone beyond speechifying and the only ones that listen to him are other bigots. He's come to my Dad a few times wanting him to 'investigate' the Japanese. Dad told him that the health department has checked on the night soil charge and determined that the Japanese farmers are NOT using it. What they are doing is using irrigation and compost, and there is no law against good farming practices."

Stanley nodded thoughtfully and then said with some caution, "I'm worried that your father may have underestimated these people, Kathleen. If Imhoff has asked your father to investigate the immigrants, he may well have done the same with the Washington State Police or, for that matter, even the FBI. In ordinary times perhaps Imhoff and his ilk could be written off as cranks, but we may be on the brink of war with Japan. If that happens, I'm worried whether the Japanese immigrants will be safe."

"I understand your concern, Stanley," Kathleen allowed, "But as long as my father is Police Chief here, I don't think they're in any danger."

"Crawford is a very small town, Kathleen, and your father's influence ends at the town limits." He reflected a bit, then added, "Hiro's family seems particularly vulnerable. His father is elderly. His mother hardly speaks English. His sisters are only teenagers. The family needs somebody to stand up for it." Stanley paused and looked seriously at Kathleen, "I propose that you and I do just that–that we appoint ourselves as Hiro's family protectors." Before Kathleen could react, Stanley went on, "I think we could do it. You have knowledge of the local situation and the people involved. Your Dad is police chief. As for me, well, I'm large! If matters look like they're going south, I can handle any of these local pukes."

Oh, my," Kathleen said with considerable surprise, "I don't know what to say. Of course I want to protect Hiro's family, but I'm not sure about how to do that. What did you have in mind?"

"I thought we could start off by going out to Hiro's farm and you could introduce me to his parents." Stanley suggested.

CHAPTER 12

Again, Kathleen was surprised. "Gee, Stanley, I have a confession to make about that. I've never even met Hiro's parents. Our relationship hasn't quite got to that point yet. And, you know, the Japanese tend to be reserved. They don't invite people into their homes like we do, and one does not just drop in without an invitation."

Stanley thought about "Polish Hill" where he was raised and the easy informality of cousins, aunts, uncles, and neighbors coming by unannounced. His family always made them welcome and his mother always had something in the ice box for them. He missed that here in Seattle, and felt a little bad for the Japanese that their culture apparently did not allow for it. "Well, I don't want to intrude where I'm not welcome, Kathleen, and I certainly don't want to create an awkward situation between you and your future in-laws. But I'm still worried. Is there anything we can do now?"

"Kathleen pondered the question, "No, Stanley, nothing occurs to me. But when Hiro returns, he plans to introduce me to his parents, and I'm sure he will want to introduce you as well. That won't be long. He arrives in Yokohama 18 November, spends a week there, then two weeks aboard ship coming home. That would get him back here about 7 or 8 December. I can't imagine anything happening by then."

Stanley nodded, but continued to look worried. "Okay, we'll wait for Hiro to get back, but in the meantime if anything does come up, call me! Now let's order. Do they have hamburgers? I'm hungry."

Later that week the phone in the Kelly residence rang one short and one long, and then again one short and one long. Kathleen picked it up and listened. She heard a woman say hello, and almost simultaneously a man say the same thing. Kathleen said pointedly, "Mrs. Fitzgerald? This is Kathleen. The call is for us. Remember? One long and one short is for us. Two longs are for you."

"Oh," came the reply, "Sorry Kathleen. I keep forgetting." Mrs. Fitzgerald was getting on in years.

Kathleen's father thought that getting a private line was an unnecessary expense, so–although she was sure that Mrs. Fitzgerald occasionally listened in on her conversations—she had to soldier on with the party line. Satisfied that this time Mrs. Fitzgerald had hung up, Kathleen said into the phone, "Stanley, is that you?"

"Yes, it is Kathy. I hope I'm not interrupting anything."

"Not at all, Stanley. I thought I recognized your voice. Is anything wrong?"

Well, Kathleen," Stanley began hesitantly, "Yesterday I was called into Mr. Hardman's office. He's our Personnel Director and the guy that usually handles contacts from outside the firm. He told me he received a visit by two FBI agents. They wanted to know about Hiro. Why was he going to Japan? When would he return? That sort of stuff."

"Really?" Kathleen responded, "Why would they want to know that?"

"That's what Mr. Hardman wondered. So he called a few friends in the Seattle Police Department and learned that the FBI is compiling lists of local Japanese immigrants whose loyalties are questionable.

"Surely they wouldn't include Hiro on any list like that. My God, I remember how he sang the National Anthem out loud at ball games back in high school."

"Mr. Hardman told the agents they were barking up the wrong tree. He explained that Hiro is going to Japan on company business, not because he wants to. Mr. Hardman said he was emphatic and when the agents left they had no doubts about Hiro's patriotism—but they did have doubts about a lot of other Japanese immigrants. His police contacts told Mr. Hardman that the FBI is compiling a list of local Japanese who might have divided loyalties. It includes all Japanese who expressed opposition to their political status, or own a fishing boat, or own a long range radio. It's apparently quite a long list."

Kathleen tried to digest this information. "Why would they do that, Stanley?"

"Maybe it's because someone is whispering in their ear that local Japanese are disloyal and will side with Japan if we go to war—someone like Imhoff and his gang."

CHAPTER 12

"I see what you mean," Kathleen said, "Can we do anything about it?"

"Well, Mr. Hardman told me that he intends to bring this to the attention of Mr. Scott, the owner of our firm. He has influence at City Hall. Maybe that will help."

"What about you and me? Can we do anything useful?" Kathleen asked.

"Well, I could do something useful," Stanley replied, "I could go look up our friend Mr. Imhoff and 'counsel' him a bit."

Kathleen smiled, "Nothing would please me more, Stanley, than to have you 'counsel' that bigoted old windbag. But it would get us nowhere. I think I'll talk to Mr. Tanaka about this. He's the informal leader of the Japanese-American community here. He may have some ideas."

"OK, Kathleen," Stanley offered, "You talk to Mr. Tanaka, and tell him if he thinks a little 'counseling' would be useful, you know just the guy to do it."

Kathleen giggled at the thought of suggesting violence to Mr. Tanaka, "OK, I'll do that. And you stay in touch, Stanley. If you hear anything more, call right away!"

CHAPTER 13

YOSHIKAWA DETAINED

"Thank you, Hiro," Captain Tanaka said, "Shigemitsu's conversation with you suggests strongly that he is a man with something to hide. Couple that with his phony passport picture, his having been seen with our missing passenger just before she disappeared, and the possibility that he's somehow involved with a supposed suicide back in Seattle, and I think we have enough reason to place him in custody. In fact, given those circumstances, I would be remiss to allow him to remain at liberty among our passengers. It looks like he's already thrown one overboard. I can't risk a second. I plan to confine him to his cabin, under guard, until we reach port. Then I'll turn him over to the Yokohama police."

Hiro acknowledged that with a thoughtful nod, then asked, "Should I remain in the cabin with him?"

"No, certainly not," the Captain replied, "I've already asked the Purser to find you new sleeping quarters." He paused, and then added, "But that does leave one loose end, Hiro: the valise. We need to see what's inside. Its contents might throw considerable light on this situation. Any ideas on how we might get it?"

"Why not just seize it, sir, when you confine him to his cabin?" Hiro asked.

CHAPTER 13

"No. I think that would tip him off that you had told us about it." The Captain replied, "I don't want him to know that. If he did he might retaliate against you, either now or after you leave the ship."

"Can we somehow contrive to have him give it to me voluntarily?" Hiro asked. "Perhaps I should be in the cabin when you place him under confinement. Maybe he'll give me the valise then, so he doesn't have to hand it over to you."

"Yes," the Captain reflected, "That might work."

⊕ ⊕ ⊕

Hiro returned to his cabin to find Yoshikawa asleep. Hiro's arrival roused him. He sat up on the side of his bed, blinked away his sleep, and turned to Hiro, "Oh, you're back. Good. I'm curious. Did your radio watch pick up anything interesting last night?"

"Well," Hiro fumbled, "On the naval scene, the British carrier *Ark Royal* was sunk by a German sub. As for army operations the German offensive to capture Moscow seems to be stalled in the mud."

"Yes, the war in Europe goes on. And what about elsewhere?" A pause, then with elaborate casualness Yoshikawa asked, "Anything on that suicide back in Seattle?"

"No, there was just that one report a day or two after leaving Seattle, and after that I was unable to get any local Seattle stations."

Just then there was a sharp rap on the cabin door and Captain Tanaka burst through accompanied by a rather large deckhand carrying a wooden billy club. "Shigamatsu-san," the Captain said using the name Yoshikawa's had assumed for the voyage, "As Captain of this ship I am placing you in custody. For the remainder of this voyage you are confined to this cabin."

"What?" Yoshikawa exploded, "Confined to my cabin? On what grounds? This is ridiculous. You don't know who you're dealing with."

"Perhaps not, but I'm sure it's not the person who's shown on your passport photo. Based on that and the fact that you're the last person to have been seen with our missing passenger, I have adequate grounds for placing you in custody. I'll turn you over to local authorities when we arrive in Yokohama. They will detain you while they sort out the details."

THE DOOLITTLE IRONY

"You're making a big mistake Captain. I work for very important people, and I'm involved in matters of grave significance, matters that I simply cannot share with you. Detaining me could end your career."

"We'll see about that," the Captain replied skeptically, "For now you will remain in your cabin. Your meals will be brought to you. This seaman or one like him will remain outside your door. If you attempt to leave they are authorized to use a billy club to stop you." Then, turning to Hiro he said curtly, "You will have to find a bunk elsewhere. Get your gear together and leave immediately." With that the Captain gave Yoshikawa a final stern glance and both he and the seaman stepped out of the cabin.

"Did you hear that?" Yoshikawa burst out, "The man's a fool. And the worst part is that he's turning me over to the local police. I know how they operate. Once you're in their jail, they leave you there for a few days just to demonstrate whose boss. I can't afford to be in jail that long. I have to deliver that valise as soon as possible." He stopped his rant and seemed to anguish over something for a moment. "Hiro, I have to ask you to get my valise to Yokosuka, just as fast as you can. I can't tell you why, but it's very important that you do so. Will you help me?"

"Sure," Hiro said, trying hard not to let his inner smile show, "I said I would, and I will. You'll have to give it to me now, though. I have to leave the cabin and probably won't see you again."

Yoshikawa was already scrambling to pull the valise from beneath his bed. "Here," he thrust it at Hiro, "Be sure to deliver it just as soon as possible!"

"I will," Hiro replied as he took the valise, "You can be sure of it!" and stepped out the door.

As he left the cabin wondering just what was in the valise. Shigemitsu's comments to the Captain suggested that it might have something to do with national security. If so, it might be something that the U.S. Government might want to know about. He decided to see what it was before he gave it to Captain Tanaka.

CHAPTER 13

Knowing that he would need another sleeping arrangement, Hiro had earlier that evening seen the purser, cited the Captain's order, and been assigned a new bunk–in the crew's quarters. The purser apologized, but explained this was the only bunk open on the entire ship. Hiro observed ruefully that it was not as comfortable as the cabin he just vacated. The bunk was a bare metal frame with a cotton mattress and situated alongside the water evaporator in the machine spaces. "Well," he mused, "At least I didn't have to worry about waking up with a knife in my chest."

He sat on the bunk, placed the valise on the floor in front of him, and began to empty its contents. Nothing seemed out of the ordinary: There was the money that Shigamatsu had promised for cab fare to Yokosuka Naval Base and a card with the name of an IJN officer on it–presumably the man he is to contact. In addition there was a change of clothes, shaving gear, hair brush, a note pad, and nothing else. What could Shigamatsu have been talking about? Hiro began to examine the note pad for evidence of some kind of secret writing, but then noticed that one of the edges of the valise's lining seemed to be frayed. He looked more closely and found the stitching had been loosened. He carefully pulled the lining back, and in so doing uncovered a paper document. He removed it, trying not to rip the stitching any further. Across the front cover was the title "PACFLT MOVEMENT SCHEDULE: Fourth Quarter 1941." The inside pages were divided into three sections, one for each month. The names of ships were listed in the left hand column, dates in a row across the top, and each ship's activities shown in the intersecting boxes. The document was a summary of the Fleet's movements, day-by-day, ship-by-ship. Hiro had no naval experience but it did not take an expert to realize that the Imperial Japanese Navy could benefit greatly by knowing where each ship of the American Pacific Fleet was on any given day. He looked about to be sure that no one had been watching him, and then slid the document under the pillow on his bunk.

He lay back on the bed and decided to think about this matter carefully before doing anything more. He regretted ever getting mixed up in this. He would much rather have been back in Crawford with Kathleen. He wondered what she was doing, and what she

THE DOOLITTLE IRONY

would think if she knew he was somehow involved in a plot involving murder and international intrigue. Crawford seemed a long way away. He must concentrate on the problem at hand: what to do with the document under his pillow?

Hiro tried to formulate options, just as he had been taught to do at the University of Washington with engineering problems. The document was obviously valuable and if he gave it to the Japanese Navy, as Shigamatsu had asked, he would be giving the Japanese Navy a big advantage over the American. God knows what they would do with it. Not a good option! What if he just threw the document overboard? Not a good option either because Shigamatsu would learn of it and retaliate, possibly keeping Hiro in Japan. What if he just turned it over to Captain Tanaka? Probably not a good option either because the Captain was a Japanese citizen and would likely just turn it over to the authorities and it would find its way to the Japanese Navy. He could alter the document's contents, but that would become evident on close examination and he might be held here in Japan. So what was left?

Hiro took the document out from under his pillow and looked at it searchingly. He noticed that each page was printed on a standard form designated in the lower right hand corner as NS-214. He also noticed that the only place a date appeared was on the tabs that separated the sections. A solution began to take shape in his mind. Why not switch the months? The document was held together by a simple two-prong fastener. The prongs could be straightened and the order of pages changed without leaving any evidence. October and December both had 31 days in them. If he switched them leaving the separator tabs in place, there would be no way to tell. Then the Japanese Navy would have incorrect information for both October and December. October was now history, but December was still important. Of course, not being able to move the November section, the Japanese would have accurate information on American naval movements for that latter few weeks of that month, but that appeared unavoidable.

Hiro smiled, quite pleased with himself. He had found a way to alter the document to prevent the Japanese from exploiting it. Moreover, he could do it in a way that would not be discovered. He

CHAPTER 13

looked carefully about. Good, no one in sight. He set about making the changes using his bunk as a desk. It proved to be quite quick and easy. He put the document back in the valise and set out for the bridge to find Captain Tanaka.

"So," the Captain said flatly after examining the document, "He's a spy. I guess that fits with his remarks about this being 'a grave matter that he could not share.' But it doesn't change my mind about keeping him in custody. I don't care if he kills in the name of the Emperor, he still kills and I can't have that on my ship."

Hiro had anticipated that. The Captain worried first about his ship. Everything else came second, even the Emperor. Hiro wasn't so sure about the next point. "What about the document, Captain? Will you just turn it over to the authorities?"

The Captain was pensive for a moment, and then responded, "No, Hiro, I don't want to do that. If I did they might think me a traitor. They might think I should have turned Shigamatsu–or whatever his real name is–loose once I had seen the document and realized how important it is. No, I think I must pretend that I had never seen the document."

"I see," Hiro said with some foreboding, "Does that mean you want me to do the same?"

"Yes, Hiro, that's what I would like you to do. Put the document back in the lining of the valise just like you found it. When we get into port, deliver it to the address on Yokosuka Naval Base, just as Shigamatsu asked. That way both you and I will be out of harm's way." He then added with a smile, "In fact, the Imperial Japanese Navy may treat you as a hero for delivering such an important document."

"Great," Hiro thought sarcastically, "Just what I wanted!"

The remainder of the voyage was uneventful. Each night Hiro would tune into whatever high frequency international news broadcast he

THE DOOLITTLE IRONY

could find, and dutifully report any new developments to Captain Tanaka at the breakfast table the following morning. There was no really dramatic news, more a continuation of the stories of the past week: a few more ships sunk, winter slowing the German offensive on the Russian Front, and Japan-U.S. peace talks continuing. But even more notable than the lack of news, was the Captain's apparently waning interest. In fact, all of the officers at the breakfast table were subdued. Hiro thought that odd. He would have expected them to be energized by the prospect of returning to Japan and a week of shore leave. He wondered if the Yoshikawa affair might somehow be at the root of the problem. Whatever the reason, the Captain and his officers were not going to share it with Hiro.

The *Hikawa Maru* came to dead slow at buoy No.1, allowing the pilot boat to come alongside its accommodation ladder. The pilot swung aboard to guide them down the Uraga Channel into Yokohama. Hiro stood on the rail of the foredeck and looked ahead. To the right was Chiba and to the left Kanagawa Prefectures. Along the west side of the Bay were the ports of Yokosuka, Yokohama, and Tokyo. Dominating the view westward was majestic Mt. Fujiyama, over 12,000 feet high, beautifully symmetrical, and snow-capped at this time of year. The mountain was 60 miles away, but could be seen clearly on this brisk November morning. Hiro paused to consider that it had been only about 90 years earlier that Commodore Perry must have enjoyed the same view from his Black Ships.

Hiro was in the middle of that historical footnote when he heard his name being called. "Hiro, up here," Captain Tanaka was shouting from the bridge wing. "Can you come up for a minute? I have news."

Hiro climbed the two ladders to the bridge and found the Captain waiting for him at the top. "Thank you, Hiro," he said, "I trust you are enjoying this brisk November morning."

Hiro smiled and nodded, waiting for the bad news he sensed that the Captain had called him up to the bridge to deliver.

The Captain was abrupt, "Hiro, the *Hikawa Maru* will not be making the return voyage to America as we anticipated."

CHAPTER 13

Hiro stared at the Captain, dumbfounded, speechless.

"I'm afraid the Japanese Government has requisitioned this ship from the NYK lines. It is to be turned over to the Imperial Japanese Navy and converted into a hospital ship. Work will begin in just a few days. We learned about his several days ago but I was forbidden to share the news with anyone beyond the ship's officers. Reason given was national security and all that stuff."

Noting Hiro's expression, he added, "Of course, so far as we know, our sister ship *Heian Maru*, will continue conducting repatriation voyages. I've asked our Purser to contact his counterpart aboard that ship and arrange your passage home. It might involve a delay, but I think you'll be OK."

Hiro felt like he had just been hit by a hammer. The Captain's news about the *Heian Maru* was not reassuring. He had used the phrase, "…so far as we know." That implied a lot of uncertainty.

"I have other news about our prisoner, Shigamatsu, or whatever his real name is. He will be taken into custody by the Prefecture Police when we arrive and they will get to the bottom of the situation. As for the valise, go ahead and deliver it to the person Shigamatsu designated. I think that will get you–and me–out of the line of fire. The less we're involved, the better."

Hiro tried to recover his composure. "What about you, Captain? Will they put you in the Navy?" Hiro asked.

"I doubt it," the Captain replied, "Not much call for an aging Captain of a luxury liner in the Imperial Japanese Navy. Don't worry about me. I still have a few options."

Hiro wished that he could be that casual about his future, but as he looked over at the shore of Tokyo Bay sliding past, he was frightened. And he had good reason to be.

CHAPTER 14

IN JAPAN

As a harbor tug nudged the *Hikawa Maru* alongside the Yokohama's Osanbashi Pier, Hiro looked down from the rail of the Promenade Deck. The pier was crowded with men in dark kimonos and women in colored ones, some with babies strapped to their backs. Men on the pier moved a gangway into place, at the base of which was a tent erected to protect the immigration officers from the cold wind. They would use it to check the credentials of the *Amerika-gaeri*, the returning emigrants. After that the passengers would go to a nearby transit shed to claim their luggage.

A crowd had assembled, apparently to greet the returning emigrants. Hiro scanned the crowd, looking for a man holding a sign with his name on it written in English. That man would be his host, Professor Ito, from the Imperial Tokyo University. He was nowhere in sight.

The ship's public address system announced that passengers should depart in the order of their stateroom numbers. In a normal passage, that meant those with suites went first, followed by the first, second and third class passengers—in keeping with the status of their ticket. Today's order of departure would be identical, even though all of the passengers had paid the same price. That meant that Hiro, with a third class cabin, would be among the very last to leave. He hoped that Professor Ito—who he had still not been able to spot—was a patient man.

CHAPTER 14

Actually, the first passenger to leave the ship was his cabin mate, Shigamatsu. He was manacled and led roughly by a uniformed policeman who carried a baton and looked like he would be happy to use it. Shigamatsu probably had a few hard days ahead.

More than an hour passed before Hiro was able to descend the gangway. The immigration officer looked at his American passport suspiciously and asked for his name and why an American citizen was coming to Japan.

"I am Hiro Yamada, and I am an American only by birth. I am Japanese by choice, and I have chosen to return to my homeland now. If I wait any longer, I might never be able to return."

The immigration officer nodded. It was a story similar to those he had heard from the other passengers who had preceded Hiro. He motioned Hiro toward the exit.

As Hiro left the tent, a rather distinguished-looking man in Western garb stepped forward and asked, "Are you Yamada Hiro," using his name in the Japanese order.

"I am," Hiro replied, "And you must be Professor Ito. I was told you would carry a sign with my name on it."

"Yes," the Professor said, leading Hiro away from the crowd, "But today it is not prudent to carry signs in English. Some of these men nearby could cause a commotion. So I stood close to the tent where I could hear the names of the passengers. I was surprised to hear you say that you are staying here. No one told me that."

"That was just a story I made up for the immigration officer," Hiro said, "Please don't believe that I want to stay here. I want to go home just as soon as possible."

"Of course," the Professor replied, "I understand, and we have passage for you on the *Hikawa Maru* when she returns to the U.S. on 18 December."

"I'm afraid not, Professor," Hiro said so others could not hear, "The *Hikawa Maru* is not going back to America on the 18th or ever. It is being transferred to the Japanese Navy and converted to a hospital ship. I just learned that from the Captain of this ship."

"Oh, my! A hospital ship! I'm sorry to hear that. It's not a good sign for Japan," the professor replied in worried tone. Then, focusing on the more immediate problem it presented, he asked, "Hiro, how will you get home without passage on the *Hikawa Maru*?"

"Possibly on the *Heian Maru*," Hiro replied, "It's another repatriation ship and the Captain of the *Hikawa Maru* said he would try to arrange it for me."

"Oh, good," the professor said, "I'm anxious to get the data I've collected back to your firm, and I'm anxious to see what data you brought for me. Is that what you're carrying in the valise?"

"No, Professor," Hiro said, "The data that my firm sent to you is in my luggage. We can get that in just a minute, but first I let me explain that I have to deliver this valise to a person at the Yokosuka Naval Base. It won't take long. I just have to drop it off, and then I can leave. How far is the base and how do I get there?"

"Oh, my," the Professor worried, "Yokosuka is less than 20 kilometers south, but your choices of getting there are not great. Trains and busses do not run frequently, and we have only a few taxies. Autos are rare here compared with the United States. But I just saw a taxi outside the pier."

"Are they very expensive?" Hiro asked, "I have 200 yen. Will that cover taxi fare to Yokosuka and back?"

"I think that will be ample," the Professor allowed, "But I think I should go with you. We should not get separated."

"Good idea," Hiro responded, "Let's claim my baggage and then get the taxi."

As the two men climbed into the taxi's back seat, the Professor negotiated the price with the driver. Hiro commented that the taxi looked like a lot like an American-produced Chrysler Airflow. The Professor agreed and explained: "This is a Toyoda AA, 1939 model. As you observed, it's a copy of the Chrysler Airflow design. In fact, most Japanese passenger cars are copies of one Western model or another. Until a few years ago almost all autos in Japan were produced by Western owned manufacturers–Ford, Chrysler, General Motors and some European manufacturers. But then the Japanese government passed legislation to protect Japanese manufacturers from foreign

CHAPTER 14

competition. It restricted auto production to Japanese-owned companies. They didn't have the knowhow to create their own designs, so they copied foreign products. It's cheaper and faster. We've done that with many products."

As the taxi drove south through the city, Hiro mentally compared it to Seattle. Yokohama did not fare well by his estimate. "The city does not appear prosperous," he said to Professor Ito," The people are not well dressed and many of the stores appear to be empty."

"You must remember, Hiro, that our country has already been at war for over three years," the Professor commented, "More than a million of our men are stationed overseas. The National Mobilization Act put Japan on a wartime footing. It's quite a drain on the economy. Rationing began recently. That's why I was so dispirited to hear that the *Hikawa Maru* is being converted to a hospital ship. It probably means we will be seeing even more war."

Will the Japanese people tolerate that?" Hiro asked.

"Oh, I think so," the Professor replied, "The Japanese people are intensely nationalistic. The war enjoys widespread support, but even if that changed the Japanese populace could do little to alter matters. This is not a democracy. The Government here is firmly in the hands of the military."

The Toyoda AA toiled the 18 kilometers to Yokosuka. The road was slow, rutted, and crowded with bicycles and horse drawn carts. The trip took almost an hour. Yokosuka was a port city, dominated by the Japanese Imperial Navy Base, built during the late nineteenth century to guard the entrance to Tokyo Bay. It had grown into an imposing facility housing an arsenal, ship repair facility, hospital, weather facility, petroleum storage tanks, and elements of the Imperial Japanese Navy General Staff. The latter was where Hiro had been instructed to deliver the valise.

"I have a valise for Captain Ogawa," he explained to the guard at the front gate.

"You must have credentials to enter the base," the guard replied with a degree of arrogance he reserved for civilians, "Leave it with me."

"I can't do that," Hiro replied, "My instructions are to deliver it personally to Captain Ogawa. Call him. Tell him I have a valise for him from Ensign Yoshikawa. He'll understand."

THE DOOLITTLE IRONY

The guard was reluctant to take orders from a young civilian. Still, this involved a senior officer so he returned to the guard shack to make the phone call. Ten minutes passed and Hiro was beginning to think the trip had been useless, when the guard reappeared. "You may go in sir," he said with considerable more deference, "But your companion and the taxi will have to wait here. Just have the taxi pull over to the side and I'll give you directions to the Captain's office. It's not a long walk."

⊕ ⊕ ⊕

Captain Ogawa stared intently at Hiro. "So," he said, "Ensign Yoshikawa sent you?"

Hiro was discomfited by the Captain's gaze. "Actually," he said in his 40-year-old style Japanese, "I do not know an Ensign Yoshikawa. I was simply asked by a man named Shigamatsu, who was my cabin mate aboard the *Hikawa Maru*, to deliver this valise to you personally. He told me that when I delivered it to use the name Yoshikawa and you would understand." Hiro handed the valise to Ogawa who looked at it briefly, then pressed a button on his desk. A junior officer appeared, took the valise without further instruction from the Captain, and disappeared through the same side door he had used to enter.

"Why did Shigamatsu not deliver the valise himself?" Ogawa asked.

"He was taken into custody aboard the ship for reasons that I don't fully understand," Hiro replied, "And when I left the ship I noticed the police were escorting him in shackles to one of their vehicles. It looked like they were taking him off to jail."

"Really," Ogawa said looking a bit puzzled, "Well I am indebted to you for bringing the valise here. Thank you."

"You're quite welcome, sir," Hiro said, glad that the visit was coming to an end, "Now I must rejoin my colleague. He's waiting for me in the taxi and we have business to take care of."

Ogawa's friendly attitude seemed to disappear and his voice took on an edge. "I'm afraid that will not be possible. We must detain you until we can clear up a few details. I will have your colleague in

CHAPTER 14

the taxi told that he should go on without you, and we will assure him that we will deliver you to your next destination just as soon as possible."

"What?" Hiro blurted, "Captain Ogawa, you can't just keep me here. I have business elsewhere. I did you a favor–and now you do this? You have no right to hold me."

"Yamada-san," Ogawa said addressing Hiro in the same condescending fashion that Western police call people "sir" when they give them a traffic ticket, "I assure you I do have the right to detain you. This is a national security matter, and you are an alien. I will use force if necessary."

"I don't understand. I have done nothing wrong?" Hiro insisted.

"You will remain in the Visiting Officers Quarters until I know exactly what's going on. You will be treated courteously as long as you cooperate. If you try to flee, we will put you in our brig and, I assure you, it's not a place you would want to be."

The same officer that had taken the valise from Captain Ogawa earlier, apparently one of his aides, reappeared at Hiro's elbow and motioned him to follow. In a state of shock, Hiro did, all the way to the Visiting Officer's Quarters, a hotel-like facility near the waterfront. The arrangements for Hiro's arrival seemed to have been made in advance. Without picking it up at the desk, the aide produced a room key, opened the door, and waited for Hiro to enter. The room was spare, even by Japanese standards–*tatami* mats, two *zabuton* cushions, a low *chubudai* table, a *futon* bed, and a single electric light.

Looking at the aide, Hiro asked, "How long will I be here?"

"Until you are told to go," the aide replied abruptly and then left without another word. Hiro looked out the room's single window, but could see only the side of the building next door. His thoughts cascaded through his consciousness. How had he gotten involved in this mess? What if he was kept here a long time? How would he get aboard the *Heien Maru* back to Seattle? Who would tell Kathleen and his family? Hiro was quite frightened. He fell onto one of the zabutons, cradled his head in his hands, and actually cried.

⟡ ⟡ ⟡

THE DOOLITTLE IRONY

After Hiro left, Captain Ogawa pondered his next moves. He would not lower himself to phoning the prefecture police. He would simply call his contact in the Kenpeitai, Japan's own Gestapo. It had originally been an element of the army military police, but had grown in size and influence to become a kind of Imperial secret police with jurisdiction over Army, Navy and civilian security matters. Its tactics were brutal, and included the use of torture. Its influence originated at the very highest level of the Japanese Government. Prime Minister Tojo was himself a former Chief of the Kenpeitai in Manchuria. Ogawa was confident that a phone call from the Kenpeitai would get the prefecture police's attention.

It did. Within two hours of the Kenpeitai relaying Captain Ogawa's request, the Prefecture Police had delivered Ensign Yoshikawa to Captain Ogawa's office. Ogawa greeted him warmly–though without a hug or other Western gesture of affection.

"Yoshikawa, *Okaerinasaimase*," he effused, using the formal expression for welcome back.

Yoshikawa stood rigidly at attention, as an Imperial Japanese Navy ensign should in the presence of a senior officer.

"You have done a marvelous job and now you are back! That is very good! We need you here. We had one report that you had taken your own life rather than have to surrender to the U.S."

"No sir," Yoshikawa replied still at attention.

"At ease, Yoshikawa, relax. We have much to talk about. Sit there," Ogawa said pointing to the chair beside his desk, "And start from the beginning. I must hear everything."

Yoshikawa sat, and was served a cup of sake by the aide who seemed to appear and disappear mysteriously. "You may have read my reporting from Oahu, Captain, but I have not been in touch since I left there. Let me fill you in on that period first. It will enable you to understand more about the document that I brought back in the valise."

"Good," the Captain said, "of course we found the document in the valise lining and have examined it. It seems to provide the location for most of the major ships in the Pacific Fleet, day by day, through the end of December. Tell me how you got it and whether you think it's authentic."

CHAPTER 14

Yoshikawa recapped the prostitute's story about acquiring the document from a drunken young officer, how he had smuggled it out of Hawaii aboard the Pan Am Clipper, his passage back home on the *Hikawa Maru*, and his need to kill two people in the process. Captain Ogawa listened with rapt attention.

"I did not want to kill either of the two people." Yoshikawa said defensively, "They were Japanese, and entirely innocent. But I knew just how important the document could be. I reasoned that we intend to attack Pearl Harbor. That was evident from the simple fact that I was sent there to collect information. I also reasoned that the attack would come soon, based on the state of our diplomatic relations with the United States. And I knew that the success of an attack would depend on having as many ships of the American Pacific Fleet there as possible, especially aircraft carriers."

"Yes, accurate on all counts," the Captain complimented Yoshikawa, "And at this point we have no current information on the American fleet's movement, so the document could be crucial. As for the killings, they were necessary. You must not allow your conscience to trouble you. The information you've brought may save the lives of many hundreds, even thousands, of Japanese. You should be proud."

Then Ogawa's eyes narrowed just a bit as he focused on Yoshikawa's facial reaction to his next question, "Do you think the document is indeed authentic, Ensign Yoshikawa?"

"I really don't know, sir," came the reply, "But we should be able to validate it easily enough. We can simply compare our knowledge of U.S. fleet movements with those shown on the schedule."

"Yes," Ogawa confirmed. I've already directed our analysts to get started on that. The problem is we don't know with any real confidence what those movements are. We're dependent on communications intelligence for that sort of thing and, frankly, our COMINT is not that good. We have not broken their encryption systems and so cannot read their message traffic. That leaves direction finding and radio intelligence as our primary sources and those can be vague. It won't be easy."

"How long have we got sir?" Yoshikawa asked.

"Not long at all," said Ogawa, "The attack fleet gets underway 26 November, and Tokyo will make the go/no-go decision 1 December.

THE DOOLITTLE IRONY

The attack itself is not slated until 0800 Sunday, 7 December, but turning it around at that late date may be impossible. No, I'd say we have to validate the authenticity of the document before 1 December, if our leaders in Tokyo are to factor it into their decision."

Ogawa paused briefly to collect his thoughts, and then shifted the focus of the conversation, "Let's talk about this Yamada fellow, the one who delivered the valise to me. What do you know about him?"

"Not much, Yoshida replied, "He was assigned to the same cabin as me on the passage here. He seems polite, well educated, and handy with HF radios. He helped the Captain of the Hikawa monitor international radio traffic. In fact, it was he who picked up the news broadcast from Seattle that reported the death of the man I had to kill."

"Really ...?" Ogawa interjected with interest.

"He said he was returning to Japan because he had been treated poorly in America," Yoshikawa continued, "Said his employer had overlooked his qualifications as an engineer and turned him into a messenger boy, just because he was Japanese. He was delivering data on earthquakes to some professor at the Imperial University of Tokyo."

"That must have been the man who came here with him in the taxi," observed Ogawa, "Are you confident that he is who he claims to be? I'm suspicious. It is unusual for a Nisei to show any allegiance to Japan. As you well know, none of them would help us collect intelligence. They have no allegiance to the Emperor. Yet Yamada claims to be returning to the homeland because of his mistreatment in America. Is that logical? A university trained engineer? With a job in an engineering firm? Complaining about a free trip to Tokyo? It sounds like fabrication."

"Yes," Yoshikawa agreed, "I worried about that too. But when I gave him the valise, I had no other choice. It was either give the document to him or have it fall into hands of the ship's officers or the prefecture police. In either case, you would probably never have got it and I'd still be in jail."

"You did the right thing," Captain Ogawa conceded, "It worked out well. But I am still suspicious. What if he set you up for this?

CHAPTER 14

What else does he have up his sleeve? What does he know about the document? How does he expect to get back to the United States?"

His reference to the United States caused Ogawa to pause and begin to muse aloud, "On the other hand, what if this man is real? I mean, what if he really is a disaffected Nisei? Maybe he would be willing to act as our agent? We could get him back into the United States via Mexico. The commercial contacts we've developed there to get around the embargo would provide him transportation and cover. You said he is from Seattle? We have no reliable sources there, especially with access to the sort of information we need. This guy is an engineer. He's technically savvy. He might be able to acquire information on naval construction, weapons development, that sort of thing. Yes, he could be very valuable."

Another pause, then Ogawa went on. "But first we must resolve any issues about his involvement with this document. That means detaining him while we look into the matter. But if we detain him, it could turn him against us, and then he might not be willing to act as our agent." Having ended his lengthy monologue, he concluded, "It's a dilemma, Yoshikawa. Do you have any suggestions?"

"Actually, I might, sir." Yoshikawa replied, "When I spoke to him on the ship I told him if he stayed in Japan he would be drafted into the army. That meant infantry duty in China–not a very pleasant prospect. I also told him I might be able to help him with an alternative, perhaps duty with the Navy. He sounded like he thought that might be a good idea. So perhaps you could find him some work here, work that would require he stay on base."

Ogawa nodded, "Yes, that might work. But for now, I want you to bunk with Yamada. Work your way into his confidence and find out what you can about him. In the meantime, I'll look around for an appropriate job to keep him here, and my staff will bend every effort to determine whether the document is authentic. I think that is a good plan, Yoshikawa. Carry on."

"Yes sir," Yoshida replied, acknowledging that he had been dismissed.

The ubiquitous aide appeared again at just the right moment to take Yoshikawa to the visitor's quarters. On the way, Yoshikawa thought this was not the kind of return he had hoped for. He had

THE DOOLITTLE IRONY

thought perhaps he would be given something of a hero's welcome. Now that appeared unlikely. His good work would be overlooked in the rush of preparations for the upcoming attack on Pearl Harbor.

Hiro was astonished when the door swung open and the young man who he had since learned was named Yoshikawa entered.

"You," Hiro blurted, "What are you doing here?"

"Well, we meet again," Yoshikawa said, trying to appear surprised, "I guess I should ask you the same question." Yoshikawa knew he would have to be especially alert for this conversation. He had a mental outline of what he would say but he realized he might have to change it abruptly, depending on how the conversation developed.

"I am being detained," Hiro responded to Yoshikawa's question, "Your friend Ogawa seems to think I'm lying to him. I told him exactly what happened–that you had been held by the authorities and had asked me to deliver your valise to him. I delivered it and that's all I did. That's the extent of my involvement."

By now Yoshikawa had sat on one of the futons, folded his legs beneath him, and was listening to Hiro closely. "So, I presume he doesn't believe you, so he wants to keep you here until he can look into the matter. Sounds a bit like my case."

"Your case?" repeated Hiro, "And what is your case?"

Hiro was wary. Certainly he was not in the same room with Yoshikawa by accident. They had been put together for a reason, perhaps to monitor their conversation or perhaps to give Yoshikawa a chance to ferret out what he could about Hiro.

"Oh, my," Yoshikawa said slowly, "It's a long story. Is there any sake? If we're going to talk, I think I need to relax a bit."

"Actually," Hiro said, there is some sake, two bottles. I found them and some glasses in the drawer of the *chabudai*." Hiro wondered if the sake was intended to loosen his lips.

Hiro took the sake from the table and poured two glasses. Yoshikawa appeared pensive.

"Yes," Yoshikawa began, "I guess since we seem now to be in this thing together, I owe you the truth." He paused again, "It's not

CHAPTER 14

altogether easy for me to tell, and when I've finished you may hate me. I ask only that you try to understand that what I did, I did for my country and my Emperor. Let me begin by admitting that I am an intelligence officer for the Imperial Japanese Navy." Yoshikawa had reasoned that the story he gave Hiro should be as close to the truth as possible. It would be easier to tell and easier to remember that way.

"I was trained as a pilot but was diverted to this duty for reasons I don't understand," he continued, "For the last several months I have been posing as a civilian while collecting information on military installations on Oahu–Pearl Harbor Naval Base, Hickam Air Force Base, Schofield Barracks, etc. But when the embargo was imposed, I was stranded. I tried various ways to get back to Japan but without success. Finally I managed to get a Pan Am Clipper flight back to Seattle, and there I learned about the *Hikawa Maru's* repatriation passage. But there were no tickets left to purchase, and none of the passengers would sell me theirs. I became desperate."

"And so you murdered that man for his ticket and tried to make it look like suicide!" Hiro accused.

"No," Yoshikawa lied, "I'm not a murderer. I thought the pills I put in his drink were knock out drops. I was simply going to leave him in the hotel room and by the time he woke up the ship would have sailed. But when he died, I had to do something so I faked the suicide note and switched passports. I never meant to kill the man."

Hiro nodded skeptically and asked, "What about the elderly woman on the boat? Did you kill her?"

Yoshikawa paused, seemingly reluctant to go on, but then conceded, "Yes, I suppose I did, but again, it was not intentional. I know you find that hard to believe. Let me try to explain. First, the woman was not that elderly. In fact, she was quite strong, probably the result of working on a farm. When she saw me she became quite excited and accused me of stealing a ticket. She would not be placated. She hit me with a walking stick that she carried. I tried to defend myself. We struggled. We fell against the rail while she continued to flail her walking stick. Then her hand slipped, the ship rolled, and her momentum carried her over the rail. It was all over in an instant. I was dumbfounded. I thought about shouting 'Man Overboard' but realized it was dark and she would never be recovered. I admit I also thought if I yelled there would be an investigation and I would be uncovered. I had my mission to complete. I could not allow myself to be discovered."

"Really? Why?" Hiro questioned, "You had already completed your mission. You had reported on military facilities in Oahu. Besides, you were on a Japanese ship. What difference would it make if you were seen to be a spy? You were a spy in the service of Japan. You would probably have been seen as a hero."

"But there would have been an investigation." Yoshikawa objected, "It would have taken time, and I didn't have any time to spare. I had to get back as soon as possible."

"Let me guess why," Hiro ventured, "There was something in the valise that you needed to get to your intelligence headquarters, something that could not wait. Am I right?"

Yoshikawa was a bit surprised at how quickly Hiro had deduced that. It probably meant that he had discovered the purloined document and had some idea of its importance.

"Yes, you are right," Yoshikawa admitted, "That is the reason I asked you to deliver it. I did not realize it would mean you would be detained."

"Well," Hiro countered, "I can understand why I've been detained, but I don't see why you have been. Why would Ogawa keep you here? I would have thought he throw a party to welcome you back."

This was a turn of conversation that Yoshikawa had not anticipated. His answer had to be convincing or Hiro would recognize he was being played for a fool. "Yes, the same thought crossed my mind," Yoshikawa said ruefully–the last truthful statement he would make.

"The answer lies in the nature of the intelligence business," Yoshikawa began. He was rather proud of the explanation he was about to offer. It had occurred to him almost spontaneously and, like many good lies, was based on the truth–just changed enough to fit the circumstances. "Intelligence is an inherently corrupt practice. We bribe people to tell us enemy secrets, but we're never completely sure about the validity of the information they've provided. After all, if we

CHAPTER 14

were able to bribe them, perhaps the enemy had also. Maybe they are deliberately lying to mislead us. You can never be quite sure of the spy's real loyalty."

Yoshikawa paused and noted with satisfaction that Hiro was listening closely. "That's the sort of thing Ogawa is worried about. You see, when an intelligence organization finds a spy, it does not necessarily shoot him right away. Instead we try to 'turn' him, in other words, get him to work for us–be a double agent. Consider this situation: You have been discovered to be a spy. Your captors tell you that you will be executed tomorrow morning unless you help them. All you need do is supply the government that sent you with false information. They would never know, and you would not be shot. Few spies turn down such an offer."

"What does that have to do with you," Hiro asked.

"There was a period when I was beyond their control," Yoshikawa explained, "It was from the time the Japanese Consulate in Honolulu closed to the time I returned here. My superiors had no idea where I was or what I was doing during those months. What if I had been uncovered as a spy by the Americans during that period? And what if I had been arrested and 'turned?' After all, I suddenly re-appear in very unlikely circumstances with information of a very sensitive nature. Should they trust me? Should they trust the information? Or would it make more sense to check both very carefully?"

"I see," Hiro said, "So you're being detained while they check you out?"

"Yes," Yoshikawa replied, "Just as you are being detained while they check you out."

"How long will that take, and what will happen when they're done?" Hiro asked.

"It probably won't take very long, "Yoshikawa responded, "And as for what happens then, that will depend on what they find. Unless you are an American spy, you don't have anything to worry about. But for now, we have no choice but to wait. It appears that you and I will be spending some time together."

CHAPTER 15

BACK HOME

Crawford, Washington, 20 November

The telephone in Kathleen's parent's home rang one-short-and-one-long. Her mother picked it up, greeted the caller with a polite "hello," listened briefly then went to the foot of the steps and called, "Kathleen, it's for you. It's Stanley."

Kathleen came down the steps two at a time, expecting the phone call to be news about Hiro. "Stanley," she blurted exuberantly, "Is he there? Did you hear from him?"

Stanley paused before beginning just a beat or two, but enough to alert Kathleen that all may not be well. "Yes, Hiro has arrived in Tokyo. Professor Ito sent a telegram saying that he had met him at the pier in Yokohama."

"Oh thank goodness," Kathleen said sounding relieved, "I thought maybe something went wrong."

"Actually, Kathleen, we're not sure about that. Professor Ito reported that Hiro had been detained at a Naval Base near Tokyo."

"Detained?" Kathleen repeated excitedly, "What do you mean, Stanley? Detained? Why would he be detained at a naval base? Did the firm ask him to go there?"

CHAPTER 15

"No, we did not, Kathleen. We don't understand this either. Professor Ito just said that he and Hiro went to the Naval Base to deliver a valise. Apparently one of the ships passengers had asked him to do so, but at the gate only Hiro was allowed to go in. The Professor had to wait in the cab. After about a half hour, a young officer came to the taxi and said Hiro was being detained and the taxi would have to leave. That's all the Professor knew."

"Stanley, that just doesn't make sense. What's going on? This is awful."

"I understand your concern, Kathleen," Stanley said, "We're worried too. Mr. Scott, our owner, has already been on the phone with the State Department. Of course, they have no information on the matter at this point, but they'll cable the Embassy in Tokyo and get back to us as soon as possible."

"I don't understand what 'detained' means, Stanley," Kathleen said anxiously, "Is that like being arrested? Why would Hiro be arrested?"

"I just don't know. I can't imagine why he would be arrested—or detained or whatever," Stanley replied frustrated, "but I'm afraid that's not all the worrisome news I have. You might want to sit down for this. Professor Ito reported that the ship Hiro was booked on for return passage to Seattle will not sail as scheduled. I don't know why, but before you get too concerned, the professor said that Hiro is being booked on another ship. It might involve a delay, but at least it's a way home."

The phone went silent as Kathleen tried to grasp what she had just heard. "My God," she said in a rare reference to the Almighty, "This is terrible Stanley. I don't know what to say. Is there anything at all that I can do?"

"Well, perhaps there is one small thing," Stanley replied, "You told me once that one of the people there in the Japanese community owned a high frequency radio that was used to send messages back and forth to Japan."

"Yes, you mean Mr. Tanaka," Kathleen volunteered.

"Contact him, Kathleen, and tell him what's going on. Maybe he can talk to someone in Japan and learn something about all this. Or maybe Hiro will send him a message. It's worth a try."

THE DOOLITTLE IRONY

"That's a good idea, Stanley," Kathleen agreed, "I'll do that right now."

She did, immediately, even before telling her parents about Hiro's situation.

Mr. Tanaka listened closely to Kathleen's story and then gave her the information he had on the matter. He explained that his brother was, in fact, the master of the *Hikawa Maru*. He also explained that he had told his brother of Hiro's radio skills, and that his brother intended to ask Hiro to help with monitoring news broadcasts about the war along the passage to Japan.

"But I have heard nothing from my brother since the *Hikawa Maru* sailed," Mr. Tanaka told Kathleen. "But that's not abnormal. I usually only speak to him when he is here in Seattle. I can't imagine why his ship is not sailing. Had he known about that when he was here, I think he would have told me. I know you are very worried, Kathleen, so I will try to contact him by radio. It won't be easy. I really don't know where he is so I will have to ask some of our mutual friends to track him down. It may take a while, but just as soon as I know anything, I'll call."

Two days passed—two days of great anxiety for Kathleen. She ate very little and phoned Stanley repeatedly at his office, but Stanley had no new information. Then on the third day, Stanley phoned to report the American Embassy in Tokyo had cabled back saying the Japanese government alleges it has no news about Hiro. "It cannot confirm that he has been detained, or offer any explanation about why he might have been detained. Very frustrating!"

Just a few minutes later Mr. Tanaka phoned. "I received news from my brother in Tokyo," he told Kathleen, "He says that Hiro had helped him uncover a murderer aboard the *Hikawa Maru*. He thinks the murderer may have been a Japanese intelligence officer operating under cover. They turned him over to the prefecture police when they arrived in Yokohama, but the man they think is a murderer asked Hiro to deliver a valise to the Yokosuka Naval Base, to a man named Ogawa. That explains why he went to the Base—but it doesn't

CHAPTER 15

explain why he would deliver a valise for someone who might be a murderer."

"Oh my gracious," Kathleen said with exasperation, "This just gets more and more complicated. I've just talked with Stanley Polasky, Mr. Tanaka. He's a co-worker of Hiro's at Scott Engineering. He told me that the owner of the firm is in touch with the State Department about Hiro's situation and the Embassy in Tokyo is investigating the matter. I think the information you've just given me should be provided to the State Department. They can confront the Japanese Government with it and maybe get some answers. Would you do me a favor, Mr. Tanaka, and call Stanley? Just tell him what you've told me and ask that he get it to the State Department? Here's his number. Oh, and one more thing. Can you ask your brother why his ship is not sailing and whether he thinks Hiro can get passage home on another ship?"

CHAPTER 16

OGAWA'S PITCH

YOKOSUKA, 24 NOVEMBER

Captain Ogawa listened intently as Yoshikawa reported to him on what he had learned about Hiro during the previous four days of sharing a room in the VOQ. "I don't think the guy is deliberately fabricating," Yoshikawa began, using the term intelligence officers use to mean lying, "But I do not think he's being entirely candid either. I told you that he had explained to me while we were cabin mates aboard the *Hikawa Maru* that he was angry with the way Americans treated Japanese immigrants—you know, prohibiting them from becoming citizens or owning property. He even saw his job with the engineering firm as a kind of insult because they had made him a menial courier. He told me that was the last straw, and he intended to stay in Japan rather than go back to the United States and subject himself to more such treatment."

Yoshikawa paused to shift rhetorical gears, "But I think that had been impulsive. By now he's had time to reconsider. In fact, it looked to me like he was a bit homesick. Why do I think that? First, he shows very little political sophistication. He talks about Japan in terms that he learned from his parents, who remember the quaint customs of the Meiji period. He seems unaware that a new, modern

CHAPTER 16

Japan has emerged, one that demands its rightful place as the leader of the East Asia Co-Prosperity Sphere. He did not come here to join our fight. He came to escape America."

"Interesting," Ogawa allowed, "And why do you say he wants to go home–back to America?"

"Yes, that was my second point," Yoshikawa continued, "On several occasions he's made oblique references to a girl. I think it's a romantic attachment, and I don't think he really wants to leave her. Perhaps in a fit of pique he might have told himself that he could start anew in Japan. But just a week or two of separation was enough to erode that. No, I think he's like most Nisei. His parent's allegiances to the Emperor dissipated long ago, and certainly none ever rubbed off on their children. By and large, the Nisei are more American than Japanese, although in this case we may have one who is disillusioned with America."

"Yes," agreed Ogawa, "that fits with information I received yesterday. The Chief of Staff phoned to say he received a note from the Ministry of Foreign Affairs inquiring about our friend Hiro. Somehow the Ministry had learned that he had come here to Yokosuka and was detained. I presume the Professor that came here in the taxi is the source of that information. But how did the American Embassy learn of it? We've checked on the Professor. He has no file, and people on the campus describe him as an academic completely devoted to his profession. I doubt he would have risked that by reporting the Japanese Navy had without explanation detained an American citizen. More likely, he told his contacts in the U.S.–I think they are working together on earthquake issues–and they then called the U.S. State Department. Next day our Foreign Ministry gets an official inquiry! Pretty quick! Probably means that the engineering firm is pretty well connected."

"What do you plan to do with him?" Yoshikawa asked.

"I don't know," Ogawa replied, as a small smile appeared at the corner of his mouth. "I'll have to think of something."

⊕ ⊕ ⊕

Ogawa had assembled his senior staff around the conference table in his office. Among the back benchers seated against the wall was

THE DOOLITTLE IRONY

Ensign Yoshikawa. This would be a very important meeting so Ogawa had adopted his official persona: aloof, demanding, and judgmental. "As I have warned you in past such meetings," he began looking around the room, "What we discuss here is extremely sensitive and must never go beyond these walls. That is especially the case today."

With that he paused for effect and then announced, "Gentlemen, the operation we have been working on for over a year has begun. 24 hours ago six of our best aircraft carriers–Akagi, Kaga, Soryu, Hiryu, Shokaku, and Zuikaku–with 359 aircraft, surface units, and submarines sailed from Hittokapu. Their mission is to attack Pearl Harbor!" A cheer erupted from the officers. This was the culmination of more than a year's worth of work for them, a matter that many of them thought would never happen given the IJN had never operated so far east.

Ogawa allowed their revelry to continue only briefly, and then shouted over the din, "Quiet!" Subdued by the outburst, the officers fell silent and turned their attention back to Ogawa. "I have more to add," he said in a more moderate tone. "Final approval for this attack has not yet been given. The carrier force is moving to a point northwest of Hawaii, and will wait there for Tokyo's final approval to attack. That approval will depend on several factors, not the least of which is–and this is where we come in, gentlemen–whether or not the American aircraft carriers will be present in Pearl Harbor when we attack." The officers nodded to one another, understanding the carriers' importance. "If they are not, the attack will almost certainly be either canceled or delayed, " Another pause, " Which brings me to the point gentlemen, we must decide today if the information we've been able to gather on this issue warrants telling Combined Fleet Headquarters that the American carriers will be present, absent, or simply admit that we don't know." He stopped and looked down the table, his eyes coming to rest on Commander Nokimura. "Nokimura, can you summarize for me what we know?"

"As you know, Captain," the Commander began, "Our primary sources on all current ship movements in and around the Hawaiian Islands are high frequency direction finding by which we use a ship's radio transmissions to triangulate its position. We also monitor the American fleet's message broadcasts. We cannot read their content

CHAPTER 16

because we have not been able to break American encryption systems, but we can read the unencrypted address lines. By counting the number of messages sent to and from the various units involved we can get some idea of the fleet's operational activity."

The commander paused in seeming frustration before continuing with his list of all the sources he did NOT have, "Of course, we do not have any aerial reconnaissance, nor do we have much human source information. We did get some reporting from casual sources in and around Pearl Harbor, but those have mostly dried up since Ensign Yoshikawa left. There is a dentist there who provides general observations about life in Honolulu, but he doesn't know much about naval operations. We have checked with our German allies to see what information they have. As I think I mentioned before, they have a source there who says he can produce information about American fleet activities, but he's unproven!"

The Commander looked pensive for a moment, and then said. "If we were entirely dependent on those sources, I fear our answer to Headquarters would be embarrassing! But there is a bright side," the commander added, "It is the PACFLT Movement Schedule that our courageous ensign has brought us. If it is authentic, then we need merely move our finger down a column to determine where the American carriers are on any given day."

The Commander paused, then with a touch of melodrama asked rhetorically, "Is it authentic? Can we be <u>certain</u> it's authentic? I can say Captain Ogawa, that we have been awake night and day for the past week trying to determine just that. We run checks on all the persons that we know who were involved in this case–Professor Ito, Captain Tanaka, Yamada Hiro, we even checked Ensign Yoshikawa! None of the security organizations I've been in touch with–the prefecture police, the Kenpeitai, the Home Ministry–have any information to indicate we should be suspicious of those people. I've also run name checks with our sister intelligence services and diplomatic services to determine whether they have any reports of these people being involved in intelligence activities. Nothing."

The commander looked up and down the table. Some of the officers had known parts of what he just reported–but none had been

THE DOOLITTLE IRONY

privy to the complete picture. They nodded in admiration of the Commander's thoroughness.

He had more. "I also had the Hawaiian news media checked for reports of a missing naval document or investigations into a breach of security at the Naval Base. Again, nothing! Allow me to quickly add that I don't put much importance on that. American security authorities would have embargoed all such information. They would reason its publication could help the enemy, plus be embarrassing to them!" That brought a knowing smile from Ogawa. "To sum up," the Commander concluded, "We have no evidence to suggest that the document has been planted by Western powers to mislead us with false information."

"On the other hand, Captain," the Commander continued, "We do have information to the contrary. We have checked the information in the document against what we know of American fleet movements. Using all of the sources I've cited above–HF/DF, communications intelligence, liaison services, open sources–we have determined that," and he paused here to select the most precise formulation, "The movements shown in the document for November appear to be largely in keeping with what we know of those movements from all other sources." That raised eyebrows around the table.

"Do you mean," asked Ogama as he leaned forward, "That you think the document is authentic?"

Refusing to be drawn into making a definitive statement, the Commander continued, "This is what we know, Captain: the document covers the last three months of this year on the Western calendar: October, November, and December. Two of those months are now almost past. Our information on U.S. fleet movements for October is sketchy and only partly matches the document's information. But for November, the match is remarkable. There are only a few minor discrepancies. Why doesn't the older October information correlate as well as November's? The candid answer is that we do not know. But the encouraging point remains that the document's more recent information covering November has been extraordinarily accurate. On that basis, we are inclined to believe the accuracy will continue, and the document's information for December will prove accurate."

CHAPTER 16

The Commander paused, content that he had phrased his knowledge of the situation as precisely as possible. He then plunged into more dangerous waters, "And the document shows that on December 8, the planned date for our attack, two of the four carriers assigned to the U.S. Pacific Fleet will be in Pearl Harbor–the *Enterprise* and Yorktown. The other two will be at sea. So our attack would get two of four carriers. General Headquarters will have to decide whether that is enough to support a "GO" recommendation to the Emperor."

Ogawa smiled. This was excellent. He would provide decision makers in Tokyo information that would support their predilection to attack. They would credit him for the work. It would get him promoted to Admiral. He looked approvingly at his senior officers up and down the table, then beyond them to the less senior officers in the seats along the wall. He noted with satisfaction that Ensign Yoshikawa was present.

"I want to thank all of you for your hard work and diligence. You have served the Emperor well. I especially want to thank Commander Nokimura for coordinating the very complicated efforts to validate the document. (He used the word "coordinating" rather than" leading" with respect to Nokimura's contribution. He would use "leading" to describe his own contribution. That would sound better in the commendations he was sure to receive.)

Ogawa then turned to Yoshikawa and added. "In particular I want to thank Ensign Yoshikawa for his courageous efforts in procuring this document and getting it securely back here to our organization. It was not easy." With that Ogawa rose and began to applaud. As one, the other officers followed suit. Yoshikawa smiled. The meeting ended. All present came to rigid attention as Ogawa departed the room, and then a general hubbub ensued as the officers discussed the news they had just learned. Faithful to Ogawa's caution, they would discuss it no more once having left the room.

After more than a week under what amounted to being held under house arrest in the Visiting Officer's Quarters, Hiro was glad to

THE DOOLITTLE IRONY

emerge into fresh air and the brisk late autumn weather. Since Ogawa's aide had taken him there, Hiro had not been allowed to go outside or converse with anyone except Yoshikawa. The two had had several lengthy conversations, even though Hiro was sure that whatever he said would get back to Ogawa. He tried to remain very guarded, but realized that he probably revealed more of himself than he would have preferred. Now the same aide that had brought him to the Visiting Officer's Quarters was taking him somewhere.

Hiro worried that his tampering with the PACFLT Movement Schedule had been discovered and he was about to be interrogated. His tampering had not been extensive. He simply switched the months of October and December, allowing November to remain in place. It had been easy to straighten the strap clamp that bound the document's pages together, change their order, and put the clamp back in place. It was unlikely they had discovered that. On the other hand, if they had checked actual PACFLT movements against the October listing—Hiro didn't know how they would do that but presumed they could—they might have discovered numerous discrepancies. He had listened carefully to Yoshikawa's conversation over the past week to catch any hint of that, but had gleaned nothing.

The aide led Hiro back into the headquarters building and, surprisingly, right to Captain Ogawa's office. As Hiro entered, he was even more surprised to see Ogawa actually stand, bow slightly to greet him, and then motion him to take a seat beside the desk. Ogawa had chosen to display an avuncular persona today, calculating that it would ingratiate him with his young visitor. "I trust you have been treated well since we last met, Hiro," he said using Hiro's given rather than surname, in the fashion that an American might.

Hiro sat, nodded, but remained silent.

"I hope that you realize that detaining you was not an action we undertook easily. Usually we Japanese are very hospitable, but in your case we had to be cautious," Ogawa explained, "You arrived here unannounced, with a valise that you alleged was sent by a man being held prisoner in a local jail. We had no choice but to check your story. We did, and I'm glad to report that our investigation confirmed it. We have no reason to doubt your veracity."

CHAPTER 16

Hiro's face brightened and he asked, "Does that mean you are going to release me?"

"It means that you and I need to discuss a few things, Hiro."

"Discuss? That does not sound promising," Hiro observed.

"Oh, I think you may find it very promising." Ogawa said in a kindly tone. Then, leaning back in his chair, he said, "You probably realize that we observed your behavior while you were being detained in the VOQ. And you probably guessed also that I've talked with Ensign Yoshikawa about his impressions of you. He was quite flattering. He believes you are a sincere and intelligent young man. He described you as a Nisei who has become disillusioned with America, but who retains emotional ties to other Japanese people who remain there. He told me that you had at one point told him you intended to remain here in Japan and never go back to America. But Yoshikawa thinks you may have changed your mind about that. I would not be surprised if that were the case. One develops strong ties to the place where they were raised. Parents, siblings, perhaps a girl friend–they would be difficult to leave."

Hiro was taken aback by Ogawa's approach. He had expected an iron fist, and instead was being treated with a velvet glove. He decided to play along. "Yes, I guess that describes my situation. I impulsively thought I would simply stay here in Japan rather than go back to the United States, but my parents depend on me. I could not abandon them. So when Captain Tanaka told me that the *Hikawa Maru* had been requisitioned by the Navy, I immediately asked if he could arrange passage for me on the *Heian Maru*, the other repatriation ship."

Ogawa raised his hand motioning Hiro to stop. "I'm afraid I have disappointing news in that regard. True, the *Heian Maru* was initially thought to be a second repatriation ship, but that did not pan out. In fact, last month the *Heian Maru*, like its sister ships the *Hikawa Maru*, was requisitioned by the IJN. It will no longer provide service between here and Seattle. It's being converted to a troop ship. A third diplomatic exchange ship, the *Tatuta Maru*, will leave soon to go to Mexico. But you would not want to leave on it." Ogawa didn't explain that last remark.

"Do you mean I'm stuck here? That I have no way to go back to the U.S.?" Hiro asked in genuine surprise.

THE DOOLITTLE IRONY

"That would seem to be the case," Ogawa replied, "You could perhaps get transportation to a third country and then back to the United States. But I must tell you that would be difficult. You are an American citizen, with an American passport. Just as soon as you leave this base, our internal security forces would likely pick you up. After all, you are a citizen of a country that has committed hostile acts against Japan. Even if the internal security people don't put you in custody, they will certainly confiscate your passport. If you attempt to leave the country, they would almost certainly discover that and detain you.

"But perhaps there is another way," Ogawa observed, "The Imperial Japanese Navy has means at its disposal to move people around the world quite beyond the control of our internal security agencies. Of course, it does so only under compelling circumstances." Ogawa paused, waiting for the implication of his remark to sink in. "Yoshikawa thought that you might be willing to help Japan, and simultaneously 'even the score' with America."

Ogawa's implication was obvious, but Hiro chose to play ignorant. "Even the score? What does that mean?" Hiro asked, "What are you getting at? You apparently want something of me."

"Your intuition is very keen, Hiro. In fact, I do have a proposal," Ogawa conceded. "To put it succinctly, if you agree to serve as our eyes and ears in the Seattle area, we will arrange to transport you back there. Our request is really quite innocent. We will ask you to do nothing dangerous, just report matters like ship arrivals and departures, military construction, that sort of thing. It would involve no jeopardy to your family or friends. In fact, they would not know of the arrangement, nor would anyone else. You would simply receive instructions from us by mail intermittently. You would respond by mail, sending an envelope with the information you've collected to an address we give you. To offset any expenses that you incur, and as a token of our appreciation, we would deposit a sum in a local bank that you can draw on. So you see, my proposal gives you a means to get back to your family and resume your normal life. Plus it gives you the satisfaction of knowing that you have not stood idly by, allowing yourself and your loved ones to be victimized. You have taken a stand against American racism in a very positive way."

CHAPTER 16

Hiro had listened to the pitch attentively, and now quietly reflected. Of course, there was never any question in his mind about actually becoming a spy for the Imperial Japanese Navy. He would never do that, but he might *say* he would. By agreeing, he could get back to America. Once there he could report all of this to the authorities or simply forget about it entirely. He doubted there was much that Ogawa could do about it.

All he had to do was agree–but he had to do so convincingly. Ogawa was a senior intelligence officer who had doubtless done this many times before. He would not be easily fooled. He would look for telltale signs that Hiro was lying–body language, facial expressions, unease, that sort of thing.

Hiro chose not to jump at the bait. "You make it sound easy, but in the United States I would be considered a traitor. They would hang me and my family would be disgraced. It sounds very risky."

Ogawa smiled, affecting a touch of patience, "Risk? No, Hiro, not much risk. There are already others like you in the Japanese community back in Seattle. We have such arrangements with them, and we have conducted these arrangements for many years–all quite safely." Ogawa wondered if his own body language reflected just how false he knew that information was. He remembered how intelligence officers in the Japanese Consulate in Seattle had tried to recruit informants from among the local immigrant community. Never had they had been able to find one who was seriously interested in helping the Emperor, much less with access to the kinds of information the Imperial Japanese Navy needed. Now Ogawa had in front of him a young Nisei who might well be suborned to serve the Emperor–and Ogawa never even had to leave his office to recruit him! Hiro was a real find. He had reason to hate the United States and work against it. Moreover, as a young engineer with a job in an engineering firm, he had access to a wide variety of technical information the IJN and other Japanese military elements would value. Yes, recruiting Hiro would be a feather in his cap. With war close at hand, there would soon be many promotions handed out. Ogawa wanted desperately to receive one.

"So, Hiro, I see it as an ideal arrangement for you. What do you think?" Ogawa asked.

THE DOOLITTLE IRONY

"Would I be able to see Professor Ito before going home?" Hiro asked, "I think he must be worried, and I suspect he has contacted my firm to report my absence. If I am to return to the United States, he would want me to take the data that I came here to collect. In fact, if I didn't, it would arouse suspicion."

Ogawa was impressed. Hiro was already thinking like an agent. "Yes, that's a good point. Let's think about that and meet again tomorrow, Hiro. I think we've made quite a lot of progress today." He then ended his pitch on an up note, "I am confident that as you consider my offer in the next 24 hours, you will come to agree that it is the right thing to do."

CHAPTER 17

TENSION IN CRAWFORD

1 December 1941

Stanley had driven out from Seattle to discuss Hiro's situation with Kathleen. They had met at Grimm's Drugstore and Stanley had ordered two coffees, simply to justify occupying the booth. Not really anxious to hear Stanley's news—she knew it would be bad—she delayed a bit by admonishing Stanley, "You know, Stanley, this is not Seattle. We don't have big city ways here in Crawford. Mr. Grimm won't throw us out if we don't eat. Teenagers sit here all evening sometimes without ordering anything. Hiro and I have done it." But small talk was not enough to relieve the tension. Not able to contain herself any longer, she blurted out, "Stanley, it's been more than a week since I've had any information about Hiro. You've driven way out here. What do you have for me?"

"As you probably guessed, Kathleen, it's not good news. Today the State Department told us two things. First; the Japanese Government has denied any knowledge of Hiro, beyond the fact that he cleared the passport check when he left the *Hikawa Maru*. They cannot confirm the report from Professor Ito that Hiro went to the Yokosuka Naval Base. The second piece of information is that the ship that Hiro was to have been given passage home on when the *Hikawa Maru* was requisitioned has now itself been requisitioned."

"Oh, my God!" Kathleen exclaimed, "Then how will Hiro get home? Does this mean he's stranded there, Stanley? Can't your firm arrange something? You were the ones that sent him there."

"We're doing everything we can think of, Kathleen. Mr. Scott, our owner, has called several of his political contacts for help. He also managed to get through by phone to Professor Ito and told him that our firm would pay any expenses involved in getting Hiro back." Stanley hesitated and then added, "But I don't want to mislead you, Kathy. America and Japan are practically at war with one another. Many of the arrangements that we have had with people and organizations in Japan have been ended. The situation is largely out of our control. Hiro is apparently on his own over there."

"Oh, Stanley, "Kathleen said, a tear beginning to well up in her eye, "I didn't realize it was so bad."

"How about Mr. Tanaka?" Stanley asked, "Has he been able to contact his brother?"

"No," Kathleen got control of her emotions and replied, "He has phoned and tried to contact him by radio. No luck. His brother seems to have disappeared."

"Well, Mr. Tanaka's radio and phone calls have not gone unnoticed," Stanley announced grimly, "There was a report about them today in one of the periodicals published by some anti-immigrant organization probably connected to that Imhoff bigot. They twisted the story around to say that Hiro had absconded to Japan with secret documents he stole from our firm, and now he refuses to come back."

"WHAT?" Kathleen exploded, "That's ridiculous. Who would believe that?"

"Yes, it is ridiculous, Kathleen," Stanley agreed, "But unfortunately there are people who will believe it–people who hate Japanese immigrants and are anxious to believe the very worst about them. That's another reason I came out here tonight. I think it's time I talk to Hiro's parents. They may be in danger. Some of these kooks may become violent."

Kathy looked stunned. "You want to meet Hiro's parents? And I guess you want me to introduce you to them?"

CHAPTER 17

"Well, yes," Stanley responded, looking a little puzzled.

"We talked about this before, Stanley," Kathleen said wrinkling her brow, "I still haven't met Hiro's parents!"

"Oh," Stanley cringed and held his hand up to apologize, "Yes, I remember now. The mother who said you probably don't even know how to cook rice. I forgot about that. Sorry." Before Kathleen could accept his apology, Stanley went on, "But this is really important. What happens if some of Imhoff's boys get drunk and decide to pay a visit to Hiro's farm? His parents have no phone so they can't call your father for help. So what do they do?"

"I don't know, Stanley, Kathleen replied honestly, "Do you have something in mind?"

"Well, I do think we should warn them. And I want them to know that if anything happens, I will find the guys who did it and make them sorry."

"Stanley, that's my father's job, not yours."

"Where I come from we take care of those matters ourselves," Stanley said with a look that made Kathy realize he meant it.

"OK, Stanley, I know Hiro would appreciate your protectiveness, but I'm not sure his parents will understand. Like most Japanese, they are submissive. Fighting back is not their way." She paused, "But I can see that you're determined to talk to them, and," she added with some trepidation, "I guess it's about time I met them also. So damn the torpedoes, full speed ahead. Let's go."

The two donned their coats and walked out through the late fall chill to Stanley's car.

The '37 Chevy bumped slowly down the mile-long dirt road that led from Crawford to Hiro's parent's house. It was not a joyful trip. Both he and Kathleen were quiet, absorbed in their thoughts. The weather was damp and overcast like Seattle normally is at that time of year. The road was barely more than two parallel ruts separated by a strip of weeds recently turned brown by a hard frost. It was rarely used by automobiles. No one who lived along it could afford a car. Kathleen and Stanley passed three small, wooden frame farm houses along the way, badly weathered, in need of paint, with tarpaper roofs. They presumed the houses were occupied by Japanese families, although they were indistinguishable from homes that poor

THE DOOLITTLE IRONY

White farmers might occupy. Hiro's parent's house looked much the same–square, with three small windows on three sides and a door and two windows on the fourth. A shade tree sat to one side of the house, a kitchen garden in front, with a wooden fence to separate it from the road.

Stanley pulled to one side of the road and opened the door to get out. As he did he looked over at Kathleen and asked, "What should I call them?" referring to the names he should use with Hiro's parents.

"Japanese people here know that Whites know little or nothing of Japanese customs, so don't use Mama-san or anything like that," Kathleen answered, "Those things are very complex and we'd probably just mess them up. So just address them as you would your own parents."

He was just about to ask about knocking on the door, when his question was rendered superfluous by two teenage girls who burst through it and ran excitedly to Kathleen.

"Kathleen!" they shouted, and looked at her as though she was a celebrity. "We are so glad you came! We knew you would," they bubbled. Kathleen smiled widely and hugged them both. It was obvious they had met and talked many times before, becoming fast friends and probably co-conspirators without either Hiro or their mother knowing of it.

A memory flashed into Stanley's mind of his father once telling him, "Women are born with more sense about romantic matters than any man will develop in a life time. So when you meet a girl that looks like 'the one,' don't worry about what to do. She'll take care of everything."

"Avaron, Natsuko, I want you to meet Stanley," Kathleen announced over the girls excitement.

"Oh, we knew who it was," Natsuko bubbled, "We know all about Stanley!" And with that she ran back into the house to announce excitedly to her mother and father that Kathleen and Stanley had arrived.

Avaron, now 18, the older of the two, stayed behind to escort the guests into the house. She surprised Stanley–and Kathleen–by

CHAPTER 17

taking Stanley's arm, smiling coquettishly, and leading him toward the front door.

Inside both Mama-san and Papa-san had stood and faced the door, surprised looks on their faces. As Kathleen and Stanley entered the surprised look turned to a perplexed one. Avaron took charge of the social niceties, "Mama-san, Papa-san, this is Kathleen and Stanley. Stanley is a very good friend of Hiro and Kathleen is his fiancée."

Avaron seemed to take some pleasure in pointing out to her mother that Kathleen status as Hiro's fiancée, and her mother reacted. Speaking in Japanese she said sharply to Avaron, "Don't be impertinent, Avaron, especially in front of others."

Avaron seemed to shrivel a bit. Stanley noted that Mama-san apparently still packed a punch.

Then, in her halting English she addressed both Kathleen and Stanley, "The Yamada family welcomes you to our humble home. Please, take seat," pointing to the table and chairs, then asked, "May I serve tea?"

"That would be nice, Mrs. Yamada, thank you very much," Kathleen said smiling. She and Stanley sat while Mama-san busied herself assembling the tea. Papa-san sat down at the table also but remained quiet. Stanley wondered if Papa-san had at some point in his life got the same advice about womanly initiative as Stanley had from his father.

As Mama-san served the tea, Kathleen saw that it was Lipton and thought sarcastically to herself, "Well, I might not know how to cook rice for Hiro, but I'll be able to manage his tea."

As Mama-san sat down at the table, Stanley began, "Mr. and Mrs. Yamada, Kathleen and I came here with news about Hiro, and to express our concern about what's happening here in Crawford. First let me bring you up to date on Hiro." Stanley started at the beginning, explained why his firm had sent Hiro to Tokyo, how matters had become confused, and now how Hiro was in Tokyo, possibly stranded, probably trying to find his way back home.

Hiro's parents sat stoically listening to Stanley's report. Avaron and Natsuko sat on futons to either side of their parents, occasionally exchanging glances of concern.

THE DOOLITTLE IRONY

When Stanley finished, Kathleen turned the focus of the conversation from Tokyo back to Crawford. "That's not the only reason Stanley and I came here tonight," she said, "Just today Stanley learned that some of the local Whites who hate Japanese are saying that Hiro is a traitor. They say that he stole information from Stanley's firm, gave it to the Japanese military, and now refuses to come back to the United States."

Stanley stepped in at that point and added, "Of course, no responsible person believes them. Everyone who knows Hiro knows he could never do that. But there are people out there who simply hate Japanese. Some are even prone to violence. I'm worried that a few of them might get drunk some night and come here."

Papa-san broke his silence at that point. In a steady, resolute voice with hardly a trace of accent, he said, "I will protect my family." Stanley and Kathleen looked at him anew. Papa-san no longer appeared the weak, aged man who listened passively while others conducted the family business. This was a man to be dealt with.

"We don't doubt that you would do just that, Mr. Yamada," Stanley said firmly, "And we're here to say we want to help you do just that! If anybody shows up and threatens you or any member of your family, I want you to contact me. Just tell Mr. Tanaka and he'll find me."

Looking a bit discomfited by the talk of vigilantism, Kathleen inserted, "Of course, the Crawford police should be told first. They will see to your safety."

"Police for White people," Mama-san retorted, "Not help Japanese. We call Stanley!"

And with that, the matter was settled. Stanley had become the Yamada's champion. All the social and cultural problems Kathleen had anticipated in dealing with the Yamadas never emerged. It all seemed so easy. She had to wish that her problems with the family could be as easily dispatched. But those would have to wait for another evening. Kathleen and Stanley took their leave. Kathleen bowed briskly from the waist, just as Avaron had taught her. Seeing her do so, Stanley tried also but with considerably less grace. Mama-san hid a smile, watched them depart, and thought to herself, "Americans are very strange people."

CHAPTER 18

TURNING THE PRISONER

YOKOSUKA, DECEMBER 1, 1941

Promptly, 24 hours after their last meeting, Hiro was again ushered into Captain Ogawa's office. "Well, Hiro, I'm pleased to see you again," the Captain began, "Sit down. Relax. Would you like tea?"

"No, thank you," Hiro replied curtly.

"Very well," Ogawa said, "I sense that you want to get right down to business, so let me ask, have you made a decision?"

"I have. The answer is yes, I do accept your proposal, Captain," Hiro stated evenly, "Subject to the consideration that I asked for at our last session—that I be able to visit Professor Ito and conduct the business that I was sent here to do. After that, I'll simply tell him that I will arrange my own transportation back home."

"Very well," the Captain agreed, thinking that the visit would be a necessary element to Hiro's cover story once he arrived home, "How do you plan to explain to him your absence for the last 12 days?"

"I'll tell him the truth: my cabin mate on the *Hikawa Maru* had asked that I deliver a valise to you. It was naïve of me to do so, especially considering he had been taken into custody when we came ashore. But I had agreed and wanted to keep my promise. When I delivered it, you were justifiably suspicious. I was an alien from a hostile country, and the man who asked that I deliver it was apparently a criminal. You detained me while you investigated. You determined that my involvement in the matter was innocent and so you chose to let me go. You even apologized and offered assistance in returning me to the United States."

"Very good, Hiro," Ogawa said admiringly, "I'm impressed! Yes, that is literally what happened–and one should always stick as close to the facts as possible in such matters. You think well on your feet. That will stand you in good stead when you get back to the United States."

Then, wishing to allay any qualms Hiro might have he added, "I am glad you've joined our cause. I think you agree that Japan has a right to eliminate White dominance in the Western Pacific. Asia should be for the Asians. Your Revolutionary War freed America from foreign dominance. We are simply trying to do the same. You are doing the right thing, Hiro"

Hiro nodded and, encouraged by the Captain's little lecture, ventured a suggestion, "With respect to my return, Professor Ito mentioned that he had heard of a third repatriation ship, the *Tatsuta Maru*. Would that be a possibility?"

An odd look came over Ogawa's face, "Probably not, Hiro, it's due to sail on 4 December and that probably would not allow us enough time. You see, after your visit to Professor Ito, we want you to return here. There are certain skills and techniques you should learn. It won't take long. With luck you will be home to celebrate an American Christmas with your family."

Hiro could not suppress a smile. "Good" he said simply.

⊕ ⊕ ⊕

Tokyo Imperial University, 4 December

Hiro's hopes that he would be allowed to take the train to Tokyo unescorted were dashed when he saw Ogawa's aide waiting in a car out-

CHAPTER 18

side the VOQ. Understanding why the aide was there, Hiro climbed into the front passenger seat and the aide began their 40-mile drive to Tokyo. They were silent until Hiro asked if the car they were driving was a Toyota Model AA, the same as the taxi that had delivered him to Yokosuka a few weeks before. That apparently got the driver's interest and he immediately responded in American English with just a trace of accent, "Yes, it might well be familiar to you. Its body is modeled on the Chrysler Airflow," he said, "Plus its engine is copied from Chevrolet and its electrics from Ford."

"Really?" Hiro responded, "Why doesn't Japan use its own designs?"

The aide was not offended by the question. "Oh, we will," he said, "but we have to learn the business first. Someday we will produce the best cars in the world."

"Well," Hiro responded with a note of skepticism, "That's a worthy goal." Then, in a friendly tone, he inquired, "Where did you learn to speak English so well?"

"I spent my childhood in the States," the aide replied, "Los Angeles. But when I was 12 my parents returned to Japan and I've been here ever since."

"So you received most of your schooling here? Is that where you learned about cars?"

"Yes, professional training is a big part of Japanese education for men," the aide replied, "But we also are given military and moral training."

"Moral training?" inquired Hiro.

"Yes, meaning our duty to the Emperor! We are all privileged to be his subjects, and we owe him our lives."

"I see," Hiro said, trying to think of a question that was appropriate under the circumstances. None occurred to him so he changed the subject. "Do you know where the Imperial University is in Tokyo?"

"Oh, yes," the aide said, "The area we are going to is near *Akamon*, the Red Gate." He said it as though the entire world knew where that was. Hiro certainly did not, but rather than pursue the subject he simply allowed the conversation to lapse into silence.

THE DOOLITTLE IRONY

The drive took nearly three hours and it was nearing mid-day when the aide pulled up in front of an apartment building near an impressive ironwork sign that read in Kanji, "The Imperial University of Tokyo."

"I'll see you back here at five o'clock," he told the aide as he was leaving the car.

"No," corrected the aide, "I must stay with you. I will go to Professor Ito's apartment and wait outside his door."

"Really?" Hiro asked. He had hoped to go to a telegraph office this afternoon with Professor Ito but the aide would probably not allow that. "OK," Hiro acquiesced, "But I'll be awhile."

The Professor opened the door with a smile and asked Hiro into his apartment. He explained that a military officer had phoned yesterday to say Hiro would visit to go over the data he had brought from Seattle. The apartment was just a single room, not unlike Hiro's room at the VOQ, but with a small table and cooking area to one side. The professor asked Hiro to be seated at the table and then apologized for being a bachelor. "I have no wife to serve tea, so please excuse me." He moved to a small stove on the far wall and spoke as he was preparing the tea. "Your people have been very worried about you," he said, "I even received a phone call from Mr. Scott."

"Really, Professor? Do you mean you have a telephone here in your apartment?" Hiro asked excitedly, thinking perhaps he could call Kathleen directly.

"Oh, no, Hiro. I am just a lowly professor. I had to go down to the telephone exchange to receive the call."

The professor handed Hiro the cup of green tea and sat down with him at the table. "I hope you don't mind but I took the data you brought from your luggage. It was left in the taxi when you were detained." Hiro noted the information he had brought was piled there on the table in a neat stack. The Professor pointed to it, "I have many questions."

"I hope I can answer them," Hiro said, "There are many graphs and displays, and I had only a few weeks to learn about them before leaving." The professor smiled politely, and then reached over to pick up the top item from the stack. "Oh, Professor," Hiro said, "Before we get started, may I give you some information on my own situa-

Chapter 18

tion and ask that you pass it along to Mr. Scott? Do you think you can call him? I know overseas calls are expensive. Can I pay you?"

"No need for any payment. Mr. Scott says he will take care of such expenses, so I will just reverse the charges. What would you like me to tell him?"

Hiro covered the high points: he had been detained but was now free; he thought he would be able to arrange transportation home but had no details about how or when; he had met with Professor Ito, discussed the data that the firm had sent and would try to take back to Seattle whatever information Professor had for them. He, of course, made no mention of his experience with Captain Ogawa. He wanted desperately to have the full story relayed to Mr. Scott, but suspected the Professor would instead report it back to Ogawa. "Oh, one other thing, Professor Ito, would you ask Mr. Scott to tell Kathleen that I love her?" The Professor smiled and said, "Of course. I'll be sure to do that."

The afternoon stretched on as the Professor posed question after question about the seismic data and engineering detail contained in the packet Hiro had brought. It was after 7:00 PM when he finally left. Just as Hiro expected, the aide was patiently waiting. They drove back to Yokosuka through a light snow, a rare event in Tokyo. Hiro thought the otherwise drab, sprawling city looked so much better in White.

⊕   ⊕   ⊕

Yokohama, 4 December

That morning the *Tatuta Maru* sailed from Yokohama en route to Mexico with 29 Americans aboard. The ship had had a long history of repatriation activities. The year before it was to have sailed from New York to Germany to repatriate the crew of the *SS Columbus,* a German ship whose crew had chosen to scuttle her rather than let her fall into British hands. But London exerted heavy diplomatic pressure so the U.S. Government canceled that voyage. This year the *Tatuta Maru* had transported Jewish refugees who had fled the

THE DOOLITTLE IRONY

Nazis, crossing Asia to Vladivostok. From there the ship had taken them to refugee settlements in Shanghai and San Francisco. The ship had been in San Francisco the day President Roosevelt signed the Executive Order directing that Japanese assets in the U.S. be seized. Federal agents removed nine million dollars in bonds from the ship, but allowed it to leave port and return to Japan. After that the two countries agreed to designate it as one of three Japanese ships authorized to conduct diplomatic exchanges despite imposition of the American embargo. That was ostensibly its mission today, but the ship's Captain had sealed orders that he was to open three days out of port. The ship's captain wondered about that. Why would he receive new orders on 7 December 1941?

CHAPTER 19

PEARL HARBOR

WASHINGTON, D.C., 6 DECEMBER 1941

A dusting of snow and a chill wind had descended on the American capital. In downtown Washington, Christmas shoppers with children in tow strolled down F and G Streets, stopping to look in each of the store windows decorated for Christmas. At 11th and F Street, Woodward and Lothrop's store windows featured a Santa with real whiskers and a Lionel Train display that boys from miles away came to see. A streetcar clanged its way past the shoppers, and men bundled up against the weather stood at corner newsstands selling copies of the Washington Post, The Evening Star, and the Times-Herald. On 6 December, 1941, Washington D.C. was still a sleepy southern town enjoying a touch of winter. That would change very soon.

Not all Washingtonians were preparing for a peaceful holiday. A few were at their desks concerned about a holiday that might be anything but peaceful. Those included Captain High and Bill Russo, who had just poked his head into the Captain's office, "I'm glad I found you in, Captain," Bill said, "Got a minute?" The Captain smiled and waved Bill in. Bill sprawled in the overstuffed chair without waiting to be asked, a liberty he would not have taken had the two not developed such a close relationship over the past few months.

"I'm worried that something big is about to happen." Bill started, "A Japanese linguist who works in the cryptanalytic section stopped by my office yesterday afternoon. She told me that she had just looked over a sheaf of cables that were a month old but had just been decrypted. One was addressed to the Japanese Consulate in Hawaii from the Foreign Ministry in Tokyo. It requested detailed information on ship and aircraft movements into and out of Pearl Harbor. It also wanted the port divided into sectors with individual ships located in each of the sectors, and information about which of the ships had to be nested side-by-side. She thought it looked like the kind of information you would use to plan a bombing attack, so she asked her boss about it. He just told her not to worry about it–her job was to translate, not analyze. But she said she didn't trust that analysts would see it as she had, so she came to me thinking that I'd be able to ensure that the information got into the right hands. Of course, she should not have done that and, if it ever became known, she and I could both go to jail."

"And now that you've told me, I could join you there," the Captain commented sourly.

"Sorry, sir," Bill responded contritely, "But it sounded really ominous so I thought you should know."

"Actually, Bill, I already did know. That message was distributed to the heavies around town and they took it to mean different things. Some saw it as just the standard sort of information that one navy collects on another, not an imminent threat. Others disagreed, especially Admiral Stark.

"So last week Admiral Turner, our Chief of Plans, sent a warning message to both the Asiatic and Pacific Fleets. It told them to expect Japan to take aggressive action in the near future, probably directed against the Philippines, Malaya, or Borneo. As for Hawaii, he also saw that as less likely. Admiral Kimmel and General Short agree. They think the big threat in Hawaii is the Japanese immigrant population so they worry about sabotage. Hell, a third of the Island is Japanese so I guess they have reason to worry."

CHAPTER 19

Bill wrinkled his brow and replied, "Sir, I doubt those immigrants are much different than the ones on the West Coast. Throwing explosives and blowing up airplanes just isn't what they do. They're submissive. They accept their lives as they are, and are just grateful for an opportunity to earn a living."

"I have another bit of information, Bill," the Captain said, "Based on the latest MAGIC intercepts, as well as a telephone intercept by the FBI, it looks like the Japanese Embassies and Consulates have begun to burn their secret papers and code material. We cabled that information to Kimmel and Short but we could not share the source with them. You intelligence guys insist on keeping knowledge of MAGIC right here in Washington."

"So what's the bottom line skipper?" Bill asked with evident alarm.

"Well, as far as I can tell, the consensus among the heavies here is that war is inevitable. Most think Tokyo will conduct a surprise attack and they'll do it soon. But they don't think Hawaii is the likely target. They expect it to be the oil fields in Borneo and possibly also the Philippines and Malaya. The field commanders have been warned. It's up to them to take defensive action." The Captain paused, then looked directly at Bill and asked, "Got any better ideas?"

"Well, sir" Bill offered, "How about increasing air reconnaissance around our bases? Or maybe disperse the fleet to sea? Or have Admiral Stark phone and talk personally about the gravity of this matter with Admiral Kimmel? And for that matter, what about warning the American public?"

"Good questions," Captain High conceded, "I can tell you that the options you offered have all been actively considered. Decisions? Well, we don't have enough fuel, spare parts, or men to sustain additional aerial reconnaissance for very long. Disperse the fleet to sea? Same answer. As for a phone call, true, it might convey a sense of urgency–but it's also a major security risk. Phone calls can be intercepted. And as for notifying the public, it might cause widespread panic. Besides, that's a political decision and I think the political strategy currently is to allow the Japs to fire the first shot. That will give the White House the excuse it wants to enter the European War. Sounds cynical, but that's the way I see things."

Bill sighed, "It's all above my pay grade, Skipper."

"Mine too," the Captain said pushing back from his desk, "But I think we've done all we can do for today. Let's go home and get ready for Christmas. I've been in the office so much my family has probably forgotten what I look like."

⊕ ⊕ ⊕

At Sea North of Hawaii

The Imperial Japanese Navy Attack Force totaled 30 ships, including oilers, destroyers, cruisers, battleships, and six aircraft carriers with over 400 planes embarked. Under the command of Vice Admiral Chuichi Nagumo, the Task Force had traveled about 3,400 miles to reach this designated stand-by point north of Hawaii on 1 December. Its orders were to wait there for a decision by the Japanese Cabinet in Tokyo whether to attack the American military complex on Oahu or return to Japan.

The next day the decision arrived by coded message: "Climb Mount Niitaka," meaning attack Sunday morning, 7 December. That set into motion carefully laid preparations for the attack. Aircraft and equipment were readied while the six aircraft carriers refueled from the oilers. Having completed their preparations, the carriers headed south, leaving the slower support ships behind. They closed to an area about 230 miles north of Oahu, from which they would launch the strike against Pearl Harbor.

Nagumo's task force was not the only one poised to launch an attack that morning. Other Imperial Japanese Navy Fleets had taken up positions to attack Malaya, Luzon, Guam, and the Netherlands East Indies. But their success depended on success at Pearl Harbor. In all, the various attacks were to constitute what Tokyo saw as a pre-emptive action, designed to paralyze the U.S. Pacific Fleet for about six months while Japan seized the Borneo oil fields and conquered much of Southeast Asia.

It was now 0550 Hawaii Standard Time, Sunday, 7 December 1941. The skies north of Hawaii were dark and the seas heavy. Under

CHAPTER 19

normal conditions air operations would have been canceled, but these were not normal conditions. This was the strike that would determine the future of the Japanese Empire. The carriers turned into the wind, the aircraft started their engines, and the first wave of attack aircraft began to launch.

✤ ✤ ✤

8 December, Yokosuka

Captain Ogawa's staff had remained at their desks through Sunday, 7 December, just in case there were last minute problems regarding the upcoming strike on Pearl Harbor. Midnight came and went and it was now about 3:00 AM on 8 December. In Hawaii, thanks to the International Dateline, it was 8:00 AM "the day before," 7 December. This was when air strikes on Oahu were slated to begin and many of Ogawa's staff had gathered around the teletype machines in the Communications Room waiting for post-strike reports.

Seeing the knot of men, Captain Ogawa walked over. "Don't expect anything from the attack force this soon," he admonished, "Vice Admiral's Nagumo's fleet must remain in radio silence until it is out of range of American retaliation. The best information we can hope for at this point are news reports from commercial radio broadcasts. So be patient." Then he added with particular rancor, "Unfortunately, commercial news reports will probably not tell us whether the American carriers were actually at Pearl Harbor."

That was the critical point for Ogawa. Based on the document Yoshikawa had acquired–the PACFLT Quarterly Schedule–he had told his superiors that two carriers would be there. If that was wrong, then his credibility with Combined Headquarters was ruined, as well as his chances for promotion to Admiral. With that thought in mind he turned to his ever present aide and snapped, "Have Both Yoshikawa and Hiro in my office tomorrow at 1200."

✤ ✤ ✤

THE DOOLITTLE IRONY

7 December 1942, Pearl Harbor Naval Base

As the first Japanese attack wave proceeded toward Oahu, two Japanese scout planes launched earlier to reconnoiter Oahu reported mixed news for the attackers. The bad was that there were no American carriers in the harbor. The good was that were no signs of U.S. readiness for the attack. When the first wave arrived over the island at 0755, its leader confirmed that all was still quiet, and sent out the now famous call, "Tora Tora Tora!" It signaled that the attack was a complete surprise!

It should not have been. There were indicators: a U.S. destroyer had just sunk a Japanese mini-sub and a radar station had detected a large number of unidentified incoming aircraft. But it was a sleepy Sunday morning and no one on Oahu connected the dots.

The first wave of aircraft roared down on the Island: 43 fighters; 51 dive bombers, 40 torpedo bombers, and 49 high level bombers. All had carefully orchestrated roles. The fighters were to establish air superiority, but there was no need for that because only a few U.S. aircraft ever got aloft to oppose them. So the fighters strafed the American aircraft on the ground at Kaneohe, Wheeler, and Hickam Air Fields, easy targets because they had been clustered together to make them easier to protect against the possibility of ground attacks by local Japanese. Concurrently, dive bombers attacked the airfields from above while the torpedo planes and high level bombers went after the battleships moored along Battleship Row.

Attacks by the first wave subsided by 0830, only to be replaced by attacks from a second wave only 15 minutes later. This time 167 aircraft struck Hickam, Wheeler and Kaneohe, as well as Bellows Field and Pearl Harbor Naval Base itself. By 0930 Hickam and Wheeler were out of action and the Arizona had capsized with over 1100 men aboard. Billowing smoke and twisted wreckage were everywhere. The seven battleships along Battleship Row had been sunk or severely damaged. Three cruisers, three destroyers, four auxiliaries and 160 aircraft were damaged or destroyed, along with 2,400 personnel killed and over 1,000 wounded. Fires would burn for days, sunken ships would take years to be repaired, and the Island was in turmoil fearing that a Japanese invasion was imminent.

CHAPTER 19

A third wave of attack aircraft had been readied by the Japanese but was not launched. It would have targeted the petroleum storage tanks; the ship and submarine repair facilities; plus conduct a search for the missing American carriers. But Admiral Nagumo chose to rest on his laurels. The Americans were showing signs of reviving from their initial surprise. Aircraft losses in the second wave had increased sharply and there was still the danger that the Americans would discover where the Japanese carriers were and inflict heavy losses on them. Nagumo played it safe and withdrew, but his decision would be regarded by Japanese military leaders as a crucially missed opportunity. He had not destroyed the petroleum storage and ship repair facilities, whereas doing so would have severely complicated America's recovery from the attack. Also he had failed to sink any of the American aircraft carriers and a search might have found and sunk the Enterprise, only a few hundred miles out at sea. (That was an omission that Tokyo would regret in only five short months!) But the major problem was the attack itself. It awoke the sleeping giant. It coalesced what had been a divided America into a nation totally committed to the defeat of the Japanese Empire. The attack set American retaliation in motion and the outcome was inevitable.

But in December 1941 that was not obvious.

CHAPTER 20

REACTION

Sunday, December 7, Crawford, Washington

It was almost noon. The Yamada family had finished its morning chores, Papa was relaxing, the two girls were outside somewhere, and Mama was preparing fish for lunch. The Yamadas did not go to church on Sunday as did many of their Christian neighbors. Mama and Papa had been raised in the traditional Japanese religion known as Shinto, but had long ago drifted away from its practices. Unlike some of their Japanese friends, they had not adopted a Christian faith in its place. It was not so much because the Christian singing or liturgy was strange, or because they felt unwelcome. Indeed, the Palmquists had invited them to attend Lutheran services. But the Yamada elders considered it excessively "Western," and they chose to eschew such practices whenever they could. In this regard the Yamadas were much like the majority of the Issei–"stand-offish." Their critics saw it as arrogance.

Suddenly Natsuko burst through the door and yelled, "Mama, Papa, turn on the radio." The 16-year-old had run all the way from town. "Japan is attacking the United States. I heard about it from the Palmquists. They said to tell you right away." Mama and Papa exchanged glances, not yet sure what to make of their 16-year-old's excited state.

CHAPTER 20

"OK, turn on radio, Natsuko," Mama said. The table model sat prominently in the center of their house, but Mama or Papa had never seen the need to master its use. The children took care of that.

Natsuko tuned it to a station in Seattle. An excited male voice was in mid-sentence, "… United Press International has issued a flash bulletin that Japan has attacked the U.S. Naval Base in Pearl Harbor in Hawaii. Details are very sketchy but personnel have reportedly been killed and U.S. ships sunk." The announcer promised to report additional information as soon as the station received it. In the meantime, showing little sense of the gravity of the moment, the station reverted to its normally scheduled program. By an uncanny coincidence, Bing Crosby began singing "The Japanese Sandman."

The Yamadas were stunned. The two elders understood from conversations with the Palmquists that governments of Japan and the U.S. were at odds, but they never suspected it could come to this. Neither knew of a place called Pearl Harbor. Papa had some background in the geography of the area because he had been to Oahu as a young immigrant to work in the Dole pineapple fields. He knew that Pearl Harbor was on the island's southern coast, but knew nothing of a naval base. He tried telling Mama that, but her mind had shifted elsewhere.

"Is Hiro in danger?" she asked of Papa.

Papa could not be certain. No one had heard from Hiro for well over a month, but he sought to reassure Mama. "No," he replied in Japanese, "Hawaii is very far from Japan."

Mama initially seemed relieved, but then other possibilities occurred to her. "What if the U.S. bombs Japan? Hiro could be killed." Papa was thinking how he might answer that when, even before Bing Crosby could finish his song, the announcer came back on the air. He repeated the news he had provided just a few minutes before, but then added, "We have received a report from a listener that a Japanese plane has been sighted over Puget Sound. We cannot confirm that, but will keep you posted on any new information as we receive it." It was only the first of many sightings reported. "We will return to our normally scheduled program as soon as we can." But that day the station never did.

202

THE DOOLITTLE IRONY

In the town center of Crawford, White citizens were standing around the front street in small knots, trying to grasp what was happening in Pearl Harbor. Some were angry, even incensed. "Where to hell do those little Jap bastards get off attacking the U.S.? I'll bet before this day is over they'll be heading back home with their tails between their legs." But as fresh reports from Hawaii arrived, the picture grew increasingly dim. News bulletins reported "heavy" casualties and the loss of "several" American warships. How could this happen to the United States? Everyone knew the American Navy was far superior to the Japanese.

As the news grew worse, Crawford's anger deepened and its citizens began looking for some explanation. Most blamed Japanese duplicity. "Damn Japs had to conduct a sneak attack–can't fight fair!" Others raised questions. "Why didn't we see them coming? Was everybody asleep out there?"

Fritz Imhoff, the president of the local Agricultural Council, had a ready answer. "The Japs had spies. How else would they know when to attack?" And, of course, all the White folks gathered around knew who Imhoff meant by "spies:" Japanese immigrants! "Sure," Fritz went on, "They were writing back to Japan all the time. They could have included all kinds of military information in those letters."

His accusations had been at the back of the townspeople's minds since the first report of the attack. Fritz just said it bluntly. "We have Japanese immigrants right here in Crawford, probably 15 or 20 families! And who's to say they're not writing back to Tokyo reporting on what we're doing? We've already heard reports of Japanese airplanes in the area."

Imhoff's accusations were familiar to the Crawford citizens. They had heard him rage about the Japanese before. He was the President of the local Agrarian Council, an avid anti-Japanese organization of White American farmers that resented the Japanese. The Council complained about "cheap labor," which it argued was the reason for the Japanese farmers' success. In California more than 40% of the agricultural product came from Japanese farms. Imhoff did not want that same situation developing in Washington State.

The townspeople understood Imhoff was just trying to protect the White farmer's pocketbook. Many discounted his charges

CHAPTER 20

on that basis. Surely the Japanese-Americans they knew personally could not be traitors. But some wondered. There had been reports of Japanese treachery. The previous summer the Washington Post published a story re-printed in the Seattle Post-Intelligencer entitled a "Confidential Report on Japanese Activities in California." It alleged that the Japanese consulates were instructing Issei and Nisei to move close to oil rigs so they could destroy them if war broke out. It further alleged that Japanese fishermen were really Japanese naval officers and that Japanese butlers and laundrymen were expected to sabotage vital bridges and tunnels. There had been other such reports, including one that the FBI was looking into the situation. Most of Crawford's White citizens had dismissed such charges as paranoia. Now, the attack on Pearl Harbor made them wonder.

As the afternoon wore on and reports from Pearl Harbor worsened, Mama worried more and more about Hiro. "We write my sister. Ask about Hiro." But Natsuko pointed out that exchanging letters would take months. "Why not try the ham radio, Mama-san?"

"Good!" Mama exclaimed in English. The Japanese community used ham radio equipment located at the Tanaka household to stay in occasional touch with friends and relatives in Japan. Natsuko wasted no time. She and her mother composed a brief note asking Mama's sister if she had any information about Hiro. Natusuko ran purposefully out the front door with the note in hand.

An hour later she returned, looking frustrated, "By the time I got there, Mama," she reported, "There was already a line of Japanese wanting to send their messages to Japan. Mr. Tanaka told me it would probably be early tomorrow before he could to ours." Natsuko had politely thanked him, left the written message, and said she would return tomorrow.

She did, quite early the next day so as to be the first in line. But an hour later she again returned home disappointed. "Mama," she explained, "Mrs. Tanaka told me we can't send our message. The FBI came last night and took Mr. Tanaka and all the radio equipment.

She doesn't even know where he is. They searched the house and left it a mess. They just upset drawers all over the floor, and they ripped the sheets off the bed. And not only that, Mama," Natsuko gushed, "Mrs. Tanaka said that we are probably going to have black outs. We'll have to turn off all our lights at night and drape black cloth in front of our windows. Mr. Grimm will even have to turn off his store lights."

"Oh, my," Mama replied, "It gets dark early. How will I cook?"

"I'm not done, Mama," Natsuko said, "I have something else to tell you: there were men in town that were carrying guns. They're not from Crawford but they knew me. One of them looked real mean at me and said, 'We know who you are. You're that traitor's sister! We'll be around to see you later."

That alarmed Mama. "Natsuko," she snapped, "We need to call Stanley."

That proved difficult. Natsuko went back to use the Tanaka's phone, being careful to avoid the town center where the armed men were. Once she arrived, she waited for Mrs. Tanaka to finish her calls. That was quite lengthy because Mrs. Tanaka was calling anyone she thought might know where her husband had been taken. No one did, so she relinquished the phone to Natsuko, who then tried to phone Stanley. But the phone by then had been taken over by Mrs. Tanaka's party line. Finally the other party hung up and Natsuko got the operator. She gave her the number of Stanley's boarding house, waited several minutes, and was then told by the operator, "Sorry but I can't get through to the switchboard in that area." Natsuko wanted to scream but Japanese girls must be reserved, so she simply said, "Oh, my! Operator this is very important. Could you try another number for me?" And she gave her Kathleen's phone. This time she got right through, probably because the Tanakas and Kathleen's family were on the same switchboard.

"Hello," a man's voice answered. It must be Kathleen's father, the Chief of Police. "So much the better," Natsuko thought. "Sir, my name is Natsuko Yamada." That's all she got out because the Chief took right over. "Natsuko? Yes, I thought you might call. I hear that one of those idiots threatened you just a little while ago. Some of the folks that were within earshot heard it and told me. If I had heard it

CHAPTER 20

myself, the guy would be in jail right now. But I didn't so all I could do was go over and "discuss" the matter with them. I told them I would be watching them and I intend to drive up the road where your house is once or twice a day. If I catch them out there, I told them they were going to jail. And I mean it. I think I could make a charge of 'inciting to violence' stick."

Surprised at Chief Kelly's declaration, Natsuko only managed a weak, "Thank you, sir."

But the Chief was not done. "One other thing, Natsuko, I want to thank you and your parents for calling me. I know our Japanese families around here have little confidence in the local police, and I understand their attitude. I also know that a friend of Hiro's has offered his personal protection to your family. I'm talking about Stanley. I met him myself and he seems like a man you would want as a friend. Good! One can never have too many friends–especially the kind that's willing to go to the mat for you. But as Chief of Police, I prefer doing things the lawful way, and so I am grateful that you called me instead of Stanley. Keeping the peace is my job, not his."

Natsuko smiled and chose not to confess to Chief Kelly that she had in fact been trying to call Stanley. "Thank you sir, I'll tell my family that. Please say hello to Kathleen for me."

Walking home Natsuko felt safer. "Wow!" she thought, "The police are on our side. Wait till I tell Mama."

CHAPTER 21

FOLLOWING THE ATTACK

1200, 9 December 1941, Yokosuka

It was the day after the Imperial Japanese Navy had attacked Pearl Harbor. Ogawa's aide had escorted Hiro and Yoshikawa to his boss's office at precisely 1200. They now sat in front of Ogawa's imposing desk, waiting for him to acknowledge their presence. Bleary eyed from having had no sleep the night before, he stared with a look of petulance at them. Then, without the slightest salutation, he began, "The preliminary signal from Admiral Nagumo is that our attack on Pearl Harbor is a major success. He believes the damage imposed is sufficient to keep the U.S. Pacific Fleet out of action for at least six months, perhaps a year. Commercial newscasts seem to confirm that. It is cause for celebration of all those who contributed to it." Then, looking directly at Yoshikawa said, "That should include you Yoshikawa, for all the useful intelligence you provided on the Oahu targets."

Yoshikawa tried to look stoically modest but was not fully successful. A hint of a smile appeared at the corners of his mouth as he anticipated good news about a promotion or even a medal. That proved to be a brutal disappointment.

"Unfortunately, that record of success has been sullied by your provision of that PACFLT scheduling document. The American car-

CHAPTER 21

riers were not "In Port Pearl" as the document indicated. I have to conclude that the document was a ruse by American Intelligence and we were unfortunately taken in by it. You should have vetted the source before bringing it back here. The prostitute who brought it to you was probably in the employ of the Americans. A few questions to the right people would have uncovered that."

Yoshikawa was crestfallen. He wanted to shout in his own defense, "I didn't have time, you had ordered me to return, I was afraid that American Military Intelligence was about to arrest me," and all the other reasons why it had been impossible to vet the source. But he remained silent. Ensigns did not argue with Captains in the Imperial Japanese Navy, even when they were right.

"I believe that failure demonstrates you are not cut out for work as an intelligence officer. I have, therefore, taken action to have you reassigned to flying duty. At 0800 tomorrow you are to report to the Fifth Fleet Support Center for transportation to your new assignment with the Naval Air Group Chi Chi-Jima."

Chi Chi-Jima? Yoshikawa was stunned. Chi Chi-Jima was a tiny, isolated island about 600 miles south of Tokyo, no place an ambitious young pilot in the Imperial Japanese Navy would want to be assigned. No, he was being sent there for Ogawa's personal reasons–to get him "out of town." Ogawa did not want him nearby when the inevitable questions would be raised about how the PACFLT Schedule document had led to attacking Pearl Harbor when the American carriers were out to sea. No, Ogawa would answer those questions himself–in a fashion that would clearly exonerate Ogawa!

Nevertheless, Yoshikawa stood erect. Even knowing that he was being railroaded did not cause him to lose his military bearing. He merely stood at attention and replied stiffly, "Yes sir." But his outward appearance belied the rancor inside. His dedication to the Imperial Japanese Navy had just suffered an irreparable injury. His fidelity to the IJN was no longer unequivocal. He better understood now that an IJN officer had to first "take care of number one." In the future he would do that. He would choose a course that served his best interests. He would no longer take risks that could later prove his undoing, even if as a result the Emperor might not be as well served. He would remember this in the future as his "Ogawa lesson."

THE DOOLITTLE IRONY

Ogawa swiveled in his chair toward Hiro. "As for you, he intoned, "I believe that you are a naïve victim of circumstances. You would not be here now had you been able to avoid it. Nevertheless, you have acted in the best interests of the Emperor. You helped Yoshikawa and you agreed to serve as our agent in America. That latter point is what I want to talk to you about today. There has been a change. The attack on Pearl Harbor–especially considering that it did not sink the American carriers–has introduced a risk that the United States will attempt to retaliate in kind. Tokyo itself is vulnerable. It's on the eastern coast of Honshu, within range of American carriers 200 miles out to sea. So Admiral Yamamoto has directed that we take precautions. We will fly air patrols all along the coast to detect any approaching American warships. We are also deploying a cordon of fishing boats and coasters well out to sea to provide continuous surveillance of the eastern seaward approaches." At that point he paused to reassure himself that Hiro comprehended his message. "That's where you come in Hiro. These boats are being refitted now with guns and military radios. The crews will mostly be the same civilians that operated them originally, but they need gunners and radio operators. You, Hiro, can operate radios."

Hiro suffered none of the military restraint that Yoshikawa did, so he interrupted, "But Captain, I should go back to the United States. If I'm here too long, people back there will be suspicious."

Ogawa brushed off his objections, "Not at all. You could simply tell them that the attack on Pearl Harbor brought additional travel restrictions. It took time for you to work around them."

Hiro offered no rebuttal, recognizing there was nothing he could say to change this matter, "How long do you think I will have to wait?"

Ogawa considered, and then replied, "I think you should be prepared to serve as a radio operator for about six months. If America has not attacked by that time, Admiral Yamamoto will probably be willing to stand down. When that happens, we will look at the situation and decide about an assignment in the U.S."

Six months! Oh, my God! How did he ever get into this mess! What would Kathleen think? How could he tell his family? They would be so worried. His only consolation was the Captain's vague

CHAPTER 21

promise that in six months he might get to go back to America. At least that was better than getting thrown into a naval prison for the duration of the war, which is what he expected would happen if he chose not to cooperate.

"The boat to which you've been assigned is right here in Yokosuka. My aide will take you there first thing in the morning. Any training you require will be provided before you sail," Ogawa concluded, "I wish you good fortune." Then, turning to Yoshikawa, he offered similar good wishes. The two younger men bowed courteously, Ogawa returned a perfunctory bow, and the meeting ended.

On the way back to the VOQ neither Yoshikawa nor Hiro spoke. Both were lost in depression. Neither yet fully comprehended what had just happened. Both knew they were the victims of Ogawa's bureaucratic maneuvering. Neither was able to do anything about it.

By contrast, Captain Ogawa was smugly satisfied. He had sent the only two people who had any first hand knowledge of the PACFLT Schedule situation to remote locations. His professional rivals—who would doubtless try to make something of this matter—would have lots of difficulty finding out what exactly happened. They would have only his version of the situation.

⊕ ⊕ ⊕

JANUARY 1942, CRAWFORD

The White community's treatment of their Japanese neighbors just after the attack on Pearl Harbor was initially benign. For the most part, the media acknowledged that the Imperial Government of Japan and the Japanese-American community were quite different, much in the fashion that local German population was quite different from the Nazis in Berlin. Yes, there were a few anti-Japanese incidents, but mostly instigated by elements that had long held grudges against them.

Unfortunately, the period of good will was brief. The loss of Guam, Wake Island, and the British Gilbert Islands, followed by Japanese conquests in the Philippines and the Dutch East Indies,

THE DOOLITTLE IRONY

Thailand, Singapore, Hong Kong Burma soured whatever good will the Japanese immigrants may have enjoyed. The Japanese seemed unstoppable. What if Tokyo next set its sights on Hawaii? Or for that matter, the West Coast? Hysterical reports of Japanese planes over Seattle and submarine sightings in Puget Sound filled the media. The word "Jap" became a slur, a synonym for evil. Doubts and suspicions grew in the White community about whether the Japanese in their midst would remain loyal to America if an invasion did materialize.

⊕ ⊕ ⊕

"Stanley, is that you?" Kathleen asked. She had phoned Stanley at his office to inquire whether he had any new information on Hiro. She was confident the answer would be no, otherwise Stanley would have already called. Nevertheless, she asked, "Is there anything new."

"No," came the reply, "Nor is it likely there will be anytime soon. Phone connections are all down. Ham radios have been confiscated. Our diplomats in Japan have all been detained by the Japanese–as well as news reporters, businessmen, and other Americans. It's not encouraging, Kathleen. We will probably have to rely on Hiro's ingenuity to get him through this. There's nothing we can do from here."

"Yes, I know–but I can't stop asking! I guess this is what a wife feels like when she gets one of those 'Missing in Action' telegrams from the War Department."

Anxious to move on to a less anguishing topic Stanley asked, "Actually, Kathleen, I've wanted to ask about Hiro's parents. I think a lot of White hostility has developed toward the local Japanese. I appreciate that your Dad is on top of the situation, but there are some things he can't control. The FBI is certainly one of those. Has Mrs. Tanaka found out where they took her husband? And why?"

"No, I don't think so Stanley," Kathleen responded, "Have you?"

"Well, I do have some information. You'll recall that Mr. Scott, the man who owns this firm, is pretty well connected around town. He learned from City Hall that the FBI detained Japanese up and down the West Coast, just like they did Mr. Tanaka. Apparently it's has been keeping lists of local Japanese they consider potential collaborators. It's not that these men have <u>actually</u> collaborated; it's

CHAPTER 21

just that they have radios that could be used to communicate with Japan, or fishing boats that could sail out to meet a Japanese ship. In some cases, they were picked up only because they were community leaders."

"My gosh, Stanley," Kathleen blurted, "That's not fair! Have many been arrested?"

"Mr. Scott says over 1,200, and they were all taken just like Mr. Tanaka. FBI agents knock on the door at any hour of the day or night. They have no warrant. They offer no explanation. They search the house and make a terrible mess. Then they take the man off in handcuffs and refuse to say where they are taking him or how the family can contact him. It's really bad, Kathleen," Stanley concluded, "It's why my father left Europe. I never thought I'd see anything like it here."

"Oh, one other thing," Stanley added, "Mr. Scott said the Japanese that were picked up from this area were taken to a federal prison in Missoula, Montana. They're being held incommunicado and he doesn't have any idea about when they might be released. He doubts that Mrs. Tanaka would be allowed to see him even if she went there. And as you probably know, the bank accounts of all Japanese here have been frozen. So even if Mrs. Tanaka wants to go see her husband, she probably can't–unless she has enough cash on hand for a rail ticket."

"Oh, Stanley, that is such bad news!" Kathleen said in frustration, and then asked rhetorically, "Can things get any worse?"

They could.

✣ ✣ ✣

WASHINGTON, D.C., FOLLOWING PEARL HARBOR

Pearl Harbor brought disgrace to the U.S. Navy. Japan had destroyed practically all of America's Pacific Battleship Fleet in less than two hours. How could that happen? It was not as though ample forces had not been available to defend the Island. Army and Navy resources on or near Pearl Harbor had totaled about 4000 aircraft, almost 1000

THE DOOLITTLE IRONY

antiaircraft guns and 43,000 men. But when the Japanese attacked, all 43,000 of those men were seemingly asleep, playing golf, or nursing hangovers acquired the night before in the bars and brothels of Honolulu. This was not what America expected of its military forces. It demanded explanations from those responsible for military readiness there. Why had they not maintained a proper alert? Why had not a more effective resistance been mounted? In the months following Pearl Harbor, Congress would convene hearings to bring those leaders to task. Heads would roll, careers would end, and personal disgrace would be meted out. In the months following Pearl Harbor, senior U.S. military leaders did not sleep easily.

Both Captain High and Lieutenant Bill Russo were exhausted. Neither had left their offices in days. They had been inundated with questions and tasks from the Navy brass, the White House, and probably half the members of Congress. The questions were endless. Why had Pearl Harbor happened? Who was at fault? What should we do now? Exactly what ships and aircraft remain operational? Where should we deploy them? How vulnerable are we? The questions went on and on, and the politicians and brass who posed them wanted their answers RIGHT NOW! Bill was convinced the Japanese would be easier to deal with than the bureaucrats in Washington, D.C.

"Lieutenant Russo," Bill's office secretary called to him, "It's Captain High for you." Bill picked up the phone but, of course, Captain High was not REALLY there. No, it was Captain High's secretary on the other end of the line, who then said, "Just a moment for Captain High." It was little bureaucratic rituals like this that irritated Bill. To make a call in the Navy, "Officer 1's" secretary had to call "Officer 2's" secretary. Then the junior of the two officers would come on the line first, followed by the senior. Why couldn't they just call and say, "Hey Bill, it's me." But, as he had done thousands of times before, Bill just suppressed his irritation and waited.

"Bill, I just attended a meeting with Admiral Stark. He wants me to go along with him to a meeting that's coming up as a back-bencher-plus-one." That was Navy jargon meaning Captain High could attend–though not as a principal–and he could bring another person. "I want you to be my plus one."

CHAPTER 21

"Well, thanks for keeping me in mind Captain, but I'm up to my eyeballs over here. You're gonna have to clear it with N-2."

"No sweat there, Bill, I already have. I think you'll find your time well spent. A lot of heavies will be there. It will be fun to see them in action."

✦ ✦ ✦

CAPTAIN High's use of the word "heavies" was no exaggeration. Just two weeks after Pearl Harbor, President Roosevelt, Prime Minister Churchill, and the most senior military officers of both Britain and the United States met in Washington, D.C. to discuss broad wartime strategy and priorities. Known as the Arcadia Conference, it produced a number of historic decisions, among them: the U.S. and Britain would closely combine their war efforts; their first priority would be to defeat Nazi Germany and only secondarily Japan; military decisions would be made jointly under the direction of a British-American Combined Chiefs of Staff; and an invasion of Africa would be launched in 1942. Perhaps the most significant and enduring product of the Conference was the *Declaration by United Nations,* a document that asserted complete victory over the Axis powers was essential. The document was eventually signed by a total of 26 nations and led to establishment of the United Nations in 1945.

Unfortunately, Bill and Captain High were not able to see this history being made first hand. As conferences frequently do, this one broke into sub-groups. The one Bill and Captain High were assigned to concerned logistics. In the context of December 1941, that really meant, "How can the U.S. meet Britain's manifold needs for military hardware, especially if an invasion of Africa is to be mounted in 1942?"

The Brits took the lead. They provided a background briefing on the political and military situation in Northern Africa, and their view of the area's strategic significance. Commodore Derrick Sterling was just finishing. "So in sum, gentleman, we Brits believe control of North Africa is imperative. It would assure us naval control of the Mediterranean and maritime access to the Suez Canal, the Middle East, and India. Moreover its northern shores provide a staging area

THE DOOLITTLE IRONY

for the invasion of Europe itself through what some call its 'soft underbelly.'"

This brought a question from one of the U.S. Army officers present, "But Commodore Sterling, wouldn't an invasion of Africa drain away resources from a cross-channel operation?"

And in those few sentences, the sub-group had been given a capsulated version of the major difference between the strategic views of Britain and the U.S. regarding the European Theater of War. Britain preferred to invade Germany from the south through Italy or the Balkans–Europe's "soft underbelly." That required securing the Mediterranean which, perhaps not coincidentally, also preserved the British Empire's line of communication with the Middle East and South Asia. The United States saw that as a sideshow. Its objective was more elegant: invade and defeat Germany by the shortest route possible. That was across the English Channel and through Northern Europe.

Commodore Sterling was already all too aware of America's view, and had the official British response ready, "Actually, Britain sees an invasion of Europe across the English Channel as excessively risky. Think of the thousands of ships and landing craft that would require. It's a logistical nightmare. Plus the weather is unpredictable. And wherever we landed on the Western Continent, it would be rather easy for the German Army to concentrate its forces there and overwhelm our beachhead."

"Well," the U.S. officer replied, "I guess for the purposes of this sub-group, that's neither here nor there. Our betters will have to decide that issue. As of this point in time, we are committed to an invasion of Africa and we're here to figure out how the U.S. can best provide the logistic support you Brits will need."

"One thing we desperately need is transport aircraft," the Commodore replied, happy to get away from the contentious strategic issue. "The distances we have to deal with in Africa are significant and there are few rail lines or modern roads. Air transport is the answer, but we simply don't have enough aircraft–and we don't have a good way to get new aircraft to where they're needed." He paused in an effort to assure their attention and then added, "But we think we have a solution."

CHAPTER 21

The room quieted in anticipation, and the Commodore got right to the point, "We want the U.S. to use its naval carriers to ferry transport aircraft to some point off of the African Continent, launch them while still out at sea, and have them fly the rest of the way to their destinations."

Several U.S. officers spoke at once. "Transport aircraft? We're talking about transport aircraft? Like the C-47? My god man, you're talking 15,000 to 20,000 lbs. empty, and a takeoff speed of 85 knots. Planes that size can't operate off a carrier!"

"But we don't want them to <u>operate</u> off a carrier," the Commodore responded, "We just want them to <u>take off</u> from a carrier. We'll load the planes onto the carriers with cranes while it's in port. Then the carrier sails toward its destination. While still 50 or 100 miles distant, the aircraft launch and fly ashore. Gentlemen, we have researched this proposal. Our aeronautical engineers think that by turning into the wind, moving the carrier to full speed, and giving the launch aircraft a few hundred feet of deck to accelerate, they can reach take off speed."

"Sounds good in theory" one skeptic blurted out, "But have you actually done it?"

"No, we haven't. As you know, we have precious few carriers, and we just can't spare one to test out this theory. But as I said our best aeronautical engineers say it can be done."

The Americans were not convinced but chose not to belabor the issue. The working group moved on to other topics.

CHAPTER 22

LOOKING FOR REVENGE

Later, at Happy Hour, the Captain and Bill pondered the matter over a draft beer. Captain High was in a modest way qualified to judge the merits of the Brits' aeronautical arguments. Like most U.S. Naval Officers of his age and rank, he had grown up in a battleship navy. But by mid-career he had come to realize that aviation would soon play a big part in naval affairs. He wrangled his way into flight training–which included instruction in aeronautics– and after 14 months qualified as a naval aviator. But he was never assigned actual flight duties. Instead the Navy saw his training as a means of familiarizing him with this strange new field so when he assumed command of a ship or shore installation, he would better understand how aviation fit in.

"You know, Bill," the Captain observed, "The Brits are right. If a planes take off speed is 85 knots, that doesn't mean the plane has to be moving at 85 knots down a runway. It just means the plane's wings have to "think" the plane is moving at that speed. So if you're aboard a carrier that's moving along at 20 knots, and you turn into a 10-knot headwind, you've already got 30 knots of wind across the airplane's wings. Then the plane accelerates down 500 feet of deck to a speed of 55 knots, and you've reached take off speed. The real issue is not speed over the ground; it's the speed of the wings thru the air."

CHAPTER 22

"I see, Skipper," Bill replied, "But then the planes can't land back aboard the carrier. They have to land ashore. That makes for a curious operation. I guess if you're going to ferry transport aircraft like the Brits want, it would work. But I'm having trouble imagining another scenario where that capability would be useful."

"Yeah, you're right Bill," the Captain agreed, "And I doubt we're going to use our carriers as delivery trucks for the Brits. So using carriers for this sort of operation would require very special circumstances. At this point, I don't know what they would be."

It was Mid-January in Washington, D.C. and a light snow was falling, giving the city a joyful post-holiday appearance. That was deceptive. Christmas and New Years had been anything but joyful. Recriminations for the disaster at Pearl Harbor were being cast about. Admiral Kimmel and General Short, the two senior officers in Hawaii, had been found guilty of errors in judgment and dereliction of duty. Wake Island had fallen on Christmas Eve and the Japanese had entered Manila on 2 January.

In the Atlantic German submarines were sinking coastal shipping along the East Coast in plain view of Americans watching from the shore. For most military personnel, wartime duties had taken precedence over all holiday festivities. Fourteen-hour workdays had become the norm. So when Admiral King–who had recently replaced Admiral Stark as Chief of Naval Operations–called a surprise staff meeting 10 January, the staffers wondered what new disaster could possibly have befallen the Navy.

The Admiral presided at the head of the long conference table. Captain High sat toward the foot of the table, befitting his lowly status amid a room full of flag officers. Bill occupied a "back bencher" chair against the wall. All expected the meeting to be unpleasant. They would not be disappointed.

"Gentlemen," the Admiral began, "I have just left the President. Our meeting was unpleasant. He is normally a civil man, not given to upbraiding senior officers in front of their peers. Today was an exception. Mr. Roosevelt does not currently hold the United States

THE DOOLITTLE IRONY

Navy in high regard, and as that service's senior representative, he made me acutely aware of that! I can't say I blame him." Then, warming to his task, the Admiral raised his voice, "The President desperately wants to retaliate in kind for Pearl Harbor. In other words, he wants to bomb Japan. We've explained to him that the Army Air Corp's closest base to Japan is in the Aleutians, and that is out of range of even our longest range bombers. We explained also that the Navy currently has only three aircraft carriers in the Pacific, and we cannot risk losing even one of them on a very risky venture like he's proposing. But he's adamant."

Then, in the fashion of a revival preacher, He laid out the challenge before them, "Gentlemen, unless we can come up with an idea to produce a victory soon and give the President some political breathing space, we can all expect reassignments to a harbor tug in Kodiak. These past six weeks have laid bare our problems. We have been slow, unresponsive, and unable to adjust to new circumstances. Gentlemen, we need to stretch our minds. We need to do something big, something that will restore the President's confidence in the Navy, and this nation's self confidence. If you've got any bright ideas, gentlemen, now's the time to float them." With that he banged the table with his fist and left the room. His performance had lived up to his crusty reputation.

Bill and Captain High exchanged glances. As they filed out of the conference room with the rest of the staff, the Captain turned to Bill and asked, "Are you thinking what I'm thinking?"

Bill responded with a glint in his eye, "Sure, bombers instead of air transports!"

"Good," the Captain smiled. We may have to make up some of this on the fly, but let's catch him now, before he forgets what he said."

Bill nodded. They would beard the lion in his den.

Twenty minutes later in the privacy of the Admiral's office, Captain High finished making his pitch. "That's it, sir. In sum, we launch bombers from a carrier well out to sea. That added distance protects our carriers. The bombers hit Tokyo and recover somewhere to the west. Maybe China. Maybe Russia. It would be only one raid, and we can't expect it to have any material effect on Japan's military

CHAPTER 22

capability. But it might knock them off balance, and we can say we evened the score for Pearl."

The Admiral was not a man who suffered fools gladly. Staring back at Captain High across his desk, he looked incredulous. "Let me get this straight, High," he said, "you want me to take one or more of our Pacific Fleet carriers, load them with bombers they were never designed to launch, drive them deep into the Pacific, penetrate Japan's homeland defenses, bomb Tokyo, and then hope our planes escape to the Asian mainland and our ships back to Hawaii?"

He paused just long enough to get his breath. "And you want me to do this mostly as a publicity stunt? Just so we can say we bombed Tokyo? Tell me. What do we do if we lose a carrier? Hell, we only got three out there. Who's going to defend Seattle if we get our carriers sunk in Tokyo Bay on some damn publicity stunt?"

He took another breath, this one shorter than the last. He was on a roll! "And what aircraft would we use? And who says the Chinese or the Russians would allow us to land on their turf? Hell, Captain, I'd say this idea of your borders on the ridiculous."

Captain High was not surprised at the Admiral's reaction. Put in the fashion the Admiral just had, it did border on the ridiculous. Nevertheless, High thought, the Admiral had asked for ideas. So he decided to press just a bit. "Sir, we know there are many problems, but we believe the idea has sufficient prospect that it that it should be looked at seriously."

The Admiral's scowl did not soften. Instead he shifted his gaze to Bill and asked with a bit of sarcasm, "Well, lieutenant, you been standing there with your teeth in your mouth. What have you got to add?" Bill shuffled his feet nervously, "Well, sir, I think we just might pull it off. I was a Naval Attache in Tokyo a few years ago. I saw the problems the Japanese Navy had with the Japanese Army, and vice versa. They hate one another. Well, the air defense of Tokyo is a joint Army-Navy responsibility, heavily dependent on the two services coordinating with one another. I'll bet there are quite a few holes in it. Plus, much of their Navy is now deployed to the Indian Ocean. After their run of successes in the Central and South Pacific, the Japs are probably feeling pretty smug. They think they have us on the ropes. The idea of U.S. carriers attacking Tokyo probably doesn't

THE DOOLITTLE IRONY

strike them as very likely. With the element of surprise on our side, I think we can pull it off."

There was a long pause. The Admiral pushed his chair back from the desk and seemed to relax just a bit and his tone wasn't quite so strident. "OK," he conceded, "The Brits gave me that pitch about using carriers to ferry transport aircraft also. It seems feasible, so maybe launching bombers is not so pie-in-the-sky. Besides, we're desperate."

He looked sternly at High. "I'll give you 24 hours to put some meat on these bones of an idea you've got. Maybe it will get the President off my back. I want you to get with the air operations people to help you work this thing."

Then he added something that suggested he didn't think the idea was quite as farfetched as his rant had indicated: "Oh, and let's keep this close hold. Just in case we decide to try this, the fewer people who know about it the better."

It was that same afternoon that Admiral King personally placed a call on the secure line to Lieutenant General Henry "Hap" Arnold, Chief of the Army Air Force. Arnold was a man of significant accomplishment–the Army's "Aviator #1," taught to fly by none other than Wilbur and Orville Wright. He had been an early and vocal advocate of a robust air capability and had even advocated for an Air Force independent of the Army. As a civilian, he helped found Pan American Airlines and even wrote a series of juvenile fiction intended to interest youth in a career in aviation.

Hap Arnold picked up the phone. "Ernie, what can I do for you?" He listened attentively, nodded occasionally, and raised his eyebrows a few times. "Damn, Ernie," he responded finally, "I like it. But risky! And you've got a lot more skin in the game than me. I stand to lose a couple dozen aircraft. You could lose a big chunk of what remains of the Pacific Fleet. This has to be your call–and, of course, the President's. But I think he'll go for it. Sounds like just what he is looking for. Let's try it out on him.

CHAPTER 22

✧ ✧ ✧

THE WHITE HOUSE

Admiral King and General Arnold were finishing their presentation. "So you see, Mr. President," General Arnold said, "If you want a dramatic strike to give America a victory it can celebrate, then bombing Tokyo is certainly it. And the only way we can do that is the way we've just outlined to you. Our air bases in the Aleutians are beyond the range of even our longest range bombers so we have to use carriers to get close enough."

"Bombing Tokyo" was just the phrase the President wanted to hear. He set his mid-afternoon martini on the table, smiled and said, "Yes, I think this might just be what we need. It'll give the Japs a taste of their own medicine."

Admiral King was pleased with that response but thought it bureaucratically prudent to highlight the downside of the proposal just so he could say, "I warned you Mr. President," if things went awry. The Admiral's job was already in jeopardy for not having warned about the Pearl Harbor attack more emphatically. He wasn't about to make the same mistake again. "Well, sir, if we lose any of our carriers in the Pacific, we must realize that we may not be able to stop the Japs from striking our own homeland, just as we plan to strike theirs. It's a bit of a crap shoot, but I think the risk is acceptable if we follow the plan we've outlined here. By using longer range Army bombers we can launch farther out to sea than the Japs probably anticipate. By the time they react, our carriers will be out of range."

"Well, I'll leave the details to you and Hap," the President concluded, "We need a victory, gentlemen. The West Coast is hysterical. The whole country is reeling with news of military defeats. We need something to cheer about for a change. I'm relying on you two to produce that."

The two left to walk to the nearby Old Executive Office Building where Admiral King maintained an office and where General Arnold's car awaited. "I guess we've got our marching orders, Hap," Admiral King commented as they walked across the White

THE DOOLITTLE IRONY

House grounds, "but if we're to succeed we've got to work together–none of that inter-service rivalry crap."

"I agree," Hap retorted, "And we're going to have to put good people in charge. I think I've got just the man." When he returned to his office, the smile that had earned him the nickname "Hap" spread across his face as he told his secretary, "Have Lieutenant Colonel Doolittle come see me."

CHAPTER 23

WAR HYSTERIA

Crawford, late January-Early February 1942

The President's use of the word "hysteria" was not exaggeration. Following the attack on Pearl Harbor, a rash of Japanese ship and aircraft sightings had been reported up and down the West Coast. Many were ridiculous, but the media published them anyway, without confirmation. Worse, the Army's Western Military District, the military element responsible for the security of the West Coast, seemed also to accept them without question—and by so doing confirm their authenticity.

As a result, in the two months following Pearl Harbor the public along the West Coast had been gradually worked into a state of near hysteria. This was evident in an incident that later became known as the "Battle of Los Angeles." In the night of 24 February, anti-aircraft defense elements there opened fire on what they thought was a Japanese aircraft. They fired over 1,400 shells at what turned out to be a weather balloon. In the ensuing confusion five fatalities occurred as the result of heart attacks and traffic accidents.

Stanley was increasingly concerned about the situation. "Kathleen," he asked at their weekly meeting at Grimm's Drug Store,

THE DOOLITTLE IRONY

"Have you seen some of the signs around Seattle? 'Japs Unwelcome' and "Japs go back to Tokyo.' They are really mean-spirited."

"I know," she replied, "Fortunately it's not that vicious out here in Crawford, but still the local Japanese read the newspapers. They see references to the 'Yellow Peril,' they are restricted from being out after dark by a curfew, their bank accounts have been frozen, they are not even allowed to go near bridges or tunnels. Just a few days ago the Japanese red caps at King Street Station were replaced by Filipinos who wear badges that say 'Filipino not Japanese.' There's even been talk about moving the local Japanese to another location, away from the Coast so they could not collaborate with a Japanese invasion."

"Yeah," Stanley nodded sadly, "My boss, Mr. Scott, has been telling us that General DeWitt is pushing hard for that."

"Who's General DeWitt?" Kathleen asked.

"He's the commanding officer of the Western Military District. He's got about four-or-five divisions of Army troops under him, mostly reserves, poorly trained, scattered up and down the Coast. They're responsible for maintaining the security of anything that relates to our military defense–ports, harbors, bridges, tunnels, roads, shipyards, etc. It was one of their air defense elements that fired on that so-called Japanese aircraft over Los Angeles the other night that turned out to be a weather balloon. And they're the ones that claim Japanese planes and submarines are constantly reconnoitering the West Coast–although they never quite come up with any concrete evidence of it. According to Mr. Scott, WMD is not really a crack outfit and General DeWitt is not really a crack general."

"You might say that about our politicians, as well," Catherine observed. "Did you see some of the recent stuff in the news? This Attorney General down in California, what's his name, Earl Warren, he's out to make a name for himself. He said the "Japanese situation" is the Achilles Heel of the West Coast defense effort. He says that unless "something" is done about it, we'll have another Pearl Harbor right here where we live."

"Yes," Stanley agreed, "And the press cooperates by giving these guys all kinds of ink. Hell, Walter Lippman the other day wrote the West Coast is in imminent danger due to a so-called "fifth column."

CHAPTER 23

He meant the Japanese here. And then he went on to say that these people have no Constitutional rights because no one has a right to reside or do business on a battlefield. Geez, I'm just an engineer, but even I can see that that's bullshit. He's just trying to build support among his readers back on the East Coast for some kind of action against the Japanese. And he's not alone. Anything with even a taint of Japanese is reviled by most Americans. Dance bands will no longer play *The Japanese Sandman*, and rowdies are chopping down the Japanese cherry trees on the Mall in Washington, D.C. Sure, there are a few voices out there urging moderation–Eleanor Roosevelt, Herbert Hoover, Attorney General Biddle, maybe some others–but they're few and far between. Things do not look good. I don't know exactly what to expect, but I'm sure it's not going to be good for the Japanese-Americans."

"Well, Stanley," Kathleen observed, "I can see them taking some kind of action against the *Issei*. They're not citizens. But the *Nisei* are. I just can't imagine that the government can do anything to them. It would be illegal."

Stanley grunted, "I wish I had your confidence. But I don't. In a war where an invasion force–real or imagined–is just over the horizon, the concept of 'rights' becomes a nicety. Survival is paramount. And survival is framed in the most basic way–'us and them.' In this case, 'us' is White European and 'them' is Yellow Japanese. "

A long pause followed while both pondered what lie ahead. Finally Stanley broke the silence, "You know, we haven't even talked about Hiro. I guess neither of us really expected anything new on that score. God, how things have changed in just a few months!"

Stanley's reference to Hiro brought a furrow to Kathleen's brow. "I really do worry about him, Stanley. I wonder if he's in prison, or worse."

Wanting to avoid the tears and emotion that seemed to be welling in Kathy, Stanley abruptly changed the subject, "It's late, Kathleen. I better go. Can I give you a ride?"

"No, thank you," Kathleen responded with a grateful smile, "I can walk. It's not far–and it's still safe out here."

The two left Grimm's Drug Store and walked into the fading light of the winter evening. Then they saw it, a big poster board

THE DOOLITTLE IRONY

on which someone had boldly lettered, "NO NANKING IN CRAWFORD!" It referred to an incident that occurred in China several years before–"The Rape of Nanking"–where the Japanese Army had committed mass murder and mass rape of the civilian population. The sheer brutality had shocked the Western world and had since been repeated in other areas of Japanese conquest. The poster board was leaning on Stanley's Chevy–an unmistakable message.

Stanley picked up the poster and spun it into the street face down. He looked around to see if there was anyone there who might want to pursue the issue with him personally but, of course, there was not. "C'mon," he said to Kathleen," I'd better give you a lift. Maybe Crawford isn't as safe as you think."

CHAPTER 24

AT SEA ABOARD *PICKET SHIP #23*

The Nitto Maru was tiny by maritime standards. It was constructed of steel, displaced 124 tons and was only about 70 feet in length. It had been a fishing boat before being impressed into duty with the Imperial Japanese Navy. The IJN had designated it "Picket Ship #23" and assigned it to the Fifth Fleet, the naval organization charged with defense of the home waters. The Nitto Maru's mission was simple: maintain visual watch for enemy ships in a patrol area about 650 miles east of the Japanese coastline. If it spotted another ship, it would seek to identify it and, if hostile, send a contact report to the Fifth Fleet Flag Ship describing the contact and listing its course and speed. If the enemy ship attacked, *Picket Ship #23* was almost certainly a goner. It was slow, had no armor, and only three small guns.

Hiro had become familiar with his new duties. Most were not difficult. The radio the IJN had equipped the ship with was a high-frequency transceiver and its functions were familiar to him. It employed "continuous wave" transmission, which meant he would have to tap out his message using "dits and dahs." Hiro could manage that well enough. He had had to develop a keying speed of about five words per minute to get his ham radio license. That would probably have been adequate, except that the IJN did not use standard International Morse Code. It used the Japanese equivalent, called

THE DOOLITTLE IRONY

Wabun, which requires knowledge of the Japanese written language. Therein lay the problem. Hiro's mother had insisted that her family speak Japanese at home; hence Hiro could manage spoken Japanese, though it was admittedly the "old fashioned" style. But Mama had never insisted that her children learn to write in Japanese, and consequently Hiro had only a rudimentary knowledge of what many consider the most complicated written language in the world. He relied on charts that showed Wabun equivalents for each International Morse signal. Using it was slow and cumbersome. He wondered what he would do if he ever had to transmit in an emergency.

The Imperial Japanese Navy seemed unconcerned about that prospect. By its reckoning, the chances of the Nitto Maru encountering an enemy ship were extremely remote. Whether its radioman was capable of transmitting a properly encoded emergency message in a timely fashion just didn't seem that important.

The Nitto Maru's operation was quite regular: leave port, spend three days getting to its assigned patrol area about 650 NM west of Tokyo; spend the next two weeks plying a race track pattern about 25 miles long; then spend another three days transiting back to port. That would be followed by a four-day period to rest and refit, so the cycle was twenty days at sea, four days ashore. Considering that the weather was frequently rough and there was nothing to break the boredom, it was a difficult grind. Still, during the shore periods Hiro rarely left the ship. Going ashore with other men from his ship would risk getting drunk and perhaps revealing his true loyalties.

The boredom of the long patrols was occasionally broken by conversations with crew members. All had previously been fishermen. Their knowledge of the world beyond their small enclaves was limited. All were intensely interested in the U.S. On an abstract level, they saw it as an enemy, but on a personal level they had many questions about life there. How big was his family's farm? Was it true that everyone had a car? Had he really gone to college? All were quite willing to accept Hiro's story about being a returning expatriate rallying to the Emperor's defense. They saw it as what they would do in a similar situation.

The crew members were not so much different than his parents and the other Issei with whom he had grown up. They worked hard, had modest expectations, and bore great love for their families. The

CHAPTER 24

single biggest difference was their adoration of the Emperor. It was unequivocal and, to Hiro, inexplicable. Nevertheless he grew to like his crewmates and they seemed to reciprocate. Their conversations had the benefit of bringing his Japanese language usage up to date. He thought now if he had to go ashore by himself, he'd be able to pass at least a nominal inspection as a native.

The Captain of the Nitto Maru was not at all like the rest of the crew. He was a young IJN officer who had just graduated from the Japanese Naval Academy at Etijima near Hiroshima. His surname was Enjo. No one knew his given name because he insisted on being called "Captain Enjo." He was a cruel disciplinarian. When displeased with a crew member, he would strike him with his fists–a practice he learned at Etijima, Japan's Naval Academy notorious for its brutal discipline. Normally a brand new officer like Enjo would have had been assigned a junior position aboard a destroyer or cruiser. But when the IJN impressed fishing vessels into service as picket ships, Enjo volunteered to command one. Though normally assigned to a senior non-commissioned officer, he saw it as an opportunity for "command at sea," a valuable experience for any ambitious naval officer.

Enjo was taken with the importance of his new assignment. He spoke to crew members only to issue orders. Hiro was something of an exception, possibly because he was a radio operator, involved in electronics which Enjo saw as a dark art. His training at Etijima had included nothing about such matters, but he knew it was a very important field. He had heard about electronic devices that could see targets in the dark, in bad weather, and at great distances.

Hiro remembered one conversation with Enjo in particular. It occurred on the bridge, where Hiro would occasionally go for a breath of air. The helmsman happened to be gone and Enjo himself had taken the wheel. He did that occasionally, and seemed to enjoy being in direct control of the ship. He rarely spoke to Hiro, but with the wheel in his hand he seemed to relax. He bragged that he came from a long line of naval officers. His grandfather had been aboard a battleship at Japan's great victory at Tsushima Straits. His father was now a Captain on the Imperial Japanese Naval Planning Staff. His family expected Enjo to be a loyal officer too, and he was determined to be just that.

THE DOOLITTLE IRONY

"I will never be captured," he asserted to Hiro, "I will give up my life before that happens." Hiro listened politely, but gave the Captain's rant little importance. In Hiro's opinion, the Captain was just another impressionable young Japanese man who had lost his independent judgment to the Bushido Code, the Japanese warrior ethic that demanded death rather than surrender.

Most of Hiro's days at sea were spent at his radio, scanning the airwaves for information on world events. He was occasionally able to find English language news broadcasts, some from the West Coast of America that had skipped across the Pacific bouncing between the earth and the ionosphere. Transmission quirks like these are typical of the high frequency radio band, but they are unreliable and usually of brief duration. Nevertheless, using these and Japanese domestic broadcasts he was able to follow the string of Japanese victories through the Pacific: the seizure of Guam; the invasion of the Philippines; the sinking of the Royal Navy's *Repulse* and the *Prince of Wales*; the fall of Hong Kong; the invasion of the Dutch East Indies. He had just listened to a fragment of British news about MacArthur's escape from the Philippines. It struck him hard. MacArthur was the commander of both U.S. and Philippine forces there. His departure signaled yet another dramatic Japanese military success. Tokyo seemed invincible. Hiro wondered whether Hawaii or even the West Coast of North America could be next on Japan's target list.

Primary among his concerns was the safety of Kathleen and his family. Hiro had heard fragments of news reports that alluded to the "problem" of Japanese immigrants on the West Coast of America. He wasn't sure what that meant. Perhaps the *Kibbie* had been making trouble. Of course the Japanese domestic broadcasts were full of hysterical accusations that the U.S. Government was forcing Japanese immigrants aboard trains and sending them off to concentration camps. They decried this as yet another in a long series of American transgressions against the Japanese people. Hiro wrote off Tokyo's claims as just another pack of lies and distortions to discredit America and justify the war Japan had undertaken against it. Surely, Hiro reasoned, the America he knew would never be guilty of such behavior. After all, it was clearly unconstitutional.

CHAPTER 25

THE TOKYO RAID TAKES SHAPE

WASHINGTON, D.C., JANUARY 1942

General Arnold had had little difficulty deciding on whom to put in charge of organizing the bombing raid on Tokyo the President had just authorized. It had to be Jimmy Doolittle. There was no man in America better qualified. At 45 years of age, Doolittle had already become a legend in aviation circles. Raised in the rough and tumble gold rush era in Nome, Alaska, he moved as a teen to Southern California. Although a diminutive 5'4" tall, he helped support his mother with prize money earned as a free-lance boxer. He joined the Army Air Corps at the outset of the First World War, was awarded a commission, and then stayed in uniform following the war's end to help popularize the new field of aviation. He barnstormed around the country, established new aviation records, and won several major racing trophies.

Doolittle was a man for all seasons. In addition to being a daredevil, he was a man of considerable intellect. He earned a Bachelor of Arts degree from the University of California, Berkely, in 1922; entered the Massachusetts Institute of Technology in 1924; and within two years had earned both a master's and a doctorate in aeronautical engineering–the latter being the first such degree issued in

THE DOOLITTLE IRONY

the United States. He was also a pioneer in instrumented flight. He tested devices such gyroscopes and artificial horizons which enable pilots to fly in darkness, through cloud cover, and other conditions of limited visibility. In 1930 he traded his regular commission in the Army Air Corps for a reserve commission, left active duty, and accepted a position with Shell Oil Corporation as head of Aviation Operations. There he was instrumental in developing yet another element critical to a growing aviation industry: high octane aviation gas. With it, airplanes could fly higher and faster than ever before.

Though a civilian, Doolittle maintained his connections with the Army Air Corps and in 1940 reentered active duty as a Major. Hap Arnold personally had him assigned to his staff as a special advisor and promoted him to Lieutenant Colonel.

Doolittle was just what was needed to lead this operation against Tokyo–technically savvy, highly experienced, and able to analyze a problem, devise a solution, and set it in place. Of course, once the plan reached that stage, General Arnold reasoned, he would put someone else in charge to actually fly the mission. After all, Doolittle was too valuable to send on some hare-brained scheme to bomb Tokyo.

Lieutenant Colonel Doolittle saluted smartly as he entered General Arnold's office. The General wasted no time on small talk this morning. "Jim," he began, "What's the biggest bomber in our inventory that can launch from an aircraft carrier?"

Doolittle was understandably stumped. It was not the sort of arcane trivia that barnstormers like Doolittle carried around in their heads.

Noting his silence, General Arnold said, "I want you to get together with a Captain High over on Ernie King's staff about an operation we're considering. He can fill you in on the details. When you've got those, and you've worked out a preliminary plan, I want you to bring it here so we can discuss it. Understand this carries the very top priority. If you run into people who won't cooperate, use my name. If that doesn't work call me and I'll put the fear of God into

CHAPTER 25

them. Now get busy." Then he added a critical admonition, "And Jimmy, keep this under your hat!"

Doolittle began mentally sorting through the possible aircraft choices even before he exited the Munitions Building. It would have to be a medium bomber. That meant the B-18, B-23, B-25, or B-26. He would have to determine how much space was available on the deck of the carrier to be used, how far the planes would have to fly, what bomb loads they would be expected to carry, and lots of other details. He wondered what the target was–probably one of the outlying Japanese Islands. God knows, he wished it were Tokyo.

Elsewhere in Washington, the Navy had begun working on its end of the operation. Captain High was the point man on the project and, with other elements of ADM King's staff, had chosen a carrier to perform the mission. It was the *USS Hornet*, CV-8, a member of the Yorktown Class. With an 825-foot deck it was large enough to launch land based bombers, displaced 20,000 tons, and carried a ship's company of about 1,350 officers and men. It embarked a total of 74 aircraft with an additional complement of about 850 officers and men. The *Hornet* had been built in the Newport News Shipbuilding Yard, commissioned only a few months earlier, and was undergoing sea trials on the East Coast in preparation for deployment to the Pacific. It had not yet been committed to any specific mission.

As General Arnold had directed, Doolittle contacted Captain High and learned to his great satisfaction that the target was indeed Tokyo. Wonderful! This was just the kind of challenge that Doolittle lived for. He and Captain High, along with High's ever present protégé Lieutenant Bill Russo, set about to outline a mission plan.

First, what aircraft to use? They considered the *Hornet's* deck dimensions, island clearances, and top speed, and then agreed on the B-25. Named for aviation iconoclast Billy Mitchell, it was a relatively new medium bomber manufactured by North American Aviation that had been operational for only a year or so.

THE DOOLITTLE IRONY

"The size is pretty good," Doolittle observed, "Its wing span is only 68 feet, and that allows for a six-foot clearance between its tip and the *Hornet's* Island. But its legs are too short," meaning the aircraft's range was inadequate. "What do you figure we need?"

"The way I see it," Captain High offered, "Is that they will launch about 500 miles from Tokyo. Add to that, the distance from there to wherever the planes will land. In that regard, there are only three possibilities: 1) after hitting Tokyo, the bombers could fly back to the carrier. But they couldn't land because the deck is not strong enough. That means they would have to ditch in the ocean alongside the carrier. What if the weather is bad and there are high seas? Not a good option! 2) They could fly to the Soviet Union and land someplace like Vladivostok. That would be within the aircraft's range but it's unlikely the Soviet Union would permit it. The country is locked in a life-and-death struggle with Hitler on its Western Front. They've signed a non-aggression pact with Japan to avoid having to fight on their Eastern Front as well. If the Soviet Union allowed the U.S. to land its planes in Vladivostok–planes that had just bombed Tokyo–Japan might well retaliate somehow. I just don't see Moscow allowing that to happen. 3) The bombers fly west after bombing Tokyo and land in an area on the Mainland controlled by the Chinese Nationalists. Chiang Kai-Shek would probably not welcome that because it risks Japanese retaliation. On the other hand, he just might relish being part of a raid on their enemy's capital city."

The Captain paused and looked at the other two. "So what do you two think?"

"I say we use the China option as a planning scenario," Doolittle replied, "It seems to be the most plausible of the three."

There were nods from the other two. "But if we do that," Doolittle went on, "that means our planes will have to travel maybe another 1200 miles after bombing Tokyo. The B-25's range is well short of that. We'd have to add perhaps another 1,000 gallons of fuel. That means reducing the aircraft's weight, and the only way we can do that is by eliminating things not absolutely necessary to the bombing mission–guns, radios, armor plating, and maybe some other stuff."

CHAPTER 25

Captain High nodded in agreement, "Yeah, I guess that's the only way–although not having guns is not very attractive when you're going to fly into your enemy's capital!"

"Anyway, " the Captain continued, "It seems like we have identified the essential elements of the mission: sail to within 500 miles of Tokyo, launch the bombers, conduct the attack, and then escape to an airfield somewhere in China. Jimmy, it looks like you've got the lion's share of the work. Getting the planes, modifying them, getting crews, training them, developing target information, that all sounds like Army Air Force business. As for the Navy, we'll get you a carrier, put your planes on it, and sail as close as we can to the target. Anything else we can do?"

"Yes," Doolittle replied emphatically, "Arrange to have the *Hornet* launch a B-25. I know it's theoretically possible, but until we can say we've actually done it, we're going to have to deal with a bunch of Doubting Thomases."

And so, on 12 February 1942, the *USS Hornet* with two B-25s on its flight deck, turned into the 22-knot wind off Hampton Roads, Virginia and increased ship speed to 20 knots. That meant the B-25s had only to gain 26 knots on their take off roll to reach their lift off speed of 68 knots. It was easy. Both planes virtually leapt into the air after a very short roll, the first one rising so sharply that it came dangerously close to hitting a part of the carrier's island overhang. So much for Doubting Thomases!

CHAPTER 26

INTERNMENT

By mid-February, anti-Japanese sentiment had reached fever pitch. The media was full of reports about an imminent invasion. White vigilantes along the West Coast were overturning the vegetable carts of Japanese farmers and looting Japanese stores. Japanese children were being threatened on the streets going to school. The Army was trumpeting that people of Japanese ancestry were a security threat. On February 14, 1942, General DeWitt wrote, "The Japanese race is an enemy race and while many second and third generation Japanese born on United States soil, possessed of United States citizenship have become 'Americanized,' the racial strains are undiluted." Politicians had succumbed to the pressure and climbed on the anti-Japanese bandwagon. It was apparent that the government would soon take dramatic action.

That occurred on 19 February 1942, just one week after the B-25s launched from the *Hornet*. President Roosevelt signed Executive Order No. 9066, "Authorizing the Secretary of War to Prescribe Military Areas." Its title was ambiguous, but its intent was unmistakable. It authorized the Secretary of War and military commanders he may designate to prescribe areas of the United States,

> "... from which any or all persons may be excluded, and with respect to which, the right

CHAPTER 26

> of any person to enter, remain in, or leave shall be subject to whatever restrictions the Secretary of War or the appropriate Military Commander may impose in his discretion."

The Army would be the sole arbiter of such matters. There were no provisions for judicial review or other safe guards of civil rights.

The Executive Order further established authority for the Army to peremptorily move people it deemed a threat.

> ".... The Secretary of War is hereby authorized to provide for residents of any such area who are excluded therefrom, such transportation, food, shelter, and other accommodations as may be necessary,..."

Just five days later the first relocation began at Terminal Island near San Pedro, CA. People of Japanese ancestry were given 48 hours to vacate the Island, and could take away only what they could carry.

On 2 March 1942 General DeWitt issued a proclamation that designated the Western portions of Washington, Oregon and California, and the southern third of Arizona to be military areas from which Americans of Japanese ancestry would be excluded. (The exclusion zone would later be expanded to include the entire state of California.)

The plan was to round up the Japanese as quickly as possible and house them locally in temporary assembly centers. More permanent sites would then be built east of the Sierras Nevada in California and the Cascades in Washington and Oregon where the internees would be held for duration of the need. Two organizations were quickly established to carry out the relocation: the Wartime Civil Control Administration would move the Japanese from their residences to temporary assembly centers, and the War Relocation Authority (WRA) would build and manage permanent relocation centers. President Roosevelt appointed Milton Eisenhower, brother of then-Brigadier General Dwight Eisenhower, to head the WRA.

⊕ ⊕ ⊕

THE DOOLITTLE IRONY

1 April 1942, Crawford

"Kathleen, is that you?" Stanley asked as a woman's voice answered the phone.

"Yes, Stanley, I'm glad you called, I was just about to call you."

"I guess you've heard about Bainbridge then," Stanley said, "I can't really believe it. Three hundred or more Japanese are being forced to leave the Island."

"Then it's true." Kathleen said, "They're really going to move the Japanese out of the area, and they've already begun!" Kathleen paused to regain her composure, "Where are they sending them, Stanley?"

"Mr. Scott says they're being sent to some desolate spot in the Mojave Desert down in California, a place called Manzanar."

"So far away?"

"Yeah, the idea is get them on the other side of the mountains. I guess some genius decided that these people are so threatening to the security of the United States that they have to be isolated in some remote area," Stanley observed dryly, "God, I hope this is not typical of the decisions we can expect from our leaders. If it is, I don't hold out much hope for winning this war."

"You sound like my father," Kathleen said, "He thinks this is all so stupid. He says with this war started, we need soldiers, farmers and factory workers more than ever before. The Japanese can do all of that, so why are we sending them to some prison out in the boonies to sit there useless?"

"Your Dad's a smart guy, Kathleen. What's his role in this mess? Is he expected to help with the internment? Will he have to force Japanese out of their homes?"

"No," Kathleen answered, "That's all going to be handled by the military. His job will be to keep the peace and protect the Japanese. Some of the local rowdies have been threatening to burn their houses after they leave–to make sure they never return."

"Burn them?" Stanley asked, "It's more likely they'll try to buy them at some ridiculously low price. The Japanese on Bainbridge are being given six days to sell all their property and belongings. The local yokels are offering pennies on the dollar. One of them offered a

CHAPTER 26

Japanese lady $1.00 for a beautiful set of china. She smashed it right there in front of him rather than sell it at that price."

"Good for her," Kathleen exalted, but then worried aloud, "Oh, Stanley, where is all of this going? Does this mean that even Hiro's family will have to move?"

"Yeah," Stanley observed, "I think that's inevitable, and I think that you and I should visit them and try to prepare them for it and offer our assistance. How about if I come out on Saturday?"

"Sure," Kathleen replied, "How about late morning? I'll meet you at Grimm's Drug Store. I'll probably see Avaron or Natsuko before then, so I'll tell them to expect us about noon."

Just before noon that Saturday, Kathleen and Stanley arrived at Hiro's parents' house. As usual, the two girls were out front waiting for their arrival, though not with the same bubbling glee that had characterized their earlier greetings. Inside Mama and Papa waited at the table, grim faced and ready for the bad news that they knew Stanley was bringing. Kathleen smiled and used one of the few Japanese words she knew, *konnichiwa*, Mama-san" meaning, 'good day.' Papa smiled kindly and responded, "*ohayō gozaimasu*," meaning 'good morning.' Kathleen's effusive nature made her want to hug both of them tightly but she knew that was not the Japanese way so she simply took a seat at the table. Stanley did his best to bow, but it turned out more like an awkward nod. He likewise sat down. Avaron and Natsuko pulled up futons and sat cross legged on them on the floor. All looked expectantly at Stanley.

"I have very disturbing news," he began, thinking he would deliver the short speech he had memorized.

But Mama was too impatient to wait for rhetorical niceties, "How soon we have to leave?"

"Then you already know that you have to move," Stanley said glad that he was not the one to break the news, "OK, let me give you what details I have. Later this month orders will be issued that all persons of Japanese ancestry will have to leave the area as soon as possible. Ultimately, the plan is to move you to an isolated area on

THE DOOLITTLE IRONY

the other side of the Cascade Mountains. Why? Some people say it's to keep you away from the coast so you can't conduct so-called 'Fifth Column activities,' meaning to collaborate with the Japanese. Others say it's for your own safety, to protect you from White vigilantes."

Stanley could tell by their cynical looks that Hiro's family did not believe they were being sent away for any altruistic motive such as providing them protection.

"What's the name of the place we're going to?" asked Avaron.

"It doesn't have a name, at least not yet," Stanley explained, "In fact it hasn't even been built. All I know at this point is that it will be located on Federal land near Twin Falls, Idaho."

"Twin Falls?" Avaron echoed, "I never heard of it but it sounds nice."

"I wouldn't get my hopes up on that score, Avaron," Stanley said, "I hear Twin Falls is upland desert–hot, dry, with a lot of electrical storms but not much rain. Don't expect a resort. I think we're talking about something that looks more like a military camp."

Natsuko raised her hand as she might have at school. "You said it hasn't been built yet. How long is that going to take and where do we stay till then?"

"Good questions, Natsuko," Stanley replied, "Mr. Scott, that's the owner of the firm where I work and the man who gave me all this information, said that it will probably be a few months at least before the permanent relocation center is finished. Until then the Federal Government wants to house you in the fairgrounds where the annual Western Washington State Fair is held. It's near Puyallup, south of Tacoma. There are a lot of buildings there that might be used for temporary shelter."

"Buildings?" Kathleen inquired after a pause, "I've been there for several of the fairs and the only buildings I remember were for the livestock. Is that what they're talking about?"

Stanley had hoped this point would not come up. He didn't want to be the one to explain it. "Yes," he agreed, "But they plan to clean them out and make them habitable."

"Clean them out?" Natsuko interrupted, "How can you clean out a pig sty? Or get rid of the smell of chicken manure? Am I going

CHAPTER 26

to have to live in a barn? This doesn't sound like a very happy situation, Stanley!"

Outspoken, like her mother, Stanley thought. "No, not happy," he said aloud, "But please don't shoot the messenger. I'm here to help."

"I just don't understand all of this," Natsuko continued, "We've done nothing wrong. We never even thought of giving information to the Imperial Japanese Navy. It's just ridiculous. Now I can't finish my sophomore year and Avaron won't be able to graduate, just because some stupid old men in uniforms who don't even know us think we might be traitors. What about the Zimmerman family? We're at war with Germany but they're not getting sent away. Or the Nataros? We're at war with Italy but they don't have to go to some stinky barn."

Then, warming to her task, she voiced the conviction that to this point had been left unsaid, "Some people say it's because we look like the enemy. Well, so do the Zimmermans and the Nataros. The difference is they are White and we are Yellow! We are a different race! And that's why we're treated differently and why we're being locked up! That's called racism, and we were taught at school that racism is wrong!" Then, frustrated with the world as only a sixteen year old can be, she shouted angrily, "I hate it!" and broke into sobs. Kathleen abandoned her reserve, knelt on the floor, took Natsuko in her arms and began to cry as well. Then Avaron joined in. It became a group hug with all three in tears. Mama and Papa looked on, wondering how their daughters had come to such emotion.

Stanley felt quite inadequate. He thought of trying to explain that it was really a matter of numbers. Interning all persons of German or Italian descent was impractical. There were too many. And it wasn't really racism either. The Japanese on Hawaii were not being interned. Why? Because there were too many of them! A third of the Island population was Japanese. Intern that many and the Island's economy would shut down.

But Stanley realized that explaining to the girls the practicalities of American politics was not really useful. Besides, Natsuko was ultimately right. The internment was being perpetrated primarily by the same sort of bigots that had denied the Japanese immigrants citizenship and the right to vote. Now they were taking advantage of war hysteria to eliminate the Japanese as the economic element that they had been unable to compete against successfully. Maybe they would even pick up a few bargains the Japanese had to leave behind!

Mama's patience with the sobbing ended quickly. She pointedly repeated her original question, this time a little louder with a bit of an edge, "When we have to leave?"

The room came to order at the sound of Mama's stern question and eyes turned back to Stanley.

"Probably the end of this month," he responded dourly, "And you'll be permitted to take with you only what you can carry. That will have to include not just clothing but pots and pans, bedding, washing utensils, and anything else you think you'll need while away. Don't worry too much about carrying things. I intend to be here and will help carry whatever you take."

Papa posed the really difficult question. Looking at Stanley, he asked, "What about farm? Who take care of it? And house?"

Stanley had no good answer but, to his surprise, Kathleen did. She spoke up, "Let me try to answer that." Eyes shifted to her, "My father is the Chief of Police. He knows already the Japanese families will soon be forced to leave. He has talked to the Mayor and the Town Council about this and they agree. While you are gone he will take steps to protect your property against vigilantes and looters. He will make sure that no one else farms your property, and he'll expel any squatters that try to move into your house."

Papa smiled, "That good, but farms need work. Tools rust. Engines break." Mama knew that Papa was worried about that tractor that he so prized.

"Maybe I can help a little there," Stanley offered, "I don't know much about farming, but I know my way around an engine. I can come out and start it up every once in a while, as long as I'm around."

Kathleen picked up on the last phrase, "As long as you're around? Are you going somewhere, Stanley?"

"Well, probably," Stanley allowed, "I am eligible for the draft, and I could receive a notice to report for a physical any day now. Or it might be several months before they get around to me."

CHAPTER 26

Kathleen frowned. She hadn't thought of Stanley's draft status. He had come to play a significant role in her and Hiro's lives. He had been responsible for getting them back together, he shared Kathleen's deep concern about Hiro's safety, and he was her conduit to Mr. Scott and his contacts in the State Department, the FBI, and City Hall. She and Hiro had even thought about calling their first son Stanley. She had come to rely on him. What would she do when he left?

Her train of thought was interrupted by Stanley's voice, "Are there any more questions?" he asked, looking in turn at each member of Hiro's family. "This is not going to be easy for you. Kathleen and I will help wherever we can, but once you leave here we won't be able to do much. Look, I'm confident you will all come through this. I know that, as a Japanese family, you will stay together and take care of one another."

Mama sneered a little at Stanley's reference to the Japanese family. What did he know about staying together? What did he know about living in a community where you were not welcome, where the local culture was so alien to your own, and from which you were now being expelled for no good reason? Mama knew. She knew all too well. She had tried to protect her family from the Whites, had tried to instill in her children the Japanese values that had seen her through many bad times. But she had failed. Hiro was gone–lost doing the bidding of a White company. She might never see him again. Even if he did return, he would marry a White girl who could not even cook rice! She expected Avaron and Natsuko had probably also strayed from her standards and adopted White values. Well, now they would see that she had been right. The Whites were not to be trusted. They turned on the Japanese just as soon as they had the opportunity.

At that point Stanley stood up and everyone took that to mean that the meeting was ending. Its purpose had been accomplished. Hiro's family now knew generally what was in store for them. They had a rough idea of where they were being sent and when they would have to leave. It was all bad news and the family was still trying to internalize it. Their mood was grim. They exchanged goodbyes with Kathleen and Stanley, and the two drove off without fanfare. No one was happy.

CHAPTER 27

BOUND FOR TOKYO

Late March, Washington, D.C.

Bill Russo and Captain High sat in straight backed chairs opposite Admiral King, who sat behind his desk looking his usual dour self. The straight backed chairs were not a part of the Admiral's otherwise comfortably appointed office. His aide had placed them there for this meeting. They indicated this would be a business session. With the exception of the coffee on the table–a necessity at any Navy meeting–the Admiral would offer no social niceties.

"Well, gentlemen," he began, "You've been working on this Tokyo thing for more than a month now. I hope you have some good things to report."

Captain High was prepared. "Yes, Admiral, we do have some good things to report. Let me tick them off: First, we have written a mission concept, which I'm told you've read and approved."

"That's true," the Admiral admitted, "But not without concern. The Navy has a lot at risk here. You're committing about half our fighting force in the Pacific. We've got real problems if this thing goes belly up."

CHAPTER 27

"Yes sir, we've thought about that. For example, we've tried to decide what we should do with the bombers if the Japs discover us before the Task Force is within striking range

"Wonderful!" the Admiral sneered, "You're worried about a few dozen Army bombers when the real problem is what we do if the Japs sink our carriers? They're the only thing between us and an Imperial Japanese Navy attack on San Francisco."

Captain High waited until he was sure the Admiral had finished his rant, and then resumed his report. "As you also know, we've agreed on a bomber–the B-25–and demonstrated that it can launch from a carrier."

"But the plane has to be modified." The Admiral corrected testily.

"Yes sir and Lieutenant Colonel Doolittle has that in hand. He's adding fuel tanks to increase range and decreasing weight by removing some of the radios and guns. Incidentally, "the Captain added with a smile, "He's replaced the tail guns with two broomsticks to keep the Zeroes off his tail." Then in a more serious tone he added, "Let me say here, sir, that whoever picked Doolittle to head up the Army end of this project sure made the right decision. The guy is smart and he can get things done. He's impressed the hell out of me."

"Yes," the Admiral observed dryly, "Everyone seems to say that. But go on. What else has been done."

"It looks like we'll try to hit targets in five cities: Tokyo, Yokohama, Kobe, Nagoya, and Yokosuka. Doolittle has arranged for the Air Corps to provide target folders on military installations in each."

"Why so many cities? Why not concentrate on just one or two? And why so far apart. Hell, it's 250 miles from Tokyo to Kobe," Admiral King noted with his usual grace.

"The logic is to spread the attack out so more people will see the bombers, and it will look like more planes are involved. We know we're not likely to inflict any real damage on the Japanese. Our purpose is simply to put them on notice that–despite all their propaganda to the contrary–even their capital city is not safe. We can hit them when we want to. I should also report that we'll hit only military and industrial targets—and, no, the Imperial Palace is not on the list."

The Admiral nodded, but had no comment. Captain High wondered if he would have been happy or angry had the Palace been on the list.

"Doolittle's also selected aircrews." Captain High went on, "He took personnel from three squadrons of the 17th Bomb Group up in Washington State. He has them training now for short take offs and overwater navigation—matters that the Army Air Corps is not big on. He arranged for the training to take place at some out-of-the way place in Florida called Eglin Air Base."

"Eglin? I've been there," the Admiral grunted ruefully, "I remember it mostly for snakes. Pygmy rattlers. All over the place—including my room in the BOQ!"

Captain High wondered to himself, "I wonder if he bit their heads off?" but what he said was, "Doolittle will have the planes flown to Alameda where they'll be loaded aboard the *Hornet*'s flight deck. The cover story will be that we're ferrying them to Hawaii. A debarkation date has been set: 1 April—not far away!"

It was now the Admiral's turn to report. "Yes, just for your info I've talked to Admiral Nimitz. He outlined the forces he intends to assign: two carriers, four cruisers, eight destroyers and two oilers. Sixteen ships all told."

"Two carriers, sir?" Captain Low inquired.

"Yes, the *Hornet* to launch the bombers and the *Enterprise* to provide air cover. The *Enterprise* is in Hawaii now and the *Hornet* will get underway from San Francisco. The two will rendezvous north of Hawaii and proceed as a single Task Force to conduct the attack. Admiral Nimitz and I agreed that Bull Halsey is the man to command the Task Force. He's aggressive but understands just how valuable the carriers are. He won't put them in harm's way if he can avoid it."

Then the Admiral dropped his surprise, "I want both of you to go along on the *Hornet*." He paused a moment to let that sink in, then explained, "High, I want you there as my eyes and ears. This is a very risky operation. If it fails, people will take cover and point fingers. I want someone there to report objectively exactly what hap-

CHAPTER 27

pened. You are uniquely prepared to do that. You've been involved in this operation from the outset. You know what should happen, so you should also know when someone departs from the script. Do you think you can do that, High?"

The question was rhetorical. If Captain High wanted to continue in the Navy there was only one answer, and he provided it, "Yes, sir."

Then the Admiral looked directly at Bill Russo for the first time during the entire meeting and said caustically, "As for you Lieutenant, I want you to go along just because High here doesn't seem able to go anywhere without you." He paused seemingly to savor the discomfort he had caused both men, and then relented a bit, "Besides, I hear you're a hotshot on Japan. You might be able to pass on a few useful nuggets to the crews in case they go down–although I hope to god that doesn't happen."

Then the Admiral dismissed the two with a curt, "Thanks for coming," and went back to the papers on his desk. Bill and Captain High left, trying to fathom what had just happened.

☩ ☩ ☩

EMBARKATION DAY, SAN FRANCISCO

It was 1 April, Embarkation Day for the West Coast component of the attack force. Physical preparations had all been completed. The ships had gathered in San Francisco Harbor: the *Hornet*, cruisers *Nashville* and *Vincennes*, destroyers *Gwin, Meredith, Monssen* and *Grayson*, and the oiler *Cimarron*. The Navy had designated the group of ships and men "Task Force 18" and placed it under the command of Captain Marc Mitscher. The B-25s had been modified to give them greater range and 16 were now lashed to the deck of the *Hornet*.

Task Force 18 would depart San Francisco and sail to a point northwest of Hawaii where it would rendezvous with "Task Force 16." That task force would also contain eight ships: the carrier *Enterprise*, cruisers *Northhampton* and *Salt Lake City*, destroyers *Balch, Benham, Elett* and *Fanning*, and the oiler *Sabine*. Admiral William F. "Bull"

THE DOOLITTLE IRONY

Halsey would command the Hawaii component and take over command of the entire Task Force once the two had rendezvoused.

A few loose ends remained, for example, the question of where the B-25s would land in China. This hadn't yet been worked out with the Chinese Nationalist Government and would have to be resolved at a higher level. Other matters that remained, however, could be worked out at this level. Doolittle, High, and Halsey met quietly at the Fairmont Hotel that evening in San Francisco to do just that.

Jimmy Doolittle had the floor. "Admiral, one of the major points we should consider is what to do if the Task Force is discovered before we reach our launch point. The *Hornet* will need to launch its fighters, but the B-25s are in the way. So for planning purposes, we offer three scenarios: 1) if the Japs find us while we're still in range of Hawaii or Midway, we'll fly the B-25s back here. 2) If we're within B-25 range of Tokyo we'll conduct the attack then ditch at sea, hoping one of our subs will pick us up. And 3) if we are discovered while the B-25s are completely beyond any range, we'll push them overboard."

Admiral Halsey listened politely, thought a moment, and then offered, "Jimmy, its well that you've outlined several planning scenarios. They give us a framework to consider what action we should take if we encounter that scenario. But in my experience, the scenarios that one plans rarely develop exactly as we anticipate. There's always some small detail that changes everything. So while I applaud your efforts to plan ahead, I warn that planning is no substitute for on-scene judgment.

Doolittle nodded. He didn't really have to be told this. His experience had taught him the same lesson.

"I want you to understand," Halsey went on, "That, as Commander of the Task Force, I will be making the on-scene decisions and they will not always be the ones you would make. Your top priority is to bomb Tokyo. My top priority is to bring the two carriers back to Hawaii undamaged. We must have them to protect Midway, Hawaii, even the West Coast. Their loss is unacceptable–but yours is. I will do my best to get you to your planned launch area, but understand that at the first hint of Japanese attack, I will decide a course of action to save the carriers–even if it means jeopardizing your B-25s."

CHAPTER 27

Doolittle was not surprised to hear that. Halsey had a reputation for being blunt, even feisty. And Doolittle certainly did not doubt Halsey's commitment to inflict damage on Tokyo. Halsey hated the Japanese. He was widely quoted in military circles as saying of the Japanese when he saw the damage they had inflicted, "Before we're through with them, the Japanese language will be spoken only in hell!"

1 April had brought an unexpected treat for the B-25 crews. Jimmy Doolittle announced shore liberty for that evening, much to the men's delight. But first he re-emphasized the need for security. "As I've told you men repeatedly since we began this mission, you must not tell any others about what we're doing–not your wives, girl friends, family or bartenders." The latter reference brought a few smiles. "Tonight that's especially true. The Hornet is out in the Bay where everyone can see it. Those B-25s on deck are not normal Navy issue. People know that. If you get questions, avoid them. Change the subject. If you're pressed, we're ferrying them to Hawaii. But in no case mention that you've been practicing to take off from a Navy carrier."

Then Doolittle paused and tried to make eye contact with each of the men. "One more thing, I've told you before and I'll repeat it here. This is a very dangerous mission. You may not come back. But it's not too late to back out. You can leave now. No questions. No repercussions. We get underway tomorrow, so this may be your last chance." There were no takers–nor had there been on any of the previous occasions that Doolittle had made the offer. From his very first contact with them, not a single man had shown any interest in withdrawing. Doolittle thought this quite remarkable. These were not men who had been selected for past bravery or aggressive personalities. These were just men who happened to be in the 17th Bomb Wing when Doolittle needed B-25 crews. They were just average Americans, and yet every man was willing to put his life at risk in a venture that no one would even describe to him. It made Doolittle

THE DOOLITTLE IRONY

very proud—and it made him very confident. If anyone could possibly carry out this mission, this group of men could!

◈ ◈ ◈

The morning of 2 April, Task Force 18 got underway, sailing one-by-one beneath the Golden Gate Bridge: four destroyers, two cruisers, an oiler, and finally at noon, the Hornet. All morning men on those ships who had gone on liberty the night before talked of having done the things that young men away from home are wont to do. This morning they nursed hangovers, talked of their amorous—sometimes imagined—adventures with the local girls, complained about the high price of prostitutes, and exchanged information about their experiences in the marvelous city of San Francisco.

"I rode a cable car from downtown to Fisherman's Wharf. Got some great pictures," one of Doolittle's airmen reported.

"Yeah," commented another, "We rode a cable car to Union Square and then just walked around the city. It's a really interesting place. We ate in Chinatown and then walked up Geary Street to Japantown. That was strange. The stores and restaurants there are all closing. When we asked why, some local folks explained that the Federal Government is moving all Japanese out of the city. He said they were being sent to Santa Anita."

"Santa Anita?" repeated one onlooker looking puzzled, "Why would they be sending them to a racetrack?"

"You guys need to read the newspaper," observed another onlooker apparently more literate than the others, "They're sending all the Japanese along the whole West Coast to camps out in the desert because they think they might support a Japanese invasion. They call it 'internment.'"

"Yeah," came a cynical voice from the fringe of the group, "And I call it bullshit. I grew up with Japanese immigrants. I went to school with them. They're as much American as any of us."

Astern, as the West Cost sank below the horizon, the ship's loud speaker came alive. "Now hear this. Captain Marc Mitscher has an announcement."

CHAPTER 27

A few seconds passed, static was heard on the PA system as someone handed the microphone to Captain Mitscher. "This is your Captain. You men have been wondering about where this mission is headed. Now that we're at sea I can tell you. This ship will carry the Army bombers to the coast of Japan for the bombing of Tokyo." Raucous, prolonged cheers could be heard all over the ship. They were going to even the score for Pearl Harbor!

The men aboard the Enterprise had to wait longer to hear the news. It wasn't until after the two Task Forces had rendezvoused north of Hawaii that Halsey took to the Enterprise's PA system to declare their destination with a more Hollywood announcement, "This force is bound for Tokyo!"

Now that the men knew their mission, Bill Russo could begin the task that Admiral King had suggested for him—preparing the aircrews for the possibility of being shot down in Japan. He had prepared packets of items that a downed crewman might find useful. Each included 1) about $100 worth of Japanese yen; 2) a map of the area printed on silk so it would remain useful even if it got wet; 3) cards printed in English and Japanese that read, "I am an airman in need. If you help me, you will be rewarded;" and 4) basic Japanese words and phrases a downed airman could use to ask for help. He had packaged these in individual packets and planned to distribute one to each aircrew member.

He had also prepared information on a few questions that might be on their minds.

Question: What treatment should I expect if I'm captured? Answer: Your chances of survival are very poor. You will likely be paraded thru the streets, tried by a kangaroo court, and executed.

Question: Is that certain? Are there absolutely no Japanese that might help me? Answer: Actually, there are. Not all Japanese are bad people. Most are simply the reluctant subjects of a militarist government. Some might help if they can do so without risk to themselves. If you have a choice, surrender to an older man or woman who lives in a rural area.

THE DOOLITTLE IRONY

Bill asked Captain High to look over his notes. The Captain did, nodding in most places, but the point about not all Japanese being bad people caught his attention. "I'm sure you're correct, Bill, many Japanese are not wild eyed butchers. But I'm not sure whether telling our crewmen that is a good idea."

"But Captain, I've lived in Japan," Bill replied, "Sure, many Japanese–doubtless a majority of them–have been swept up in nationalistic furor. But many have not. They have no ambitions of empire. They only want peace and security for their families–just like us."

"I agree," the Captain acknowledged, "And most of our aircrews are from families like you describe. But Tokyo made peace impossible. It attacked Pearl Harbor, killed over 2,000 Americans, and overran our troops in Guam and the Philippines. They're trying to dominate the entire Western Pacific. If we don't stop them, maybe San Francisco is next. America has to fight back. That means asking young American men who have been raised with Christian values and believe that taking a human life is wrong, to fly war machines over the enemy and drop bombs that they know will kill military and civilians alike. They can't do that in good conscience if we tell them some of the enemy are innocent. We must demonize the Japanese, show them as deserving of being bombed. And God knows, that's not a difficult task given the brutality they've demonstrated in places like Nanking."

Again, the Captain paused to reflect, "No, now is *not* the time to be equivocal about our mission. We are at war. Logic and reason are suspended. Hatred and violence have taken their place. When this war is over, maybe we'll have time to look back, reflect, and realize how utterly wrong much of what we did in the name of patriotism was. Maybe young men like you will be able to put the nation and the world on a more peaceful course."

Again the Captain paused, and then looked squarely into Bill's eyes, "But for now, we're at war, and we may be sending these young men off to risk their lives. Let's give them no reason to doubt the righteousness of their cause. Let's tell them to hate the Japanese so they can bomb them without compunction. That's one reason why we have a firebrand like Halsey in command. He says he hates the Japanese, all of them. He says the only good Japs are dead Japs. I

CHAPTER 27

don't know if he's sincere or just posturing for the men. But that seems to be the order of the day."

Bill sighed. Of course, the Captain and Admiral Halsey were right. Killing Japanese meant first demonizing them. He would have reason to remember that before the mission was over.

CHAPTER 28

THE RAID

Approaching Japan

TF 16 from Hawaii and TF 18 from San Francisco had rendezvoused 12 April at a point well north of Midway Island. The two merged into a single task force designated TF 16 under Admiral Halsey, and set a course toward Japan. Security became increasingly important as they approached the target area. Strict radio silence was maintained, and although the task force was well north of shipping lanes, the Enterprise launched regular reconnaissance flights to search for other ships. The men aboard, both air crewmen and ship's company, realized that they were about to engage the enemy. Few had ever actually been shot at in anger. Some became introspective and wrote letters home. Others sought to divert themselves with craps or poker. The earlier excitement of avenging Pearl Harbor settled into a more somber appreciation of what they were about.

By 17 April the Task Force had reached a point about 1,000 miles east of Honshu, the Japanese Main Island on which Tokyo is located. There, in heavy weather, the oilers refueled the two carriers and four cruisers. Those six ships then began a high speed, 25-knot run toward Tokyo. The two oilers remained behind because they could not keep up with the carriers pace and the eight destroyers stayed to conserve fuel. The plan called for the fast ships to sail to within about 400 miles of Honshu. Early on 19th, they would launch the bombers and immediately turn eastward back to Hawaii. The bombers would conduct their attack and fly westward to airfields in Nationalist controlled areas of China.

That evening the air crews were summoned to the flight deck for a small ceremony. As the men looked on, Captain Mitscher and Jimmy Doolittle attached three medals to one of the bombs that would be dropped on Tokyo. The medals had been awarded to American seamen for various reasons by the Japanese Government in earlier years. After Pearl Harbor those men had returned the medals to the Navy with the request that they be sent back to the Japs "in an appropriate fashion." Some of Doolittle's men painted their own greetings on the bombs, such as on one incendiary: "I don't want to set the world on fire, just Tokyo."

Early on the morning of 18 April the weather seemed to be abating, but the anemometer still showed wind gusts of 35 knots and waves were cresting at 30-feet. The Task Force was confident it had not been discovered; nevertheless, when at 0310 the radar watch aboard the *Enterprise* picked up two contacts about 10 miles dead ahead, Halsey directed the task force to turn north and evade them. About a half hour later the two contacts disappeared from the radar screen so the Task Force again turned west.

⊕ ⊕ ⊕

The Waiting Trap

Ensign Takeo Yoshikawa had by now been assigned to the Chichi-Jima Air Group for about four months. During that time he had done well. He qualified as a command pilot aboard the IJN's medium bomber G4M3, the plane the Allies nicknamed the "Betty." Takeo realized that much of the credit for his rapid ascendency was the hostilities with the Western powers. It meant huge new areas of ocean had to be patrolled. Pilots were in short supply, and instruction hours had been truncated to get more pilots into the fleet. So here he was, on his first patrol as command pilot aboard his own aircraft with a crew of seven and four 250-lb bombs in the bomb bay. His mission this morning was to help with the search that had been mounted by Admiral Yamamoto to detect any American Naval Force approaching Honshu.

Takeo's pre-flight intelligence briefing had provided useful background. On 10 April Japanese Intelligence had intercepted a communication emanating from an American naval unit in the north central Pacific. It was a fragmentary intercept, probably sent in error. Any American naval element there would certainly be maintaining radio silence–but sometimes a 19-year old communications mate would slip momentarily and press the wrong switch. This slip had been caught by two of Japan's HF/DF stations and they were able to triangulate its location with reasonable accuracy. It was too far west to be headed for the Aleutians and too far north to be headed for the Marianas. Moreover, the header of the intercept indicated it was from a task group of significant size, probably containing at least one carrier. Given those factors, Captain Ogawa's Intelligence Group had estimated the American Task Group's most likely target was Tokyo–just as Admiral Yamamoto had predicted. Knowing that the recent American carrier raids on the Marshalls had been launched from 200 miles at sea, Intelligence expected the same tactic to be used here. It had "dead reckoned"–a navigational term meaning extrapolated from the Task Force's current likely course and speed–to estimate the task group would be about 200 miles off the Japanese coast, in position to launch strikes by the morning of 19 April, tomorrow.

Takeo had taken his plane to 18,000 feet to get above the weather. He looked down into the thick, heavy Pacific cloud cover below and wondered why his operations officer hadn't simply canceled this patrol. For as far as he could see in any direction, there was just solid overcast that extended from the surface to about 14,000 feet. Then he saw it, a hole in the cloud cover had opened, maybe a half-mile wide that allowed one to peer down to the ocean with only a wispy cloud to distort one's view. Takeo banked left to get a better look. Yes, he could see the ocean and for a few fleeting seconds he could see two carriers and several smaller ships in formation around them. One of the carriers looked especially strange with large objects

CHAPTER 28

lined up on the after end of her flight deck. But then the hole closed and he was left with only a vague impression. He asked his crew if they had seen anything but none had even seen the hole, much less two carriers and support ships. He could tell by their follow-on questions that they thought this was perhaps just the illusion of a green plane commander who wanted to hit the jackpot on his first outing. Takeo circled, thinking the hole might reopen. It did not, so he continued along his assigned track.

A few months ago, a more innocent Takeo might have reported this sighting, even in the face of his crew's apparent disbelief. But he had learned at the hands of Captain Ogawa that bold, independent action is not rewarded in the Imperial Japanese Navy. Anyway, he was beginning to doubt his own vision. Maybe he was just seeing what he wanted to see. Why take a chance? He remained silent.

After his patrol ended Takeo sat mentally reviewing what happened. Then it came to him. Those strange objects on the after half of that one carrier's flight deck were airplanes, larger than the airplanes that carriers usually carried, so large that they could not get them down the elevators to the hangar deck. Why would they have such large planes aboard? Maybe the Americans had designed a completely new aircraft that would carry bigger bomb loads a greater distance. That would give them an advantage against Japanese carriers–and then he realized it would give them a similar advantage in bombing Tokyo. Instead of launching from 200 miles at sea, they could launch from probably 400 miles, or even more. That meant the Americans needn't wait till the 19th to launch the attack as Japanese Intelligence had predicted. They could do it today, on the $18^{th.}$

Takeo considered going right to his squadron's commanding officer with his observation, but again remembered Captain Ogawa. If Takeo was right and the attack did occur a day early, it would discredit Ogawa. For the second time in as many months, Ogawa would be responsible for a bad intelligence call: first the absence of the U.S. carriers at Pearl Harbor; now the mistake about when to expect the American strike. It could cost him his career. Takeo smiled with satisfaction. Yes, he would remain quiet about his sighting and his theory, and let the bureaucratic blowback fall on Ogawa.

Revenge was sweet.

THE DOOLITTLE IRONY

✦ ✦ ✦

Morning, 18 April Aboard the Nitto Maru #23

It was dawn but the early morning sun had not yet broken through the heavy overcast. Glancing at the clock, Hiro decided it was time to start the day. He stood up and stretched, not an easy matter in the cramped radio shack. He had had little sleep the night before due to the high winds and 30-foot seas. As was his custom on such nights, he had simply wedged himself between two communication racks and indulged his mind with memories of home. The images were fresh and vivid: Mama-san cooking rice, Papa-san working in the fields, his two teenage sisters giggling, and pleasant nooks on the University of Washington campus where he used to relax with friends between classes. He thought about neighbors and friends in Crawford. He even thought about Stanley and some of the people he had worked with in his brief tenure at Scott Engineering.

But most of all, he thought about Kathleen. He could see her face as though she were there with him. He remembered the freckles (that he never mentioned because they embarrassed her), the reddish tint of her hair, her deep blue eyes, her lighthearted smile and quick wit. He knew that she was not beautiful like a Hollywood starlet, but when she walked into a room, everything seemed to brighten. He remembered her gentle touch and the disturbing effect she had on him when they embraced. Sometimes on nights such as the one just past he would fantasize about having sex with her. That usually led to a wet dream and the need to wash his shorts. But the attraction she held for him was more than just sex. It was much deeper. He felt incomplete when she was not with him–and she had not been with him for more than four months.

That reminded him of why he was aboard the *Nitto Maru #23*. Captain Ogawa had said that he would send Hiro back to Seattle as an agent for Japanese Intelligence if Hiro would first serve six months as a radio operator aboard the Nitto Maru. Hiro had agreed. Of course, he had no intention of spying on the United States, but if agreeing to do so would get him back home, then he was quite prepared to lie. Once home he could easily enough go to the FBI and explain the

CHAPTER 28

situation. Now, only two months remained on his "hitch." When that was completed, he would go see Ogawa to remind him of his promise.

The four months he had spent on board the Nitto Maru had been miserable. The weather had been wet and the sea rough; the food was little more that rice and whatever fish the men could catch; he was bored but could not even keep himself busy by helping the crew operate the ship because he was the only one on board capable of monitoring the radio nets. Not that they needed to be monitored! The guard frequencies were to be the means headquarters would advise of any naval or maritime vessels expected in Nitto Maru's area. But IJN ships had no reason to come this way and the patrol area was off the beaten maritime track. Consequently the *Nitto Maru #23* had NEVER received any traffic. And he was not allowed to transmit because the Americans might intercept it and thereby uncover the existence of the patrol barrier. Nevertheless Captain Enjo made sure he was on watch continuously. Reflecting on this he had thought on many occasions, "I do nothing–but it takes 24 hours a day to do it."

Hiro expected that routine to continue for the two months remaining of his time aboard the Maru. Certainly the prospect of the Americans showing up was close to zero. Based on what he had heard on international radio broadcasts, Tokyo was still on the offensive and America was reeling backwards. Washington would have to build a whole new military machine before it was again strong enough to challenge Tokyo in its home waters. That would take much longer than a few months.

He sometimes wondered what he would do if the Americans did show up. He resolved he would not be a party to springing the trap that the Japanese had set for them. If ever asked to transmit information about a U.S. Navy Task Force, he didn't know exactly what he would do. Probably he would simply fake sending the report, or he would transmit false data. No one would ever know. The report would be in Wabun, the Japanese equivalent of Morse code. Neither the ship's captain nor any of the crew would be able to read what he sent. But such matters were unpredictable. He would have to wait and see!

THE DOOLITTLE IRONY

He decided what he needed was fresh air. He exited the radio shack, went down the short passageway and out the leeward door to the deck. The polar cold front that had been the source of last night's ugly weather had nearly passed. Visibility had improved to just over a mile, cloud cover was about nine tenths, and the ceiling had lifted to about 1,000 feet. But even with the superstructure shielding him from the wind, the weather was still cruel. The prospect of going overboard was frightening, and he held tight to the handrail.

By now it was nearing 6:30 and the brisk wind had sharpened his senses. He peered up at the sky, fascinated by the changing formations of the dark scud little more than 1,000 feet above. That's when a hole in the overhead opened and through it he saw a plane, rather high, on a northerly course. "Maybe a transport," he thought, "It's too high to be a patrol plane." Anyway, the *Nitto Maru* was not interested in planes. It was out there to watch for ships. In fact, the four crewmen who would man the first lookout watch were just then taking their positions at each quarter of the boat. Depending on the weather, they would stand one- or two-hour watches throughout the daylight hours.

Just then a smaller, fast aircraft appeared briefly to starboard. Hiro saw no markings but concluded it must be Japanese. The plane did not reappear and neither Hiro nor the four men on watch were concerned enough to notify Captain Enjo.

It was now about 6:30 and visibility was improving noticeably. Just as Hiro was about to go below, out of the mist to his left he saw appear like a ghost in a Hollywood movie the outline of a ship. It seemed rather close, maybe a few miles although estimating distances over water is difficult. Just then another shape caught his eye. It was larger than the first, flat along the top with a kind of upward protrusion in the center. Hiro was untrained in ship recognition but concluded that what he was seeing was unmistakably an aircraft carrier. Moreover, since Headquarters had not advised that a Japanese carrier would be nearby this morning, it was almost certainly American. Then, just beyond that, another large flat shape appeared. Another American carrier!

The two lookouts on his side of the Nitto Maru were stunned at the sight and shouted to one another excitedly, pointing toward

CHAPTER 28

the carriers. Then both came running to Hiro talking so rapidly he had trouble understanding them. "Quick," he understood one to say, "Radio headquarters. American warships!"

"Wait," Hiro shouted over top of their excitement, "First you must tell Captain Enjo." That brought a sudden silence and fearful looks from both.

"No, you tell Captain Enjo," they insisted, "He'll hit us."

"Yes, he probably would," thought Hiro, "Once he sees those carriers he's liable to do anything." Then he thought with unusual bellicosity, "If the sonofabitch tries to hit me I'll deck him. I've wanted to do that ever since I got here."

He ran down the single ladder to the Captain's quarters. Not bothering to knock, he burst through the door to find Enjo sitting on the side of his bunk, not yet fully awake. "Captain Enjo," Hiro shouted, "You must come to the deck at once. There is something you must see." Enjo was apparently too startled to object to Hiro's breach of decorum and quickly pulled on his pants. He ran up the ladder and over to the rail. The lookouts had returned to their watch positions, intending to stay out of his way. The sight of the carriers apparently took some time to register with him. Both carriers and at least two surface combatants were now clearly visible. An airplane flew by at high speed, obviously reporting back to the carrier a description of the *Nitto Maru*. Enjo stared intensely from one ship to the next. His appearance seemed to change. He looked first crestfallen, then angry, then thoughtful, and finally resigned.

At least five minutes passed and Hiro was beginning to think that Enjo had been shocked into inaction. But Enjo tore himself away and went up to the bridge. He checked the navigation chart and chronometer, then grabbed a large tablet and began writing. After several minutes, he ripped off the page and handed it to Hiro. "Here," he said sharply, "Get this off to Fifth Fleet Headquarters immediately." He paused and looked at Hiro oddly. "I have told you what I must do. Now it is time." With that he left the bridge and went down the ladder to his cabin, avoiding the sight of the American ships.

Hiro didn't have time to ponder the meaning of Enjo's look. He glanced at the note. It was in Kanji and Hiro was not sure he knew

THE DOOLITTLE IRONY

enough Kanji characters to trust his own reading. He motioned for one of the lookouts to help him. The note read, "Two American carriers and two cruisers 650 miles east of Inubo Saki, heading 270, about 15 knots. One carrier conducting flight ops, the other has ten or more large two engine planes on aft end of flight deck, possibly bombers. American recon aircraft have sighted *Nitto Maru #23*. Will continue to monitor and report enemy movements as long as possible."

Hiro was impressed. In his haste, he had not even noticed the large planes. Enjo had summed up the situation rather well. It was the kind of information that the Japanese were waiting for. With the huge number of aircraft and ships within attack range, they could easily overwhelm and sink the American fleet. It would be yet another bitter defeat for America and glorious victory for Japan. "And here I am," Hiro thought, "About to send the message that will set all of that in motion."

The lookout that had helped him read the note jostled his elbow. He was anxious for Hiro to go back to the radio shack and begin sending the message. Hiro started below, thinking he would destroy Enjo's message once inside the radio shack, but the crewman followed him. "Maybe you should go back to your post," Hiro suggested to the lookout.

"No, no need for lookouts anymore," the man said logically enough, "I will help you send the message."

Hiro grimaced. Shaking the lookout would not be easy. He returned to the radio shack and sat down at the transmission key. The lookout began asking questions. How does the key work? What is a frequency band? How do you select a frequency? How do you send the message? Hiro tried to be patient. "You first key the message, and the machine holds it until you're ready to send. Then you just hit this button and it sends what you've already keyed, but it does so quite rapidly. That reduces the amount of time you use the frequency and the possibility that the Americans will be able to triangulate your position."

"Triangulate?" the lookout repeated, obviously ready to ask a bevy of questions about triangulation.

CHAPTER 28

Hiro headed him off, "Stop. This is not the time or place for instructions on operating a radio. I have to key this message. Let me get started."

Then an idea hit Hiro had about how to get rid of the lookout. He glanced up at him and said, "Captain Enjo forgot to say whether we will go to general quarters. Go up to his cabin and ask him so I can put it in the message." The man hesitated, obviously worried about getting anywhere close to Ito. "Go on," Hiro urged, "I'll key in this message while you're gone."

The lookout reluctantly left for the Captain's cabin, and Hiro considered his options. First, he could send the message as Enjo had written it. No, that was absolutely unacceptable. Second, he could simply not send the message at all. No, that would not work. Other patrol ships had already–or would soon–sight the Americans and report. If the *Nitto Maru #23* did not, the omission would be conspicuous. Third, he could alter the message to provide erroneous data. Yes, that might work. He would change what he could and omit the rest. He first keyed in, "Three enemy carriers sighted. Position 650 miles east of Inubo Saki." Changing two carriers to three might confuse the Japanese response, but changing the carrier's position was impossible. Headquarters already knew where the Nitto's patrol area was–approximately 650 miles east of Inubo Saki. Reporting some other position would make headquarters immediately suspicious.

He had keyed the sentence, but he had not encoded it. He considered doing that but his thoughts were interrupted when the lookout burst back into the radio shack with a look of horror, "Come quick. Please, come quick. Captain Enjo …" The man could not finish the sentence, and Hiro saw the panic on his face.

Hiro ran to the Captain's cabin and stopped at the open doorway, horrified by the scene before him. Enjo's body lay slumped on the bed, a gun in his limp hand, the back of his head missing. On the bulkhead behind him was a smear of bone, blood and brains. Hiro remembered Enjo's comment just a few minutes ago as he was leaving the bridge: "I have told you what I must do. Now it is time." He also remembered an earlier conversation when Enjo had pompously asserted, "I will never be captured." Well, he was right about that. He had kept his Bushido vow never to be taken alive by an enemy.

THE DOOLITTLE IRONY

Hiro was sickened by the scene and turned to leave, but by then other crew members had arrived and were blocking the doorway. Hiro saw no remorse in their eyes. They hated Enjo and would gladly have thrown his corpse overboard. But they were frightened by the plight Enjo had left them in. They were leaderless, in a small ship, with a powerful enemy in sight, and no idea about what to do next.

An older crewman looked at Hiro, "What should we do?" he asked. The other crewmen listened for an answer. It was apparent they were willing to have Hiro be their next commanding officer.

"Oh my God," Hiro thought as he realized what the man's question meant. What should he do? He didn't want these men to die. He didn't want to die either.

"Have the ship come to general quarters," he responded without thinking, He wasn't really sure what general quarters meant on board the *Nitto Maru #23*, but the crew apparently did. They took off in all directions, a klaxon sounded throughout the ship, and by the time Hiro came back on deck they had manned the guns.

The lookout that had been with him in the radio room and had discovered Ito's body was suddenly at his side again, tugging at his elbow. "Captain," conferring on Hiro the title that Enjo had held, "I sent message."

"You what?" Hiro asked astonished.

"I pushed the button to send the message," the man said obviously proud of himself, "I knew that's what I should do."

"I see," Hiro responded, trying to recover from his initial shock. Then he added in a voice befitting his new position as captain-elect of the *Nitto Maru #23*, "Very well, carry on."

At 0500, Jimmy Doolittle entered the bridge of the Hornet. Captain Mitscher was already there, looking his usual gaunt self beside the plotting table. He smiled at Doolittle and motioned one of the young men on watch to bring coffee for their Army guest. "Black and bitter," Doolittle told the man, hoping that the coffee would sharpen his senses amid the dark Pacific morning.

CHAPTER 28

"We're about 670 miles off the coast of Honshu," the Captain said to Doolittle, pointing to a spot on the chart, "We had two radar contacts a few hours back and that's worrisome. We're not near any shipping lanes, and the weather is too bad for them to have been fishing boats. Halsey is launching some extra recon, just in case."

Doolittle nodded, hoping the steaming cup of coffee he had just been handed would awaken his brain. It was typical Navy coffee: strong, bitter, and had probably been sitting in a big 20-cup urn since before the watch started. "When do you estimate we'll be at our launch area, Captain?" Doolittle asked.

"Well, Jimmy, that all depends on how many contacts we have to avoid," Captain Mitscher replied, "We've had to slow because of these seas. Our SOA—that's 'speed of advance' to you Army types—is probably not much more than 13 knots currently. If we maintain that we should be 400 miles off Honshu in about 20 hours. So you're looking at a possible launch early tomorrow morning, assuming all goes well."

The atmosphere on the bridge was tense. Captain Mitscher and Jimmy Doolittle exchanged only occasional remarks. Personnel on lookout—all of whom were 19 or under because teens had the best eyesight—strained to pick out any suspicious shapes amid the gray morning light.

Aboard the *Enterprise*, one of Halsey's search planes appeared out of the early morning gloom flying up the ship's wake. It seemed to be making a landing approach but its wheels were up and the Landing Ship Officer, known simply as the LSO, was not out on the flight deck waving his paddles to help the pilot land. As the plane passed over the flight deck a hand appeared from its canopy and dropped a weighted bean bag with a note in it. This was the way search planes reported their contact information during periods of radio silence. The note explained that pilot had spotted a ship about 42 miles ahead and thought that the ship had seen him too. Admiral Halsey grimaced a bit and directed that general quarters be sounded. He then ordered the Task Force to a more southerly heading to avoid the contact.

As the Task Force turned to its new heading, Captain Mitscher commented to Doolittle, "I don't like this. Why are these sampans out here in such bad weather? They could be lookouts. If that's the case, the Japs are expecting us."

About two hours later, at 0744, Captain Mitscher's suspicion proved to be well founded. Lookouts on the *Hornet* reported sighting a small ship about five miles west southwest. Considering that the Hornet had sighted the smaller ship, it was almost certain that the smaller ship had sighted the 800-plus foot *Hornet*, and probably the rest of the Task Force as well. Then the radio watch on the *Hornet* confirmed the worst. "Sir," came the voice on the squawk box, "We've intercepted a message on one of the Japanese military frequencies. It was broadcast in the clear to the IJN Fifth Fleet Headquarters, and its signal strength indicates it originated somewhere nearby, probably that sampan that's in sight. It reads, 'Three enemy carriers sighted. Position 650 miles east of Inubo Saki,'" referring to the land promontory that juts into the Pacific from the eastern shore of Honshu, about 60 miles east of Tokyo.

The Task Force had been discovered. Its position was now known to the Japanese, and its intent was obvious–bomb Tokyo. The Japanese would respond like a nest of angry wasps. Halsey was in a vulnerable position. If Tokyo had placed picket ships to detect an oncoming American force, it probably also had planes on standby to investigate and attack whatever contacts the pickets reported. Japanese aircraft could be overhead very soon.

Halsey took quick action, "Tell the *Hornet* to launch those bombers right now," he commanded, "When the last one is airborne, bring up the Wildcats. We might need CAP very soon." Halsey was referring to the fact that the *Hornet* could not launch its own fighters with B-25s blocking the deck. "And tell Doolittle I said good luck."

The OD took pencil in hand, paused a few seconds, and then wrote, "Launch planes. To Col Doolittle and Gallant Command: Good Luck and God Bless. Halsey" He showed the note to the Admiral for his approval. Halsey smiled as he read the OD's more theatrical syntax. Halsey glanced up at the OD, nodded his approval of the note, and commented facetiously, "You'll go far, Lieutenant!"

Halsey wasn't done. "Tell the Wildcats to sink that damn sampan before it can transmit anything more," he said in reference to the *Nitto Maru #23*, "And just as backup tell the *Nashville* to drop out

CHAPTER 28

of formation and sink that damn sampan if the Wildcats don't. We sure as hell don't want it reporting that we have long range bombers aboard. Tell 'em also to pick up any of the Jap crewmen that they can. I'd like to know more about what these patrol boats are doing out here!"

♦ ♦ ♦

Trying to behave like the Captain of a ship should, Hiro started on an inspection tour of the Nitto Maru. He looked around the deck to see where the men had positioned themselves for general quarters. Two were at each of the Maru's three deck guns. That included a 20-mm cannon forward and two 50-caliber machine guns at each side of the deck amidships. He walked to the two men at the 20-mm cannon and asked, "When is the last time you fired this gun?"

They looked at each other, concerned. One spoke up, "We never fired this gun. The instructor told us how to load it, but we never actually fired it. Captain Enjo said it would be a waste of time. If a plane attacks, we're done for." The other man nodded in agreement.

"Captain Enjo was probably right about that," Hiro ventured, "How about the other gun crews? Did they ever fire their weapons?

"No," was the answer, "None of the weapons have ever been fired."

"Then move away from the gun," Hiro told them, "Even if you fire it you'll never hit anything and you're unnecessarily exposed there on the open deck. Go below and tell the engineer that I said you are to be his damage control party. Tell the other gun crews to do the same. He'll tell you what to do."

Hiro was rather pleased with himself. With one action he had eliminated the possibility of shooting down an American plane and got the Japanese crewmen–really just fishermen–off the deck and into a safer area below. Maybe with a little luck, the Nitto Maru would survive this encounter with the menacing naval force just a few miles away.

Hiro went below to the radio shack and found an incoming message from Fifth Fleet Headquarters. It was not encoded–probably because his message to them had not been encoded. It read: "Nitto

THE DOOLITTLE IRONY

Maru #23. Good work! Understand three carriers 650 miles east of Inubo Saki. Need info re course, speed, air activity, ship identities. Send urgently. Report situation every 15 minutes. Acknowledge."

"Acknowledge?" Hiro said aloud. "Me?" Hiro thought sarcastically, "I never intended to send the first one. I'm sure as hell not going to send anymore."

Just then he realized the incoming message presented a significant danger for the Nitto Maru. If the US Navy had decided previously that the little ship was too small to bother with, when they intercepted this incoming message from Fifth Fleet they would change their minds. They could not tolerate a spy in their midst reporting their every movement. He went to the bridge and told the helmsman, "Come left to a course directly away from the carriers. Let's not give them any reason to think we're shadowing them." The helmsman complied immediately, looking relieved at the prospect of getting away from the American warships. The Bushido Code was not something that Japanese fisherman thought applied to them.

That's when the first of the American fighters, a star emblazoned on the side of its fuselage, made a pass on the Nitto Maru. It was the same type of aircraft that had flown by earlier but this time it was much closer and much louder. It had flown up the Nitto Maru's wake and was almost on it before Hiro heard the noise. As it flashed past the bridge he could see the face of the pilot turn toward him. He raised his hand in a gesture of friendship but was too late for the pilot to have seen it. Hiro hoped that the pilot noted the Nitto Maru had not fired on him and, in fact, that its deck guns were not even manned. Hiro wasn't sure what the airplane's close pass meant, but he called down to the engine room and asked that two men be sent topside with binoculars to watch for approaching aircraft, one to look forward, the other aft. Hiro didn't want to be surprised again.

Five minutes later the aft lookout shouted and pointed astern. Another plane, or perhaps the same one, was approaching at a somewhat higher altitude. As they watched the plane nosed over and began a gradual descent directly toward them. The leading edge of its wings seemed to twinkle and angry eruptions of water rapidly stitched their way up the Maru's wake. The plane was strafing them! It intended to sink the Nitto Maru! Everyone on board who could

CHAPTER 28

see what was happening took cover. But the little ship was not an easy target. The sea was rough and it bobbed with every swell. Just as the machine gun fire reached the Maru, the Pacific wrenched it to one side and out of the path of the attacking aircraft's 50-mm machine gun fire. The plane roared overhead, climbing to altitude and banking gradually left.

For a brief moment the men on the bridge breathed easier, but then another fighter appeared. Again, it came from behind in a gradual dive, and again the men above decks took what cover they could. The fighter held its fire this time until it was only about 500 yards astern. This time there was no long line of splashes racing toward the Maru. This time the water just in front of the ship seemed to explode in a hundred or more splashes in the same small circle. It was close, but it was a miss. The fighter had led its target just a little too much. Like its predecessor, it climbed out and banked gradually left. Hiro sensed what that meant. They were going around for another run at the Maru.

Thinking the little ship might make a harder target were it perpendicular to the attacker. Hiro had the helmsman come left 90 degrees. This put the ship athwart the movement of the sea, a dangerous attitude because it risked the ship capsizing. But it had the advantage of hiding the Maru intermittently in the trough between 30-foot waves. If the attacking fighters lost sight of the ship, perhaps it would spoil their aim.

That proved to be the case. On the next pass the Maru bobbed up as the wave peaked beneath it. The fighter took aim and fired, but then the Maru sank out of sight and the fighter's long burst missed overhead. The second fighter was luckier. The wind blowing against the broadside of the Maru this time kept the Maru in sight just a few seconds too long. A portion of the fighters burst struck the bow of the Maru. It sounded like an air hammer at a construction site. There was no fire or secondary explosion, and Hiro hoped the fighter pilots would get no luckier than that.

About five minutes passed without another strafing run, but before Hiro began to breathe easy again the lookout watching astern shouted and pointed, this time at a plane much higher in the sky. Like the two planes before him, this one approached from astern. As it was almost directly overhead, it dipped one wing sharply and dove

THE DOOLITTLE IRONY

straight for the Maru. Hiro shouted to the helmsman, "Hard aport," but the Maru was in a trough and was sluggish answering the helm. The plane was only a few thousand feet overhead when it released two canister-shaped objects, one from below each wing. They plummeted to either side of the little ship and suddenly two large geysers erupted close aboard each side of the Maru. As the plane pulled up in a slow climb, Hiro saw a twinkling from the after end of the planes' cockpit. He ducked instinctively as he heard the rat-a-tat of machine gun bullets impacting the ship's superstructure. This time they had been attacked by a dive bomber, not a fighter, and dive bombers carried rear gunners. That's where the machine gun fire had come from. Hiro called to the engine room thru the speaking tube to have the damage control party look for problems to the hull the two bombs may have caused.

Before he could get a reply a second dive bomber appeared. It used the same tactic to deliver its weapons but this time the helmsman was able to turn the Maru enough that both bombs landed to starboard. Again, the dive bomber's tail gunner sprayed the Maru as the plane climbed out. He hit the ship squarely but seemed to do no damage.

Hiro again asked for a damage report but received no reply and before he could go below to check for himself another dive bomber appeared–or maybe it was the first dive bomber on a second pass. This time it released a larger bomb that it carried directly beneath the fuselage. The bomb struck the sea only a few hundred feet behind the Maru. It exploded with a monstrous roar and lifted the stern of the ship completely out of the water, swamping the aft deck with a geyser of water probably fifty feet high. Hiro scrambled down the ladder to the engine room to check for damage. Several men were there looking shaken but unharmed. He asked if there was any damage to the hull. The engineer said the damage control party was checking and he would report just as soon as he knew.

Hiro climbed back up the ladder and just as he was emerging onto the deck, another dive bomber dropped another large bomb from beneath its fuselage. This time the bomb fell ahead of the Maru. Its geyser towered over the little ship, and then dropped tons of water on its forward deck. Hiro had to cling to a stanchion desperately to

CHAPTER 28

avoid being washed overboard. On the bridge he found the helmsman in a state of shock, unable to respond to Hiro's commands. The Maru's condition was serious and about to get much worse.

Four and-a-half miles away the captain of the *USS Nashville*, a light cruiser, was reading Halsey's directive just handed him by the signalman to "detach and sink sampan ASAP." Understanding that Halsey wanted the Maru sunk before it could send another report, the Nashville's captain ordered a course to close the *Nitto Maru* and directed that the three forward turrets "open rapid fire" immediately. The range to the Nitto Maru at that point was about 9,000 yards, roughly four-and-a-half miles. That was well within range of the Nashville's six-inch guns but, as the attacking aircraft had learned, the *Nitto Maru* was not an easy target bobbing among the Pacific waves. Moreover, the Nashville's guns were loaded with 130-pound armor piercing shells. These were designed to be used against armored enemy combatants. Used against the thin-skinned *Nitto Maru*, they could easily pass through the ship completely, leaving little more than a hole in the hull that could be patched by a damage control party. The Nashville began 'rapid fire' just before 0800 and delivered on the Nitto Maru an astonishing 31 shells per minute for the next 29 minutes–928 shells! At the 29th minute, the Maru was still afloat, but now dead in the water, issuing billows of smoke, and going down rapidly by the stern.

Following the air attacks Hiro had tried his best to rally the crew, but then shells began to rain down, first far away and then progressively closer. Panic ensued. Above decks became a maelstrom. Fifty-foot geysers of water erupted violently all about. The ship shuddered under repeated hits. Then a shell struck the engine room, the ship lost way, and fire erupted. Some of the men dove overboard, others remained aboard thinking it was safer than almost certain death in the water from hypothermia, being killed by hydraulic shock waves

THE DOOLITTLE IRONY

from the impacting shells, or simply drowning. Hiro remained on board not because he had thought through those alternatives, but merely because the bridge offered some small degree of protection from the hell around him. In the 29th minute the shelling stopped. Hiro waited, then stood on shaking legs and looked around. The ship was a wreck. Its masts and kingposts had been toppled, the ventilators turned into jagged shards of metal, the funnels were bent, and the ship was sinking by the stern.

It was obvious the *Nitto Maru* would go down within minutes. The water had reached amidships and the bow was rising precariously. The heat from the fire was overwhelming and leaping into the frigid Pacific was Hiro's only way out. He grabbed the life preserver that hung on the bulkhead just inside the bridge and leapt. The cold ocean water stunned him. He ducked his head into the hole of the life preserver and began to kick and paddle away from the burning ship. He looked about but saw no other crewmen.

Hiro watched the *Nitto Maru #23* lift its bow high in the air and slip rapidly into the sea. Large bubbles appeared where the ship had been, and a slick of diesel oil spread and flotsam floated to the surface. The wind howled and Hiro bobbed helplessly as the Pacific swells passed beneath him. His arms were stretched akimbo over the life preserver or he would have slipped under. Time passed. The cold water was numbing his hands and feet and he could feel himself getting weaker. His mind was shutting down and pictures of home appeared, then he saw Kathleen smiling, then nothing, as he slipped into unconsciousness.

CHAPTER 29

INTERNMENT HITS HOME

Crawford, 18 April 1942

"Stanley?" Kathleen spoke loudly into the phone, "Is that you?" Stanley had just picked up the office phone, having been summoned to it by the receptionist, "Yes, Kathleen," he responded, "What's wrong."

"They're nailing up the Evacuation Notice here in Crawford," Kathleen said obviously near tears, "Avaron and Natsuko just ran here from Grimm's Drug Store. They said there were two men in uniform doing it, and it says the Japanese have less than two weeks to pack up and leave."

"Really?" Stanley responded a bit puzzled, "Mr. Scott said the Army probably won't post notices here in Seattle for another week. I guess they must have started earlier with the outlying areas, like Bainbridge and Vashon Islands."

"Stanley," Kathleen said, "I think you should come out here to Crawford. You and I should go to Hiro's parents and see how they are coping and what they need. Avaron and Natsuko seemed in control when they were here, but I don't know what they'll be like when they get home. You know, Avaron will not be able to graduate high school because of this. She's very upset."

THE DOOLITTLE IRONY

"You're right, Kathleen. I had planned to come out anyway. I'll leave work. Mr. Scott is very worried about both Hiro and his family. He feels responsible. He told me to take whatever time I need to help out."

"OK. I'll meet you at Grimm's in about an hour." Kathleen said as she hung up.

Rather than wait the hour at her house–which would mean having to fend off her mother's remarks about how Kathleen should not get involved–she walked the several blocks to Grimm's. A knot of people were gathered outside the store looking up at two White papers that had been tacked on a telephone pole. In bold print one read,

"Western Defense Command and Fourth Army Wartime Civil Control Station, INSTRUCTION TO ALL PERSONS OF JAPANESE ANCESTRY LIVING IN THE AREA OF CRAWFORD, WASHINGTON… all persons of Japanese ancestry, both alien and non-alien, be excluded from the Military Area or be liable to criminal penalties… and subject to immediate apprehension and internment."

Kathleen was struck by the euphemisms. "Non-aliens?" What they meant were American citizens! And "military area?" That meant these people's homes. And where would the non-aliens taken from this military area being forcibly sent? "Camp Harmony!" That's what the Army was calling it in their press releases! Kathleen thought it unforgivably hypocritical. She hoped that the U.S. Army fought with greater courage than it wrote. An image flashed through her mind of the scene from the movie *Wizard of Oz*, where Dorothy uncovers the Wizard to be just an ordinary man behind a curtain making himself seem Wizardly by pulling levers to release puffs of steam and using a microphone to make his voice sound portentous.

There was a second posting. It read:

> "**Japanese Exclusion Order No. 17, dated April 18, 1942. All** Japanese persons, both alien and non-alien, will be evacuated from the Crawford military area by 12:00 PM, 1 May 1942." It explained they would be evacuated in

CHAPTER 29

family units, and each family was to designate a head-of-household to serve as its representative. "Evacuees" would be allowed to take only two suitcases containing their clothing, bedding, dishes, cooking utensils, medicines, etc. They were to report to Fourth Army Wartime Civil Control Administration Office in Seattle on 1 May. Busses would load in Crawford for the trip to Seattle at 12:00 PM.

The townspeople gathered about reading the Proclamation were all White and all somber. As they gazed up, they thought this was a matter beyond their control. They may not approve of it, but they were not going to risk opposing it. Their concerns were on the personal level: I wonder how Mrs. Tanaka is going to manage without her husband? Have the Akita's been able to sell their car? Well, we all knew this was coming but it's going to be hard for them.

"Yes," Kathleen thought resignedly as she stepped away from the knot of people, "It's not anything any of us can change. If the Japanese don't submit they will be, 'liable to criminal penalties… and subject to immediate apprehension and internment.' And if any Whites interfere, they will be dealt with forcibly. The government has sent men in uniforms with guns here to make certain of that."

Just then Stanley drove up and parked across the street.

"Let's get a Coke before we go out to Hiro's," he said as he joined her, "We need to talk about what we plan to do."

They sat at their usual table. Grimms's had just one other customer, a lady in the back of the store getting a prescription filled. The stools at the soda counter were all vacant. Being a weekday, Crawford's teenagers were at school—except for the Japanese.

"First," Stanley began, "bring me up to date on Hiro's family, Kathleen. Have they figured out what to do with the house and farm?"

"Based on what the two girls have told me," Kathleen replied, "The answer is no. You see, the fields have not been planted because Hiro's dad has been ill and Hiro had taken a job with your outfit. It's too late to do any spring planting now, so other farmers aren't interested in taking over the land. As for the house, it's rather humble, far

THE DOOLITTLE IRONY

from town, and the market is very poor for a seller. The people who would be most likely to be interested in it are other Japanese, and they're all being 'evacuated' just like Hiro's family."

"What about their personal property?" Stanley asked.

Kathleen grimaced and said, "Well, they have few possessions of value–a radio, some dishes that Mama had inherited from her mother, maybe the stove and ice box. The one item that Papa prized was the tractor, and I'm sorry to report that he has already sold it."

"Really!" Stanley said with surprise, "I thought he would never let that go."

"Nor did I," Kathleen responded, "I think it's very discouraging. It probably means that Papa has given up on any prospect of returning to the farm."

"How's his health?"

"The girls tell me he rests a lot. He tried to help Mama tend the garden a few times, but got tired and had to go into the house and sit down. My Dad says Papa has a heart condition, probably because he's had to work hard all his life. Dad said he doesn't know any Japanese men who have lived past 70, and Papa's already 65 I think."

"Not a very encouraging picture," Stanley allowed, "What can we do to help?"

"I've been thinking a lot about that, Stanley," Kathleen said, "And I've tried to get from the girls some sense of what the family might want. The answer, briefly, is that the family doesn't want anything. They have the usual independent Japanese attitude. I'm not even sure they will accept help if we offer it."

"OK," Stanley said slowly, "We both knew that going in. So what have you concocted?" He asked, knowing full well that Kathleen had very likely given this a lot of thought.

Kathleen smiled wryly, "Yes, I do have a few thoughts," she admitted. "First, I think we should go to their house the morning that they board the bus to Seattle. We should not allow them to carry their luggage the mile from their house into town. We should load it into your car, put Mama and Papa in the back seat, and drive them into town. The car will be loaded with the eight suitcases they're allowed to take, so there will be no room for Avaron, Natsuko and I in the car. We will walk."

CHAPTER 29

"OK" Stanley said, "What else?"

Kathleen looked a bit wary as she offered her next suggestion, "The family will have to board the bus and, of course, you and I will not be permitted to do so. So–subject to your approval–I suggest we jump in your car and follow them down to the assembly point in Seattle." Then, before Stanley could raise an objection, she added, "They will need us down there. The luggage will be heavy and Papa will have to act as head-of-household. He'll be tired. We should be there to help."

Stanley smiled, "I agree. We <u>should</u> be there and we <u>should</u> help. But I'm not sure how much the Army will <u>let</u> us help. They may rope off the area and allow only Japanese beyond a certain point. I've read that over 7,000 are to be evacuated, so it's possible we may not even be able to find them in such a large crowd. Let's give it a try, but not tell the family that we'll be there. I wouldn't want them to be disappointed."

"Umm," Kathleen mused, "I think you're right. We should not raise their expectations. Besides, they might just tell us that they don't want us there."

Stanley smiled, "Yeah, That's a possibility! Got any more suggestions?"

"Yes," Kathleen offered, "I think we should reassure them that we will take care of their property while they're gone. My dad has already told me he would have his men patrol their road regularly. I can go by every week or so myself."

"I don't know how much I can help with that," Stanley said ruefully, "I'm draft bait. I could be summoned any day now."

"You've done a lot already, Stanley," Kathleen said, trying to assuage any guilt he might feel, "You've been a very good friend to Hiro. I know he will be grateful." With that Kathleen paused, realizing she had used the future tense, "… he will be…," not the conditional, "… he would be …" A furrow appeared on her brow and she asked the same question she always asked each time she spoke to Stanley, "Do you have any news of Hiro?"

"No, Kathleen, none," Stanley replied, "Mr. Scott says all channels of communication with Tokyo are down. No postal exchange, no telegraph, no voice circuits, no ham radio connections, no third-

THE DOOLITTLE IRONY

party communications. We have no way of knowing anything about what's going on inside Japan, and it could be a long time before we do. This war could go on for a year–maybe even two. That's a long separation, Kathleen. And you have to face the possibility that Hiro may never return."

Kathleen had, of course, thought about that previously but hearing Stanley say it gave it a hard-edged reality. Her shoulders slumped and she dissolved into tears. Hiro had been gone only four months but it seemed an eternity. Being separated from him for two years was unimaginable.

Stanley tried to cheer her up a bit, "You know, Kathleen, it's probably just as well that he's not here. I don't think Hiro would take well to being sent to a prison camp."

"No, that's for sure," Kathleen agreed with a smile, "But he wouldn't be going alone, Stanley. We would get married and I'd go with him. You can be sure of that."

"OK, enough of this sad stuff," Stanley said, "Let's go see Hiro's family."

They did, and found it in a much better frame of mind than Stanley and Kathleen had expected. Mama was cooking rice, Papa was resting, and the girls were discussing where they could get some more suitcases. Mrs. Palmquist had already agreed to give them three. Stanley immediately offered another, and Kathleen thought she could find two. The two girls thought six might be enough because they planned to put the dishes and cooking utensils in two duffel bags and then pack the bed linens and towels around them so they would not get broke. The duffel bags had come from friends at school whose fathers had served in the Army.

Stanley announced he would be there 1 May to drive Mama-san and Papa-san to town, along with the luggage. Neither Mama nor Papa objected, and the girls happily welcomed the luggage part. Apparently Mama had put them in charge of not just packing it, but carrying it as well. The prospect of having a car to move it into town, and having big, strong Stanley there to help carry it lifted a big weight from their shoulders, literally! Stanley did not mention that he and Kathleen would try to be at the Wartime Civil Control Administration Office in Seattle when the bus arrived.

CHAPTER 29

Mama turned to Avaron and said something in Japanese. Avaron nodded and looked at Stanley, "Mama-san asks if you have any news of Hiro?"

"No," Stanley replied, "I have nothing new to report." Remembering Kathleen's tears earlier in Grimm's, he did not offer the Mr. Scott's comments about all communications with Japan being cut, and he especially did not mention the possibility that Hiro would never return. Instead he simply reassured them saying, "But no news is good news. Hiro is probably warm and safe, hoping his family is not worrying about him too much."

CHAPTER 30

GOOD LUCK AND GOD BLESS

Aboard the *USS Hornet*, April 18

"LAUNCH PLANES X TO COL DOOLITTLE AND GALLANT COMMAND, GOOD LUCK AND GOD BLESS. HALSEY." Doolittle was on the bridge of the *Hornet* when the signal arrived. He hurriedly shook hands with Mitscher and clambered down three ladders to the flight deck. An ear splitting klaxon rang throughout the ship and the loudspeaker blared, "Army pilots, man your aircraft." The announcement came as a surprise to most of the Army aircrews. They hadn't expected to launch until later in the day or early tomorrow.

Much had to be done before the planes could takeoff. Engine covers and the tie-downs had to be removed. Fuel had to be added to every aircraft because the Task Force was still 150 miles short of its planned launch point. Without more fuel, the planes could not make their recovery airfields in China. That meant adding every possible drop of fuel to each plane's tanks, rocking the planes back and forth to eliminate air bubbles in the tanks, and loading 10 five-gallon cans of gas aboard each aircraft. Those would be added to the fuel tanks while in flight.

CHAPTER 30

Doolittle and his co-pilot, Dick Cole, climbed into their B-25's cockpit just a few minutes after the *Hornet's* klaxon had sounded. While deckhands moved their plane into takeoff position they went through the pre-flight checklist, ran up the engines, checked the magnetos, made certain the flaps were down and trim tabs in neutral, and then gave the LSO the thumbs up. This was not a good morning for flying. Winds were gusting to 30 knots and the ceiling was only 1,000 feet with nine-tenths cloud cover. Pacific swells were rising to 30 feet and the Hornet was pitching violently as green water occasionally broke over the flight deck. Doolittle checked his watch: 0820. Only 20 minutes had passed after Halsey's directive and he was ready to launch. Pretty good! The flight deck began to pitch upward as the *Hornet* climbed the next 30-foot swell. As the LSO dropped his arm with the checkered flag signaling takeoff, Doolittle released the brakes and the B-25 began to roll forward.

The Hornet's speed through the water at that point was about 22 knots, and it was heading directly into a northwesterly wind of 24 knots. That meant Doolittle needed to be moving only 22 knots across the deck to take off. The airspeed indicator reached that easily and as the flight deck neared its highest angle, he eased back on the yoke and was aloft. He gained altitude and then nosed over gradually to gain airspeed.

"Not bad for the first time, sir," Dick Cole commented dryly to Doolittle.

"Thanks, Dick," Doolittle smiled, "I could probably use some more practice. On the other hand I'm not sure I want any."

Doolittle banked left in a 360-degree turn to come back over the *Hornet*. He flew up its wake, directly in line with the ships heading. He did this so his navigator, Henry Potter, could check his magnetic compass and adjust his gyroscopes. Sitting alongside the *Hornet's* steel island for the last 16 days could have induced magnetic variations. Accurate navigation was essential if the planes were to find their airfield destinations in China. Doolittle leveled off at about 200 feet. Speaking into his throat microphone, Doolittle said to his navigator, "Hank, gimme a heading for Tokyo."

At about that same time in the radio shack of the Enterprise, two radiomen were monitoring an English language broadcast from Tokyo.

THE DOOLITTLE IRONY

The announcer was ridiculing a claim made by a foreign observer that Tokyo was vulnerable to air attack. "It is absolutely impossible," the announcer declared, "For enemy bombers to get within 500 miles of Tokyo. Instead of worrying about such foolish things, the Japanese people are enjoying the fine spring sunshine and the fragrance of cherry blossoms."

"Sir," Hank replied, "Course to Tokyo is 268 magnetic. Tokyo is about 615 miles distant and we are running into 27 knot headwinds. At this consumption rate, fuel is critical. We may have to ditch well short of the China coast."

"OK, Hank, keep me posted." Doolittle replied looking undisturbed by that news.

"Sir," Dick Cole asked of Doolittle, "What do you think our chances are of being intercepted by Jap fighters?"

"Pretty good I'd say," Doolittle observed, "They know we're here thanks to that picket ship, and it doesn't take a genius to figure out we intend to bomb Tokyo. They deployed those picket boats so they probably also got other stuff ready as well. That would likely include fighters. On the other hand, they probably don't know we're coming in Army bombers. That changes a lot. Let's hope that throws them off somehow."

The *Hornet* launched the last of the B-25s one hour after Doolittle took off. All 16 had launched successfully and all 16 were headed for Japan at low altitude. At 0927 Halsey turned his Task Force 180 degrees to due east at 25 knots, intent on outrunning what would certainly be a frenzied effort by the Japanese to retaliate for the bombing of Tokyo.

About 30 minutes after launching, the second aircraft piloted by Travis Hooper, joined with Doolittle in a loose formation. The two flew together the next four hours all the way to Honshu, making landfall at a point about 60 miles north of Tokyo. They saw hundreds of fishing boats and overflew several Japanese naval ships, but none had fired on them. The only aircraft they encountered was a Japanese float plane that flew close overhead going in the opposite direction, and probably never saw the B-25s. Doolittle's hope that the Japanese fighter defense would be thrown off somehow by the American's use

CHAPTER 30

of Army bombers rather than Navy aircraft was apparently coming true.

The weather had now improved and was CAVU–clear and visibility unlimited. Having reached Honshu, Hooper turned south along the coast toward his target. Doolittle chose an alternative route. "Hank, let's go inland a ways and then head south," he said to his navigator, "Probably less AAA that way." He was largely right. They encountered little ground fire until reaching the Tokyo suburbs, but there heavy flak forced Doolittle to drop to tree top level, flying so low that he disrupted a baseball game in a Tokyo suburb. Pedestrians and bicyclers looked up and waved, mistaking the B-25 for a Japanese plane. Tokyo had just conducted an air raid drill that morning and many people thought this was just a part of that exercise. As he got closer to the city center flak exploded in black puffs to either side of Doolittle's plane but he was too low for the AAA guns to be accurate.

"There's our target ahead," Doolittle said, as they approached the North Central Industrial area of Tokyo. "Fred, I'm going up to 1,200 feet," he announced to Fred Braemer, the bombardier. Braemer opened the bomb bay doors, sighted the target, and at 1230 Tokyo time, released in quick succession the four incendiary weapons they were carrying. The weapons had been specially designed and produced for Doolittle. Each weighed about 500 pounds and contained 128 four-pound incendiary devices. The original bombing plan had called for Doolittle to precede the other 15 aircraft over Tokyo by about an hour. He was to arrive at dusk, find the target area in the daylight, and drop the incendiary weapons. The remaining 15 aircraft were to arrive under the protection of darkness and be guided to the target by the fires that Doolittle's plane had set. Of course, the *Nitto Maru*'s contact report had changed that. Doolittle dropped back down to 100 feet and began to make his escape toward the coast.

By now Japanese fighters had appeared overhead though none had yet attacked. Then Paul Leonard, the gunner, spoke up, "Sir, there are about five fighters converging on our tail." Doolittle saw two hills just ahead. He flew in an S-turn around them and lost the

THE DOOLITTLE IRONY

Japanese fighters on the second turn. Relieved, he crossed the coastline, flew out to sea, and then turned southwest.

The remaining B-25s attacked their targets in groups, hitting steel works, oil refineries, oil tank farms, ammunition dumps, dock yards, munitions plants, and airplane factories. Like Doolittle, they encountered occasional heavy flak but little fighter opposition. They struck ten targets in Tokyo, two in Yokohama, and one each in Kobe, Osaka, Nagoya, and Yokosuka.

Seeing the B-25s overhead was cause for celebration among the various Western diplomats that had been interned by Japanese officials in Tokyo. American diplomats rushed to the rooftop of the hotel where they were being held and cheered mightily. The British also cheered, and used the raid as reason to get pleasantly inebriated drinking champagne toasts to the American fliers the rest of the afternoon. Western journalists and businessmen also cheered but they had been interned in less congenial facilities—mostly jails—which did not offer champagne for toasting. An Argentinean commercial attaché wrote, "I ran up to our roof and saw four American bombers flying in over the rooftops. They couldn't have been more than 100 feet off the ground. I looked down the streets. All Tokyo seemed to be in panic.... I could see fires starting near the port."

Although the 32,000 pounds of bombs dropped were hardly enough to dent Japan's overall war effort, it was not completely insignificant. The last of the B-25s reported flames and smoke belching over much of the city. Perhaps the most telling effect was the damage inflicted on the aircraft carrier *Ryuho*. It was in the dry dock at the Yokosuka Naval Base and took direct hits on its bow by a 500-pound high explosive bomb and farther aft by several incendiary weapons. The dry dock itself was also damaged, trapping the Ryuho inside and preventing it from joining the IJN attack on Midway that June.

Having completed their bomb runs, the B-25s turned southwest toward China. They had performed a remarkable feat of arms. They had penetrated to the very heart of the Japanese Empire, eluded its most formidable defenses, and outwitted its best military minds.

CHAPTER 30

They had bearded the lion in his own den and exposed the mighty Japanese military machine as vulnerable—and they had done so without the loss of a single aircraft. In their wake they left Tokyo burning.

At 1345, a radio broadcast from Tokyo offered this somewhat hysterical report: "A large fleet of enemy bombers appeared over Tokyo this afternoon and did much damage to military objectives and some damage to nonmilitary objectives and some damage to factories. The known death toll is between three thousand and four thousand so far. No planes were reported shot down over Tokyo. Osaka was also bombed. Tokyo reports several large fires burning."

The Doolittle Raid had served notice to Tokyo that attacking Pearl Harbor was a major mistake. If Tokyo expected America to sue for peace and abandon the Western Pacific to Japanese hegemony, Doolittle's raid proved that a significant misjudgment. The sleeping giant had awoken. American ingenuity, determination, and courage had carried the day. Halsey would later say of Doolittle's raid, "I do not know of any more gallant deed in history…"

Captain Ogawa arrived in his office late-morning of the 18th. He had been at the senior staff meeting at Fifth Fleet Headquarters that morning and stopped by the communications office on the off chance that the Nitto Maru had been heard from again. It had not, but there were reports from some of the search aircraft about catching glimpses of American twin-engine bombers flying westward over the Pacific toward Honshu. Ogawa wrote them off as hysterical, and made a mental note to improve the aircraft recognition training for pilots.

The Staff meeting's principal topic of discussion had been, of course, the American naval force. Ogawa fancied himself a major architect of the trap that was about to be sprung. He had been the one who contributed the intelligence that led to locating the American force. Even more notably, he was the first one who had calculated the day of attack to be 19 April. The Chief of Staff had lauded his work at the meeting and Ogawa basked in his praise. He believed it was his due. He recalled bitterly how he had suffered misfortune with his earlier estimate that the American carriers would be at Pearl Harbor

THE DOOLITTLE IRONY

on the morning of 7 December 1941. But as he had told others, the error was not his, "If only that idiot Takeo Yoshikawa had done his job properly, I would not have made that prediction!" He smirked as he wondered how Takeo was enjoying the night life on Chichi-Jima

That's when the ear-shattering explosions occurred. They came from the direction of the Yokosuka Arsenal, the section of the base where ship repairs were performed. Initially he thought a steam boiler had exploded. He ran outside and saw the black smoke rising in a pall above the dry dock where the light carrier *Ryuho* was being worked on. Simultaneously he saw men pointing in the air at a black plane climbing to altitude from what must have been the low level bombing run that hit the *Ryuho*. The Americans! He looked at the plane again. It was a two engine bomber much like Japan's own G4M3. A bomber? "It must have come from China," he thought, "It could not possibly have come from the American carriers." But then he remembered the reports from what he thought had been hysterical pilots. Twin-engine bombers! In a flash of insight he realized the Americans must have somehow launched bombers from their aircraft carriers. The bombers' greater range allowed them to launch from much farther out than the 200 miles he had expected. And that greater range had allowed them to do it today, not tomorrow as he had predicted. Ogawa was dumbfounded. He simply couldn't believe it was happening. The Americans showed up a day early and ruined the trap that had been set for them. He went back to his office, fearful of the summons to his superiors' that he knew would follow in the next few hours.

This was a failure of epic proportions! For the first time since the Thirteenth Century, the Japanese Homeland had been struck by foreign military forces. The Japanese political and military leadership had proclaimed to the world this could never happen. Japan was too strong! Now those powerful men would be deeply embarrassed. They would be looking for scapegoats. Ogawa would undergo a Court of Inquiry, probably a Courts Martial. He would be shamed and suffer loss of face. Under *Bushido*, a Samurai who had been guilty of such abject failure was expected to take his own life. Tradition dictated that he commit *Seppuku*, ritual disembowelment. But Ogawa was not of that temperament. He immediately began looking for others to blame. Nothing occurred to him immediately, but he was confident he would think of something. He always had before.

CHAPTER 31

INTERNMENT BEGINS

While Doolittle and company were demonstrating America's courage and gallantry over Tokyo, others were demonstrating less attractive facets of American character in Crawford, Washington.

The busses that were to carry the Japanese from Crawford into an assembly point in Seattle had just pulled up in front of Grimm's Drug Store. About 40 Japanese were waiting. The drivers opened their cargo bay doors for the Japanese to load their own luggage. There was bumping and jostling to get it all on board. Avaron had volunteered to load the family's luggage, but at 102 pounds she had proved inadequate to deal with the scrum. She was left standing with all six bags on the street.

"You can't leave those bags there," a somewhat overweight US Army reserve private snapped at Avaron, "You gotta load them aboard the bus."

"But there's no room on this bus," Avaron replied weakly.

"Then you'll just have to do something else with them, but you can't leave then there." The private declared, feeling quite dominant in front of this meek Japanese teenager.

"OK, just give me a minute to find another bus to put them on," Avaron pleaded.

THE DOOLITTLE IRONY

"Look, maybe your kind don't understand English, but I said you can't leave them there." The guard shifted his rifle in a vaguely menacing way.

Stanley was standing a few steps away and overheard the exchange. "Why," he wondered bitterly to himself, "Are soldiers carrying rifles in tiny Crawford. I hope they're not loaded." He did not voice those thoughts. He simply stepped into the private's line of sight and asked with just a touch of edge, "Is there a problem, private?"

The private looked up at Stanley's six-foot-two muscular frame and became significantly more polite, "Well, sir, I have orders to keep this space clear."

"So you have, private," Stanley agreed in a friendly tone, "And this young lady is trying to help you follow those orders." Then without waiting for the soldier's approval, he motioned Avaron to go and search for room on another bus. "That OK with you private?"

Not happy about being contradicted by a civilian but unwilling to start an argument with a man of Stanley imposing stature, the soldier sought to save face, "OK, but you'll have to stay by those suitcases until she gets back."

"Why, sure," Stanley smiled, confident that the soldier fully appreciated he had just lost this minor encounter. Stanley hoped it would prompt him to be more civil in the future.

Avaron returned from having checked the other two busses. She grabbed two suitcases and said to Stanley, "I think we can fit them in the first bus up front." Stanley put one duffel bag under each arm and followed Avaron. The cargo bay beneath the seats was crammed but inside the bus there were vacant seats. Stanley piled the four pieces of luggage in one of the rear seats. As he was doing that, Avaron retrieved the last two suitcases and Stanley piled them precariously atop the first four.

As they were leaving the bus the same soldier they had earlier confronted stopped them and smugly declared, "You can't put luggage inside the bus. That's for passengers only."

"Private," Stanley said as though the word was distasteful, "You know that all the cargo bays are full. What do you propose we do with these bags?"

CHAPTER 31

Seeing his chance to get back at Stanley for their last encounter, the private replied rudely, "I don't know. That's your problem. All I know is that you can't put them inside the bus."

Just then the corporal in charge of the detail walked over, "Denkins," he said in a loud voice.

The private looked over at the corporal. Stanley thought of the dog in the RCA advertisement and wondered if Denkins was going to tilt his head to one side. "Denkins, we don't have enough goddam room underneath for all the luggage." He pointed to a number of bags still on the sidewalk. "I wantcha to get the owners of these bags to put them inside the first bus. There's still room in there."

Stanley smiled. Denkins took note of that and looked angry. He mumbled something under his breath about 'goddam slants,' and walked over to the Japanese standing beside the luggage on the sidewalk. "What the hell are you people doin'? You waitin' for a red cap to load your luggage? Get this junk off the sidewalk and put it on that first bus, and do it now!"

Denkins typified to Stanley the sort of men that had fostered hatred of the Japanese. Small, unaccomplished men who found that intimidating someone smaller made them feel less inadequate. The same kind of guy that went home and kicked the dog after screwing up on the job and getting chewed out by the boss. Like the dog, the Japanese could not fight back. They were the lowest on the cultural food chain here, socially unacceptable and politically powerless. Denkins was nothing more than a school yard bully.

Stanley had worked himself into a bit of a lather when he glanced across the street and saw Fritz Imhoff and one of his cronies pulling signs from the trunk of their car. One read, "And don't come back, Slants!" and "Good Riddance Yellow Peril. Stanley strode across the street and spoke to Imhoff, a paunchy, middle aged man with the look of a nervous squirrel. "This is not time to be putting up signs like that," Stanley said levelly, "These people are leaving. You got your way. So just go home and kick the dog."

It took a minute for Imhoff to understand the "kick the dog" part, and his face reddened as its meaning dawned on him. "I don't give a damn what you think. I've got a right to put up these signs. This is a free country and I'll do what I please."

THE DOOLITTLE IRONY

Stanley tried again, "Look, these people are losing everything. They have been forced out of their homes, their farms, their businesses. They'll be imprisoned out in the desert somewhere. What have they ever done to deserve that? Did they threaten your family? Did they rape your daughter or rob your son? Do they run in gangs and rob banks? No, they're peaceful people who have asked nothing more than to be let alone. They haven't been sending military secrets to Tokyo any more than you've been sending them to Berlin."

"You just don't get it, do you?" Imhoff snapped, "These people are foreigners. They're not like us. They never should have been allowed in the country and they sure as hell can never be real Americans. We're getting them out of Crawford and I hope they get shipped back to Japan. You're a White man. You should understand that."

"Yeah, I'm a White man," Stanley said trying to be patient, "But I'm also a Nisei in my own way. I'm second generation Polish. What about you? Imhoff? That's German isn't it? I'll bet it wasn't that long ago when your family was eating knockwurst in Essen. Maybe we should be locking you up so you don't spy for Hitler."

"Get outta my way, you dumb Polack," Imhoff snarled, "I'm putting these signs up whether you like it or not."

That was too much for Stanley. He moved directly in Imhoff's path, leaned in close to him so others would not hear and said, "Listen you goddam little kraut bastard, you're going to put those signs back in that trunk and drive off. If you don't I'm gonna wreck both your knees with these steel toed shoes I got on. You'll never walk again. And if I ever hear that you tried any of this Nazi bullshit again here in Crawford, I'll come back and break your goddam elbows too. You want to call the cops? Go ahead. I can break your knees before they get here. "

Stanley was an impressive figure and Imhoff estimated that he was not bluffing. Insulting these damn Japs was not worth losing one's knees, so he put the signs back in the trunk, motioned for his friend to get in the car, and the two of them drove off. Imhoff was not contrite. He would continue this in another venue when he had better advantage.

CHAPTER 31

Stanley rejoined Hiro's family and Kathleen caught his eye, "I noticed you having a conversation with our 'friends' across the street."

"Yeah, they decided to go home," Stanley replied nonchalantly.

The Japanese in Crawford had been spared the derision for now. In Seattle it would be different.

CHAPTER 32

ESCAPE TO CHINA

WITH THE B-25S CROSSING THE EAST CHINA SEA, 18 APRIL

Doolittle's planners had chosen Yaki Shima, an island just south of Kyushu, as the navigation point the B-25s would overfly to begin their crossing of the East China Sea. Doolittle arrived there at 1700, with the other 14 aircraft strung out behind him. They were all low on fuel, facing bad weather and confronting the prospect of headwinds over the East China Sea.

"Sir," the navigator spoke into his throat mike to Doolittle, "Our fuel situation is critical. With these headwinds we'll not be able to reach the mainland."

"Thanks, Hank," Doolittle responded, and then to the whole crew via his ICS (Internal Communication System) said, "You all heard that. If it turns out we can't make the Chinese Mainland, we'll have to ditch. If possible, I'll do so alongside a fishing boat. Once aboard we'll ask to be taken to a friendly port."

As Doolittle brought the plane to a course of 260 degrees true, he chose to think beyond the possibility of an ocean ditching and anticipate the situation that awaited them in China. Doolittle had been told that State Department and military officials back in

CHAPTER 32

Washington had arranged for a landing field about 70 miles inland from the coast at a place called Chuchow. It would be equipped with a homing beacon, lights for night landings, and enough aviation gasoline for the planes to refuel and fly on to Chungking, the Nationalist Government's wartime capital. There the planes would be turned over to General Claire Chennault's forces and the aircrews returned to the United States. At least that was the plan.

Doolittle knew that there was ample opportunity for the plan to go awry. "I'm not optimistic about anything on the Chinese end of this," Doolittle remarked to his copilot, "Chiang Kai Shek's people are difficult to deal with. Their organization is riddled with spies and you can't share anything with them that you don't want others to know about. So we've been very stingy about sharing information with them. Chiang himself doesn't know that our mission was to bomb Tokyo. Washington was afraid that if they told him that he would refuse us permission to land out of fear of Japanese retaliation."

"I guess if I were Chiang I'd worry about that too," Hooper chimed in, "The Japs did a job on Nanking."

"Nothing we can do about any of that," Doolittle commented, " It's all being handled by diplomats, Admirals, and others well above our pay grade. For now, let's just make sure we're ready to ditch if that becomes necessary. Check life vests, rafts, rations and water–and make sure your ditching station is clear of loose material. When we ditch we'll hit that ocean mighty hard and anything that's not secured is going to turn into a missile hazard. Be a shame to have survived bombing Tokyo only to have been killed by a flying can of beans."

The flight across the East China Sea was uneventful. Doolittle kept the plane at about 1,000 feet and 160 knots, conditions that would yield the best mileage. About half way across the winds began to shift. Soon the headwind became a tailwind and Hooper piped up in the ICS, "We've got a tailwind, sir, and it looks like we have enough fuel to make landfall. That's the good news. The bad is that we're heading into bad weather. Let's hope we find that Chuchow homing beacon soon. Otherwise you're going to have to make some tough decisions."

They did not find the homing beacon. Due to snafus in both China and America, it was not activated that night. In fact, when

THE DOOLITTLE IRONY

personnel at Chuchow heard the B-25s overhead, they thought it was a Japanese air raid, turned all the airfield lights off and sounded an air raid alarm! Not that it mattered. The weather had deteriorated to the point that finding the airfield and making a safe landing was probably impossible. Doolittle had to decide whether to ditch the aircraft in the ocean close to the shore or have the crew bail out from altitude. He opted for the latter.

Their map showed a range of mountains just to the west, so he climbed to avoid them. At 8,000 with just minutes of fuel remaining, he slowed the plane, released the escape door in the front of the aircraft and announced to the waiting crewman, "OK, one at a time, in close intervals, so we stay together and can find one another on the ground." He was the last one out. The night was dark and visibility was zero. Doolittle had parachuted once before with bad results, fracturing both ankles on rocky terrain. This time the landing was a little softer, though less dignified. This time he came down in a wet rice paddy that had been recently fertilized with night soil!

The other crews trailing behind faced the same weather conditions and confronted the same decision. Bail out or ditch? It had been a tough day. Twelve hours earlier they had taken flight in a very precarious manner, then they bombed Tokyo a very precarious mission, and now they would have to return to earth in a very precarious jump. Most crews opted to bail out, a few to ditch.

The following morning practically all of the crewmen who had come down in territory controlled by Nationalist Chinese were able begin their overland journey to Chungking. They would travel by river boat, by rail, by foot, and even by sedan chair. Some would be aided by Chinese peasants or militia. Others would be robbed by Chinese bandits. Some would encounter an American Missionary who was himself attempting to elude the Japanese. He served as their interpreter and provided them critical help getting to Chungking. He was killed by Chinese Communists just after the war officially ended. His name was John Birch, the man for whom an American anti-Communist political movement was later named.

Two of the crews came down in Japanese occupied territory. Of the ten crew members, two drowned and eight fell into Japanese hands. They were sent back to Shanghai and in August, tried, found

CHAPTER 32

guilty of having murdered Japanese civilians, and sentenced to death. Three were executed but the other five were sent to a POW camp. One of those died of malnutrition. The others were imprisoned for three brutal years until the Japanese surrendered in August 1945. Miraculously, 67 0f the 80 crewmen who bombed Tokyo survived the ditching and bailouts and made their way across 800 miles of Chinese territory to Chungking. There they were feted by the Chinese Government, met Chiang Kai Shek and his famous wife Madam Chiang, and given Chinese medals.

In the United States news of the raid became public based on information not from U.S. Government sources but from Japanese news broadcasts. The New York Times headlined its 18 April edition (the morning of 19 April in Tokyo): JAPAN REPORTS TOKYO, YOKOHAMA BOMBED BY 'ENEMY PLANES' IN DAYLIGHT. But it wasn't until 21 April that Doolittle managed to get his own report of the raid back to Generals Marshall and Arnold through Chinese communication channels. He reported that the raid had achieved surprise, delivered its bombs, and escaped to China, though probably at the cost of all of its planes. Hap Arnold was initially not happy with that news, remarking to the President that any mission that lost over 10% of its planes was considered a failure. But he was wrong! News of the raid lifted both civilian and military morale dramatically. Men and women rejoiced in the streets. Newspapers ran extras. Politicians loved it. After a litany of defeats, the U.S. had bombed the reviled enemy's own capital. Doolittle became an overnight hero.

During a Presidential press conference on the afternoon of 21 April, reporters pressed FDR for details of the raid. Where did the planes originate? Where did they go? The President finally relented with a remark that has since become widely quoted, "Yes, I guess the time has now come to tell you. They're from our new secret base in Shangi-La!" That was, of course, a facetious reference to the fictional valley in the mountains of Asia described in James Hilton's novel *Lost Horizon*, a story that Frank Capra had just turned into a popular motion picture.

Of course, Doolittle had no way of knowing any of that. It took his crew over two weeks to get to Chungking, during which he had

THE DOOLITTLE IRONY

expressed much concern about his future in the Army Air Force. "I expect to be court martialed," he told his flight engineer, "We lost every plane. The flight was a complete failure."

"For chrissakes, sir, you're a hero," Leonard retorted. You bombed Tokyo. They're probably gonna give you a medal and promote you to general!"

As it turned out, Cole's prediction was spot on. Not only was Doolittle awarded a Medal of Honor, the President himself personally pinned it on. And Hap Arnold promoted Doolittle not just one rank, but two. From being a Lieutenant Colonel, he skipped over the rank of Colonel to become a Brigadier General–an extremely rare event. And Doolittle's crewmen also were recognized for their bravery. All 80 airmen who participated in the raid were promoted one rank and awarded Distinguished Flying Crosses. Those who were captured and tortured subsequently received Purple Hearts.

Sadly, the Tokyo Raid brought disaster to China. As Chiang had feared, the Japanese exacted horrific retribution. The Japanese Imperial Army undertook a brutal campaign to punish the Eastern coastal provinces of China for the support they gave the American airmen. Over the summer of 1942, Japanese soldiers laid waste to some 20,000 square miles and killed an estimated 250,000 Chinese. They raped women, burned cities, pillaged towns and villages, drove away or slaughtered thousands of farm animals, destroyed vital irrigation systems and set crops on fire. They destroyed bridges, roads, and airfields. They even employed germ warfare, using the Chinese population to test the effectiveness of their biological agents. China paid dearly for its assistance to the Doolittle Raid.

CHAPTER 33

ESCAPE TO HAWAII

The *Nashville* was rescuing survivors of the third picket ship it had sunk that day. The first had been the ship that radioed the contact report. That had been about 0830. The second and third occurred in the early afternoon hours. In each case, the Nashville attempted to pick up survivors for questioning but had been unsuccessful on the first two. On the third, however, a number of men were spotted jumping overboard and the *Nashville* was now dead in the water trying to rescue them–very risky with Japanese submarines nearby. It had lowered its accommodation ladder and several seamen had five survivors up and out of the water. Then other seamen helped them up the ladder to the deck of the *Nashville*. As the last one cleared the rail, the Chief Bosun directed the rigging of the accommodation ladder back into its place and the *Nashville* immediately got underway. The unconscious survivor was loaded on a stretcher and taken to sick bay. The other four were taken to the Nashville's brig.

"Lieutenant," the Nashville's Captain said to his Officer of the Deck, "Send a semaphore signal to Admiral Halsey when we get within sight. Tell him we have aboard five Japanese survivors but cannot interrogate them because no Nashville crewman speaks Japanese. If he wants them interrogated, he will have to provide a Japanese speaker." And then he mused sarcastically to the men nearby, "You

THE DOOLITTLE IRONY

know, if you're gonna go to war with somebody, you oughta have a guy around who speaks their language—just in case they want to give up or something! Surely there are guys in the United States that speak Japanese. What about all those Japs in Japan Town? We could use one of them right now. Instead they're sending them off to summer camp." The men nodded seriously. It was always good policy to agree with the Captain.

Halsey was not ready to grant the *Nashville's* request for a Japanese speaker. When the last of Doolittle's bombers had launched that morning, he had immediately turned the Task Force due east at 25 knots. His intent at this stage of the mission was to escape what was sure to be a frenzied search by the Imperial Japanese Navy for the American Task Force that had just bombed their capital city. Three days would pass before Halsey, with nearly 2,000 miles of Pacific between him and Tokyo, would be willing to slow the Task Force enough to rig a breeches buoy and transfer Bill Russo from the *Hornet* to the *Nashville*.

Three days later Bill and Captain High stood near the rail of the *Hornet's* hangar deck, waiting for the Chief Bosun to supervise the rigging of a breeches buoy to transfer Bill to the *Nashville*.

"Bill," the Captain said, "You might not get much from these POW's. Considering that they're from converted fishing boats, they probably don't have much information we can use."

"Yes, sir" Bill agreed, "But whatever they do know I'll try to get down on paper so we can submit an information report right after getting back to Pearl."

"Good," The Captain allowed, "I understand we are due to make Pearl on the morning of the 25th, so that gives you about three days. Don't bother trying to get back to me before then. We're still under radio silence. I'll read your reports when we get ashore." Then, with a smile, he added, "And good luck with that highline transfer."

Bill had never been in a breeches buoy before. It looked like fun, but it also looked dangerous as hell. It's basically just a seat—called a bosun's chair—fabricated of canvas straps and suspended on a pulley

CHAPTER 33

that runs along a cable strung between two ships. It's a mechanism that's used frequently to transfer mail, supplies and occasionally men between ships at sea. It is risky. Both ships must be moving at exactly the same speed on exactly parallel courses. Minor variations can result in dunking the person or material being transferred. Major variations can cause the loss of life and collision of the two ships.

At the Chief's signal, Bill stepped into the bosun's chair; two deckhands strapped him into the safety harness and then signaled the *Nashville* that all was ready. Bill felt the seat swing out over the Pacific as the Nashville winched him over. He had donned foul weather gear but the wind and spray from the Pacific 40 feet below drenched him. The ships were moving at about 12 knots, and looking down at the Pacific rushing between the two ships was like looking at the Niagra River just before it plunges over the falls. The bosun's chair rose and fell with the rolling of the two ships, and Bill was glad that he only had to travel about 200 feet. When his feet touched the deck of the Nashville and he climbed out of the safety harness, he wondered if he could reproduce a breeches buoy as a thrill ride in an amusement park. It would make him a ton of money.

In keeping with navy protocol, Bill saluted the flag on the fantail, then turned and saluted the Officer of the Deck who had come down from the bridge to welcome him aboard.

"Lieutenant William Russo," Bill introduced himself.

"You're the Japanese speaker," the OD stated matter-of-factly. Then without waiting for confirmation added, "The Captain wants me to take you to sick bay right away. We've got a surprise in store for you there."

"Really? A surprise?" Bill was puzzled. This wasn't normal for the U.S. Navy. Surprises were for six-year-olds. Navy officers hated surprises. They were too orderly to value disorder. Bill stifled his curiosity and followed the OD down into sick bay.

As they entered, two corpsmen were at the bedside of a young Japanese seaman who looked drawn and exhausted. "Lieutenant Russo," the OD said, "I want you to meet one of the Japs we pulled out of the drink a few days ago. He was unconscious then and just woke up this morning."

THE DOOLITTLE IRONY

Bill looked directly at the man and said in a friendly voice, "Konichiwa," and then continued in Japanese, "I am Lieutenant Russo, an intelligence officer. I am here to get your story: who you are, how you got here, what you did in the Japanese Navy, that sort of thing."

The young man looked up and replied in astonishingly clear, American English, "Sure. I'll be happy to tell you everything I know, Lieutenant, but can we speak in English? It's my native tongue."

Bill was speechless. He looked over at the OD and said, "I see what you mean by a surprise. Wow!"

The OD nodded, "OK, I'll get out of your way now and let you two talk. My Captain asks only that you brief him on what you learn, before you get back to Pearl and slap a classification on it that he's not cleared for."

Bill smiled a bit guiltily. Yes, that's probably what would happen.

The OD waved a hand, signaled the two corpsmen to leave the area, and as he stepped into the passageway said, "I'll let you two alone. If you need anything, the corpsmen will be nearby."

Bill pulled a chair over to the bed and said more casually than he felt, "So, what's your name?"

"My name is Hiro Yamada and I'm from the Seattle area," was the reply, "If you want to hear my story, I hope you have a long time. It's rather complicated."

Bill Russo took his pen and notebook from the waterproof bag in which he had brought them, smiled and said to Hiro, "I'm ready to copy." He did, for the next two hours. When it looked like Hiro was done, Bill could only shake his head in amazement, "Wow! Nobody's going to believe this."

"But every word is true, Lieutenant, I swear," Hiro said sincerely.

"Oh, I believe you, Hiro," Bill replied, "Hell, nobody could make up a story like this! But others will be skeptical. I'll have to run checks with law enforcement, intelligence agencies, your community leaders, the University of Washington, your employer, etc. "

"Can you notify my family and Kathleen that I'm safe?"

Bill thought about it. "No, I don't think I can promise that right now," he replied, "What you've told me affects a lot of things—some that may not yet be apparent. No, I think that until we get this sorted

CHAPTER 33

out we'll have to hold you incommunicado. But after what you've been through, a few more days or weeks should be tolerable."

Hiro was obviously disappointed. "Will you promise me you'll hurry? I'm really worried about my family."

✢ ✢ ✢

USS Nashville, **21 April**

Following his two hour session with Hiro, Bill Russo had gone up to see Captain Erikson, commanding officer of the *Nashville*, as he had told the OD he would. He gave the Captain a sanitized version of Hiro's story, deliberately changing part of it: "Basically, he's a kibbie who got caught up by the Japanese draft. They stuck him in the Navy as communicator because he had been a ham radio operator and they needed radiomen aboard the picket ships."

"Kibbie, huh?" the Captain commented.

"Yes sir, a Nisei who had been sent back to Japan for his education."

"Oh, I know what a *kibbie* is. I grew up near Seattle and there are a lot of Japanese-Americans up there."

"Really? Ever hear of a little town up there called Crawford?" Bill asked.

"Oh, sure," the Captain smiled, "I went to the University of Washington with a guy from there. Japanese guy. I think his name was Tanaka."

"Really!" Bill said with raised eyebrows.

"Thanks Lieutenant," the Captain smiled, "I know damn well you didn't tell me everything but maybe I'll read about it in the newspaper."

Bill returned the smile and thought, "I like this guy's style."

With that Bill went to the cabin he had been assigned and began drafting his report while the details were still fresh in his mind. Then he went below to the brig and spoke individually to the other four seamen taken prisoner. As he and Captain High had suspected, they were innocent fisherman caught up in a war that rapacious Tokyo

THE DOOLITTLE IRONY

militarists had started. One of the seamen claimed to be an officer in the Imperial Japanese Navy, but his claim was unconvincing. He had probably heard that captured officers treated better than ordinary seaman and was just angling for a more comfortable captivity.

All four of the seamen did corroborate one important detail of Hiro's story. He claimed to have no memory of the time between he leapt off the *Nitto Maru* and the time he awoke in the sick bay of the *Nashville*. The four seamen each reported that they had hauled Hiro out of the sea after their ship came on the scene of the Nitto Maru's sinking. There was flotsam, an oil slick, and there in the middle of it all was Hiro, wedged into a life preserver. They pulled him up on the deck and left him there for dead, still in his life preserver. A few hours later their own ship was attacked by the Nashville. As it sank, Hiro apparently drifted off the deck into the Pacific, still in his life preserver. That's when he was picked up by the *Nashville*.

The morning of 25 April, Task Force 16 returned to Pearl but there was no victory parade. Most of the officers and men were confined to base, which the Navy justified as a security measure. But the story was being carried in all the Hawaii newspapers, based on information garnered from Japanese newscasts. Being confined to base did not go down well with the returning seamen, especially considering they all had expected to be greeted as returning heroes.

Just as soon as Bill left the *Nashville*, he hurried with his handwritten report to see Captain High who had been given a small suite in the Visiting Officer's Quarters. "Sir," he said as he burst through the door, "I think we have a situation."

A bit startled by Bill's sudden entrance, Captain High looked up from his chair and asked, "Really? Whatchagot?"

"Maybe the best way to explain is for you to first read my interrogation report from the *Nashville*. Then we can talk."

"OK," the Captain replied accepting the report from Bill's outstretched hand, "I'll do that right now. Have a seat. I think there's a beer in the refrigerator."

CHAPTER 33

Gratefully, bill accepted both offers and waited patiently while Captain High waded through the 12-page report. He read it the first time without looking up. Then he went back over it, pausing to reflect on parts of it. Finally he looked back at Bill, "Have you been able to verify any of this?"

"No sir," Bill responded, "I thought we'd get off inquiries to the FBI, Seattle Police Department, Naval Intelligence, the Army's Western Command, and so on."

"No," the Captain said emphatically, "I don't want this handled through routine channels. The stuff in this report is sensitive and could affect a lot of very senior people. I'm going to call Navy Counter Intelligence directly. I know a few people there who can run these checks in private channels, and do so in a hurry. We need to get this thing sorted out quickly. I'm going to have to talk directly to Admiral King about this, and I can't keep him waiting much more than a day." A pause then, "Have you talked to anyone else on this?"

"Yes," Bill admitted, "The Captain of the *Nashville*. He insisted on knowing, but I gave him a sanitized version."

"You mean Jonathon Erickson? Yes, Jon's an old friend. I'll give him a call and explain to him. Incidentally where is this Hiro fellow now?"

"I left him on the ship, sir, in sick bay. He's much recovered and doesn't really have to be there, but I just couldn't put him in the brig. Besides, those men are going to be transferred to Army custody. The Army's responsible for incarcerating POW's I'm told."

"We don't want this guy talking to the Army before we're ready," the Captain said, "Tell you what, I'll ask Captain Erickson to transfer custody of the man personally to me. You bring him here to this suite. You're going to have to outfit him with an officer's uniform or he'll raise all kinds of suspicion. Once you get him here, keep him here, and don't leave him. I'll be gone all day but hopefully by tonight I'll be back with news from Washington."

Captain High grabbed the report and ran out the door, leaving Bill to say, "Aye aye, sir," to an empty room.

CHAPTER 34

CAMP HARMONY

CRAWFORD, 21 APRIL

Hiro's concern about his family was well justified. The process of interning all Japanese from Western Washington had begun. On this date evacuation notices would be posted throughout the city. Today also, busses would arrive from outlying areas where evacuation notices had gone up earlier. The busses would bring the Japanese to the Fourth Army Wartime Civil Control Administration in Seattle. After being administratively processed there–names recorded, family units identified, etc–they would again board busses to the Fair Grounds at Puyallup, about 30 miles south. The Fairgrounds would serve as a temporary "Assembly Center" for the Japanese before being sent along to their permanent internment camp, then under construction at Minidoka, Idaho.

With so much evacuation activity going on, the local anti-Japanese bigots were out in force. A number had gathered near the Civil Control Center where they thought the busses would be arriving. Many carried vile signs. Some were drinking from bottles inside paper bags. As the busses of Japanese residents from Crawford arrived, a few of the hecklers who had been drinking and were no longer satisfied with carrying rude signs stepped forward to confront the Japanese

CHAPTER 34

face to face. Several of the soldiers nearby directed them to step back and most did. A few seemed determined to persist.

One was Fritz Imhoff, who saw it as his responsibility as self-appointed leader of the anti-Japanese rabble to push the issue. "Get your Yellow asses out of Seattle and stay out," he snarled at a small knot of Japanese waiting to get into the Control Commission building. Again, one of the soldiers warned him to stand out of the way. He did not, and continued his drunken diatribe. Concerned about the prospect of violence erupting, this time the soldier roughly dragged Imhoff to an alley around the side of the building and pushed him into a military truck parked there.

"Stay there until you sober up, goddamit," the soldier commanded and returned to his post around the corner of the building.

Predictably, Imhoff did not heed the soldiers command. As he was clumsily try to climb down from the truck's tailgate he felt a hand on his shoulder spinning him around and then a violent pain in his stomach. He doubled over and wretched violently. Then his legs weakened and he fell in his own puke. He never saw the assailant that had punched him in the gut, but he didn't have to when he heard, "Just be glad I didn't break your knees."

Stanley rejoined Kathleen where he had left her outside the building. "Sorry for stepping away like that. I just wanted to say hello to a friend."

Kathleen was oblivious to what had just happened in the alley. She was intent on finding Hiro's family among the Japanese entering and leaving the building across the street. Then all four emerged and Kathleen ran across the street to them yelling "Mama-san, Papa-san,"

They all looked up, surprised when they saw her. The girls came running. Mama actually smiled at her and Kathleen thought, "This is the first time she's ever been happy to see me."

The girls hugged her, then ran to Stanley and did the same with him. Mama and Papa maintained their Japanese dignity but couldn't hide their delight completely.

"How did it go in there?" Kathleen asked, "Are you all OK?"

"Everything went well," Natsuko bubbled, "Papa did it all. You should have seen him. He answered all the questions and one of the soldiers even called him sir."

Avaron added, "I was so proud. I didn't know he could do that."

Then Mama said in her broken English, "Of course. Why you think I marry Papa?" They all broke into laughter. Mama actually had a sense of humor!

Kathleen had to choke back a tear. "Oh my God," she thought, "I am actually becoming a part of this family, just when they have to leave."

"What happens now? Did they tell you inside where you go from here?" Kathleen asked.

"Yes," Avaron responded, "We are going to get back on the busses and go down to the Fairgrounds at Puyallup."

"Can we go too?"

"No, just Japanese." Avaron said, "It seems we will be among the first to get there. They said that was good because we might have some choice in where we stay."

"Yes," Natsuko chimed in lamely, "I'm going to pick the Ferris Wheel." Her sister was the only one who laughed.

"Will we be able to visit you down there?" Kathleen inquired.

"They thought there would be provisions made for visitors," Avaron said, referring to the men who had processed them inside the building, "But they would be limited." Then she looked over at the busses and noted that the soldiers were motioning the Japanese to board. "Oh, look, it's time we got back on."

There was a moment of silence. Their emotions were close to the surface. Even Stanley frowned and looked at his shoes. Then Papa, in his heretofore unaccustomed role as family leader, said, "We must go. Stanley and Kathleen, you have been very kind. Now we all must be very brave."

That was it. Mama, Papa, Avaron and Natsuko walked to the bus. The two girls occasionally peeked back, but once on the bus they were out of sight. As the busses drove off, Kathleen said a silent prayer and Stanley swore under his breath.

⊕ ⊕ ⊕

CHAPTER 34

29 April, Puyallup, Washington

When President Roosevelt signed Executive Order 9066 authorizing the movement of West Coast Japanese to locations east of the Rockies, there was no place to move them to. Camps had to be built and, considering that over 120,000 Japanese had to be moved, that would take months. Until those facilities were complete, the interned Japanese had to be housed somewhere, so the Army requisitioned large public facilities, mostly race tracks or fair grounds close to major cities. The Japanese were housed there in existing buildings or, if those were inadequate, the Army built temporary shelters. Construction was sized to allow 50 square feet of living space for each occupant, the size of a small bathroom. Toilets were communal latrines and dining was done communally in mess halls. The Japanese were held in 13 of these "assembly centers" along the West Coast through the summer of 1942. That fall they would be transported to ten "relocation centers" located inland on the other side of the Rockies.

Puyallup was the Assembly Center for the Seattle-Tacoma area. Located about 30 miles south of Seattle in the shadow of Mt. Ranier, Puyallup was a town of about 7,000 in 1942. Since 1900 it had served as the site of the annual Western Washington State Fair, a highly popular event that attracted 400,000 attendees or more. The Fair was primarily a family event, featuring agricultural and domestic exhibits, but it also had amusement rides, an art gallery, and even a dance hall. It spread over 160 acres and included numerous buildings, most of which were used to house the livestock being exhibited. The Army deemed it appropriate for use as an assembly center.

29 April 1942

> *Dear Kathleen,*
>
> *We have been here for four days now. When we arrived we found that—contrary to what we had*

THE DOOLITTLE IRONY

been told at the office in Seattle—getting here before most of the others was a <u>disadvantage</u>, not an advantage. It meant that we were assigned space here in the Main Fair Ground in a building that had HOUSED CATTLE. The soldiers said that the smell wasn't nearly as bad as the building that had been used for pigs, and that we would soon get used to it. But had we arrived later we might have got some of the new shelters being built. People say they are very small but at least they don't stink.

The camp—they call it Camp Harmony—is quite large and encircled by barbed wire. There are no private bathrooms or kitchens, just communal toilets and mess halls that serve what the soldiers call B-rations that are prepared in field kitchens. It's all American food. How I long for some of Mama's rice! Our beds are wooden planks and our mattresses are feedbags that we stuffed with straw.

It's been raining heavily since we arrived. The paths between buildings are muddy and the roof over our cubicle leaks. Papa is beginning to cough and I'm worried that he'll catch pneumonia. Mama seems to be holding up but asks incessantly about Hiro. Have you heard anything of him? Natsuko and I are bored. There is nothing to do and we can't visit our friends because the camp is divided into four sections and we are not permitted to move from one to another unless escorted by a soldier. We've only been here four days and already I'm looking forward to moving on to wherever they send us. Some people say it a place called Minidoka in Idaho. It couldn't be any worse that this place.

CHAPTER 34

Sorry to be so down. I miss home, Crawford High, and you.

Love,
Avaron

P.S. Say hello to Stanley for me.

CHAPTER 35

DAMAGE CONTROL

0100, 30 April, 1942, Pearl Harbor

Bill Russo had spent most of the day getting Hiro into the guise of a naval ensign. The chief petty officer who ran Uniform Issue looked more than a little puzzled when the two showed up and asked to outfit Hiro with a Tropical White Long uniform. He looked over Hiro who was dressed in civvies borrowed from Bill. "Do you need a whole new uniform, sir?" he asked of Hiro.

Before Hiro could respond Bill jumped in with the cover story he had devised, "Yes, a complete uniform, Chief. This is the very first ensign to graduate from the new Intel Language School in San Francisco. He's going to be working communications intelligence. I'm his sponsor and I'm supposed to introduce him to our Commanding Officer in just one hour. But the Army lost his gear on the flight over and all he has are the blues he traveled in, so he needs a Tropical White Long to be in the proper uniform to meet the CO."

Still puzzled, the chief leaned in to Bill and asked in a low voice, "Sir, are you sure about this? This guy is Japanese and I didn't know we had any Japanese officers in the Navy."

"Things change all the time, chief," Bill responded.

CHAPTER 35

The chief nodded, still not fully convinced, "OK, Lieutenant, whatever you say." Then turning to Hiro said, "But you're going to have to pay cash. As I'm sure you know, officers are entitled to only one uniform allowance and that's when they're commissioned. After that it's pay as you go."

Bill intruded again and asked, "How much will it be for the entire uniform, devices, shoes, belt, socks, etc."

The chief reflected a bit and then said, "I'm not really sure of the exact amount, but I think we're talking in excess of forty bucks."

Hiro looked at Bill, and Bill at the chief, "Well, we don't have that much, chief. We'll have to come back."

"Just a minute, sir," he said with a touch of cheer, "I don't want no hotshot intelligence officers mad at me so if you'll give me $20 now, I'll give you the uniform and you agree to have the cash here by tomorrow."

"Chief, you are a man of wisdom and compassion," Bill said gratefully as he handed him two fives and a ten. "Measure him up and put it all in a bag. We don't have much time."

Bill and Hiro returned to the VOQ, drawing a few prolonged looks along the way. If Bill had not been there, Hiro likely would have been detained by some security conscious passer-by, then questioned by a security detail, and probably held in a local facility until his story could be checked. Bill made a mental note not to allow Hiro to wander about alone, even after he donned his ensign uniform.

Back in the Captain's suite at the VOQ, Bill showed Hiro how the new uniform was to be worn: placement of the epaulettes, how to attach the brass buttons, etc. When he was finished he had to admit that Hiro cut a fine figure as a naval ensign. He said that to Hiro.

Hiro backed up from the dresser mirror to get a better view of his new outfit and had to agree, "Wow, I wish Kathleen could see me now."

"Yes," Bill agreed, "I think she would be impressed. But let's not get too far ahead of ourselves. This situation is more complicated than you and I understand. Captain High is trying to work it out now. Until he does, we're just going to have to be patient. Right now we need to get you a navy haircut. Let's do that downstairs at the VOQ barbershop, then get some chow, and then come back here to wait for Captain High."

THE DOOLITTLE IRONY

⊕ ⊕ ⊕

It was after 2:00 AM when Captain High finally returned looking frustrated and cranky. He looked at a sleepy Bill who had just awakened to let him into his own room. "Never again," the Captain started, "Never again do I want to be the messenger that so many of my superiors want to shoot!"

"Uh oh," Bill said, "I take it things did not go well?"

"We need to talk about that. Where's Hiro?"

"He's sleeping on the cot in the bedroom. Do you want me to get him?" Bill asked.

"No, quite the opposite," Captain High replied, "He shouldn't hear what I've got. Let's just talk in here. If he wakes up, we'll have to continue the discussion later."

"Sounds bad!" Bill said.

"Yes and no." the Captain retorted, "Let me start at the beginning. When I left you earlier today it was with the intention of first establishing Hiro's *bona fides*, i.e., is he who he says he is? That was not easy. With the eight-hour time difference by the time I got through to Washington it was the wee small hours there. The only person awake was the Duty Officer in the Command Center. I had to explain to him who I was and that I was acting at the personal direction of Admiral King. I gave him the names of some people to call and told him to get them into the Center so I could talk to them on the secure line. They weren't happy getting called out of bed, and they weren't happy with what I asked them to do. Anyway, you don't care about all that. I just mention it so you can understand how my day went: hectic, uphill, like pulling teeth!"

"I think I get the picture," Bill said, "And all I had to deal with was the Chief at Uniform Issue!"

"Huh?" the Captain said, looking puzzled.

"Never mind, we can talk about that later. Now tell me, what did you learn? Is Hiro for real?"

"You bet, right down the line," the Captain replied with some satisfaction, "We seem to have on our hands a guy who has lived the last six months in an adventure right out of a dime novel. But first let me explain what I did. I had the FBI check their Seattle Field Office.

CHAPTER 35

I asked if they knew of a man by the name of Hiro Yamada. Initially they said he had absconded with information from his employer and went back to Japan. That scared the hell out of me. But just about an hour later they called back to reverse their story. Yes, they apologized; Hiro is an employee in good standing with an outfit called Scott Engineering. Seems the Scott guy who owns the place is a heavy hitter with contacts in City Hall and was not very happy when he learned of the FBI's initial report. The agent who handled that one is probably looking at a transfer to Nome."

"Anything else from Seattle?" Bill asked, hoping to get information about Hiro's family.

"Yes, a couple things," the Captain replied, "The FBI checked with the Chief of Police in the little town where Hiro lives and he confirmed that Hiro is a local citizen of good reputation with no outstanding warrants. The University of Washington confirmed that Hiro graduated from there last year and the local Draft Board confirmed that he's properly registered. The only negative comments made were about him dating a White girl."

"Yeah," Bill confirmed, "That would be Kathleen. I think they intend to marry. He's very anxious to get in touch with her."

"But," the Captain interrupted, "We can't allow that–not for awhile anyway." He paused as though to collect himself and then added, "And the reason is just what you feared would happen when we first talked months ago: some 7,000 Japanese from around Seattle, including Hiro's family, are being 'interned.' That's a polite word for imprisoned. They're in a place near Tacoma the Army calls 'Camp Harmony,' waiting to be transported to some isolated place in Idaho."

"I'm not surprised," Bill said, "We saw the same thing happening in San Francisco before we left. Remember the men saying how Japan Town was empty?"

"Yes, I do," the Captain said with a shrug, "And it's all over the newspapers. But so far I don't think Hiro knows about it, and I'm afraid of his reaction when he finds out."

"Well, sooner or later he's bound to find out," Bill observed.

"I'd rather it be later," the Captain said worriedly, "Consider the impact his story could have. Back home Americans are rejoicing in

THE DOOLITTLE IRONY

the streets about Doolittle's raid. They see it as a daring feat of arms and a demonstration of America's unbeatable will. But Hiro's story would show that to be horse feathers."

The Captain paused, troubled by his own realization of what had happened, "In fact, the Japanese had read our souls. They knew we couldn't resist taking a shot at Tokyo so they set a trap for us. They positioned a large defensive force of ships and aircraft around Tokyo. Then they strung more than a hundred picket boats along their coast 600–700 miles out to sea to detect any approaching U. S. force."

Again a pause while Captain High seemed to summon a will to continue. "The picket string did its job. It sighted us 650 miles out. But we got lucky. It was Hiro's boat that saw us first and when the boat's captain tried to send a detailed contact report, Hiro acted like the American patriot he is and altered it. In particular he omitted the part about one of the carriers having Army bombers on the flight deck. Had the Japanese known that, they would have figured out that we could launch from 500 or 600 miles out rather than closing to 200. And when Halsey realized we'd been discovered, he took advantage of the bombers greater range and launched from about 600. Consequently we hit Tokyo 24 hours before the Japs were ready. Had we carried out the raid as originally planned and waited until the next day to launch, the bombers would almost certainly have been shot down and the Task Force sunk. So the vaunted American military victory is uncovered as just the product of a ton of luck and a patriotic American of Japanese descent uncannily being in the right place at the right time."

"I think it's kind of inspiring, Captain," Bill said, "Hiro should get a medal."

"I agree, but if you're a politician who has just ordered all Japanese-Americans be imprisoned, it would be embarrassing as hell to admit that our great military victory was due in large part to the actions of a Japanese-American," Captain High observed ironically, "And talking about medals, in just a few days they're going to give the Medal of Honor to Lieutenant Colonel–excuse me, GENERAL Doolittle. He's been promoted TWO grades."

Then the Captain finished, "So you see, Washington politicians have made Doolittle into a great hero. They wouldn't like Hiro's story

CHAPTER 35

on the front page of the evening newspaper. It would diminish their idol. And let's not forget Halsey. Do you think old '*The only good Jap is a Dead Jap*' would be happy crediting a Japanese-American for saving his ass? Unlikely!"

"Yes," Bill mused, "I can see Hiro might be a problem of sorts for Washington. What are they going to do about it?"

"Damned if I know," the Captain conceded, "I spelled this all out for Admiral King. He got angry. Said he sent me out here to keep things under control and now I bring him this large pile of crap."

"But there was nothing you could do," Bill pointed out somewhat gratuitously.

"He was just venting, Bill," the Captain said with patience that he really didn't feel, "He told me he would have to discuss this matter with other people tomorrow and I was to call him at 0700 tomorrow–about 1500 our time. So until then we need to keep Hiro away from newscasts and newspapers." Then with a flourish he declared, "Enough for now! I'm bushed. Let's get some rest"

⊕ ⊕ ⊕

1 May, Pearl Harbor

Admiral King had told Captain High to phone him at 0700 Washington time on the secure line. He did so, promptly. It took some doing because secure voice communications with the Mainland were in short supply and one normally one had to go through a lot of wickets to get a phone reserved for a particular time. But the mention of Earnest King did wonders to remove bureaucratic obstacles. The call was placed at exactly 1500 Hawaiian time, 0700 Washington time. As always, the Admiral's directions were brief, direct, and unequivocal. The phone call ended at 0704.

Captain High returned to the VOQ lobby and sat in one of its bamboo chairs with the overstuffed cushions. He remained there, pensive, for more than a half hour. He was considering the guidance that Admiral King had given him on how to handle this matter. There were only a few major points: the Admiral was willing to concede that the major aspects of Hiro's story were probably true; Hiro was very likely a patriot, and had acted as such on several critical occasions; his actions were meritorious and deserving of America's gratitude; however, if made public Hiro's story had the potential to diminish the stature of the Doolittle Raid and by extension diminish the improvement in national morale it had brought; that outcome was unacceptable to Washington so Hiro would have to be "controlled."

That, the Admiral had concluded, is to be Captain High's task. He could use any combination of carrot and stick he thought necessary. The Admiral would support whatever actions he took–within reason–as long as they kept Hiro and his explosive story under wraps.

Captain High had conceived a tentative plan, and he wanted to run it by Bill Russo. Bill knew Hiro much better than the Captain and would be better able to assess how Hiro would react. The Captain stepped to the lobby phone, called his room, and asked Bill to make up an excuse to leave the room, then come down to the lobby. A few minutes later Bill descended the steps looking worried.

"Captain, I guess you don't want Hiro in on this conversation. I hope that doesn't mean we're going to throw him in the brig."

"Hmmff," the Captain grunted, "I guess that might be one option, but let me tell you of the CNO's guidance on this matter." He did so, and added the Admiral's admonition that this guidance had come from "the highest sources."

"OK, these are my ideas. You know Hiro a lot better than I, so tell me whether you think they'll work. First, we praise his patriotism and thank him for his bravery. We tell him also that he has acquired valuable knowledge and skills that the U.S. Navy can use. Consequently we want him to join us and we offer him a commission as a Navy ensign. He would continue to serve right here in Hawaii."

"Can we do that?" Bill asked, remembering all the years of preparation he had to go through to get his commission as an ensign.

"Sure," the Captain replied, "With Admiral King's authority, we can provide him a direct commission."

"OK," Bill agreed, "I think he might actually like that. But first he's going to want to go home and see Kathleen and his family."

CHAPTER 35

"Yeah, that's a tough one," conceded the Captain, "If we allow him to go back to Washington State, he'll get locked up with the rest of the Japanese back there. And we sure as hell can't get his family out here. That would create attention and that's not what we want. Do you think he would settle for a phone call?"

"Maybe," Bill replied, "If he understood the situation. But that would mean we would have to tell him about the internment and I don't think he's going to like that at all."

"Well, we're going to have to tell him about the internment sooner or later. We can't keep him cooped up in here for the rest of the war."

"No," Bill agreed, "And there's no way we can sugarcoat it. What about his girlfriend? Even if he agrees to a phone call with his family, he's going to want to see Kathleen."

"OK. I'm stumped on that one. Got any ideas?"

"Actually, yes," Bill smiled as he said it, "She is a nurse, just graduated from University of Washington. Could we bring her out as a nurse? Hell the Navy needs nurses, and I'm absolutely sure that Hiro would like that idea."

The Captain sensed why Bill had smiled as he made that suggestion. He had had it up his sleeve waiting for the right minute to spring it. "Hmmff," the Captain reacted with one of his patented grunts, "That's a lot more difficult. It involves matters that are out of our control, like would she be willing to come? Would she be willing to leave her home? Maybe she has a job." But then his attitude became more positive. "But if she's willing, I think I can arrange it. God knows, there is a need. We have hundreds of wounded personnel. The Navy Hospital is expanding, we just got a Mobil Hospital here on base, and the Hospital Ship *Solace* has just left port. So there's plenty of need for nurses."

"Yes sir, if we offer him that I think he'll do just about anything we want."

"That's good, Bill," the Captain replied soberly, "Because his alternatives are pretty grim. Let me tell you about what else came out of my phone call with the Admiral. The real reason why Washington thinks offering him a commission is a good idea is because if he's in the military they can control him. One false step and he's in the brig. And let me tell you about what will happen to Hiro if he turns down our proposition. He'll be turned over to the Army as a prisoner-of-war and held in custody for the duration. Washington wants to see this young man treated right–but only if he stays mum about his story."

"Wow, that's pretty cynical, Captain!"

"True, so let's be especially persuasive. It's a good deal and we want him to buy it as though we are representatives of a grateful nation seeking to reward him for his courageous, patriotic actions. We never want him to know that there are grim alternatives."

"Yes sir," Bill replied with a bit of sarcasm, "I understand and will obey."

The Captain noted Bill's undertone of resentment, "Bill, what we are about may be unsavory, but it could be much worse. I suspect before the war is over this little bit of deceit will no longer even register on our scales of injustice. So let's now go talk to Hiro, and hope he gives us the right answers."

Hiro loved the idea of being able to continue wearing his uniform. "I planned on volunteering for military service anyway, so this is fine and added he could now use the uniform allowance to pay back the chief. And when the Captain told him of the possibility of having Kathleen join him in Hawaii, he actually jumped out of his chair and shook the Captains hand so vigorously that Bill had to step in to restrain him.

"Understand, Hiro," the Captain warned, "None of this is final. We have to talk to a lot of people and get their cooperation to make this happen. It will take time."

"And Hiro, along with this good news," Captain High added, "I have some bad news. Don't worry, nobody has died. All are safe and healthy… but your family has been relocated as a part of defensive measures taken on the West Coast against the possibility of a Japanese invasion."

"What do you mean, 'relocated?' Don't tell me all that stuff I heard on the international new broadcasts was right! Did they put my family in prison?"

CHAPTER 35

"No," the Captain quickly reassured Hiro, "They are merely being detained in a camp south of Seattle. I doubt this will go on very long–just until the threat of invasion passes. Understand Hiro, this is all just war hysteria. America will soon recover its senses."

"Maybe I should go back and help set the situation straight," Hiro said worriedly.

"I don't think you understand Hiro. You can't go back. They'll put you in the camp with your family and keep you there."

"But I'll be an officer in the Navy. They won't be able to do that."

"Hiro," the Captain explained with obvious embarrassment, "Right now the American Armed Forces are not allowing men of Japanese descent to serve. Those that were on active duty when the war broke out were sent home."

"Sent home? That's insane."

"I agree," Captain Low said, "But it's true–like I said, war hysteria. The crazies are in charge. Don't worry, Hiro, you're safe as long as you're here in Hawaii under the aegis of the Navy. But if you go back to the Mainland we won't be able to help you. The crazies will take you immediately into custody."

"I don't know, Captain, I'm responsible for my family now. My father is sick, and my mother and sisters depend on me. I've got to think about this."

"Just keep in mind, Hiro," the Captain offered, "There is nothing you can do to improve your family's situation. Nothing! The matter is out of your hands–and it's out of our hands. All we can do at this point is to try and win this war as quickly as possible and end all this internment foolishness."

"Yes, but this war could go on for a year or even two. That's a long time. My family needs me."

"Look," the Captain replied, "You need to talk about this with your girlfriend. I've made a reservation for a phone call tomorrow to Crawford Washington at noon our time, 0900 their time. You'll have to give me Kathleen's phone number. I think you need to talk to her about this. You won't have time to tell her about your experiences in Japan and how you got picked up by the U.S. Navy. The longest you'll be allowed on the line is 15 minutes so you'll have to deal only

THE DOOLITTLE IRONY

with the bare essentials. Simply explain that (1) you are now a Navy ensign, (2) that you can arrange to have her come out to Hawaii as a nurse if she wants to, and (3) you are extremely worried about your family but if you go back there you'll be interned as well. Ask her to send details about their situation, and tell her from now on you'll only be able to communicate by mail. I'll give you the FPO address to use."

"Wow, that's a lot to talk about in 15 minutes!" Hiro exclaimed, "And shouldn't I talk to my family too?"

"Yes, you should, Hiro, but they're in a camp with 7,000 other Japanese-Americans. The Army runs the camp and that means it would probably take a day to get through all the Army red tape. So I think you're going to have to talk to your parents through your girlfriend. She'll have the pleasure of telling them you're still alive."

"Wow" Hiro said again, "Just a few days ago I was floating around the Pacific in the Imperial Japanese Navy wondering if I would ever get home, and now I'm in the U.S. Navy but still wondering if I'll ever get home."

"Hiro, erase all thoughts of going back to the Mainland," the Captain admonished, "I can't emphasize strongly enough that it is simply not an option. You would end up interned in some godforsaken Army camp." Captain High carefully avoided any mention that the Navy would not even let him leave Oahu. "I've arranged to have you share a room with Bill in the BOQ for the next few days. Naturally, there will be a lot of paperwork to complete before you are formally inducted into the Navy as a commissioned officer. In fact, Bill and I have to go over to Headquarters to get started on that right now, so we'll be gone awhile. Don't leave the VOQ, and don't start any conversations with the other officers. If anyone asks, just tell them you're a Japanese linguist–and for god sakes, do NOT mention anything about being on the *Nitto Maru #23*! You can't discuss that subject with anyone but Bill and I."

"Sure, Captain, whatever you say," Hiro replied. He was still so overwhelmed with gratitude that he would have agreed to anything.

CHAPTER 36

ON THE HOMEFRONT

Kathleen set down her pen, not entirely pleased with the letter she had just written. She reviewed it one more time:

1 MAY 1942

> *Dear Avaron,*
>
> *Thank you for writing. It's important to us to know how you are doing down there at Camp Harmony.*
>
> *I'm sorry that your first days there have been so disappointing. The Camp sounds dreary and I'm proud of you for bearing up so well. I know that you and Natsuko are taking good care of your parents. That's so important. Papa-san is frail, and even though he put up a good show when you checked in through the office in Seattle, I fear he may not be able to stand much stress.*
>
> *Stanley and I have inquired several times about visiting, but were told that visits are on hold until most of the evacuees have arrived and get settled.*

THE DOOLITTLE IRONY

Everyone here asks about you and your family. I saw Mrs. Palmquist and she wants to send you a package of food. Even Mr. Grimm at the drugstore is concerned. He asks if you need any medicine.

When we are allowed to visit, I'll bring you some books. I saw Mr. Smith, your chemistry teacher. He said he has a text you should have. He also said he's trying to get your diploma, even though you have not been able to finish the school year.

No, I have heard nothing of Hiro. It's been more than five months now. Sometimes I despair.

Try to be strong. We will all get through this somehow.

Love,

Kathleen

"Kathleen, your father's on the phone. He wants to talk to you."

"OK Mom, Thanks." Kathleen walked to the hallway where the phone was located, "Hi Dad, what's up?"

"Kathleen, I just got a call from the FBI Field Office in Seattle. They wanted to know what I know about a man named Hiro Yamada."

"What?" Kathleen exploded, "Hiro? Why would they want to know about Hiro?"

"I don't know and they wouldn't tell me. I thought maybe you had some idea about it."

"God, no Dad, I have no idea at all. But I'll call Stanley and see if he has anything."

"Okay. Let me know."

As she called Stanley, her mind produced all sorts of conjecture. Had he drowned and his body washed up on the shores of Puget Sound? Was he being exchanged by the Japanese Government for some Japanese person here? Were the Japanese holding him and

CHAPTER 36

wanted information on their prisoner? Had the FBI captured him and were going to charge him with treason?

After the usual exchange with the office secretary in Scott Engineering, Stanley came on the line. "Kathleen? I was just about to call you."

"Stanley," Kathleen cut him off, "The FBI called my father to ask about Hiro. Do you have any information on that?"

"Yes, I do. Mr. Scott just told me he also got a call from the FBI inquiring about Hiro. They thought he had stolen information from our firm and gone to Japan to sell it."

What? How did they ever get that?" Kathleen asked.

"Probably from one of those anti-Japanese twerps running around the city," Stanley replied, "Anyway, Mr. Scott set them straight. But the FBI was its usual arrogant self and refused to tell Mr. Scott why they were asking."

"I'm frightened that Hiro is dead, Stanley." Kathleen said beginning to cry.

"I don't know what's going on," Stanley said, "But apparently SOMETHING is. I guess we're just going to have to wait and see what. Let's stay in close touch."

CHAPTER 37

INCENTIVIZING HIRO

Bill and Captain High walked through the wreckage that had not yet been cleared from the Japanese attack on 7 December. They entered the PACFLT Headquarters Building where the Intelligence Section was located. It had not been damaged in the attack.

"Captain, was that information you gave Hiro about Japanese-Americans not being allowed to serve in the Armed Forces true or just so much hogwash to keep Hiro from going back to the Mainland?"

"It does sound preposterous, doesn't it," the Captain said, "But it's the truth. Japanese-Americans serving on 7 December were separated out of their outfits. Some were sent home, others to remote areas. And the War Department has announced it will not draft Japanese-Americans. Hell, they're even talking about moving the Japanese Language School out of San Francisco because it's in the so-called 'exclusion zone.'"

"What a waste!" Bill sighed, "We could sure use some translators."

"Like I said, Bill, the crazies are in charge. But don't despair. Pretty soon the War Department is going to start running out of men and then the Nisei will start to look pretty good."

"Captain, if there are no Japanese being taken into the War Department now, how is it that we can provide Hiro a direct commission?"

CHAPTER 37

"RHIP," Captain High replied, "Rank Hath Its Privileges. And when you're the CNO like Earnie King is, and you have the ear of the President, you get a lot of privileges. Admiral King can make Hiro an ensign if he says it is in the national interest, whether or not the War Department likes it. Of course, there are limits to even the CNO's privileges. For example, I don't think he could exempt Hiro from internment if Hiro were back in Seattle. That would become an Inter-Service issue, because West Coast security is the Army's responsibility. Who knows how that would turn out? But here on Naval Base Pearl Harbor, Ernest King calls the shots."

"Incidentally," the Captain added, "There will be no commissioning ceremony. We don't want to call attention to this. It would just raise questions. But a message was sent to the personnel folks over at BUPERS and a file has already been opened on Ensign Hiro Yamada. As of now, Hiro is a commissioned officer in the United States Navy."

"OK," Bill said, "The commission is the carrot. What about the stick? What do we do if Hiro decides that the U.S. Navy be damned and tries to go back to the Mainland on his own?"

"We'll have to throw him in the brig, Bill," the Captain replied reluctantly, "I've already instructed the Marine Security Guard Detachment that if a man answering Hiro's description tries to leave the Base that he's to be detained. In other words, we're dead serious about this. If Hiro chooses not to cooperate with us, we'll treat him as a prisoner-of-war."

"That's pretty harsh, Captain. Hell, even if he did tell his story to the press, no one would believe him!"

"Maybe. On the other hand, the political opposition could use it to create an uproar. The Administration has enough to worry about now. They don't want any more. To them, Hiro is no more than a fly on the wall. They'll swat him without a second thought."

"And what about those 15 minutes?" Bill asked, "If the CNO can move mountains, why can't he get another 10 or 15 minutes on a phone call?"

"OK. You've caught me, Bill. Actually, that's my doing. I limited it to 15 minutes because I didn't want Hiro on the phone long enough to talk about his experiences in the Japanese Imperial Navy."

THE DOOLITTLE IRONY

"Really, Captain," Bill said wryly, "I had no idea you were so conniving."

"I'll take that as a compliment, Bill!" the Captain smiled as they arrived at the Headquarters Building.

Inside the Captain explained to the Lieutenant Commander in charge of the Intel Section what he wanted. The officer nodded smartly, acknowledged that he already knew the request was coming, and directed the yeoman to get the necessary forms. "This sort of request is a bit unusual, sir," he said to Captain High, "We had to research exactly what had to be done to issue a direct commission here in the field. But my orders were to do exactly what you want. Apparently that came right from Washington!" The last sentence was voiced with apparent disapproval.

The Captain looked at Bill and smiled, "It's like I said, RHIP! Which reminds me, you can forget about paying the Chief in Uniform Issue. His boss said he would just "write it off." He wasn't real happy that the Chief had let a Japanese guy walk out in the uniform of a U.S. Naval Officer, but when I told him the CNO was personally grateful, he changed his tune. Then the Chief became a hero."

Bill slouched on the bed in the BOQ, with his head on a pillow and his stocking feet splayed out in front of him. "Hiro, we got to get you some more clothes, some soap, a razor, a comb, etc. You're going to have to look sharp for this commissioning ceremony coming up."

"Bill, you have no idea just how wonderful it is to be back here in America, with real plumbing, hot water, a soft mattress, good food and people who speak English. Japan is so different. Give me the good old U.S. of A."

"Hmmf," Bill grunted, realizing he was picking up some of Captain High's mannerisms, "Listen, are you all ready for your telephone call to Kathleen tomorrow? Maybe you should make some notes just to be sure your cover all the points you want to discuss. Incidentally, one problem will be just getting her to believe you. It's been almost six months since you left. She has lost track of you,

CHAPTER 37

maybe thinks you're dead. Now all of a sudden you just call her on the phone and casually say, 'Hi Hon, it's me. How have you been?'"

"Yes, I've thought about that. I hope she doesn't feint. We've only got 15 minutes."

"You'll do OK, don't worry. Just stick to the business at hand. Don't get off on tangents about floating around in the Pacific."

"What can I tell Kathleen to say to my family? How can I possibly explain that I can't come back and be with them? And how can I tell them that Kathleen will be coming out here to Hawaii, but they won't? What if the Army camp they're in is terrible? How can I tell them that there is nothing I can do to make their lives better? Mama will think that I've forgotten about her, that I'm no longer her Japanese son."

"Let's not talk about any of those problems until we get you settled here on the Naval Base. You know, you've got a job to do here. You're going to have to translate Japanese-to-English and English-to-Japanese."

"Is that all I'm going to do? Just translation?"

"No," Bill replied, "But first I have to figure out how I can convince our Security Officer that we should give a Top Secret clearance to a guy who has been in the Imperial Japanese Navy for the last few months."

"Yeah," Hiro grinned, "I can see how that might be a problem."

⊕ ⊕ ⊕

2 MAY 1942

The next day at 1150, Hiro, Bill, and Captain High arrived at the Communications Section of the Headquarters Building. The Communications Chief told Hiro to sit at the vacant desk and wait for the phone to ring. "When it does your party will be on the other end. You may have to wait. The few lines we have are not always available right when we need them. Oh, and remember, this is a simplex line. Only one person can talk at a time and when you're done you have to say 'over.'"

THE DOOLITTLE IRONY

"Oh, Kathleen's going to have trouble with that." Hiro said worriedly, "She even has problems with her family's party line." He sat at the desk with the phone on it, as the Chief had instructed, and noticed that Bill and Captain High pulled up nearby chairs to sit on either side of him. "Are you two going to listen? Some of this may be personal."

The Captain raised his hand as though to call for patience, "Don't worry, Hiro. We're just here to answer whatever questions may come up. We won't listen to the gooey stuff!"

Hiro flushed with embarrassment, and both Bill and the Captain laughed at him.

In Crawford, the phone in the Kelly household rang one short and one long, one short and one long. Kathleen's mother picked up the receiver and listened while Mrs. Fitzgerald said hello. "No, Mrs. Fitzgerald," Kathleen's mother said, "It's our ring, not yours."

"Oh, I'm sorry dear. I'll hang up right now."

Kathleen's mother said politely, "This is the Kelly's residence."

The flat, unemotional voice of a female telephone operator announced, "This is the overseas operator. I have a call for a Miss Kathleen Kelly. Is this she?"

It took a few seconds for the request to register with Kathleen's mother, "Uh, no, it's not but I'll get her right away. Hold on." She rushed to the stairs and shouted, "Kathleen, come right away. You have an overseas call."

"I have a what, Mom?"

"Kathleen, get down here this very second. You have an overseas call. Hurry!"

She did. Two steps at a time. Her mother pushed the phone into her hands and Kathleen said, "Hello?"

"Is this Kathleen Kelly of Crawford, Washington?"

"Yes"

"I have a call for you from Hawaii. Hold on and I'll patch you through."

"Patch?" Kathleen wondered to herself, "What's that mean?"

A man's voice then came on, "This is the communications watch at CINCPAC." He pronounced it the Navy way, *Sink-Pack*.

"Sink-Pack?" Kathleen was getting confused.

CHAPTER 37

The male voice continued as though he had not heard her. "Ma'am, this call is being conducted on a simplex line, which means that only one person can talk at a time. When you're finished talking, you must say 'over' to signal the other party that it's his turn to talk. Do you understand? Over."

Kathleen paused but then comprehended, "OK. I have to say 'over' when I'm done talking. I'll try to remember that." A long pause ensued and Kathleen finally remembered,"Oh, I'm sorry! Over, over!

"Don't worry Ma'am, you'll get the hang of it. Just a minute while I patch you through to your party."

And then the terrible potential of the call hit her. Hiro was dead! Her legs became weak and she collapsed into the telephone chair behind her. Why else would they call? He must have died at sea. That's why they were calling from Hawaii.

"Hello," came the vaguely familiar voice through the background noise of the TransPacific call, "Kathleen? This is Hiro. I'm calling from Hawaii to tell you that I'm alright and to talk to you about some matters, but before I get to that I have to know that you're alright and you understand me. Over."

Kathleen was shocked. She was trying to fathom what she had just heard. Hiro? In Hawaii? What was he doing in Hawaii? Suddenly a welter of thoughts all came bubbling out. "Hiro? Is that really you? Are you OK? I thought they were calling to tell me you were dead. Oh my God, Hiro, you're alive. Where have you been? Everyone is so concerned about you. Why didn't you write? Hiro? Hiro? Why don't you say something? Oh, yes, I have to say 'over.' So over, over."

"Kathleen, we only have a few minutes to talk about some very important matters, so I'm going to try to ask questions, and you just answer yes or no, then say 'over' do you got that? Over."

"Hello, Hiro. Yes. Over."

"Wow," Hiro thought admiring the brevity of her answer, "I guess she really does understand."

"Kathleen, I'm now an Ensign in the U.S. Navy. Do you understand? Over."

"Hiro, what is an Ensign and why are you in the Navy? Over."

"So much for the yes-or-no answers," Hiro thought, "I wonder if this is the way our married conversations will go?" But all he said

THE DOOLITTLE IRONY

aloud was, "An ensign is a rank of an officer in the Navy, and I'll explain the rest later. For now, remember, just yes or no. My next question is: will you marry me? Over."

"Yes, over"

"Well," Hiro thought, "That may be the shortest proposal and acceptance on record." Then he asked aloud, "Would you be willing to come to Hawaii to marry me? Over."

"Yes, over."

"Would you be willing to work as a nurse here in the Navy Hospital? Over."

"Yes, over."

"Has my family been interned?" Over.

"Yes, over."

"Are they OK? Over."

"No, over"

"OK, Kathleen, you can drop the yes-no stuff now and tell me about them. Over."

"They're in a place the Army calls Camp Harmony, down near Puyallup. I haven't been able to visit them yet but Avaron sent a letter saying they had to stay in a cattle barn, their beds were just straw mattresses, the food was bad, and they were unable to visit with friends in the same camp. In a few months there going to be moved to some remote location in Idaho. I'm worried about them. Over."

"A cattle barn? Did you say a cattle barn, Kathleen? Over."

"Yes, Hiro, that's what Avaron wrote, a cattle barn. Over."

"Mama and Papa in a cattle barn? Oh that's terrible! Over."

"Can you come back, Hiro. They will want to see you. They ask about you all the time. Over."

But Hiro never had a chance to respond. Instead the voice of the Chief of the Communications Watch came on the line, "Sorry, sir. Your 15 minutes have expired."

"But I wasn't on the line 15 minutes." Hiro retorted.

"No sir, but the 15 minutes includes the time we used to place and set up the call. Sorry, sir."

"It doesn't matter anyway," Hiro thought as he put the phone down. He had heard Kathleen confirm what he had feared! His fam-

CHAPTER 37

ily torn out of their home, imprisoned in an Army Camp and being held in a cattle barn! He had to do something!"

Hiro was quiet on the way back to the VOQ. Bill knew it was because Hiro was worried about his family, and he understood that. Even though he had no family himself, Bill envied those who did. His parents were long dead and he had no siblings, cousins, aunts or uncles. He remembered the previous December when he spent an evening trimming the Christmas tree with Captain High and his family. He had felt welcome and secure in their house, and hoped that someday he would ever have his own wife and children.

Although Bill sympathized with Hiro, that was not an emotion he could act on now. Now his clear duty was to make certain that Hiro's emotions did not overcome his judgment. Captain High had assigned Bill to be Hiro's "minder." He was to stay with him 24 hours a day and make sure he did nothing foolish–defined as anything that Washington would disapprove of. Bill was trying to think of ways to keep Hiro busy as they entered his BOQ room.

"You know, Hiro," Bill said as he sprawled on one of the two beds crammed into the small space, "We mentioned earlier that we need to get you some civvies. The exchange here is pretty small and probably won't have clothes to fit you. I think we'll have to go into town to do that."

"Town?" Hiro looked puzzled.

'Yes, Honolulu," Bill said, "They have a pretty good shopping area there and, since there's a lot of Japanese on the Island, I would guess they'll have clothes that fit you."

"You mean even with the war going on they would still have clothes for sale?"

"Sure," Bill answered.

"That sure wasn't the case in Japan. Everything was in short supply. And they blamed it all on the war."

"Well, we haven't got to that stage yet," Bill observed, "And before we do, we need to get you into Honolulu and get you outfit-

THE DOOLITTLE IRONY

ted. I'm going to go down stairs and call Captain High. I should tell him we're going ashore and I should also get some money from him."

"Money?" Hiro frowned, "I don't want to take money from the Captain. That would not be right."

"Don't worry, Hiro," Bill smiled, "He has what the Navy calls discretionary funds. And he's not giving you the money. You'll have to pay him back."

Hiro smiled, "Darn! I knew there'd be a catch."

◈ ◈ ◈

"You're gonna do what?" Captain High asked with amazement.

"Captain, Honolulu is the only place that will have clothes that fit Hiro. With so many men here on base now, the Navy Exchange has very little stock. They practically sell out the same day a new shipment arrives."

"What if he decides to just wander off and head for home?"

"With no money, no ID, no passport?" Bill asked rhetorically, "I don't think he'd get very far. And I don't think Hiro would deliberately shaft us. He's a decent kid and appreciates what we've done for him."

"Yeah," Captain High observed, "But he hasn't yet figured out that we are not doing this out of the goodness of our hearts. What will his attitude be when he does?"

"Yes, I agree Skipper," reverting to the term that Navy people use to address their commanding officers, "We need to give that some serious thought. Sooner or later he's going to come to realize just what political impact his story could have. We need to get out in front of that."

"Marvelous," the Captain said sarcastically, "I never would have thought of that. When you figure out just how we can do that, let me know."

"Uh, Yes Sir," Bill replied weakly.

"As for going into Honolulu, go ahead–but NEVER let that kid out of arms length and if you have to, get the Shore Patrol to restrain him."

CHAPTER 37

✧ ✧ ✧

The next day when Bill and Hiro exited the Main Gate at the Pearl Harbor Naval Base, Bill wondered about just how effective the Captain's message to the Master-at-Arms had really been. The Captain said he had ordered all the gate guards to watch for and detain a young Japanese man in an ensign's uniform trying to leave the Base. But Hiro, obviously Japanese in an ensign's uniform, had just walked between two Marine Guards and neither raised a suspicious eyebrow. "So much for our vaunted Base security," Bill thought, "I guess Captain High's reach isn't quite what I thought it was."

Bill and Hiro boarded the commuter train to Honolulu, a small steam locomotive that pulled 15 or so passenger cars. The rail line had been built initially to transport the many field hands that worked the pineapple and sugar plantations, and now it hauled civilians traveling between Honolulu and Pearl City, or sailors going into Honolulu for a night's liberty. The trip into the city was highlighted by a traditional stop at the Dole Pineapple Plantation Depot, where every passenger was offered a free glass of fresh pineapple juice. Even in the midst of war the Dole stop continued.

Hiro had been quiet during the train ride, but as they arrived at the Honolulu station he commented, "Hawaii is quite a beautiful place. I've never been this far south before. I love the palm trees and the all the flowers."

"Yes," Bill agreed, "And the weather is really nice too." The two had to walk several blocks to find an appropriate clothing store, so Bill elaborated on Hawaii. "But Hawaii is not the same place it was before the attack. Now there are no tourists. Instead there are armed soldiers on most every block–and they're authorized to use their weapons. The Island is under martial law, all civilians must carry an identification card issued by the Army, and there's a curfew: 7:00 PM to 7:00 AM."

"Oh my," Hiro allowed, "It doesn't sound like a real fun place."

"Oh, that's not all," Bill continued, "All of the hotels have been taken over by the military. Serving liquor is prohibited, there are air raid drills, and windows must be blacked out. I could go on, but you get the picture."

THE DOOLITTLE IRONY

"Yes, but what I don't get, Bill," Hiro said, "Is why all of these Japanese that we see on the streets are free when my family and the rest of the Japanese-American community back in Seattle have been thrown into Army prisons?"

"Damn good question," Bill conceded, "The situation doesn't make me proud to be a White American." He paused to gather his thoughts, and then continued, "You see, a lot of the Whites here on the Island did want to intern the Japanese—wanted to put them on another island or send them to the Mainland. But after thinking about it for awhile, they realized they could not do that. For one, the economy would collapse without the Japanese. For another, the sugar and coffee grown here is needed for the war. Third, there were not enough ships to transport the Japanese to be evacuated. They were being used to transport all the American military dependents out of harm's way back to the Mainland. I'm sorry to admit, Hiro," Bill added ruefully, "That nowhere among those reasons were concerns about the Japanese-American's civil or constitutional rights, even though over three quarters of the Japanese were citizens,"

"I don't get it, Bill" Hiro said evenly, "Why don't they intern you. The U.S. is at war with Italy. You're Italian. But no one wants to intern you."

Bill flinched a bit, "I wish I had a good answer for that one, Hiro, but I can't tell you anything on that score that you don't already know through personal experience."

By now Bill and Hiro had arrived in the retail section of the city and located a likely-looking men's clothing store. It turned out to be operated by a Japanese family who were quite curious about Hiro. Being careful not to confront him on the subject, they did obliquely inquire how it was that a Japanese man could be a commissioned officer in the American Navy. Japanese-Americans in Hawaii were not even allowed to volunteer for military service. In fact, the two Hawaiian Reserve Units that existed at the outbreak of war were being stripped of their Japanese members.

"I don't know why I've been made an officer in the Navy," Hiro admitted, "I guess I'm special somehow." He shrugged his shoulders and looked at Bill oddly. Bill quickly turned the conversation back

CHAPTER 37

to the clothing they were buying and handed Hiro some trousers to try on.

Some minutes later, having completed their purchases Bill and Hiro left the store and emerged into the bright Hawaiian sunlight. Bill squinted and looked across the street at a Japanese restaurant. "Hiro, I'm hungry. What say we try that restaurant over there?"

They entered the restaurant, which catered to Japanese locals and the occasional American. The two seated themselves in a booth against the wall and glanced over the menu. "Bill," Hiro looked across the table with guilt, "I have to confess, I've never eaten at a Japanese restaurant before! My family was poor and we never ate at <u>any</u> restaurants. If we had, it certainly would not have been a Japanese one. My mother would never tolerate her family having a basis for judging her own cooking."

He looked over the menu for a minute or two, then back at Bill, "I guess you're not familiar with Japanese dishes, so let me suggest that your Western palette would like the beef sukiyaki and maybe a Sapporo beer. I'll try some udon. That's like a noodle soup. Also I'll get the Tekkadon, which is a rice dish with tuna. And some green tea–whatever kind they serve here."

By then a waiter had found his way to their table. Hiro ordered in Japanese.

"Well, thanks for ordering for me, Hiro," Bill smiled, "But in fact I lived in Tokyo for two years and became familiar with Japanese cuisine. I have to admit I never became fond of it. In fact, I think I would have ended up eating that hamburger they put on the bottom of the menu for American tourists afraid to order anything Japanese." The two laughed at that.

Hiro started to get up from his seat and said, "Bill, please excuse me. I have to use the bathroom," He said and walked back to the door on which "Men" appeared in both English and Japanese. A moment later he emerged, glanced around the room, and made his way to a table where two Japanese men were seated. They seemed to know Hiro and spoke with him for a few minutes. Bill noted that when Hiro left they bowed rather than shook hands.

Hiro nodded toward them when he returned to the table. "Some people I used to know back home. Seems they came here before the attack and now can't get back."

THE DOOLITTLE IRONY

"Oh, really?" Bill said. "I guess that's because the military are sending all their dependents back Stateside. Probably that's taken up a lot of passenger space."

After Hiro had made himself comfortable at the table, Bill looked across at him and said casually, "Hiro, listen, I want to make a small confession. I brought you to Honolulu today so you could buy some clothes. That's true. But I had another reason also."

Hiro looked expectantly across the table but said nothing.

"I know you are worried about your family, rightfully so. And I know you are angry that they have been interned. I presume that it must affect your attitude toward the United States. After all, why should you be loyal to those who will not be loyal to you? Why support a government that imprisons your own family? All good questions—and I have no good answers. But I wanted you to see today that there are many others who, like your family, are being treated unjustly. The people here in Honolulu—Japanese, Korean, Philippine, Hawaiian, and American—are in that category. They are ruled under martial law and have no civil rights; they have to observe curfews; they have soldiers patrolling their neighborhoods. And for that matter, what about the soldiers themselves? A lot of them are draftees, yanked from their homes and families to fight a war they had no part in starting. What if they're killed? Who will take care of their wives and children?"

Bill paused briefly to engage Hiro's eyes directly, "I guess my point is that there are many victims of this war. All of us are, in one way or another. Your family is one sort of victim. The rest of us are other sorts. None of us asked for this war. It was started by ambitious men in Tokyo which in turn has spawned this terrible war hysteria here and in the Mainland. I ask that you be patient with your country while it suffers through that hysteria. It will regain its moral footing and the wrongs we see today will be righted."

Bill paused, looking for some sort of understanding on Hiro's face. "So that's it. I guess that's my little message for today."

Hiro remained quiet, reflecting on Bill's message. Just about then the food arrived and the two men realized they were hungry. Both dug in, abandoning the philosophical for the sensual. The beef sukiyaki was very good, Bill thought. He'd try to remember this

CHAPTER 37

restaurant the next time he came into Honolulu. Hiro was likewise pleased with his rice bowl, but stopped eating long enough to ask a question.

"Bill, why I am so special that I deserve this privileged treatment. I've been made a commissioned officer. You bought me a new uniform and civilian clothing. You've given me use of Navy communications to call my girlfriend, and you're arranging for her to come to Hawaii. What have I done to deserve all that?"

"Hell, that's not hard to answer," Bill said confidently, "First, you deserve it because you risked your ass sending a fake message to save our fleet, then you almost froze to death in the cold Pacific Ocean. Second, you've spent the last few months in the Imperial Japanese Navy, during which time you picked up knowledge of its code capabilities and its operating routines. There aren't many guys in the U.S. Navy that can say that! Don't you see, Hiro, you are what intelligence officers call an 'asset.' And if you've read any spy novels, you know that Intelligence officers treat assets quite well. We spend time and money to recruit them, and more time and money to keep them. That's what I'm doing–trying to retain a very valuable asset that has fallen into our hands by mere chance. "

Hiro thought about that and nodded tentatively, "OK, I guess that makes sense. I hope I prove smart enough to justify all that effort."

"I've got no worries about that!" Bill asserted, "Now let's finish up and get back to Base before curfew. I don't want to have to explain to some 19-year old carrying a lethal weapon why I haven't observed his blessed curfew!"

Approaching the Main Gate, Bill wondered how he would get Hiro back on base without an identification card. He went through the pedestrian gate first, showed the Marine sentry his own ID, and then pointed to Hiro behind him, "Ensign Yamada has not yet been issued an identification card," he said as though that was not an unusual matter.

"You're Lieutenant Russo," stated the guard, matching Bill's face against the picture on his ID card, "And that's Ensign Yamada, you say? Just a moment please, sir." The sentry walked the few steps back to his guard shack. His gait was noticeably stiff legged. He returned

THE DOOLITTLE IRONY

with a clipboard holding both Bill and Hiro's pictures and written instructions. "Go ahead, sir, you can both pass."

Bill thought to himself, "Wow. I underestimated the Captain's horsepower. He really did have the gate covered."

As he and Hiro walked away, Hiro looked over at Bill and asked with a puzzled look, "Why was that guy walking like a duck?"

Bill laughed and said, "He's a Marine. Marines take special pride in their uniforms, particularly when they are on duty at the Main Gate. He was 'walking like a duck,' as you put it, so as not to break the crease on his freshly starched khaki trousers."

"Really?" Hiro responded, suspecting that perhaps Bill was pulling his leg.

"Really!" Bill confirmed, "You know, as a Naval Officer you'll be working with Marines a lot. Let this be your introduction to the Corps. Marines are weird—but also first rate! You'll learn to like them!

Bill deposited Hiro back at the BOQ, then made up an excuse to leave, cautioning Hiro not to leave the room. Then he walked over to the VOQ and knocked on Captain High's door. "Evenin' Skipper," he said as the Captain opened the door, "Just wanted to report on our trip to Honolulu."

"OK" the Captain replied, "Did you get him some socks and jocks?"

"Well, actually my reasons for taking him into town were a little more devious. I wanted him to see that even here in Honolulu the Japanese—as well as all civilians—were no longer leading normal lives. You know—martial law, curfews, armed guards, that sort of thing. I gave him a pitch that we all were victims of war hysteria, just like his family."

"Did it work?"

"I think so, at least partly."

"Has he figured out why he's so important?"

"Not completely," Bill opined, "But he did ask me why he was getting so much special treatment. I told him it was because he was such a valuable intelligence asset."

"That wasn't a complete lie, Bill," the Captain observed.

"No," Bill conceded, "But it wasn't the whole truth either."

CHAPTER 37

"Don't go soft on me, Bill. We're playing in the big leagues now. If we blow this somehow, we're looking at duty in Alaska for the duration."

"Yes, sir," Bill grinned wryly, "Roger, wilco. I understand and will comply."

The Captain registered Bill's reluctance. It was evident that Bill and Hiro were becoming friends. Not good. That could lead to complications.

"I better say good night, sir," Bill said, "I don't want him to be alone too long. He might wander off."

The next morning Bill visited the Intelligence Section in the Administration Building to make arrangements for Hiro's desk and security clearance.

Lieutenant Commander Wright, the Intel Section Administrator was perplexed. "Sure, a desk is no problem, but a security clearance? Hell, he hasn't even had a background check."

"Oh yes he has. A good one. Conducted by the CNO himself! Do you want me to tell him that you don't trust his work?"

"Yeah, I heard all about that from the N-2, but my neck is on the line if I do this without the usual paperwork."

"And your neck is on the line if you don't!" Bill observed dryly, "So what is it? Does he get the clearance or do I call Captain High and ask him to call the N-2."

The Officer sighed, "OK, I'll start the paperwork, but it might take a week or so. Until then he can handle only unclassified material, and he'll have to remain in the outer office with the typists."

Bill walked back to the VOQ thinking how good it was to be able to bandy about the CNO's name. When he entered the lobby he was surprised to see Hiro sitting over by the radio.

"Bill! Did you know about this?" Hiro asked excitedly, "They call it the Doolittle Raid, although one Navy guy said they should call it the Doolittle-Halsey Raid. It's all about the carriers we saw. Did you know they bombed Tokyo? Boy, I'll bet Captain Ogama is mad! I wonder if he knew anything about this."

THE DOOLITTLE IRONY

"I haven't heard the news recently," Bill lied.

"Jimmy Doolittle. That's the guy's name who led the bombers. They said he just yesterday arrived in Chungking. Is that in China, Bill? I wonder why he was in China. And get this. He was a Lieutenant Colonel and they made him a general. Wow. They're even talking about what kind of a medal they should give him."

"Some guys get all the luck," Bill commented, hoping that would end the matter. It didn't.

"Tomorrow let's get a newspaper, Bill, "Hiro enthused, "Might be more details in there. Wow! Just think, Bill, I actually saw those carriers. And one of the ships with them sunk my ship. That's amazing!"

CHAPTER 38

IN THE U.S. NAVY

5 May 1942.

The following morning Hiro went to his first day of work as a U.S. Navy ensign. He was excited about it, and more that a bit apprehensive.

"Bill, do you think I will be considered a spy? I mean because I'm Japanese?"

"No, Hiro, but I think you'll be something of a curiosity. You'll get a lot of questions. None of the officers will have read my report of what you told me during your debriefing. We've put that on a very restricted dissemination list. But they will have read a sanitized version -- which makes no mention of the contact report that you changed. We want to keep that quiet."

"Why?" Hiro asked.

"Because we don't want it to get out that we have a person knowledgeable of Japanese code activity. If Tokyo heard that they would change all their codes. So please don't talk to anyone about it, even if they ask."

"I see," Hiro said, thinking that this new world he was entering called "Intelligence" was more complicated than he had thought.

THE DOOLITTLE IRONY

The desk assigned to Hiro was small, metal, and appeared to have been squeezed into a space previously occupied by filing cabinets. As Bill had predicted, he was something of a curiosity to the rest of the staff. He had not been seated more than two minutes before a middle-aged lady walked over.

"Hello sir, I'm Mrs. Farabaugh. I'm the office manager here, you know, run the typist pool and such."

"Hello, Mrs. Farabaugh, my name is Hiro, and you don't have to call me sir."

"Oh, but I do have to call you sir," Mrs. Farabaugh corrected, "This is the Navy and you're a commissioned officer and I'm a staff employee. That means I have to call you sir."

"Oh, well if that's the custom, I guess we'd better do it. But Hiro is my given name. Yamada is my surname. So I guess Ensign Yamada is the correct address. But I mostly answer to Hiro."

"Well thank you. That's quite friendly of you, but I'd better call you Ensign Yamada, and I'll tell the other girls to do the same."

"Thank you, but I'm not used to such deference so if I don't look up right away when you call me Ensign Yamada, just yell, 'Hey, Hiro!'"

Mrs. Farabaugh smiled broadly and thought to herself that she would like this young man.

Just then another young ensign appeared beside Mrs. Farabaugh.

"Hi, I'm Justin Myers. Welcome aboard, Hiro."

Hiro looked at Mrs. Farabaugh quizzically. Understanding his look she said, "It's OK that he calls you Hiro because he's an officer too."

"I think I understand," Hiro smiled, and then to Ensign Myers responded, "Glad to meet you Justin. Thanks for stopping by to say hello."

"Who're you having lunch with, Hiro? There's a few of us who want to ask a bunch of questions. Thought maybe we could do it all at once rather than drag it out."

"Great. I'd like to meet everyone," Hiro replied.

"Good. 1200," Justin said, pronouncing it "twelve hundred."

The morning passed quickly. Many people stopped by to meet him. Most were pleasantly surprised to find an American in Japanese

CHAPTER 38

guise. A few asked questions about the Imperial Japanese Navy. Was he really in it? There were a few questions about intelligence: did the Japs really put coded messages in their fleet weather broadcasts? (Yes, they did but Hiro knew only a few of the codes.)

When Justin came by at 1200 he had four other junior officers (ensigns and lieutenants junior grade) with him. They did not go to the Officer's Mess for lunch. Instead they went to the 'Gedunk,' (Sounds like 'G' as in geese with a 'dunk' on the end). Hiro had no idea what the name meant but was pleased to see that the place looked a lot like Grimm's Drug Store. They crowded into a booth and Hiro ordered a hamburger and milkshake.

The questions began: *"How do we pronounce your name?"* Actually it was very close to the English pronunciation of 'hero' but Hiro knew they would never get it quite right. "Just call me Harry. That's what everybody called me in college."

"College? What college?"

"University of Washington. I was an engineering major."

And so it went. Many personal questions, especially about his family who Hiro explained was imprisoned in an Army camp. *"Why are they in a prison camp? None of the Japs here are? Crap, that's kinda rotten."*

When it was over, there wasn't much his new colleagues didn't know about 'Harry.' But, in keeping with Bill's request, he had not shared with them any information about the contact report.

He later asked Bill why he was not supposed to talk about that. "Because they don't have a 'need to know,'" Bill replied, hoping Hiro would not probe further.

"But I told them everything else, including that I was a radio operator. And they do have clearances."

"But not the right clearances, Hiro! It's like I said earlier, we don't want any more people than is absolutely necessary to know you have any information about Japanese codes."

"Uh oh, I already talked to one guy about messages being encoded in weather reports."

"Well don't do that again," Bill admonished, "Just tell them you handled only plain text material. The Japanese Navy didn't trust you with coded messages."

THE DOOLITTLE IRONY

"OK. I'll try to be careful," Hiro agreed, though his puzzled look remained.

◆ ◆ ◆

Later that evening Bill visited Captain High in the VOQ. "Skipper, it's just a matter of time. His questions keep getting closer to the truth. More information about the Raid is becoming public every day. I think he's just one good newspaper item away from figuring out that his changes to the contact report saved our asses–and made Jimmy Doolittle a hero."

"Yeah, I agree," the Captain said, "But the real question is will he try to tell others about that. Maybe Hiro will want to be a hero–and get a medal just like Doolittle."

"I don't see him doing that, Skipper," Bill said, "The kid's a patriot. Despite everything, he's still red, white, and blue. I don't think he'd intentionally do harm to the United States."

"Well, Bill," the Captain observed, "If you're right, we don't have long to wait to find what he'll do."

◆ ◆ ◆

6 May 1942

A tall, thin officer who looked like he had worked all night was waiting at Hiro's desk when he arrived. "Good morning." He said, "I'm Joe Rochefort from the COMINT Station. We call it Wypo." Hiro would later learn that Joe Rochefort was actually the Commander of Wypo and that he actually had worked all night, just as his rumpled uniform suggested.

Hiro noticed he was wearing the insignia of a Commander, a rank well above Hiro's in the naval pecking order. Best to call him sir! "Good morning, sir. How can I help you?"

"Harry–may I call you Harry?"

CHAPTER 38

"Yes, sir." Hiro responded tersely. He had learned that the Navy prefers communication to be brief and to the point. "But may I ask what COMINT is?"

"Well, let's not get into that until you have proper clearances. For right now, let me ask you a question based on your experience in the Japanese Navy. Why do you think a radio operator would request additional aircraft radio equipment for, let's say, something he calls the 'AK campaign?'"

Hiro thought for a moment and then replied, "I learned in radio school at Yokosuka that the Japanese Navy uses digraphs—two letters—as abbreviations for some of their major operations. So I would guess that AK is a major operation." Hiro paused a bit and then went on, "You said that he needs 'additional' equipment, so I'd guess he's not talking about replacement or repair parts. He means an additional number of radio sets. He also says 'aircraft' radios, but I doubt he's talking about radios that go into aircraft. Radio operators would not be involved with that. No, I think he's talking about additional sets of ground-based radios that are used to communicate with aircraft." Hiro paused, and then concluded, "So, I think this is a radio operator at an aircraft base somewhere that's going to be involved in a major operation that involves more aircraft than that base has handled previously."

Commander Rochefort nodded appreciatively. "OK, now let me extend the question. How would you figure out where that major operation is?"

"Oh, my," Hiro said with a frown, "I take it from your question about 'AK' that you're listening to his radio nets because that's the only place a digraph would be used. I think I'd try to narrow the possibilities to a few of the most likely places, and then focus on their communications. Maybe someone will talk about 'AK' in a different context and you'll be able to cross the two and figure out what 'AK' is all about." Hiro paused and then added, "It sounds like a very interesting problem."

Commander Rochefort smiled, admiring Hiro's analysis, "Yes, it is rather interesting. I appreciate the insights, Harry. I look forward to the time when they move you behind the green door. We can use you back there."

"Sure, sir. I look forward to getting back there too."

When Hiro later learned that Rochefort was the commander of Wypo, he realized that his visit was intended to get a reading on Hiro–to find out more about this young ensign that had been assigned to Wypo by some mysterious order from Washington. Hiro wondered if his performance had met Rochefort's expectations.

"Oh, one other thing, Harry, the guys told me about your family being interned and I just want to say that I think that's really rotten. Makes me wonder who the hell's in charge back there!"

"Thanks, sir. I wonder the same thing sometimes."

The Commander left to return to the basement where all of the information that Hiro was not yet cleared for was kept.

During the morning other officers drifted by to introduce themselves and ask a question or two about details of the IJN. Word had apparently got around that Hiro was a person who could help.

The other officers were appreciative and several more junior officers joined the original Gedunk luncheon group. By the end of the week it had swelled to about ten, so they had to pull a couple of tables together to eat. "Harry" seemed to fit right in.

✧ ✧ ✧

12 May 1942

More than a week had passed since Hiro began work. He had been busy. The office worked seven days a week, and several officers seemed to work 16 to 20 hours a day. Hiro's duties were not that demanding. He mostly just transcribed recordings of Japanese civilian radio broadcasts and answer random questions that the officers behind the green door in the basement might pose. He enjoyed doing that.

"Hiro," Bill commented at breakfast that morning, "I hear good things about you. You provided a few ideas that helped with JN-25."

"JN-25? What's that?"

"Oh, it's a code their Navy uses. You'll learn all about it soon."

"I'm glad I was helpful. Everyone has been very nice to me. It's quite a different atmosphere than the Japanese Navy. There most

CHAPTER 38

everybody seemed afraid. There was no joking and good humor like here."

"Good! And to top that I have something else that I think you'll like. This came into the VOQ. The man at the desk gave it to me just as we were leaving for breakfast." He reached inside his shirt and pulled out a small envelope edged in oblique red-white-and-blue stripes.

"Is it official? Is this my clearance?" Hiro asked looking puzzled.

"Well, let's see," Bill teased holding it up, "I note the return address is a place called Crawford, Washington," he said smiling like a Cheshire cat.

Oh, my gosh!" Hiro exclaimed as he reached across the table and snatched the letter from Bill's hand, "It's from Kathleen."

Hiro used a table knife to open the envelope and then carefully removed the letter, noting that it was written in Kathleen's graceful, feminine script. "Excuse me, Bill, but I've got to read this right now."

Dear Hiro,

The man at the post office said I can only write one page because this is going to a Fleet Postal Address, so I must write small.

I wish you could have been there when Stanley and I told your family that you are still alive and in Hawaii. I don't think I've ever seen your mother excited before but this time both she and your father jumped up and down. And Avaron and Natsuko went wild. They ran up and down the hallway shouting, 'He's alive! Hiro is alive!' The whole building seemed to know who you were and they all rushed over to hug Mama and Papa. Can you imagine? Japanese Issei hugging one another? After the hubbub settled down, I told your Mother that I would be going to Hawaii to join you. She immediately asked if she and the family could go too. I told her I didn't know but would ask you.

THE DOOLITTLE IRONY

You asked about their living conditions. I don't want to worry you, but I have to say they are not good. Camp Harmony is really just a prison. It's surrounded by barbed wire and armed guards. Your family has a very small space to live in. Their beds are just straw mattresses. They have to share toilet facilities and eat at long tables with lots of other people. But, you know, your family is very strong. And it looks to me like this experience has actually pulled them together even more. You would be so proud of Avaron and Natsuko!

I'm running out of space. So just let me add that my Mom and Dad are proud that I'm going to Hawaii as a nurse. Oh, I should also tell you, I got a call from a Navy recruiter. He asked if I would be interested in joining the Navy. They would make me an ensign, just like you. Did you arrange that?

I love you, Hiro, and I so want to be your wife. Let me know as soon as you can about the arrangements. Stanley says hello!

With all my love,

Kathleen.

When Hiro lowered the letter, Bill noticed a tear streaming down his face. "Not bad news, I hope," Bill said quietly.

Hiro tried to answer but was choked up and had to wait to gather himself. "Both good and bad news, Bill," Hiro replied, "If you don't mind, I'll just walk ahead to the office. You finish your breakfast. I've got to think a bit."

At his desk Hiro re-read the letter–twice. What could he do to help his family? There was no appealing their internment. The President of the United States himself had authorized it. Hiro had heard on the news it was called Executive Order 9066. It directed the Army to designate an "Exclusion Zone" and remove all Japanese

CHAPTER 38

from it. Well, it didn't really specify "Japanese" but everybody knew that's what it meant. Anyway, the Army designated the whole West Coast as an Exclusion zone and ordered all Japanese to be moved inland. No exceptions. Helping his family seemed impossible.

He decided to discuss it with the lunch group. They were smart. Maybe one of them would have an idea.

◆ ◆ ◆

After they had eaten their usual orders of hamburger and pie, Hiro asked for the group's attention and outlined his problem to them. They listened carefully and a few made disparaging comments about Washington and the Army, but then a Lieutenant asked how far inland did the Exclusion Area extend.

"It's basically Washington, Oregon, California, and a chunk of Arizona." Hiro replied.

"So, if you moved your parents further east than that, they'd be in compliance with the Executive Order. They would not be in the exclusion zone."

"Yes," Hiro replied slowly, "I think that's right. But how do I do that? I'm out here and can't go back or the Army will put me into Camp Harmony also."

Just then the "Noon News" came on the radio and Hiro's discussion ended so the officers could listen. It began with the usual depressing stuff: the Japanese Army continued to advance in Burma and a German submarine sank an American tanker near the mouth of the Mississippi. But then it switched to news of General Jimmy Doolittle's successful bombing of Japan.

In a deep, authoritative voice, the radio announcer intoned, "We've learned that America's hero, Jimmy Doolittle, will be receiving even more recognition for having led the daring raid on Tokyo. Already promoted two grades from Lieutenant Colonel to Brigadier General, Jimmy Doolittle is apparently going to receive the Medal of Honor, our nation's highest award. He is expected to return to Washington, D.C. soon and the President will personally drape the medal around his neck next week. A large public event is planned to celebrate Doolittle's heroic deed."

THE DOOLITTLE IRONY

"Hey, Harry, you should get a medal too. You were there," one ensign called facetiously to Hiro.

"Yeah, but Harry was no hero," another said, "He just waved as Doolittle flew by."

"Well, I did a little more than that," Hiro said defensively. Then he remembered his promise not to tell anyone of having altered the contact report, "I waved and then got blown out of the water by the *Nashville*."

They all laughed and thought Harry was a good sport. But that afternoon at his desk Hiro wondered about the matter. Why wasn't he allowed to speak of his action? If you thought about it, what he did might have been very important. Maybe it even contributed a bit to Doolittle's success, although Hiro was not quite sure how that would be. He decided to talk to Bill about it that evening.

After dinner back in their BOQ room, Hiro decided now that Bill's stomach was full and he was relaxing in the one cushioned chair in their spartan room, now might be a good time to raise the subject. "Bill," Hiro began, "I heard on the noon news today that General Doolittle will probably receive the Medal of Honor."

"I'm not surprised," Bill replied, "That was a hell of a gutsy thing he did. And it also proved to be a real morale boost for America. In fact, it probably saved the jobs of some of the muckety-mucks back in Washington, so now they're all lining up to get their pictures taken with him. I guess politics don't stop just because a war starts."

"So they want him to be a hero?"

"Sure. Wars need heroes. They're like a flag. People rally behind them," Bill philosophized.

"What about Doolittle's crewmen, and the crews in the other planes? Will they get medals?" Hiro asked.

"Probably–and they'll probably also get promoted," Bill answered.

Then came the question all of this had been leading up to, "Will I ever get a medal, Bill?"

CHAPTER 38

Bill had been expecting the question, or one like it. It meant that Hiro had come to understand that his alteration of the contact report was not just a random act in the Doolittle story. It had contributed to the success of Doolittle's mission and consequently was worthy of recognition. It probably also meant the Hiro was wondering why his contribution was being covered up. Why had Captain High and Bill made him agree not to tell others of the altered contact report?

Hiro had expected such a question and had rehearsed an answer, "Well, it's not in the works right now, Hiro. You're an intelligence officer in the U.S. Navy now, just like me. We don't get medals because medals bring attention and we don't want that. We 'court anonymity.' That's the phrase our instructors use in basic intelligence training. The business of intelligence is conducted in shadows, and that's where we must live."

Bill realized his answer was a bit melodramatic and wondered whether Hiro would buy it. He didn't.

"Gosh, Bill," Hiro said, "I can understand the need for secrecy in communications intelligence, like what we do here. If the enemy learns that you've broken his code he just changes it and you can no longer read his mail. But I didn't have access to codes. All I had was a "one-time pad" which is not a code at all."

"I can also understand the need for secrecy in dealing with human spies. If the enemy learns who they are, they shoot them and you've lost your source." Hiro paused, "But I was no spy. So if my actions became public it would not compromise a spy network. I was just some guy who happened to be in the right place at the right time, and did what he thought was his patriotic duty."

"I had lunch today with the usual group over at the Gedunk. The radio announced that General Doolittle will be given the Medal of Honor and the other guys asked if I had done anything heroic there. I remembered your warning not to say anything about the contact report, so I just said, 'Yeah, I got blown out of the water by the *Nashville*.' They all laughed, but it made me wonder why you don't want me to tell them. I mean, after all, they're intelligence officers too."

THE DOOLITTLE IRONY

"I hope you weren't too embarrassed, Hiro," Bill replied, realizing that some additional explanation was necessary. "OK, let's talk about this. Remember what I told you before? Your friends may have clearances but they don't have a 'need to know.' Please understand, Hiro, your story about altering the contact report is very sensitive. Right now in Tokyo the IJN senior officers are worried about a repeat attack. They're bringing units from the South Pacific back to Honshu to help defend against that prospect. That reduces their offensive capabilities significantly. If they learned that the success of our bombing raid rested on a simple fluke–a contact report altered by an American Nisei who just happened to be in the right place at the right time–they would stop reinforcing their homeland defense. So we can't let them know that."

Bill was pleased with himself. He had rationalized a cynical directive from Washington and made it sound reasonable. He wondered if any of the people who were responsible for issuing that directive had ever thought about the situation in those terms, or whether they were just trying to cover their butts.

"Bill, you have a way of explaining things!" Hiro conceded, "When you put it like that, it makes sense. I will keep my silence. But I do have a few other questions on another subject," Hiro hastened to add, "Did Captain High arrange to have a Navy recruiter call Kathy? She said in the letter I received this morning that one had offered her a commission as a nurse. Is that the way he plans to have her sent here?"

"I don't know," Bill answered, "But I'll ask him."

"And another question," Hiro added, "This one has to do with the terms of the internment. I heard from one of the guys at lunch that the Army is authorized only to remove the Japanese from the 'Exclusion Zone,' which covers only the Western half of California, Oregon, and Washington. What if I could get my family to some other part of the country? Would they be released?"

"That's an interesting idea," Bill responded, "I don't know the answer, but I'll try to find out."

The next day Bill reported back to Hiro the answer about the phone call from the Navy Recruiter. "Yes, Captain High is trying to determine how best to get Kathleen here, as a civilian nurse or as a

CHAPTER 38

Navy nurse? When you write to her, ask her what she prefers, but tell her also that she may not have a choice."

The answer about whether Hiro's parents would be allowed to leave the Exclusion Zone to go elsewhere was not so easy. "It started off one way, Hiro," Bill explained, "But then the Army reversed itself and went another way. I'm really not sure what the current situation is, but Captain High is going to try to clarify it. I'll keep you posted."

✣ ✣ ✣

14 May 1942

The next day Hiro's clearance authorizations arrived. They had not come through normal channels. They were signed by some Commander back in Washington and sent directly to CINCPAC–Commander in Chief Pacific. "You know, Harry," one of the junior officers observed, "You must have friends in high places. I don't know anyone else that gets personal attention from Washington."

The area behind the "green door," i.e. in the dark, dank basement of the CINCPAC Headquarters building, was not what he expected. He had thought there would be radio receivers and exotic electronic equipment. Instead he found disorderly metal desks piled high with paper, crammed together against filing cabinets with combination locks, typewriters, and a few IBM card readers; but, mostly, there were stacks and stacks of printer paper containing raw intercepted IJN message traffic. Enlisted men, junior officers and a few civilians populated the desks, all studiously examining the papers in front of them. A few seemed to be making notes in the margins.

Hiro had already met most of them, and they greeted him with the kind of locker room remarks typical of masculine settings: "Geez, Harry! They let you back here? There goes the goddam war." Harry loved it. These were his kind of people. They reminded him of the men he had worked briefly with at Scott Engineering.

The tour and introductions ended and Hiro and Lieutenant Godek, his new boss, found a quiet corner to talk over the inevitable cup of Navy coffee. "Harry, we've got various types of specialists here at Wypo: cryptanalysts who try to decipher the Japanese radio communications we intercept; linguists who translate whatever they manage to decipher into English; traffic analysts who look for patterns in Japanese Naval communications that might suggest what the IJN is up to; and finally, general analysts that try to put all the various pieces together to produce intelligence that will be useful to our command element."

He paused to give Hiro a chance to digest that. "Let me tell you a little more about each: Cryptanalysis is extremely specialized. It calls for training and a special mindset that few people have; translation calls for knowledge the Japanese language and IJN jargon; traffic analysis is like reading the outsides of mail envelopes without ever opening them; and general analysis calls for people with a broad knowledge of the IJN and Japan. They're the ones that put all the pieces together," the lieutenant smiled, "That's where I think you can make a real contribution."

Again he paused trying not to overwhelm Hiro with too much information, "The IJN currently uses an encryption system we call JN-25. It has over 50,000 code groups. We can read only about 5,000 of those, so our translations of intercepts are fragmentary. That's what I want you to help with. Take these fragments and try to fit them together into something meaningful."

"A bit like putting together a jigsaw puzzle?" Hiro asked.

"Basically, but you never have all the pieces! You have to make an educated guess about what's missing. That's tough sometimes."

"Oh, and one other thing, you needn't call me 'sir.' I'm Lenny. 'Sirs' are for the other side of the door. Back here behind the green door we like to be able to talk among ourselves freely, without worrying about the niceties of rank–or for that matter other niceties as well, such as uniforms. Our own Commanding Officer, Joe Rochefort, can be seen on occasion wearing a purple bathrobe. It's not really a fashion statement on Joe's part. It's just that he works around the clock and sleeps on the floor beside his desk."

"Really, sir? I mean Lenny," Bill stumbled.

Lenny smiled briefly at Hiro's reply, and then continued, "Now let me tell you about the main problem we're facing right now."

CHAPTER 38

Bill sat upright and tilted his head slightly as one does when trying to pay close attention.

"You were on a picket boat, Harry. You were there because Admiral Yamamoto was sure that the United States would retaliate for Pearl Harbor. He figured we'd come right back at them with our own carriers, and he was right. Well, now the tables have turned again. We've hit their capital city and humiliated the IJN. So a lot of people think the Japs will come right back at us. We just don't know how. That's what I want you to be especially alert for: how are the Japs going to strike back? All these papers you see littering everybody's desk are raw intercepts of Japanese Naval communications. Our job is to pick through them, find the few words we know, fit them into that jigsaw puzzle you talked of, and estimate what Tokyo is up to. We have been working day and night to do that. If we succeed, then maybe our guys can cut them off at the proverbial pass and kick their butts."

"I can see that," Hiro said appreciatively, "Advance warning provides a real tactical advantage. That's what the Japanese instructors said also. In fact, that's what they said our purpose on the picket ships was to give warning of U.S. Navy attack. But it didn't work." Then, choosing his words carefully Hiro asked, "Why do you think it failed, Tom? What went gone wrong for the Japs?"

Lenny touched his hand to his head in a pensive gesture, "I've wondered the same thing. We know that one of the pickets did send a contact report. That provided plenty of warning. So why weren't the Japs waiting to slice up both Doolittle and Halsey? Some say it was because we used Army bombers instead of Navy aircraft. That gave us the capability to launch earlier than the Japs expected. But surely the Picket Boat would have noted that there were bombers on the deck of the Hornet. They would have stood out like a sore thumb to any Navy person. And with that information the Japs should have figured out we could launch earlier, from farther out. But the picket boat's report didn't mention bombers—at least not the report that we intercepted. Maybe that means they're dumb—which I doubt—or maybe it means they never received information about the bombers."

"How could that have happened?" Hiro asked.

"Well, it wasn't anything we did," Lenny replied, "I've read the after-action reports and we did not jam the picket boat's transmis-

THE DOOLITTLE IRONY

sion. And it probably wasn't the fault of the Japanese Headquarters because we intercepted their request for an amplifying report. If the original report had been garbled they would have asked for a re-transmission of the original message, not an amplifying report."

"So what other explanation could there be?" Hiro asked innocently.

"If the problem didn't arise at Japanese Headquarters, and was not caused by us jamming the message, there's only one other answer. Something must have happened aboard the picket ship. It transmitted part of the contact report, but not all of it–not the part about the bombers being on the flight deck. Maybe it got sunk before it could transmit the whole message."

"Yes, I guess that might have happened," Hiro allowed.

"I'm only guessing," Lenny said, "Transmission error? Operator error? Whatever the cause, we should be grateful for it. If it hadn't happened, Halsey and Doolittle would almost certainly be at the bottom of the Pacific."

"Really? You think one little omission was that important? Kind of like that, 'For want of a nail' thing? Wow," Hiro said, "Thanks, Lenny."

That evening Bill made another of his nightly visits to see Captain High. This time he bore genuinely important news. "Skipper," Bill said as he settled into one of the two cushioned chairs in the Captain's room. (Senior officers got two chairs.) "I think our cat is out of the bag–or at least has one paw poking through a hole."

"Uh, oh. Doesn't sound good," the Captain said with mild concern, "What's happening?"

"Lenny Godek, down at Wypo, phoned me this afternoon. He's Hiro's new boss and he wanted to ask a few questions. He explained that he and Harry–everybody calls Hiro Harry–had discussed the Doolittle Raid, particularly the part about how the Japs seemed to be caught flatfooted. Hiro wanted to know what Lenny Godek figured was the cause. They kicked it around for a while and Lenny ended up speculating it was because the picket boat's contact report never men-

CHAPTER 38

tioned the bombers sitting on the *Hornet's* flight deck. After Hiro left, Lenny started putting two and two together. That's when he called me."

"Yeah, they call that analysis," Captain High said dryly, "It's the sort of thing he gets paid to do."

"Well, in this case he did it well. He said that based on Hiro's questions and the interrogation report that I prepared, it must have been Hiro that sent the contact report from the picket ship."

"Hmmf," The Captain grunted, and then asked sarcastically, "Did he have any other flashes of brilliance?"

"Actually, yes," Bill allowed, "He noted that you and I seem to be pretty close with Hiro and that ensigns don't usually get that sort of attention. He also noted that Hiro's clearances were authorized by some highly placed element in Washington–also very unusual. He concluded that Hiro was being given special treatment and he was able to think of only one reason for that–we were trying to cover up Hiro's real involvement in the incident."

Bill paused a moment to let that sink in, then continued, "He figured there was only one reason we would do that–because Hiro had been a U.S. spy in the Japanese Navy. Through sheer luck he was on the picket boat that discovered Halsey. When it sent a contact report, he secretly deleted important information from it."

"Not bad!" Captain High said admiring Lenny's chain of deduction, "In fact, it was great right up to the point that he fumbled on the five-yard line. What did you tell him?"

"I played dumb," Bill replied, "But I know he interpreted that to mean he was right, that Hiro had been a spy in Japan and we were now fitting him back into the Navy."

"Let him think that," the Captain instructed, "I suppose in a way it's a compliment to Lenny that he wasn't cynical enough to have come up with the right answer."

CHAPTER 39

DAWNING REALITY

When Bill returned to his crowded BOQ room after leaving the office that evening, he found Hiro waiting for him, ready to go to dinner. "I'm pretty hungry," Hiro announced, "I was just about to abandon you for the rice I hear is on the menu tonight."

"Rice? Don't get your hopes up Hiro. This is Navy rice, not your Mom's."

As they walked through the pleasant late afternoon sun, Hiro reminisced. "I miss my mother's rice. I miss my home too–although if you can't be home Hawaii is probably the next best place to be. The weather is warm, the breeze is pleasant and the oleander is fragrant."

Right," Bill agreed, "And May is one of the best months of the year. It seems a long way from the war right now."

The rice dish turned out to be red beans and rice–not exactly a Japanese staple. After sampling it, Hiro allowed, "You're right Bill, this is not my Mom's rice. But it's not bad."

Then, sensing that Bill was in a mellow mood, Hiro began the discussion he had planned for this evening. He feared it would become contentious, so he chose to approach it gingerly. "I had an interesting first day behind the door, he said, I think I'm really going to like it: nice people to work with; a challenging job; and a very important mission."

CHAPTER 39

"Good," Bill allowed, waiting for what he suspected Hiro really wanted to talk about.

"I had a really interesting discussion with Lieutenant Godek, my new boss. He seems to be a very bright fellow."

"Yes, I agree," Bill nodded, "Very bright guy."

"We talked about the Doolittle Raid and I asked why it had succeeded so well, especially since one of the picket ships had sent a warning of its approach."

"What did Bob say?" Bill asked aloud while silently thinking, "Uh,oh. Here it comes."

"Of course, he was not sure but he thought it was because the Japanese Navy never knew that Halsey was carrying longer range bombers. So they waited another day for the Americans to get closer. If they had known of those bombers, they would have realized the Americans were already in launch range, and gone to full alert. He thinks that single omission saved the Task Force from being sunk."

"He might be right," Bill conceded.

"Bill, not to seem unduly immodest, but I am the one who deleted the part about the bombers from the contact report."

"I realize that, Hiro, and so does Captain High and many people back in Washington, D.C. It's the reason you've been rewarded with a commission in the Navy and why we are arranging to bring Kathy here to Oahu. We are truly grateful."

"Then why are you keeping it a secret? Why can't I tell people about it? Oh, I know: 'need to know' and all that stuff. I'll admit that argument has some merit, but consider the alternative. If we tell people that a Nisei played an important role in Doolittle's raid, don't you think that it would soften America's attitude toward Japanese-Americans? I don't want to be a hero, Bill, and I don't really care about a medal. But I do love my family and this could lighten their burden. If Americans knew that a Nisei had contributed to Doolittle's bombing of Tokyo, don't you think they'd drop all those stupid suspicions about us helping Japan invade America? This whole internment thing could be turned around. And the people who instigated it would be shown to be just knee-jerk racists?"

THE DOOLITTLE IRONY

There was a long pause while Bill digested Hiro's message. It was an angle he had not thought of before. He had seen this little cover up as strictly a measure to protect the butts of some biggies back in Washington. Being a part of it was unsavory but, given the circumstances, somehow acceptable. "It's the way of the world" he had told himself. In the terms of his Catholic upbringing, it was a venial, not a mortal sin. Now Hiro had cast it in a different light and Bill would have to regard his part in this charade as possibly contributing to the continued imprisonment of over 100,000 people. Maybe now it had become a mortal sin! This was something he had to talk to Captain High about.

"Yeah," Bill said, nodding his head slowly, "I see your point. I'll talk to the Captain about this and let you know."

"Thanks, Bill. Oh, and please stress to the Captain that this is something I feel very strongly about."

"Sure. See you back at the 'Q.'" Bill thought he heard an ominous note in Hiro's last sentence, but chose not to inquire into it.

Bill went directly to the VOQ and found Captain High in his room. After a brief recap of his dinner conversation with Hiro, Bill said, "So that's it, Skipper. Hiro has figured out that played a decisive role in the Doolittle Raid. He thinks we should make it public because that would soften attitudes toward the Japanese-Americans and possibly help free his family as well as other Japanese-Americans."

The Captain had been sitting with a scotch in his hand listening politely until Bill finished. Then his calm exterior darkened. "Well I'll be damned!" he exploded, "So Hiro has taken the moral high ground on us! A few weeks ago he was just a homesick young pup we had dragged out of the Pacific. Now he's a goddam social reformer who wants to change the course of national policy. This kid is delusional."

The Captain was working himself up into a real rant, "Just think what would happen if we released this story. The only people who would believe it are already interned. The public would pooh-pooh it. The press might not even print it because there is no proof.

CHAPTER 39

Politicians would deny it. And as for ending the Japanese internment, forget it! America is in no mood to turn squishy on Japs. We could probably announce that Japanese immigrants had taken Jesus off the cross and the American public would still want them locked up."

"And think about the Navy," the Captain went on. "Our much-ballyhooed raid on Tokyo would look more like a stroke of luck than a feat of arms! Hell, we're supposed to be fighting Japs, not conducting a social crusade."

Bill was surprised at the Captain's wrath. Most Navy officers learn how to raise their voice and throw a judicious tantrum. It was a tool they used occasionally when subordinates needed additional incentive. But this outburst appeared sincere. Captain High was angry because Hiro had been unappreciative.

"Sir," Bill said abandoning use of the more familiar "Skipper" for the time being, "I think you might be coming down a little too hard on Hiro. I don't see him as insubordinate or even unappreciative. It's just that he thinks his family got a raw deal and this might help them somehow."

"So he wants me to release information that will magically change a situation that the President himself ordered? Jesus, Bill, I'm just a Captain, not a goddam miracle worker. And if I recommended to the powers-that-be back in Washington that we do such a thing, I wouldn't be a Captain very long either.

"What do you want to do about this, Skipper?" Bill asked. I don't think we can ignore the request. Hiro pointedly told me to tell you that he felt strongly about this."

"Tomorrow evening after dinner I'd like you and he to come by and see me. It sounds like Hiro is beyond persuasion on this issue, but I've got to at least try."

"Will do, sir," Bill agreed, "See you tomorrow evening."

CHAPTER 40

CARDS ON THE TABLE

The following evening Bill and Hiro showed up at Captain High's room. There were few social niceties to begin their meeting, and it was evident to the two visitors this would be a business-only session. The Captain got right to the point, "Hiro, Bill tells me you want me to release information describing your contribution to the Doolittle Raid in hopes that it would somehow work to stop the internment of Japanese-Americans on the West Coast. Is that right?"

"Yes sir," Hiro replied nervously. It was obvious that Captain High was not pleased with him and Hiro wondered whether he'd be able to stand up to such a formidable figure.

"Well, then I have to explain a few facts to you, Hiro. First, I cannot personally release this information. I don't have that authority. Given the sensitivity of the information, I think someone in Washington would have to do that. My second point is that if I did refer this matter to someone in Washington, it would almost certainly be refused. The President ordered the internment; he would have to be at least consulted about any development that could possibly turn it around. Frankly, I can't imagine anyone close to the President approaching him to say, 'Mr. President, there's this Japanese-American guy out in Hawaii who did us a good turn and now wants us to tell

CHAPTER 40

everybody about it so they'll realize that Japanese-Americans are not all bad guys and so should not be interned?"

"Captain," Hiro spoke up, "I know it sounds impractical but ..."

Captain High interrupted, "Impractical? How about ridiculous? You seem to think that the President could turn this thing around with the nod of his head. Well that's not how our government works. If you had studied political science rather than engineering you would know that authority in the U.S. Government is highly fragmented. The President is not a dictator. He may govern the country, but the country also governs him. And at this point in our history, this country is in no mood to reverse the internment. Call it unjust. Call it mean spirited. You can call it a lot of things but in the minds of Americans, it's warranted. Tokyo's attack on Pearl Harbor and its conquests in the Western Pacific have embittered America against Japan and all things Japanese. My personal opinion is that most American's accept the internment because they see it as a way of punishing Tokyo. The American reaction is emotional, visceral, and irrational. And it's well beyond our capability to control."

"But Captain," Hiro objected, "Americans are intelligent, reasoning people. If we give them an example of a Nisei who performed a patriotic act, don't you think that will affect their thinking about the Japanese-Americans in general?"

"Under normal conditions I'd say yes. But with the West Coast fearing a Japanese fleet is just over the horizon waiting to invade, I have to say no. The country has been overtaken by war hysteria. This is not a time to expect rational thinking."

Hiro was not ready to concede. "Captain, the government has imprisoned over 100,000 people in harsh conditions just because they are of Japanese descent. That's simply not fair!"

"No, it's not fair," the Captain agreed, "Nor is it fair that the government drags a man from his home and family just because he is between the ages of 18 and 40, and sends him into combat where he might well be killed. But we do that too. We call it the draft. Fairness seems to be the first casualty of war."

"But we Japanese-Americans are willing to go to war and fight with you, side-by-side. But you won't allow us in your military services. To me that means the internment is racial."

THE DOOLITTLE IRONY

"I don't see it that way, Hiro. The U.S. is allied with China and the Philippines. They're both Asian, and both have large enclaves of immigrants here in Hawaii and Stateside. But they are not interned."

Frustrated, Hiro exclaimed, "It's not your family that's suffering. You don't have to worry about a sick father dying in a prison camp."

"Don't mistake my comments for a lack of sympathy, Hiro," the Captain replied, "But you must understand that we are all now 'prisoners of war.' We are no longer free agents, able to follow our own moral course. Now we must accommodate to the imperatives of this war. Our only escape is to end it as quickly as possible."

"Well, I don't agree," Hiro countered, "We don't excuse Hitler for putting political prisoners in concentration camps. Yet we do the same thing with Japanese-Americans and you say it's because we are all 'prisoners' of this war. I don't think so. We still have free will. We are not the captives of some evil force that you call the 'imperatives of war.'"

Captain High sighed. "You're a tough guy to argue with, Hiro. I'm obviously not going to convince you of my opinion, and you're certainly not going to convince me of yours. So let's stop arguing. Instead, let's bargain. Here's my deal. I will get Kathleen out here. That should happen very soon. Also, I will try–no guarantees–to get permission from the Army for your family to leave the Exclusion Area. In return, you will remain silent about your role in the Doolittle Raid. That's my deal. Your answer can only be yes or no."

Hiro was silent for a very long moment. "OK," he finally said, "I guess if I don't take the deal you'll throw me in the brig, so I'll be quiet. But if matters don't develop as we hope, I just want you to know that I too have an alternative."

"Really? That sound's ominous," the Captain said leveling his gaze on Hiro, "Would you care to elaborate?"

"Captain High," Hiro said returning the Captain's gaze, "I am very appreciative of what you have done for me. But I know full well that you have not done it simply to express the nation's gratitude for my contribution to the success of the Doolittle Raid. Your motives were far more practical, and probably dictated by some authority figure in Washington, D.C. You wanted to suppress the fact that the success of the Doolittle Raid hung on the actions of a Japanese-

CHAPTER 40

American. It would make the idea that Japanese-Americans are a security threat to the West Coast look silly. There would no longer be justification for the internment, and a lot of powerful Americans are responsible for the internment, especially the President. So, to avoid embarrassing them, you've been instructed to keep me quiet. You see, Captain, I did take a course in political science while I was at the University, and I learned the meaning of *Realpolitic*."

"Hmmmf!" Captain high grunted, "I guess now you expect me to be contrite, now that you think you've uncovered our little ploy. But I'm not. You know, Hiro, we could have easily let you be treated as a prisoner of war. You would have been put behind barbed wire and your silence would have been sealed for the duration of the war. But we didn't. We–and I include here those authority figures in Washington you spoke of–wanted to do the right thing, at least in so far as we could. And we still do, Hiro. But I must caution that this situation has been considered and a decision rendered. If you attempt to contravene it, my orders are unequivocal: I am to do whatever is necessary to keep this story private."

Bill had been quiet through this whole discussion, but he chose to speak up now. "Hiro, what is this so-called 'alternative' you speak of? Have you given the details of your story to one of the other officers?"

"No!" Hiro asserted, "I told you I would not do that, and I have not. But if something happens to me–like being thrown in a POW camp–then the story would be made public."

"And how did you manage that?" Bill asked.

Hiro grimaced a bit and then answered, "It's too late for you to stop it, so I might as well tell you. Do you remember the little Japanese Restaurant we visited in Honolulu? Maybe you remember also that I spoke to two Japanese gentlemen there after I visited the men's room? One of them was named Tanaka. He was the Captain of the *Hikawa Maru*, the ship that I sailed to Tokyo on. He's now the Captain of a Mexican cargo ship registered in Panama. We are friends and he agreed to hold in safe keeping a sealed envelope that I would send him. If something were to happen to me, he agreed to turn it over to the Mexican Press. Inside is a detailed account of my experience, including my dealings with you. One of my friends–unknowingly, of course–later delivered the envelope to Captain Tanaka for me and, by now, his ship has left port."

"Hmmmf!" the Captain grunted again, "So you had this figured out a while ago and were just stringing us along?"

"I had hoped it would never get to this point."

"Well, frankly Hiro, now that it has, I don't think it changes much. We've still got a deal and I hope you are still committed to keeping it."

"Yes sir, I am!"

The three men parted quietly, each with a more realistic understanding of their relationship.

CHAPTER 41

MIDWAY LOOMS

17 May 1942

It was Sunday, the one day of the week that Wypo personnel managed to take a few hours off. But this morning Commander Rochefort chose to use an hour of that time to brief the staff officers on current naval operations in the South Pacific. This morning he was in proper uniform, not the purple sleeping robe that his all night work habits sometimes produced.

"As all of you know,' Rochefort began, "During the last few months Wypo has been concentrating on Japanese communications in the South Pacific. We had detected indications of an impending Japanese offensive operation there, and concluded the Japs were probably planning an attempt to take Port Moresby. We reported that to Admiral Nimitz and he dispatched two carriers–the Lexington and the Yorktown–to the Coral Sea area to head off the Japanese effort. As you may already know, those two carriers met and engaged the enemy force on several occasions between the 4th and the 8th of May. The attacks were conducted entirely by aircraft–the first time in history that a major naval battle occurred without a shot being fired by a surface combatant. I regret to inform you that we lost the Lexington,

THE DOOLITTLE IRONY

plus an oiler and a destroyer. Moreover, the Yorktown has been badly damaged and is on its way back here to the West Coast for repairs."

The room fell silent. Most of the men there had had friends on one or the other of the sunken ships.

Commander Rochefort continued, "On a happier note, I can also report that our losses were not in vain. Intercepts of Japanese communications indicate that the IJN lost at least one major carrier and has had to call off its invasion of Port Moresby." That brought a round of mild applause.

"Which brings me to a major new development," Rochefort continued, "Many of you already know that we have been looking hard at the threat of another major Japanese offensive here in the Central Pacific. We had some inkling of its timing and scope, but until recently we knew only that its objective was referred to in Japanese traffic as 'AF.' We did not know what those two letters meant so we devised a ruse to help us figure it out. We had the installation on Midway–with whom we're connected by undersea cable–transmit in the clear that its fresh water evaporators are out of commission. A few days later we saw IJN logistics traffic transmitted in a low level code that more fresh water should be planned for an upcoming invasion of "AF." We put two and two together and concluded that the upcoming invasion was targeted for…" the Commander paused for dramatic effect, "… Midway Island! That's right. The Japs are going to try to seize Midway." That prompted a series of worried looks among the audience.

Commander Rochefort continued, "We think Jimmy Doolittle's raid probably embarrassed the Japs so much they feel like they have to eliminate our carriers. We think their intent is to lure our fleet into battle on the assumption that IJN superior numbers will guarantee victory. The way they've chosen to do that is by threatening a piece of real estate they know we're willing to fight about–Midway! They expect that if they invade and occupy, our carriers will have to come out and fight. Well, Admiral Nimitz is willing to accommodate them!"

Normally, Wypo personnel were quite reserved but this time they stood and cheered. The Commander asked for quiet and then announced, "This is just the beginning of the story. I'll keep you posted. And remember, this is very sensitive! Once we leave this room we no longer mention it!"

CHAPTER 42

GOOD NEWS

That afternoon Captain High invited Bill and Hiro over for an afternoon drink in his room. Hiro thought this odd, given that they had parted the evening before on rather tense terms. But none of that was evident in the Captain's demeanor as he greeted them.

"Hi, guys!" he exuded as they arrived. "I'm really glad you're here. Sit down. I dragged in another chair so we can all take a load off. I'm going to fix us some Mai Tais. We're in Hawaii, so we might as well drink like it."

Neither Bill nor Hiro ever drank alcoholic beverages this early in the day. In fact, they rarely drank alcoholic beverages at all. But they were in the Navy after all, and alcohol was a staple of Navy social life. They watched the Captain as he went through the ritual of pouring white rum, lime juice, and orange curacao into the mixer, shaking it vigorously, pouring it into tall glasses with a garnish of lime, and then adding dark rum on top. He handed a glass to each of his visitors and sat down looking pleased with himself. Bill and Hiro had been silent, waiting to see what this strange behavior on the part of the Captain was leading up to.

"Gentlemen," the Captain began, "This is a rare occasion. Today I have only good news to share with you, so I suggest we drink

THE DOOLITTLE IRONY

to that." Then, holding his glass aloft he offered a toast, "To good news gentlemen. May we never have any other!"

Bill and Hiro both responded with the usual "Hear, hear," sipped their Mai Tais, noting that they were really very tasty, and realized that this was a different side of the Captain than they had seen before.

"I won't draw this out in the interests of drama, gents. I'll get right to the point. First, I have secured permission for your family, Hiro, to be removed from Camp Harmony."

Hiro burst out of his chair, spilled a bit of his Mai Tai and shouted, "Oh my gosh, that's wonderful!"

But the Captain had more to add so he raised his hand to restrain Hiro's outburst. "There are conditions, Hiro, so sit down and let me go over them. First, this is to done under the guise of a cover story so that the other Japanese there do not think they might be able to arrange a similar release. Second, your parents are not to know of this in advance. They'll be told that they are being transported to another place called Camp Minidoka in Idaho. It's still under construction but all of the Japanese families will be sent there when it's finished. Third, this is to be done at no cost to the U.S. Army. You'll have to arrange for their transportation and support once they are released. Fourth, they must be removed from the Exclusion Area, which in this context means they have to be moved east of the Mississippi."

"Don't worry, sir," Hiro interjected excitedly, "I'll work that out somehow. Does Kathleen know about this? She can handle things on that end."

"Yes, she does know about it, Hiro. In fact, she was instrumental in handling it–but I'll let her tell you about that when you see her. Which brings me to my next piece of good news; are you ready?"

Hiro took a long sip of his Mai Tai and said, "OK, sir, but I don't think you can beat that last news."

"Then hold onto that drink tightly this time, Hiro, because Kathleen arrives here tomorrow afternoon!"

"WHAT!" Hiro exploded, spilling more of his drink despite the Captain's caution, "Tomorrow? Oh, my gosh, tomorrow?" Hiro was stunned. He had thought it would be weeks, probably months before Kathleen got to the Island.

CHAPTER 42

"Yes, tomorrow," the Captain repeated, "Now sit back down and I'll tell you about it." Hiro sat and finished what was left of his Mai Tai. "Here, let me fix another round for us while I tell you." This time the Captain's ritual making the Mai Tai was somewhat abbreviated–mostly just pouring rum and curacao. The garnish and niceties were forgotten. "Kathleen is probably now aboard a flight from Seattle to San Francisco. Tomorrow morning she'll board the old Pan Am Clipper and 15 hours later arrive here at the sea terminal across the channel."

"Oh, my gosh," Hiro exclaimed again. How did she get on a luxury flight?"

It's no longer luxury, Hiro, the Navy has bought the Clippers and my guess is by now it's been made pretty spartan. Moreover, it's a 15-hour hop, so she won't arrive until late in the evening."

"Will I be able to meet her, Captain?"

"At that time of day, I'd guess you could, but that's assuming you're not needed at your job. You can work that out with your boss."

"OK. That should work out. Lenny Godek is a good guy. Besides, I'm usually out of the office by 2000."

"Good," the Captain said, "I won't go to the sea terminal with you but Bill, if you don't mind, I'd like you to go."

"Sure," Bill said with enthusiasm, "The whole Japanese Navy couldn't keep me away."

"Hiro, you may not recognize Kathleen," the Captain went on, "She'll be in Navy Whites wearing a brand new set of ensign insignia."

"A Navy nurse? Wow. I'll bet her dad is proud."

"The recruiter in Seattle who swore her in yesterday said they outfitted her already. He said she looked really sharp, so you better keep your eyes out for lonesome sailors making a move on her."

"She is a very pretty girl, Captain, and I know that other men look at her, but she's going to marry me!"

"But not right away, Hiro. Here's a bit of bad news. Navy nurses cannot marry. Navy regs!"

"Oh, I didn't know that, sir." Hiro said with a disappointed look, "But that's OK," he added quickly, "She'll be here and that's what matters."

"Which brings up another piece of good news, Hiro. Assuming that some handsome young Navy officer hasn't turned her head on the flight here, and considering that you can't get married right away, I presume you'll want to get formally engaged. Is that right?"

"It sure is, Captain," I know that will be what Kathleen wants."

"You understand, Hiro, you may have to put off marriage for quite awhile, and that when you do marry Kathleen will have to resign her commission and leave the Navy?"

"Yes, I know that, Captain. But that will be OK for the time being. I want to send an allotment to my mother and father. I know the U.S. Government is supposed to provide them food and shelter at Camp Harmony, but I know they'll need money for other things. Kathleen is in a similar situation. Her Mom and Dad are not rich. They sacrificed a lot to get her through college. She's always planned to pay them back after she started working."

"That's admirable, Hiro," the Captain commented, "And I'm sure it will work out. In any case, there's a war on. For the next couple of years our lives will not be our own."

Bill watched the Captain closely. There was no evidence of his rant of last night. He saw a father advising his son and realized that the Captain has developed a paternal affection for Hiro. This was no longer just the conduct of Navy business–keeping Hiro happy to keep him silent. The Captain was now invested personally in Hiro's life.

"Hiro, I anticipated that would want to get engaged soon," the Captain said, "So I've taken a few liberties. I hope you won't mind."

"Liberties, sir?"

"That's right. Of course we can cancel them if you and Kathleen prefer, but let me tell you about them first." The Captain smiled, obviously pleased with himself, "I've reserved the banquet room in the Officer's Club Saturday night the 23rd to have a little engagement party."

"Oh, that sounds great, sir," Hiro exclaimed," Kathleen loves parties. And I've never even been to the O' Club, so it'll be a treat for me too."

"I think you'll like it, Hiro. But that's not all," the Captain went on, "The Army now operates the Royal Hawaiian Hotel at Waikiki.

CHAPTER 42

They are converting it to military billets for R&R. It's no longer quite so plush, and Waikiki Beach is lined with barbed wire. But it's still a pretty nice place so I got you and Kathleen two rooms for the three days following the engagement party."

"Oh, my gosh," Hiro blurted, "The Royal Hawaiian! Wait until Kathleen's mother hears about that. It might change her mind about my suitability as a son-in-law." But then he added quickly, "You did say <u>two</u> rooms, Captain? That's good because I don't think Kathleen or her mother would approve otherwise.

"You can tell them to relax, Hiro," the Captain laughed, "The rooms are on separate floors."

"OK, I hope that'll keep Mom happy."

"Also," the Captain added, "I spoke to Commander Rochefort and Lieutenant Commander Solomon Kathleen's new boss as well. They've OK'd 72 hour leaves for both of you. Incidentally, Solomon is the Chief Nurse over at the Base Hospital where Kathleen is assigned. She's a great person and she is impressed that Kathleen has a Bachelor of Science in nursing from Washington U."

Hiro started to speak, "Captain, I can't believe all this good news. I feel like I've just won the Irish Sweepstakes! I owe it all to you, so let me offer a toast," and with a flourish he raised his glass, "To Captain High, the best doggone Captain in the whole U.S. Navy!" With that he finished his Mai Tai in one long swig. Sir, do you think we could have another drink? You mix a great Mai Tai!"

The Captain smiled and glanced over at Bill who was looking at Hiro with amusement. Bill asked, "Have you ever had a Mai Tai before, Hiro?"

"Actually, no," Hiro admitted, "But I certainly should have."

"OK," the Captain agreed and he began to mix a third round of drinks, "Incidentally, we've got a local Hawaiian Band to come in and play at your party. Can you Hula, Hiro?"

Hiro Hula?" Hiro repeated as he started on his third Mai Tai. "Hey, that's a little hard to say after two Mai Tais."

"Skipper, I think maybe we should cut off his Mai Tais before he starts to hula right here." The three laughed and talked amiably for a while longer. Altogether it was a very good afternoon, one they would remember fondly.

CHAPTER 43

KATHLEEN ARRIVES

It was Monday, the day Kathleen was scheduled to arrive aboard the Clipper. The flight was to have left San Francisco at 0800, fly 15 hours, and–after subtracting three hours for the change in time zones–land in Hawaii at 2000 local. Bill and Hiro had both spent a normal workday at the office and then caught the harbor ferry to Pearl City to meet her aircraft.

As they passed Ford Island, Bill pointed over to Battleship Row where the Japanese had sunk or damaged eight of the Pacific Fleet's capital ships. Some had already been raised. Bill pointed to the closest berth. "There's where the *USS California* was sunk. It's already been refloated and moved over to the dry dock."

Looking down Battleship Row beyond the California's berth, six other battleships lie in various states of damage. Bill pointed to the far end where the superstructure of the *USS Arizona* protruded. "Her forward magazine was hit by a bomb," he explained to Hiro, "That set off a huge explosion and the ship sank within minutes, killing almost 1,200 men–practically half of all the deaths that occurred that day." Seeing the sunken hulks in the fading light of late evening unsettled both men. They were pensive the rest of the trip.

The ferry dropped them at the former Pan Am Seaplane Terminal at Pearl City. It was now operated by the Navy and so was spartanly furnished. They sat on a crate waiting for the Boeing 314B

CHAPTER 43

to set down on the seaway that ran up the center of Middle Loch. As they waited, Hiro became increasingly nervous about what to say and how to act when Kathleen arrived. "It was a long flight, so she'll be tired and maybe she won't want to talk. Maybe she'll just want to go to the Naval Hospital and go to sleep. What do you think, Bill?"

"I wouldn't worry about it, Hiro. Just relax. The man over there says the plane is on time, so we have only a few minutes to wait."

Then, as if on cue, the plane appeared low on the horizon. It was big, and when it touched down a huge spray of water erupted to either side of its V-shaped hull. "Oh my gosh," Hiro worried, "I wonder if she was frightened by that?" He stared intently as the big plane slowed, settled into the water, and then turned toward the pier.

"Should I help her get off the plane, Bill?"

"You won't be able to, Hiro. We're not allowed out on the end of the pier. But don't worry, she's quite safe."

The huge plane taxied close to the pier, shut off its port engines, and gently eased its port side to the pier. A crewmember tossed lines to two men on the pier who secured the plane with two hawsers fore and aft. A minute later the passenger door opened and one of the crew stepped out onto the plane's sponson. He pulled up a short gangway from the pier and motioned to the passengers waiting inside the door that they could disembark. The first out was a white uniformed young woman holding onto her hat with one hand and the gangway handrail with the other.

"Oh my gosh," Hiro exploded. "It's Kathleen, KATHLEEN! KATHLEEN!"

Kathleen looked toward the shout, spotted Hiro and came racing down the pier. Hiro could not be restrained by the simple rope that had been strung to keep back the crowd. He burst through it, past the civilian guard and met Kathy halfway down the pier. Bill thought for an instant that they would collide violently, but instead they seemed to melt together into a single clump of white uniforms. They remained that way for a very long minute and Bill could tell they were both crying. The other passengers streamed by, smiling approval at two young people so desperately in love.

For Bill it was a reflective moment. The image of the sunken battleships was still with him and he was beginning to realize that the war would probably not be over in just a year or so. It could well be longer, and it would bring grief, not happy reunions like Kathleen's and Hiro's. No, there would be a visit by a chaplain or maybe a simple telegram that began, "I regret to inform you ..." But the euphoria of the moment was enough for now. Hiro came running back to Bill, towing Kathleen by the hand.

"Bill, this is Kathleen," Hiro announced excitedly, drawing Kathleen up in front of him.

Bill smiled, "Yes, I had guessed as much. Hello Kathleen, I'm Bill, a friend of Hiro's."

"And I had guessed as much also," Kathleen smiled, "And I know all about you. Hiro has written to me about how much he owes you. I am so grateful for your friendship. Would you mind if I gave you a hug?"

"Mind?' Bill laughed, "I'd love it!"

And with that Kathleen wrapped her arms around him and squeezed. "Really, Bill, both Hiro and I are so grateful. We'll name our first son after you!"

"Oh, wait, Kathleen," Hiro laughed, "I've already promised that to Stanley! But it's OK because we're going to have at least four sons! That means I still have two more to promise."

Bill laughed louder this time, "Now wait Hiro, you may want to talk that over with Kathleen."

"Yes," Kathleen asserted, "I would like to have something to say about that."

They laughed. "OK," Bill said raising his hand, "It would be fun to continue this family planning, but it's getting late. We're out after curfew–Hiro can tell you all about curfew later, Kathleen–and the last ferry leaves at 2100."

"2100?" Kathleen looked puzzled, "Wait, I have to figure that out."

"It's 9:00 PM civilian time, Kathleen," Hiro chided, "You're Navy now so you got to learn the lingo. Let's go pick up your gear."

"Gear?"

"Never mind, Kathleen," Hiro said, "It will all come in good time."

CHAPTER 43

Bill looked at the both with a more serious expression, "I know you two want to be alone together. You have a lot to talk about. Bill has a few things to tell you Kathleen, and I know that you have a lot to tell Bill. So I am going to pick up your 'gear' Kathleen, while you two talk. See you both aboard the ferry."

Bill got Kathy's gear from the pile of luggage spread on the pier–a small suitcase, with proper ID tag, weighing less than the 44-pound allowance permitted a junior officer. Another officer standing nearby caught Bill's attention as he picked up the suitcase. "Are you Kathleen's fiancé?' he asked.

"Oh no, he's over there with her now."

"Well, tell him he's a lucky man. I sat beside her on the way out and she's absolutely charming. If I were 15 years younger and didn't already have a wife and three daughters I'd ask her for a date myself."

Bill noticed he had Commander's stripes. "Yes, I just met her and she seems quite nice."

"She must certainly love that guy. You know she went to every passenger on the plane and asked if she could be first off. When she explained why, everybody smiled and said, 'of course.'"

"Oh, that's funny," Bill laughed, "I wondered about that!"

Kathleen and Hiro stood by the rail during the trip across the harbor, their faces reflecting the serious conversation they were having. She gave Hiro a parting kiss and got off the harbor ferry at Hospital Point. She was still on the dock waving when the two men lost sight of her.

"Did you get everything settled, Hiro?" Bill asked as the ferry turned into Southeast Loch, "Did Kathleen agree to the engagement party?"

"Agree? Oh she loved the idea. She's so excited about everything. You know, she's never been far away from home before. She's thrilled about it all–being in Hawaii, a new career as a nurse, being a Naval Officer, and having an engagement party at the Officer's Club. It's all an adventure for her. She told me that some sailors saluted her in San Francisco and she didn't know what to do but then she remembered soldiers saluting in some movie so she faked it."

The two leaned on the ferry's rail and looked down Battleship Row. It was now dark and the hulks of the sunken ships were only

THE DOOLITTLE IRONY

dimly visible in the moonlight. Repair crews on barges moored alongside the hulks worked around the clock. The flicker of their welding torches gave the scene the appearance of a 1920s silent film. It was ominous and left the two men unsettled, just as it had on the trip across the harbor earlier. It would be a long war.

CHAPTER 44

DISAPPOINTMENT BACK HOME

"Good Morning, Mr. Scott," Stanley said, entering the boss's spacious office, "Thanks for seeing me on such short notice."

"Oh, glad to, Stanley. In fact I was just about to call you." Mr. Scott was a man in his early sixties. He looked every bit the successful engineer and businessman: well groomed, fit, with a thatch of gray hair atop a face weathered by years of outdoor work. He was what young engineers like Stanley aspired to be. "But let's hear what you've got first, Stanley, then we can get to my business."

"Well, sir," Stanley began, "It has to do with Hiro. As you know, his parents have been interned, along with all the other Japanese-Americans in the area."

"Yes, not one of our prouder civic moves," Mr. Scott said cynically.

Stanley continued, "As you also know, the Navy has intervened in this case to get Hiro's family released to go to the East Coast."

"Yes, but I'm not clear on why the Navy did that. I presume Hiro did something to earn the Navy's gratitude."

"I'm not clear on that myself, Mr. Scott, but I presume it was significant because they've been taking pretty good care of him. They just got his girlfriend a commission as a Navy Nurse and flew her out to Hawaii."

THE DOOLITTLE IRONY

"I heard about that, but then I thought maybe the Navy was really doing itself a favor. They need nurses desperately, especially out in Pearl Harbor."

"Yes, I guess so," Stanley admitted, "Maybe it wasn't altruistic. In any case, Kathleen–Hiro's girlfriend–thought the release of Hiro's family was a done deal. She asked me to pick them up from Camp Harmony and take them back to Pittsburgh when I go for my draft physical. I agreed but when I went down to tell them to get ready, the Army commander down there said he wouldn't let them go."

"Really?" Mr. Scott said looking puzzled, "Did he explain why?"

"In a way," Stanley answered, "He rather self righteously told me that just because these people have connections in Washington don't mean they should be exempted from internment."

Mr. Scott took that in with a knowing smile and then opined, "Sounds like Service politics to me."

"Yes, it does," Hiro agreed, "That's the reason I'm here. I wondered if you had any influence in such matters."

"The short answer is no, Stanley. I'm just a Seattle guy. Washington D.C. is the big leagues. I do have a contact in the State Department, but he's not that heavy. Of course, we have two Senators in D.C., and a Congressional Representative. Sometimes a call from one of them can move things along." Mr. Scott thought for a minute, nodded to himself as though registering an idea, and said, "Yeah, I guess I have a few options, but it will take time to sort out. On the other hand, considering what I have to discuss with you, maybe that's not all bad."

"How so, sir?" Stanley said looking puzzled.

Mr. Scott leaned back in his upholstered leather chair, put his hands behind his head, and began a spiel he had probably used many times before: "As you well know, this country is at war. As you also know, the war is not going all that well for us. We lack adequate guns, planes, tanks–practically everything it takes to fight a modern war. That doesn't worry me. We have a very robust industrial base and I'm confident we'll soon remedy those shortages."

Mr. Scott paused to gather his thoughts, "The question is, when we do produce them, how do we get all those weapons to Europe and Asia where the war is being fought? There are two oceans between

CHAPTER 44

here and there so the answer has to be 'ships.' But right now, the Germans are sinking our ships faster than we can build them. The Navy will eventually take care of the U-boats, but somebody else has to take care of building ships–a LOT of ships! One guy who has stepped forward to do that you've probably already heard of–Henry J. Kaiser. This guy does things in a big way. He oversaw the construction of the Hoover and the Grand Coulee Dams. He built the San Francisco Bay Bridge. Now he has a new design for ships that can be built on a mass production basis. He's already got a shipyard operating down in Richmond California, and now he is developing another one down on the Columbia River near Vancouver, Washington. It's going to be huge. He already has over 35,000 on the payroll. I tell you, Stanley, this guy can get things done!"

"I've read about him, Mr. Scott," Stanley said, "He has an impressive record."

"But what you haven't read about, Stanley, is that he wants this firm to send people down to Vancouver to help him. Says he has problems bending metal and thinks we might be able to help."

"Wow," Stanley exclaimed, "That's a real feather in your cap, Mr. Scott. From now on you'll be more than just a little Seattle guy."

"The feather belongs to the whole firm, Stanley, including you. You've done a real workmanlike job here. That's the reason I wanted to talk to you today, to ask if you would join the team I'm sending down there. Your resume shows that you had experience working metal problems at a steel mill in Pittsburgh. Plus your work here has shown you to be a hands-on guy that gets things done. That's what we need. You would have a responsible position and there would be a raise in pay."

Stanley was dumbfounded, "That's very flattering, Mr. Scott, but I'm afraid my Draft Board already has plans for me."

"I know that, Stanley. So I called and talked to a member of your Board. I explained the situation and asked if the job I have in mind would make you eligible for a deferment on the basis of being in a critical defense-related function. His answer was unequivocal. 'Yes,' he said, 'he'll be a hell of a lot more valuable to the war effort there than slogging around Europe with an M-1.'"

THE DOOLITTLE IRONY

"Well, ..." Stanley hesitated, "This is all very sudden. I don't know what to say."

"Don't say anything yet, Stanley. Go home and think about it. I want yours to be a considered opinion, nothing impetuous. And I want you to know that I'll be working on the problem you brought about Hiro's family. Let me know within a day or two. I have to get this team together and down to Vancouver within a week."

"Thanks, Mr. Scott, I really appreciate your confidence in me–and your help with Hiro's family. I'll let you know my decision in a day or two."

Hiro received both letters on the same day, 26 May.

19 May 1942

Dear Kathleen and Hiro,

I have bad news. The arrangement you thought was in place to have the Army release your parents from Camp Harmony so I could transport them to Pittsburgh has fallen through. I don't know why, but the Commander of the Camp will not release them. Mr. Scott thinks Army-Navy rivalry is at the root of it. He is working to correct the situation, but seems to have little influence in such matters. The point is that while we thought I would be driving across country with them today, they are still in Camp Harmony with no immediate prospect of being released. Thank goodness we didn't tell them in advance about this. They would be terribly disappointed!

That brings me to my second point. Mr. Scott has arranged a draft deferment for me. He's sending me as part of a team of engineers to Vancouver in

Chapter 44

the southern part of the state. Henry J. Kaiser is building ships down there now and I guess the Draft Board considers that more important than having me carry a rifle. But Mr. Scott said that if he can get your parents out of Camp Harmony, he would find a way to get them to Pittsburgh. Incidentally, my relatives there are still quite willing to provide your family food and shelter when they arrive.

I'm limited to one page and almost out of room.

Hope you are both well.

Stanley

⊕ ⊕ ⊕

20 May 1942.

Dear Hiro,

We received a letter from Kathleen, telling us that she has become a nurse in the Navy and may soon join you in Hawaii. She wanted to tell us in person but visits are still restricted. We think her news is wonderful! Even Mama is happy for you two and said she would teach Kathleen how to cook rice the way you like it. But she hopes you stay in Hawaii because if you come back here they will put you in prison, like they have us.

I don't want to complain, Hiro, but being here is not much fun. We are treated like cattle. We live in what used to be cattle pens with mice and rats. We have to wait in long lines to eat. We have no privacy, and we are given no information about our future. We know only that we are to be moved to

THE DOOLITTLE IRONY

the other side of the Rocky Mountains, but we're not sure where, we don't know when, and we don't know what conditions we'll find there. Papa is not well and even Mama is discouraged—though she tries to put on a strong face. Avaron and I wonder if we'll ever be able to graduate high school. We've only been here a month but it seems like forever! Kathleen said she would send us some books to read. That's great because we have nothing to do and are terribly bored.

But please don't worry about us. Just stay safe so you can come home when this terrible war is over.

Love,

Natsuko

    Hiro smiled at Natsuko's letter. After reciting a litany of heart breaking complaints, she blithely says, "… don't worry about us." Only a 16-year-old would do that, Hiro thought affectionately.

    He read both letters repeatedly, each time becoming more discouraged with his family's situation. He would talk to Kathleen about this tomorrow. Maybe she would have some suggestions. He <u>must</u> do something!

CHAPTER 45

MIDWAY TAKES SHAPE

What would become known as "the Battle of the Coral Sea" had ended as something of a standoff. The IJN lost one of its major carriers and suffered minor damage to another. The U.S. lost the *Lexington* and suffered major damage to the *Yorktown*. So tactically Japan seemed to have had the upper hand, but strategically that was not the case. Tokyo had to cancel its planned invasion of Port Moresby because the loss of the two carriers meant their invasion force would not have adequate air cover. The Battle of the Coral Sea marked the high water mark of Japan's expansion into the South Pacific. It would never again mount efforts to capture Port Moresby by sea, and it would abandon its strategic intent to isolate America from Australia by seizing Pacific outposts between the two. After six months of rampaging through the Western Pacific, the Japanese advance had finally been stopped. But that was not obvious at the time. It became evident only in hindsight. In May 1942, Japan still looked like a monster on a rampage, greedily intent on conquering the entire Western Pacific.

⊕ ⊕ ⊕

THE DOOLITTLE IRONY

27 MAY 1942

Commander Rochefort looked out over his staff. They had pulled up desk chairs, boxes, and crates and were scattered in a rough circle around him. Each was intent, knowing that they were on the verge of a major battle with the Imperial Japanese Navy.

Rochefort began in a deliberate voice, "The last time we met I outlined much of what happened in the Coral Sea engagement. Since then, there have been important developments. As most of you know, we have been successful in breaking a surprising amount of IJN communications. Because of that we have a very good understanding of what the Japanese have in store, and we have conveyed all of that to Admiral Nimitz. He has given our intelligence high credibility and made it the basis for his plan to defeat the Japanese."

He was particularly proud of the last sentence. The business of intelligence did not stop when the product was typed up in a report. You didn't just drop it on the Commander's desk and walk away. You had to make sure it was put to good use. Rochefort had learned that the hard way. Much of the intercept work Wypo had done prior to Pearl Harbor had been sent directly to Washington, D.C. and held very closely there to assure its security. It was never sent back to Admiral Kimmel or General Short in Hawaii, so they never were able to factor it into their readiness decisions. Had they done so, the Japanese attack on Pearl Harbor might have had another outcome. Rochefort did not want that to happen a second time. He tried hard to make his product persuasive and assure that it got into the hands of the men who needed it. He had succeeded and Nimitz based his plan on it.

Rochefort paused, gazing down from the small crate on which he had stood so as to make eye contact with each staff member. "Using a naval force centered on four aircraft carriers," he continued, "The Japanese plan is to attack Midway from the air, bombard it from the sea, and having neutralized its defenses, land troops to occupy the Island. With Midway in their grasp, the Japs could launch land based air strikes against Pearl Harbor, Hickam and our other military installations here on Oahu. Now here is the hook: knowing we could not allow that, the Japanese believe we would dispatch our aircraft carriers to drive them out. It would produce the so-called "decisive

CHAPTER 45

battle" that they tout in their naval strategy. They think they would win that battle because they have more carriers than we, their fighters are faster, and their carrier pilots are more experienced." Rochefort paused, "But they didn't reckon with the men and women of Wypo."

The audience smiled weakly, not convinced that their Commander's flattery was entirely warranted. He continued, "You see, we now know with high confidence about when the enemy will attack, the direction from which he will attack, the number of planes he will employ, and the rough location from which he will launch those planes." Rochefort paused for emphasis, "Basically, we know as much about the enemy's plans as he does!"

Another pause to let that sink in, and then Rochefort continued, "With that information Admiral Nimitz has put together a very clever plan. The Japanese will approach the Island from the northwest and launch strikes on the morning of 4 June. Before then Nimitz will have positioned three carriers to the north of their launch point. Our planes will pounce on the Japs just as they are launching their first strikes. It will be a surprise and we stand a good chance of being successful. In addition, Nimitz has reinforced the Island's defenses. If the enemy mounts an attack, he'll find a hornet's nest waiting for him."

An ensign in the back raised his hand a bit timidly. Rochefort pointed to him, "John, you have a question?"

"Yes sir," the young man said as he stood up, "You said Admiral Nimitz will position <u>three</u> carriers? But the Lexington was sunk in the Coral Sea and the Yorktown badly damaged. It's returning stateside for repairs so we only have two carriers."

"Well timed question, John," Rochefort said approvingly, "Because it brings me to my next point. Admiral Nimitz has decided that he <u>must</u> have the *Yorktown* in this upcoming battle. He has directed that the *Yorktown* return here to Pearl Harbor for emergency repairs. In fact, a plane load of our repair people have already flown out to inspect the *Yorktown* and reported that the damage is significant. It would normally take three months to repair it but we'll have only three days. She's arriving as we speak and must leave before the first of June."

Even to intelligence officers who knew nothing of ship repair, doing 90 days of work in just three days seemed impossible. The group looked skeptical.

THE DOOLITTLE IRONY

"Not only must the ship be repaired, but the ship's crew must also be brought up to strength. We are being asked to provide one officer to go aboard and help the intelligence element. If any of you want to volunteer, see me after the meeting. Okay, now let's get back to work."

⊕ ⊕ ⊕

Ten minutes later, Hiro sat opposite Commander Rochefort in his tiny office. "Hiro," the Commander said patiently, "It's admirable that you're volunteering to join the *Yorktown's* crew temporarily, but I wonder if that's a good decision given that your fiancée has just arrived on the Island and you have a big Engagement Party set for Saturday night. Maybe this is not the right time."

"I understand, Commander," Hiro said quite seriously, "For most men, that would be good advice but, you see, I'm of Japanese descent. I don't look like the rest of you here. I look like the enemy! And my family has been put in prison because they look like the enemy. I have to prove to everybody that I am a true American, no matter what I look like. This is a chance for me to do that. The *Yorktown* is going to meet this country's enemy face-to-face, and I want to be aboard when she does. If I am, and if I acquit myself properly, maybe White Americans will begin to realize that people of Japanese descent can be just as American as if we had come from Ireland."

Rochefort was himself of Irish descent, but dismissed the idea that Hiro had meant his comment as a barb, "Okay, Hiro, I recognize that you have a unique problem and I probably don't fully appreciate it. You've chosen your own way to deal with it, and I guess I have to accept that. So yes, you can join the *Yorktown's* crew until she returns to the States for repairs."

Hiro broke into a big smile.

"But after that, it's back here for you," Rochefort declared, "We need you here and, frankly, we don't give a damn if you're Japanese, Irish, or Presbyterian."

Rochefort noted Hiro's smile at his comment and was glad that he had in some small way relieved the young ensign's anguish. Then

CHAPTER 45

he added, "But right now you better get over to the Dry Dock #1. I just heard that the repair crew is already boarding. I'll call over and tell them to expect you."

The *Yorktown* had suffered brutal damage in the Battle of the Coral Sea and just after the battle had limped into Tonga to assess the damage. A direct hit by a 500-lb. bomb had penetrated deep into the ship before exploding. It had heavily damaged the forward engine compartment, destroyed six other compartments, damaged the #2 elevator, cut off power to much of the ship, and left it without radar or refrigeration. In addition, eight near misses had ruptured the ship's fuel compartments and it was leaking oil. On board experts estimated that repairs would take 90 days.

Despite that, Admiral Nimitz ordered the *Yorktown* to leave Tonga and return to Pearl Harbor. He needed it desperately if U.S. forces were to have a chance against the Japanese. The IJN had sent four of their best carriers. Against that, Nimitz had only two–the *Hornet* and the *Enterprise*. The U.S. forces on Midway would constitute a third–an "unsinkable" carrier–and the *Yorktown* would have to make up the fourth.

Gamely, the *Yorktown* had made the long trek back to Pearl, trailing a 10-mile long stream of fuel oil but nevertheless arriving one day ahead of schedule. She steamed up the Pearl Harbor Channel and directly into Dry Dock #1. Admiral Nimitz was waiting with an inspection party. In waders they sloshed through the flooded compartments viewing the damage. On completion, the Admiral looked around at the various ship repair technicians with him and declared emphatically, "Gentlemen, we <u>must</u> have this ship back in three days." There were wide eyes and sober nods all around.

With that, 1400 civilian yard workers swarmed aboard to restock provisions and make emergency repairs. They worked furiously night and day. The power demands of their arc welders and other electric equipment were so high that a temporary blackout had to be imposed in Honolulu. Its citizens accepted that little inconvenience gladly. They understood that Hawaii was in the crosshairs of Tokyo and only the U.S. Navy could save it.

⊕ ⊕ ⊕

When Hiro reported aboard the *Yorktown* workers were everywhere. The Officer-of-the-Deck was at the top of the gangway, trying to make sure no unauthorized persons entered. He seemed to be losing control as workers streamed around him. Nevertheless he did have Hiro's name on one of his lists and directed him to the ship's communications area.

"C'mon in, Ensign Yamada," the Yorktown's Communication Officer said looking up from the papers in front of him. Hiro stepped thru the hatch and stood at attention. The Commander sat at a small metal writing surface that folded down from the bulkhead (Navy talk for wall) and served as a desk. Hiro almost saluted but then remembered that there was no saluting below decks.

The Commander was businesslike, "You needn't stand at attention, Ensign. We've temporarily set that sort of thing aside–more important things to do."

Hiro relaxed a bit but remained standing.

"I'm Jim Eason. I run Division 'K', the Communications Division. For the next couple of weeks I'll be your boss. First, let me thank you for volunteering to help us out. I've talked to Joe Rochefort about you." He raised his eyebrows and declared, "He tells me you were in the Jap Navy just a few months ago? That's astonishing! Is it true?"

Hiro wanted to give him the full story, but sensed this was not the time. So he just said, "Yes sir, in a way."

"It's okay, Ensign," Eason said, "I understand. Joe said he doesn't really know your story but the scuttlebutt is that you were a spy inside the IJN. I don't have a need-to-know about that sort of thing– although I will say that's a pretty gutsy thing to do. And I'm really glad you're here because you have just the kind of talent we need."

"Talent? What talent is that sir?" Hiro asked a bit puzzled.

"Commander Rochefort said you were a radio operator. So I figure you'll be able to understand a lot of the Japanese chatter we pick up on their tactical nets. We're not going to have time to send it

CHAPTER 45

back to Wypo for analysis. We have to be able to tell our command element what's going on <u>now</u>."

"I see, sir" Hiro responded, "But I have to warn you that I have had no experience listening to pilot communications. Maybe I can help with the surface stuff. I do know that Japanese radio operators are young and tend to lose their discipline in emergencies."

"Yeah," Eason observed wryly, "They share that with their American counterparts!"

"Anyway," the Commander continued, "I'm assigning you to Radio Central. That's where all our radio equipment is located. Your job will be to serve as a roving linguist and an instant analyst. When our operators can't follow an exchange, they'll turn their headset over to you. Maybe you'll be able figure it out."

"I'll do whatever I can, sir," Hiro promised.

"Good," the Commander said, and then in an almost apologetic tone said, "Commanded Rochefort told me that your fiancé arrived in Hawaii just a few days ago. I understand she's a Navy nurse. Great! I also understand that a party has been set up in the 'O' Club this coming Saturday to celebrate the engagement. Not so great!"

He paused, looked contrite, and said, "I'm afraid the Yorktown is scheduled to leave Saturday. That evening we will be well on our way to rendezvous with Enterprise and Hornet."

Hiro could not hide his disappointment. His face fell and his shoulders drooped. Commander Eason quickly tried to save the situation, "But wait, I may have a fix for this—not a 100% fix, but maybe 50%. Captain Buckmaster, our skipper, has promised the entire crew at least one liberty before we leave port. If I gave you that Friday night, do you think you could change all the arrangements in time and have your party Friday instead of Saturday?"

Still somewhat in shock Hiro replied, "I'll sure give it a try, sir."

"Good. Get on it. You only have about 24 hours. But right now I want you to go up to Radio Central and make your presence known. Tell them I sent you and what I want you to do. Oh, and Hiro, I don't want you to take no crap from anyone up there about being Japanese. Just tell 'em to see me if they don't like it. And don't worry. Once they find out you've been a spy and served in the IJN, they'll think you're a damn hero!"

CHAPTER 46

THE ENGAGEMENT PARTY

Hiro was frustrated by the sudden change, but he had no choice other than to adjust. When he left the *Yorktown* in Dry Dock #1, he walked quickly to the Naval Hospital just across Hospital Point. He had fewer than 36 hours to make the necessary changes. The place to start was with Kathleen!

She entered the Hospital waiting area looking a bit impatient. "Hiro, why are you here?" Kathleen asked, "I can't take time off in the middle of the day to see you."

"I understand that, Kathleen," Hiro explained, "But this is an emergency. We have to change the engagement party."

"WHAT?" Kathleen blurted? "Why would we want to change the Engagement Party?"

"Because I'm shipping out on the *Yorktown* that same day."

"WHAT?" Kathleen repeated, "Shipping out? What are you talking about?"

"They needed a person to go out on the *Yorktown* and help with the intelligence job. I volunteered."

"WHAT?" Kathleen said for the third time, "You volunteered? Even though you'll miss our Engagement Party?"

Before Kathleen became totally exasperated and walked out as she had at graduation when he tried to explain about going to Tokyo–a memory that still made him cringe–Hiro reached over,

CHAPTER 46

touched her hand gently and said in a soothing voice, "Well, I didn't plan it that way, Kathleen. Things just kind of got away from me."

She seemed to respond, "Oh, Hiro, I just don't understand. Maybe we better sit down and you can explain."

Hiro started with the two letters he had received the day before. She read them both and immediately felt guilty, "I should not have come out here, Hiro. I should be back there where I might do some good for our family." Hiro caught her use of the possessive with respect to his family. He was touched that she considered Mama, Papa and the two girls "her" family.

Then he explained about the return of the *Yorktown* and how Commander Rochefort had asked for a volunteer to go aboard and help the crew for a week or two. "I thought about the letters and I figured this is something I can do that might help. Maybe it will help change people's minds back Stateside about Japanese-Americans. Maybe they'll let them out of prison." He also explained about how Commander Eason had suggested he could still have the Engagement Party if he just advanced the time 24 hours.

Kathleen listened without interruption. Her countenance changed from frustration to patience to sympathy. "Oh, Hiro, I feel so sorry for you. You have so many burdens–your family, your Japanese heritage, this war. I don't want to add another one. I never want to be a burden to you. So, yes, I agree to change the date of our Engagement Party, or to cancel it if that's necessary." Then with emotion in her voice she added, "We'll have many parties in our lives. I'm just happy that I'll spend my life with such a caring individual as you." With that, tears welled up and she reached across and hugged Hiro.

As with most men confronted by a crying female, Hiro did not know quite how to react. He patted her back feebly and then was grateful to sense that she was regaining her composure.

"Oh, my," Kathleen said wiping her eyes, "I shouldn't cry. The other nurses say it's not very Navy!"

"I bet the other nurses cry on occasion," Hiro ventured, "Although maybe not in the middle of the hospital reception room!"

They both giggled a bit, and Hiro added, "I'm really glad you're the girl who's going to be at my Engagement Party with me."

THE DOOLITTLE IRONY

✥ ✥ ✥

Hiro hurried off to see Captain High at the VOQ to make another frantic explanation.

The Captain took the news in stride. A lifetime in the Navy had inured him to sudden disruptions in one's personal life. He was nevertheless sympathetic, "I'm really sorry to hear that, Hiro, not just because of the party but because it also cancels out your weekend at the Royal Hawaiian; nevertheless, we <u>will</u> have a party!" the Captain promised, "It may not be as grand as the one we would have had on Saturday night. The band probably won't be able to make it, and the caterer may have to abbreviate the menu. But by gosh, we'll put something together."

"I'm really grateful, Captain. It's a lot of extra work for you–and probably extra expense!"

"Don't worry about the extra expense, Hiro," Captain High said slyly, "It's taken care of by a magical pot of money I have access to that's called a 'discretionary fund.' Lowly Captain's like me don't normally have such access but four star admirals do, and the four-star admiral in question here has given me his checkbook. Frankly, I get kind of a kick out of spending it."

"Four star Admiral?" Hiro repeated, "I guess he's the one who would have thrown me in the brig had I tried to leave Base and tell my story to the press. Since that's the case, I won't feel guilty about the expense.' Then with a wry smile added, "Do you think that Kathleen and I might be able to have that weekend in the Royal Hawaiian when I get back?"

"I think we might be able to swing that," the Captain replied with a similar smile, "But for now you better get back to the ship. Don't worry about the party, I'll set it up and notify the guests of the change. Tell your boss you need to be here at 2000 Friday night and may not be back until the wee small hours of Saturday morning. But you <u>will</u> be back before the Yorktown gets underway. I don't think he'll have any trouble with that. His skipper, Captain Buckmaster, and I were classmates at Annapolis. I'm going to call him right now to explain."

CHAPTER 46

"Whatever you say, sir," Hiro replied. "See you Friday evening at 2000."

The Captain picked up the phone and directed the VOQ operator to connect him on a secure line with a series of figures around the base: Captain Buckmaster; the Chief of Nurses at the Hospital; the Supply Officer who ran the O' Club; and Commander Edwin Layton, a senior intelligence on Admiral Nimitz staff who worked closely with Commander Rochefort. In the ensuing conversations he explained that he was calling about a seemingly minor matter but which had considerable significance to Admiral King. That never failed to get their attention. He further explained that the young ensign on whose behalf he was calling was of Japanese descent. With the exception of Captain Buckmaster who had been at sea for many weeks, each of the people he called immediately asked, "Is that the guy who was a spy for us in the IJN?" Captain High did not disabuse them of that. He merely replied, "Well, we don't talk about that." The mystique was irresistible. In each case, the person was more than happy to attend and asked if they could perhaps bring a colleague to meet this young man.

Having finished the call list, Captain High phoned Commander Rochefort and introduced himself.

"Oh, yes sir, I know who you are," the Commander said, "Hiro's mentioned your name," and then, in the occasional overly bold fashion that Joe Rochefort was known for, he added, "And you're also the guy from Admiral King's staff who everybody is wondering about. They want to know just why you're out here so far from Main Navy."

Captain High smiled to himself. So the Commander's reputation was not exaggerated. "Actually, Commander," the Captain replied in the fashion that a superior speaks to a subordinate, "That's what I called about. I need to meet with you privately. Please be in the lobby of the VOQ at 1700." With that the Captain hung up. He was confident Rochefort would be there, even though his phone call did not carry the weight of a direct order–after all, he was not in the Commander's chain of command. But the Captain knew he could rely on Rochefort's curiosity.

⊕ ⊕ ⊕

THE DOOLITTLE IRONY

As expected, Rochefort arrived at the VOQ promptly at 1700. Captain High was at his window on the second floor as Rochefort arrived, and waited just a minute before joining him in the lobby. After all, Commanders waited for Captains, not the other way around.

The two didn't bother introducing themselves. "Let's go for a little walk, Commander. I want to be sure we have privacy." Captain High made his way to a small grove of palms and signaled that the two should take a seat on a bench there. He began, "You were right, Commander, when you indicated that I work for Ernest King. You were also right when you suggested that I was here for him on some special mission. That mission started out to be one thing but changed gradually to another. Let me explain."

Joe Rochefort listened closely but was skeptical. He wondered if Captain High was just another bureaucrat from Washington that would go back and write a report that no one would ever read.

"I came here because the Jimmy Doolittle raid was a total crap shoot. The heavies in Washington wanted a dramatic victory that would take the pressure off them for having blown Pearl Harbor. Doolittle came up with this crackpot scheme to risk two of our very precious carriers here in the Pacific to conduct a raid that was little more than a publicity stunt. Against all odds, he pulled it off, became an overnight hero, and was promoted two ranks to brigadier general. America loved him. What they didn't realize, and what even most of the heavies still don't realize, is that he really should have been shot down and both of the carriers sunk. The fact that they weren't is due to one man: Hiro Yamada. He was in the right place at the right time and he did he did right thing. America owes him a great debt."

"My god, really?" Rochefort exclaimed, "What did he do?"

"I can't give you the details, Commander. You don't have a need-to-know." The Captain paused to watch Rochefort's reaction. Yes, he could see that Rochefort had interpreted the remark just as he hoped he would, i.e., that the rumors were true. Good. That was just the impression the Captain wanted to convey.

"The special treatment that Hiro has received out here," the Captain continued, "Reflects the Navy's gratitude. We've had to do

CHAPTER 46

it *sub rosa* because if it ever became public that we had a spy actually inside the IJN, all our other agents there would be jeopardized."

"Yes, I suppose so," Rochefort observed, then stopped to reflect a bit, "But there might be other reasons why the heavies in Washington want to keep this under wraps."

Captain High was beginning to understand why Rochefort had a reputation for being shrewd. "And what would those be?" the Captain asked innocently.

"From the political standpoint, Washington politicos would not want the American public to think their big victory was just a fluke," Rochefort added, and then, "Especially if it became known that the fluke was the handiwork of a Japanese-American. Hell, we're putting them in prison."

The Captain nodded, thinking Rochefort was in the right profession. He would be difficult for an enemy to deceive. He decided not to discuss Rochefort's observation. He would instead deflect it. "Well, we're Naval Officers," he said to Rochefort, "We concern ourselves with Navy matters. Politics is another world, one which I'm glad not to be a part of. My job has been to protect the informant network in Japan–and that brings me to why I asked you here."

The Captain paused, looking intently at Rochefort, and announced, "I am now turning that task over to you, Commander. I will return to Washington D.C, shortly and when I do, I want you pick up this task. Put very simply, you will be responsible for assuring that Ensign Yamada does not share his role in the Doolittle Raid with anyone, even you."

Rochefort thought for a bit and then asked, "And what do I do if Hiro does try to tell others?"

"Stop him. Have him arrested on some charges that you can trump up on the spot. Then contact me. I'll handle the matter from there on."

"There are a few other points," the Captain added, "You are not to divulge to anyone, even those in your chain of command, that you are doing this, or that the U.S. Navy has spies in the IJN. I assure you that those who need to know about this already do. And I want to emphasize that I am directing you to do this under the personal authority of Admiral Ernest King."

THE DOOLITTLE IRONY

"Okay, Captain," Rochefort agreed, "Sounds spooky, but I guess it's important. Frankly, I never had any inkling that we had spies in the IJN. That's a field of intelligence I know nothing about. Maybe I can get briefed up on it someday."

"It's a highly specialized field, Commander," Captain High replied noncommittally, "But I'll see what I can do." He was a bit ashamed of making such an empty promise, and he hoped he would never have to explain the minor deceits he had just used to get Rochefort's cooperation. But he consoled himself with the knowledge that he had just recruited his replacement–a replacement who was shrewd, competent and trustworthy. He had done what he had been ordered to do. He and Bill Russo could now return to Washington with reasonable confidence that Hiro would not become a national embarrassment.

But first he must host an engagement party.

The O' Club itself was not an imposing structure. It had been built during the period when Pearl Harbor was just a coaling stop for Naval ships en route to Asia, but the officer in charge of the O' Club had managed to hide the Club's faded glory. The banquet room was bedecked in paper streamers and balloons, tables were covered with linen clothes, a bar had been set up at one end of the room, trays of *hors d'oeuvres* were positioned strategically, the lights were properly dimmed, and there were even a few music stands set up. Apparently someone had managed to hire a small music group, despite the short notice. Overhead a tasteful sign reading "Congratulations Hiro and Kathleen" was strung across the ceiling. Captain High mused to himself that mention of Ernest King did indeed get one special attention.

The guests began arriving early. A few were in dress whites but most wore work uniforms, having come directly from their 12-16 hour workday that was then the rule. A few were in civilian attire– probably enlisted men from Wypo who Rochefort had told that, since enlisted men were not allowed in the Officers Club, just come in mufti (civvies).

CHAPTER 46

There was no formal guest list. Captain High had simply asked the people he called to bring along anyone they thought appropriate, no upper limit. Considering that food and drink were free, the Captain anticipated a good showing. He was not disappointed.

Bill Russo had joined the Captain early, thinking he might help with last minute details, "Wow, Captain, it's not even 2000 and there's a line at the bar!"

"Yes, looks like we're going to have a good crowd," the Captain replied, "I just asked the Club Officer to set up another bar on the other side of the room."

"What do you have planned for the evening, Skipper?

"I thought I'd start with a welcome speech, then introduce the new couple and set up a reception line. That's traditional, gives everyone a chance to meet them. While that's going on, everyone else will get a few drinks under their belt and schmooze with their bosses. About 2100 or so, we can push back the tables and have the new couple dance. Then, since we'll have a bunch of nurses here, maybe we can prevail on them to dance with all these lonely guys."

"Hey, that sounds like a pretty nice agenda, Skipper. Sounds like you put some thought into it."

"Thanks, Bill, but I just copied my own Engagement Party—even though that was more than 25 years ago."

Hiro arrived at the party promptly at 2000, in dress whites, accompanied by his new *Yorktown* boss, Commander Eason. Bill and Captain High met them at the door but before they could exchange greetings, Kathleen arrived with a flourish. She looked stunning in dress Whites, in the company of at least ten other nurses also in dress Whites, all of whom were in high spirits. Bill wondered if they had got an early start on the evening with some of the hospital's medicinal alcohol. Social gatherings had been rare in the last six months since the Pearl Harbor attack, and they had obviously arrived ready to party! As the nurses filed in, conversations among the men stopped. The newly arrived females immediately became the center of attention."

Hiro pulled Kathleen over to Bill and the Captain. He spoke loudly to be heard over the hubbub, "Kathleen, you've met Bill and now I want you to meet our host, Captain High."

THE DOOLITTLE IRONY

Uncaring of military decorum, Kathleen rushed over and hugged the Captain tightly, then blurted, "Captain, I feel like I already know you. Hiro has talked about you so much, and he has such respect for you! We owe you and Bill so much already … and now this!" She gestured toward the party. "I'm so excited. I've never seen anything like this."

Kathleen was just what the Captain expected–bright, bubbly, a girl who lights up a room with just her presence. "Kathleen, I am so pleased to meet you," he shouted over the party noise which, with the arrival of the nurses, had become intense, "Hiro has talked about you also, so I feel like I know you too. But before we get into all that, we first have to get this party started. I'm going to introduce you and Hiro to the crowd."

Then he leaned over to Hiro and whispered, "Some of these people think you were a spy for us in the Japanese Navy. Don't agree, don't disagree. Just smile and change the subject."

"Okay, Captain. I think I understand. I've already got a few remarks like that."

The Captain took Kathleen's hand and led her and Hiro to the small, raised platform where the band would play. He raised his voice to get the crowd's attention, "Ladies, Gentlemen." Not loud enough. Half the room didn't even notice. He tried again, this time in full throat, "LADIES AND GENTLEMEN, MAY I HAVE YOUR ATTENTION!" This time it worked. Conversations stopped, the room quieted and only an occasional clink of glassware was heard.

"Thank you all for coming here tonight," he began, "I promise to keep this short and let you get back to the serious business of the evening–getting drunk!" The guests shouted and waved their glasses in approval. The Captain waited for silence to return, "But first I think a few remarks are appropriate. As you know all too well, this war has disrupted many lives. It's brought grief and hardship. It's separated us from our families and loved ones. It leaves us no choice but to bear the burden and do the best we can. That's what the two young people we honor here tonight are doing. They would have preferred this be a wedding reception, but we know that Navy nurses are not permitted to marry."

CHAPTER 46

Again the crowd erupted, but this time in disapproval. They booed and shouted, and the nurses were among the most vocal. The Captain smiled, waited patiently, and said, "Thank you, I'll pass that along to Admiral King when I get back to Washington." This time the shouts shifted back to ones of approval.

"So tonight it's my duty to apprise all you single young studs out there that this beautiful girl beside me is no longer on the market." Disappointed "aahs" filled the room. The Captain smiled, "I say that because tonight I have the honor of announcing that Ensign Kathleen Kelly is now engaged to be married to Ensign Hiro Yamada!"

Again, loud shouts of approval erupted along with chants of "Kathleen and Hiro, Kathleen and Hiro." Hiro took Kathleen's hand and the two smiled and waved like a pair of politicians.

Laughing at the crowd's raucous behavior, Bill leaned over and said to Captain High, "If there this the way they are 30 minutes into the party, look out for midnight!"

The Captain had one more announcement. He clinked a glass with his spoon and shouted above the tumult, "One more thing. I'm going to ask Hiro and Kathleen to stand here in front of the platform so you can personally wish them well, and after that we've got some music to dance to!"

More cheers for the dancing, and then everyone queued up in the standard Navy reception line to congratulate Hiro and wish felicitations to Kathleen. (In 1942, polite guests did not "congratulate" a bride. That would imply that she had "accomplished" something. It was more gentile to offer one's felicitations.)

Kathleen and Hiro were a handsome couple standing there receiving their well-wishers. Kathleen was radiant and, in his dress whites, Hiro no longer "looked like the enemy." The two were gracious, accepting each greeting with a smile and thank you. There were a few references to spying: "Good to have you back from Tokyo," and "We owe a lot to people who do what you've done." Hiro just smiled and thanked them for coming.

The reception line eventually spent itself and the musicians set up to play. The guests pushed tables out of the way to make room to dance, and the four piece band began with renditions of the day's popular songs like "Stardust," "Amapola," and "Green Eyes."

THE DOOLITTLE IRONY

Kathleen and Hiro had the first dance, and then others followed. When the band went up tempo to "Take the 'A' Train" and "Boogie Woogie Bugler Boy," the guests really got into the swing of things and the nurses demonstrated they knew a thing or two about cutting a rug. Of course, four musicians couldn't reproduce a Big Band sound, but for a crowd already half lubricated, the music was just great. The nurses seemed inexhaustible. Some of the men asked Kathleen to dance and, after getting a smiling nod from Hiro, swept her onto the floor being sure to hold her at a respectful distance. Kathleen relished the music, the party and high spirits. She had never before been the subject of so much attention.

By 2300, those who had to go back to work had already left, and those who were determined to make a night of it were well on their way to doing so.

Kathleen and Hiro found Captain High and Bill leaning against a wall trying to talk above the party's din. Hiro interrupted, "Sir, if you think it would be okay, Kathleen and I would like to leave. We would like some time to ourselves."

"Sure, Hiro," the Captain replied, "At this point I don't think anyone's going to miss you. But don't be too late. Remember you have to deploy tomorrow."

"Thank you, sir," Hiro shouted, "Commander Eason said I have to be back at the ship by 0200 and I promised not to be late." Kathy gave a wave to Bill and the Captain and whispered to Bill, "Take good care of Hiro." Bill nodded and smiled. He would later remember that promise under very trying circumstances.

Hiro shouted, "See you tomorrow, Bill." Then he and Kathleen took off out the front door like a pair of kids on the first day of summer vacation.

"See you tomorrow?" Captain High repeated to Bill, "What the hell does that mean?"

"I've been waiting for an opportunity all evening to tell you, Skipper," Bill replied, "I volunteered to go out with the *Yorktown* also."

"When did this happen?" the Captain asked, and why didn't you even check with me first?"

CHAPTER 46

"Actually, it came up just tonight." Bill responded, a little taken aback by the Captain's apparent disapproval, "Commander Eason cornered me earlier in the evening and told me he's desperate for officers who speak Japanese. Hiro told him I spent two years in Tokyo so he asked if I would man an intercept position for him. I thought you would approve because I could keep an eye on Hiro."

"Hmmmmf," the Captain responded with one of his usual grunts, "I guess you're right. But that actually brings up another subject I've wanted to talk to you about, Bill. I think we've done just about all we can do with respect to Hiro. I think it's about time we bow out."

"Really!" Bill said with surprise, "You don't think there is any chance he might still try to go public?"

"Kathleen is out here with him now. I doubt he would do anything to jeopardize that."

"But his family situation is still a problem. What if his father dies because of health conditions in the camp? Or his sister gets raped by a guard? Or something else like that?"

The Captain smiled slyly, "Well, I've recruited a "minder" to keep an eye on Hiro after we leave: Joe Rochefort"

"Rochefort? Are you sure that was a good idea Captain? Joe's a maverick. He might take Hiro's side and call the press himself."

"I gave him a story that I think he bought," the Captain said, "I told him that Hiro had been a spy for us, and there are more like him still in Tokyo. If Hiro's story ever leaked, the others would be tracked down and shot."

"Captain," Bill said, I'm surprised at you! That was a lie."

"What do you expect, Bill? I certainly couldn't tell him the truth–although he came pretty close to figuring it out for himself. Anyway, when we go, we'll leave behind a guy who will be seeing Hiro every day and can notify us if his behavior becomes erratic. I told him if he did that, we'd handle it from there."

"Okay, Skipper, whatever you say. But right now I've got to get a few things together and catch the tender out to the *Yorktown*. She's already out of dry dock."

"Okay, get going," Captain High said lightly, "Oh, and Bill, try to keep an eye on Hiro while you're out there. He's pretty young."

"Sure, Skipper, I'll do what I can."

CHAPTER 47

MIDWAY: THE MOST SIGNIFICANT NAVAL BATTLE OF WWII

Almost miraculously, three days after its return to Pearl Harbor the *Yorktown* had been patched up and was headed back to sea. It had been deemed by experts to be sufficiently "combat-worthy" to operate for a period of about two weeks, long enough to participate in the upcoming battle.

"Combat worthy" was an optimistic phrase. Major repairs had been put off until the ship returned stateside. Lesser repairs had been "jury rigged"–the Navy term for a temporary improvisation. Even some of that work remained unfinished. Civilian yard workers were still hard at it when the *Yorktown* got underway. They had to go ashore in small boats as the carrier moved down the channel.

Other problems had been jury rigged also. Aircrews and aircraft had been cobbled together from other ships to bring the *Yorktown's* Air Group up to strength. The ship's company was augmented from shore elements that could spare a few personnel. Regardless of deficiencies, the *Yorktown* got underway. It would rendezvous north of Midway Atoll with the *Hornet* and the *Enterprise*, both of which had left port several days earlier.

CHAPTER 47

Kathleen watched from a hospital window as the *Yorktown* sailed back down the long Pearl Harbor channel to the Pacific. The young man she wanted to spend her life with was on it. She had left him at the pier very early that same morning, anxious to prove himself in battle, and totally confident he would return safely. She had tried hard to match his optimism and put on a brave face so he would not have to worry about her. But as the tender pulled away from the pier to deliver its load of men returning from liberty to the *Yorktown*, she had broken into tears.

The past year had been a whip-saw of emotion for Kathleen. First her impetuous break with Hiro because of some cockamamie scheme of his mother's to find a wife in Japan, then their reunion on Whidbey Island, followed soon thereafter by their separation for Hiro to go to Tokyo on "business." (She had since heard from others that he had gone on a spy mission!) Then came the anguishing months when he disappeared, followed by the sudden exaltation of his return.

Now she was a Navy nurse charged with awesome responsibility of caring for men who had been injured in the Japanese attack on Pearl Harbor and the Battle of the Coral Sea. Moreover, her fiancée was determined to prove all by himself that Americans of Japanese descent were just as patriotic as any other Americans. She yearned for her home and the stable life she had been accustomed to.

As the *Yorktown* disappeared down the channel, Kathleen's heart was heavy with fear that the worst had not yet occurred. She wondered what she would do if anything happened to Hiro.

Captain High also watched the *Yorktown* leave harbor, and he also had a sense of foreboding. For him, this was a change of roles. Previously it had always been he that was leaving on the ship, while his wife and daughters watched from shore. The Captain did not welcome the change. He had come to regard both Hiro and Bill as the sons he never had. He was proud that they had volunteered to go, but realized that neither understood the real danger. At their ages, mortality was still something that applied to others. They would live forever.

The Captain had decided that he would watch the battle unfold in Admiral Nimitz' own Flag Plot. It was a not-really-spacious room in Headquarters with a small six-person conference table at its center and a phone positioned on the table at each chair. Maps covered two walls; the third was made up of blackboards on which recently-arrived information was displayed; and the fourth held status boards for each ship in the Pacific Fleet, showing its position, fuel status, and a variety of other data important to their operation. Flag Plot was where all the information was assembled that enabled Admiral Nimitz to command the Fleet. It was off limits to all but a few.

Captain High was a visitor to PACFLT and would not normally have intruded, but these were special circumstances. Plus, he WAS Ernie King's emissary and who was going to ask the CNO's man to leave? Certainly no one who cared about his next promotion! Even so, Captain High chose to minimize his presence by taking a seat against the wall, out of Admiral Nimitz' vision. He would say nothing during the coming action, but his pocket contained a small wallet-sized notebook on which he would jot notes on matters which he thought Admiral King might be interested. Strictly speaking, Admiral Nimitz' management of the upcoming battle was not something that Admiral King had asked him to do, but Captain High knew well that the CNO would listen very closely to whatever report he took back.

Captain High had carefully read CINCPAC's Op Order 29-42, Nimitz' Operation Order outlining how he expected the enemy to attack and how he wanted U.S. forces to defend. Captain High considered it a remarkable document. Op Orders were supposed to give subordinate commanders enough information and guidance to have them understand their mission, but not so much to interfere with their ability to employ their forces as the situation dictated. This delegation of authority was wryly encapsulated in the Naval axiom that, "The Commander should issue the Op Order, then go on leave."

Op Order 29-42 outlined the enemy attack plan. The IJN would converge on Midway from three directions: a landing force of troop transports from directly west; a battle group of surface com-

CHAPTER 47

batants from west-northwest; and a strike force of four carriers from the northwest. The Op Order also provided the objectives for U.S. forces: prevent Midway's seizure by Japan, and inflict as much damage as possible on Japanese naval forces while avoiding undue risk to U.S. forces.

Captain High observed that Nimitz' Op Order was based firmly on Joe Rochefort's intelligence estimate. Others had taken issue with that. OP-20G, the Washington headquarters element that oversaw Rochefort's office, thought perhaps Pearl Harbor was Tokyo's real target, not Midway. General Emmons, the Army Commander in Hawaii, agreed, arguing that Rochefort had made his estimate based on intentions, not capabilities—a classical error according to many military intelligence specialists.

But Nimitz had studied the intelligence closely before accepting it. He had even appointed one of his staff to play Devil's Advocate and present alternative interpretations. After close scrutiny, he was convinced Rochefort was right. He accepted the intelligence and built his Op Order on it. That was gutsy.

But as Rochefort's intelligence estimate was well defined and timely, and Nimitz' Op Order well calculated and precise, the actual conduct of the battle by U.S. forces turned out to be anything but. The dramatic American victory was the product of mishap, serendipity, and just plain good luck. Several historians of the Battle have quoted this famous line by Otto Von Bismark: *"There is a Providence that protects idiots, drunkards, children and the United States of America."*

Sitting like the proverbial fly on a wall, Captain High watched over the shoulders of Nimitz' Battle Staff as the Battle of Midway unfolded. Taking breaks only as nature required and his stomach demanded, catching catnaps in a chair in an outer room, he jotted the following:

2 June–With Nimitz Battle Staff awaiting attack:

THE DOOLITTLE IRONY

Enemy: three-pronged attack expected. Force of four carriers from northwest, Force of Surface Combatants from west-northwest, and Landing Force from west.

Friendly: Hornet and Enterprise are TF 16 under Rear Admiral Spruance. Enterprise and supporting ships are Task Force 17 under Rear Admiral Fletcher. The two TFs will operate separately with Fletcher in overall command. Both TFs have moved to positions about 300 miles northwest of Midway to ambush approaching Japanese Carrier Strike Force.

3 June–Patrol aircraft from Midway sight formation of Japanese ships 700 miles due west. It is the Japanese Landing Force. Report removes any remaining doubt that Rochefort's intelligence estimate is accurate.

4 June 1942–High altitude bombers from Midway conduct early morning bombing of the Japanese Landing Force. No hits reported.

0600–Navy patrol aircraft sights the four-carrier IJN carrier Strike Force. Midway launches torpedo planes and dive bombers to attack them, but holds back fighters to defend Island.

0630–Japanese carriers launch strike against Midway to eliminate its beach defenses in preparation for troop landing.

0708–Midway torpedo planes arrive over Japanese carriers and begin attack. U.S. torpedo bombers slow and, without fighter cover, are easy prey for Jap Zeros. Almost all U.S. aircraft are shot down.

0700–Enterprise and Hornet launch six squadrons of fighters, dive bombers, and torpedo planes to conduct coordinated strike against IJN carriers. Aircraft proceed to position where they thought Nagumo would be, but Jap carriers apparently changed course. The strike aircraft get separated. Torpedo planes turn north searching for IJN but fighters and dive bombers head south.

CHAPTER 47

0730–Japanese air strike on Midway reports unexpectedly stiff resistance by Midway defenses. Leader of Japanese attack radios message back to IJN carriers that a second strike is necessary.

0925–29 torpedo planes from Enterprise and Hornet locate Japanese carriers. Again, attack is made without fighter cover. All but four aircraft are shot down. No Jap carriers are hit by torpedoes.

1000–12 Yorktown torpedo planes attack IJN carriers. This time they have light fighter cover but it is quickly outnumbered and overwhelmed. Ten of twelve are lost. No torpedo hits.

Note: So far today, 51 American torpedo planes conducted attacks and only nine survived.

⊕ ⊕ ⊕

WITH THE IJN STRIKE FORCE

Aboard his flagship carrier *Akagi*, Admiral Nagumo was worried. Japanese planners had anticipated American forces on Midway would be taken by surprise and put up little resistance, as had been the case six months earlier at Pearl Harbor. They were wrong. Midway had proven quite ready and quite stubborn. A second strike was necessary so Nagumo had ordered that planes on the carrier's decks, which had been armed with torpedoes for use against U.S. carriers, be rearmed with general purpose weapons to use against Midway.

While that was going on, another wave of torpedo planes arrived and commenced a second attack. It was futile, of course. The Japanese combat air patrol fighters shot down every one of the slow, lumbering American torpedo planes.

Then came the fateful report. One of Nagumo's scout planes spotted a formation of ships, among which they reported was at least one aircraft carrier. Nagumo was astonished. An American carrier within striking distance! He remembered the underlying purpose for capturing Midway Island discussed in IJN planning sessions. It was

THE DOOLITTLE IRONY

not just to acquire a base from which to attack U.S. military targets on Oahu, it was to draw the American Navy into battle and sink the Pacific Fleet's carriers. Now, he was presented with an opportunity to do just that even before capturing Midway. At least one American carrier was within range of his powerful fleet. He would deal with it and let Midway wait. At 1000, Nagumo countermanded his earlier order, and directed that the aircraft on his carrier decks be rearmed a second time, this time going back to torpedoes. Deck crews swung into action. General purpose bombs that had already been hung on the wings of aircraft were now downloaded and set aside while torpedoes were brought up from below.

1020–American dive bombers arrive undetected over the Japanese Strike Force–six aircraft from the Enterprise and 17 from Yorktown. Jap fighters had failed to detect their approach because the Jap aircraft had descended to 1,000 feet to defend against low level torpedo attacks while U.S. aircraft arrive at 20,000 feet. U.S. dive bombers attack without opposition and score numerous hits. Leave three IJN carriers burning.

> *Note: Astonishingly, the two groups of U.S. aircraft arrived together through sheer luck. The Enterprise dive bombers had missed the Japanese carriers completely, but then saw a lone Japanese destroyer steaming rapidly north. The Americans reasoned correctly that it was trying to catch up with the Japanese carrier force and used its course as a vector to the Japanese carriers. When it found them, it attacked not knowing that the Yorktown force was there also. Again through sheer serendipity, the two groups selected different carriers to attack. Talk about luck!*
>
> *Learned later the flight decks of the IJN carriers' were packed with planes that were being rearmed to attack the U.S. carriers. American dive bombers*

CHAPTER 47

scored direct hits. Secondary explosions set the IJN carriers Akagi, Kaga, and Siryu ablaze. All three subsequently sank. One carrier, Hiryu, eluded the attackers.

1054–The Hiryu launches strike aircraft.

Note: Some believe the Hiryu aircraft found Yorktown by following the U.S. aircraft that had just attacked Japanese carriers back to Yorktown.

◈ ◈ ◈

Aboard the *Yorktown*

Hiro and Bill's duty stations were in Radio Central, usually referred to as the Comms Shack, located just below and aft of the bridge. It held racks of communications and RDF (radio-direction-finding) gear. There were three operator "positions," small metal desks pushed against the bulkhead with communication equipment stacked in racks in front of each desk. A voice pipe connected the Communications Shack to the Duty Officer on the bridge.

Normally, each position monitored a set of assigned USN frequencies. On receipt of a message addressed to the ship, they would copy the transmission and pass it to a communications officer who would then decode and deliver it to the Captain or another officer. They did not routinely monitor enemy tactical frequencies, except during combat or in areas where they might encounter an enemy. That certainly would be the case for the next few days.

Today they would begin to monitor Japanese air-to-air and air-to-ship communications. Most naval movements were conducted in radio silence, to prevent the enemy from using the radio signal to locate them. But once an attack began, some radio communications became absolutely necessary. For example, leaders of an air strike had to be able to direct their aircraft and report results back to the carrier. Pilots had to be able to communicate with their wingmen.

THE DOOLITTLE IRONY

Communications of this sort were usually by voice, and time did not permit the use of encryption. Simple codes and authentication measures were used to provide a modicum of security, but an acute enemy would usually be able to see through them. That is what Hiro and Bill hoped to be able to help with.

During their first few days at sea, enemy frequencies were quiet. But at dawn on 4 June air-to-air frequencies came alive with Japanese chatter. The RDF equipment indicated they were coming from the Midway area. The attack Rochefort had predicted was underway.

The remainder of the day was packed with both Japanese and American aircraft communications. Bill and Hiro translated the Japanese and passed it to Commander Eason or one of his assistants. They would synthesize both enemy and friendly activity into a single report and pass it to the Battle Staff.

They chronicled the dramatic events of the day: the Japanese attack on Midway; its leader's assessment that another strike was needed; the PBY sighting of the Japanese carrier force; the disastrous torpedo attacks on the Japanese carriers; and then the convergence of *Enterprise* and *Yorktown* dive bombers and their successful attack. Bill and Hiro both heard the alarmed Japanese voices that first saw the American SBD Devastators diving on them, scoring direct hits with their 500- and 1,000-pound bombs. They heard the alarmed cries from other Japanese ships and emergency directions from carrier personnel seeking to control the infernos that erupted on the three carriers.

Bill and Hiro both stood and excitedly translated aloud what they were hearing. Commander Eason stood by the voice tube giving the bridge a blow-by-blow account. One of the operators put the Yorktown pilots chatter on loudspeaker, and all heard the report that three enemy carriers were on fire. The Comms Shack erupted with cheers–but their elation was short lived.

1152–Yorktown's radar detects 18 fighters and 18 dive bombers from the Hiryu 32 miles out. Yorktown's combat air patrol intercepted them and shot down 11 bombers. Intense anti-aircraft fire from the Yorktown and her escorts got several more, but three bombs hit the Yorktown.

CHAPTER 47

When the Japanese aircraft got within range of the *Yorktown's* guns, the noise became deafening. Hiro stepped outside and as he looked up saw a Japanese dive bomber coming straight at him. But then the shipboard guns caught the aircraft in crossfire and the plane disintegrated. But it had already released its bomb. It hit the *Yorktown's* flight deck, bounced, and then exploded just aft of the island.

The blast blew Hiro back through the hatch into the Comms Shack where he lay on the floor stunned. When he looked up he saw Bill's face. His lips were moving but Hiro heard no sound from them. In fact he heard no sound at all. Bill propped him against a bulkhead and returned to his headset. Hiro lay there dazed for a few minutes as his hearing slowly returned.

Hiro felt okay otherwise and so stood and, without a word to anyone in the Comms Shack, went back out on deck. The scene was a maelstrom of smoke and noise and confusion. Somehow, flight ops were continuing, even as a damage control party covered the hole the bomb had created. Hiro looked around and saw a dozen or more bodies strewn about, some mangled and dismembered. Sailors who rarely set foot on the flight deck had turned out to help. Cooks, stewards and musicians from the ship's band were gathering human remains into canvas bags. Fires were burning along the base of the Island, and a stench filled the air that he realized must be the smell of burnt human flesh. He retreated into the Comms Shack and sat back down at his desk trying to regain his composure.

1320–Hiryu launches another 12 fighters and 10 torpedo planes against Yorktown. Yorktown's combat air patrol intercepts them but five manage to launch torpedoes before being shot down.

In the Comms Shack the shock of the previous bomb explosions had left the radio receivers practically useless. They picked up no Japanese chatter as the Hiryu launched its second strike so they could issue no early warning of the incoming aircraft. The *Yorktown* crew's first indication of the attack was the klaxon sounding. A few minutes later they felt the Yorktown veer hard to starboard, then back to port. Captain Buckmaster was attempting to steer the Yorktown between

THE DOOLITTLE IRONY

the torpedoes streaking toward them. Then came an ear shattering roar and two explosions in quick succession, so powerful they seem to pick the *Yorktown* up and then smash it down into the Pacific.

This time Hiro was knocked out briefly but did not lose his hearing. As he came to, he noticed the entire Comms Shack seemed to be leaning toward him and he could hear Bill shouting urgently, "Hiro, we have to abandon ship. Let's get to hell out of here."

With Bill's help Hiro stood. It was quite dark. Power was off and the deep rumble of the ships engines had gone silent. As the two climbed down the ladder onto the flight deck they noticed men lined up along the port side of the ship waiting to climb down lines that had been thrown over the edge. It was obvious that Captain Buckmaster had ordered "abandon ship." There was no panic although a few of the men chose to jump the 30 feet or so rather than wait.

"That's too high for me," Hiro told Bill as they peered over the edge."

"Yeah, me too," Bill replied, "Let's go aft. It looks lower back there."

They did, traversing the tilted flight deck, hanging onto whatever they could, and skirting the parked planes that seemed on the verge of sliding into the Pacific.

Bill was right. The fantail was only about ten feet above the water so the jump into the Pacific was not so dangerous. As they stood on the edge, Bill reached over and tightened Hiro's kapok life vest. "It's an easy jump," he told Hiro, "Once you're in the water swim away from the ship as fast as you can. When it goes down it could suck us down with it if we're too close. I'll be right behind you. Now go."

Not willing to risk any hesitation on Hiro's part, Bill pushed a startled Hiro into the Pacific and jumped in after him. Both swam strongly about 100 yards, not an easy task in the bulky vests. They rested, floating with other survivors all about. He tried not to think about sharks or the possibility that Japanese fighter pilots would strafe this large group of survivors. Bill tried to stay near Hiro and wondered, incongruously, why he felt so protective of him. Because Captain High had asked him to do so? Or because Kathleen had? Probably both, he thought, but mostly Kathleen.

CHAPTER 47

Then he heard shouts and whistles, and then the thrum of marine diesels as a rescue boat from one of the destroyers arrived on the scene. It pulled in about 20 survivors and reassured those still in the water that it would be right back for them. After three boatloads, Hiro and Bill were pulled into the craft and taken back to the destroyer, the *USS Hughes*. The two had to climb up a Jacobs Ladder to board the ship. Neither realized just how tired they were until then. Strong arms of the *Hughes* sailors had to pull them up and onto the deck. There were friendly 'Welcome Aboard' shouts from the *Hughes* crew and blankets were tossed over their shivering bodies. A few minutes later they were given hot chocolate and dry clothes that the crew itself had donated. Very soon thereafter both Hiro and Bill were asleep.

1445–American scout planes locate Hiryu.

1700–American planes attack and sink Hiryu.

5 June–0020: Admiral Yamamoto calls off the Japanese effort to seize Midway. All three of the Japanese forces–Landing, Surface Combatant, and what's left of the Strike Force–turn and head home.

Yamamoto was stunned. He had conceived the attack on Pearl Harbor primarily to destroy the heart of the American Pacific Fleet–its carriers. Then Jimmy Doolittle demonstrated that America could use those carriers to strike at the heart of Japan. The attacked had shamed the IJN. Unwilling to risk that happening again, Yamamoto devised the Midway operation to draw those carriers into combat and destroy them. He committed over 200 ships to the effort, the bulk of the IJN combat force. But, inexplicably, it had failed. Despite his advantages in numbers and quality of equipment and personnel, the Americans had in the space of a few hours destroyed four fleet carriers, 322 aircraft, and probably 2500 men. Surely, the gods had conspired against him.

Now, having lost virtually all of his air power, he knew he could not successfully seize Midway. He must return home in shame, without the victory he had so confidently expected. His decision to cancel

THE DOOLITTLE IRONY

the invasion signals the high water mark of the Imperial Japanese Empire. Never again would it regain the military initiative.

5 June, dawn—The stubborn Yorktown did not sink overnight as expected. It remains afloat. An ocean-going tug from Pearl Harbor takes it in tow and four destroyers establish a screen around it.

After a hearty breakfast, Bill and Hiro stood at the Hughes rail admiring the gritty Yorktown still afloat in the distance. As they watch, the heavy cruiser Astoria pulls alongside. Captain Buckmaster is on a bull horn, asking for volunteers to re-board the Yorktown and resume damage control efforts. He believes the ship can be saved.

Hiro brightens and says, "C'mon Bill, let's do it."

"What?" Bill asks incredulously, "For crying out loud, Hiro, we just got pulled out of the drink. Isn't that enough heroism for now?" His voice raised a few decibels and he blurted, "That ship is a goner. It could go under any time. Do you want to be on it when it does?"

"You heard Captain Buckmaster," Hiro retorted, "He thinks the ship can be salvaged. He needs help."

Bill was a bit irritated by Hiro's attitude and chose to be frank, "Are you sure you're not just trying to be a hero?" he asked, "You know, no matter how brave you are, you're not going to change the treatment of your people back in the States. If you go down with that ship, no one's really going to notice. You're just one little guy in a great big war."

But Hiro had already made up his mind. "If you don't want to go, Bill, that's okay. It probably is just a dumb stunt. But I'm going!" With that he started off toward a nearby knot of men gathered around an officer with a clipboard.

Bill gritted his teeth. Hiro truly did not know the risks involved. He was completely new to the Navy and did not even know his way around a carrier. He could get lost below deck. The passageway behind him could flood and he would not know alternate routes to get back. With a grimace, Bill turned reluctantly to follow Hiro.

Captain Buckmaster was apparently a very popular commanding officer. Bill heard his name mentioned by several of the sailors who were volunteering to go back aboard the Yorktown. "If that's

CHAPTER 47

what the Captain wants, that's what the Captain gets," said one. "I'll follow him anywhere," said another.

The officer with the clip board took Hiro's and Bill's name and file numbers, and motioned for them to wait with the dozen or more other survivors who had also volunteered to go back. A boat was lowered and the volunteers were transferred to the *Astoria*. It then moved to another destroyer where Captain Buckmaster repeated his pitch on the bullhorn. By the time the *Astoria* completed its recruiting effort, it was too late in the day to re-board, but early the next morning the *Astoria's* launch began to ferry the volunteers back to the crippled *Yorktown*.

6 June–A party of volunteers re-boards the Yorktown to resume damage control measures. They appear to be succeeding when a Japanese submarine eludes the Yorktown's destroyer screen and fires four torpedoes. One misses entirely, one hits the destroyer Hammann which was alongside helping with damage control. The remaining two strike the Yorktown. Captain Buckmaster orders "abandon ship" for the second time.

The *Yorktown* was by now so low in the water that Bill and Hiro were able to step from the Astoria's launch right onto the carrier's hangar deck. From there they made their treacherous way back to the Comms Shack. They had been given instructions to put all classified material, code books, code machines, etc., in a weighted bag and throw them overboard. But after reflecting on the matter, the two decided that was not very productive. After all, if they just left it in place and the ship sank, the material would be the same place as if they had thrown it overboard. If the ship did not sink, then the material could be recovered when it reached Pearl. In neither case was it in danger of falling into enemy hands. So Bill and Hiro chose to volunteer their efforts elsewhere.

Much had been done already to save the *Yorktown*. A salvage crew had jettisoned aircraft, cut away an anchor, and pumped seawater into empty fuel tanks to right her list. The destroyer *USS Hammann* had come alongside and was providing electrical power to the salvage effort. The ocean-going tug, *Vireo*, was towing the

THE DOOLITTLE IRONY

Yorktown toward Pearl Harbor at about two knots and, altogether, the ship's prospects were looking better.

But not all of the Japanese fleet went home when Admiral Yamamoto canceled the operation. The submarine I-168 shadowed the crippled *Yorktown*, looking for a chance to finish it off. At about 1330 on 6 June it penetrated the destroyer screen around the carrier and fired a pair of torpedoes followed quickly by a second pair. Bill and Hiro were at the edge of the hangar deck tending the power cable that ran from the *Hammann*.

Bill saw the wakes of the torpedoes and tried to shout a warning to the destroyer. He didn't have to. Its crew had already seen them and sprang into action. Two sailors with large hatchets began chopping the mooring lines that tied her to the *Yorktown*. Two other sailors ran to the depth charges stacked on her rear deck, apparently intending to disarm them. It took a minute and 20 seconds for the torpedoes to traverse the 1,350 yards to the Hammann, not enough time to disarm the depth charges. The first torpedo missed, but the second caught the destroyer amidships, sending up a huge column of water and violently wrenching the destroyer in half. Sailors leapt overboard and tried to swim away, but the stern half of the destroyer sank almost immediately. A minute after that the depth charges went off and the blast, as one observer put it, "swept the swimmers from the water like a windshield wiper cleans a windshield of water droplets."

Close behind, the second pair of torpedoes ran beneath the crippled *Hammann* and struck the *Yorktown*. It shook the ship violently. Bill was knocked off his feet and struck his head against a stanchion as he fell. He lost consciousness and when he came to, men were already moving past him to abandon ship.

Bill stood and looked around for Hiro. He was nowhere in sight. Bill searched for him on the hangar deck and then awkwardly climbed the tilted ladder to the flight deck, but Hiro was not there either. Bill clawed his way against the ship's list to the passageway that led to the Comms Shack. It was completely dark, but then a quartermaster burst out of the chart room carrying what Bill guessed was the ship's navigation log. "Get outta here!" he shouted a bit hysterically. "The Captain ordered abandon ship. It's sinking fast."

CHAPTER 47

"Is there anyone inside?" Bill demanded.

"Not a soul. I'm the last one," the quartermaster yelled over his shoulder and disappeared down the ladder.

Bill didn't know where else to look. He guessed that Hiro had left Bill to help somebody else and when he got back, Bill was gone. Hiro was now probably abandoning ship himself. Bill had little choice but to follow. He made his way back to the hangar deck, plunged into the Pacific, and swam toward the nearby *Vireo* that was picking up survivors

Once aboard, Bill searched for Hiro among the other survivors, asking many if they had seen him. One of them related the story about how the *Hammann's* depth charges had apparently exploded underwater and the grim effect it had had on survivors floating nearby. Bill remembered that he and Hiro had been at the edge of the Yorktown's hangar deck when the torpedo hit. He had been blown against a stanchion. He supposed it was possible that Hiro had been blown into the sea. If so, he would have probably become a victim of the depth charges. Not an encouraging thought!

Sunday, 7 June 1942, 0700: the Yorktown finally slides beneath the Pacific, the victim of three bombs and four torpedoes.

CHAPTER 48

THE AFTERMATH

Just six months earlier the Imperial Japanese Navy had attacked Pearl Harbor Naval Base and left the bulk of America's Pacific Fleet in smoking ruins. Now, as the U.S. Navy's combatants steamed back into Pearl from the Battle of Midway, many noted with grim satisfaction that they had exacted a down payment on the revenge that the Japanese Empire so richly deserved. But Pearl Harbor's victorious mood was tempered by the recognition of its own losses: the *Yorktown*, the *Hammann*, 145 aircraft, and at least 300 men.

As the smaller ships returned, they deposited whatever survivors they had plucked from the sea on the pier at Hospital Point. A doctor examined each as they debarked and sent those who required medical attention directly to the Naval Hospital. Bill was among those. He had suffered a gash on his head when the torpedo explosion threw him against a stanchion. A medic aboard the *Verio* had bandaged it but the doctor decided that it needed a few stitches and clean dressing.

Bill loathed the idea of going to the hospital. He knew that Kathleen would be looking at every survivor, searching for Hiro. Bill wondered if she would even recognize him. He was dirty, disheveled, in an enlisted work uniform, with a bandage over his right forehead. But Kathleen picked him out of the crowd almost immediately.

CHAPTER 48

With an excited smile she raced toward him and screamed, "Bill, oh my god, it's good to see you!" She threw her arms around him and squeezed, tears on both cheeks. The men nearby watched in envy. She relaxed her embrace and looked him squarely in the face, "Oh Bill, I was so worried," then asked the questions he knew she would, "Where is Hiro? Has he got back yet? Have you seen him?"

Bill had decided to be candid with Kathleen, "Bill and I got separated, Kathleen. I haven't seen him for almost 24 hours. He must have been picked up by one of the destroyers." He saw a look of puzzlement cross Kathleen's face and realized that she did not understand his comment because she knew none of the events of the last week while he and Hiro were at sea.

"Kathleen, I have lots to tell you, but this is probably not the right time or place. You go back to work, I'll get my forehead stitched up, and we'll meet for dinner–1700 in the Officer's Mess. Meanwhile we'll both keep our eyes open for Hiro."

Kathleen looked worried, but agreed to Bill's suggestion, "Okay, 1700."

It was almost 1700 by the time Bill got his stitches, a shower, and a fresh uniform. He called Captain High to join him and Kathleen for dinner. As he did so, he realized that the Captain did not yet know he was back.

"Bill?" the Captain shouted into the phone, "My god, I'm glad you finally checked in. I've been trying to find out what happened to you. Joe Rochefort said he knew only that you and Hiro had volunteered to go back aboard the Yorktown, which incidentally he didn't approve of. Called it a dumb stunt–nothing that two intelligence officers with your rare skills should have done! I want to hear all about it!"

"That's why I called Skipper. Can you meet Kathleen and I for dinner–1700 at the Officer's Mess?"

"Sure," the Captain replied, "Will Hiro be there too?"

"We can talk about that at dinner, sir."

THE DOOLITTLE IRONY

⊕ ⊕ ⊕

All three of them arrived early. Kathleen hugged Captain High tightly. Bill observed that she was adjusting to Navy ways–she no longer had to ask when 1700 is in "real time." But she had not yet grasped that ensigns do not hug captains, especially in the Officers Mess. Bill doubted that Kathleen's bubbling personality would ever allow her to accept that proscription.

As they took their seats, Bill asked, "Well, do we want to get our food first, or listen to my little report?"

Kathleen and the Captain were impatient, "We want to hear everything," the Captain said for both of them, "But before you get to the nitty gritty, where to hell is Hiro? That's the most important part."

Bill recapped events beginning with the first abandon ship through to the second. The Captain was astonished. Abandoning a ship and then re-boarding it, only to abandon it a second time? Unheard of!

Kathleen was more interested in Hiro's activities. When Bill recounted their decision to volunteer to re-board the Yorktown, Kathleen's face reflected her suspicion that Hiro had been the driving force behind that decision. She was all too aware of his determination to prove that he was more American than Americans.

Both Kathleen and the Captain pressed for details about how he and Hiro became separated. He did not offer his speculation that Hiro had been blown into the water, and he did not report the information about the depth charge explosions underwater.

More than an hour later they had still not eaten. Bill had painted a rather detailed picture of the week he and Hiro had spent at sea. Kathleen and Captain High had listened closely and posed many questions, especially one that Kathleen had already asked in several ways. She asked it again now, "Bill, do you think Hiro is still alive?"

As he had tried to do before, Bill carefully phrased his answer so as to be optimistic but not give her false hope, "At this point, we just don't know Kathleen. Before we jump to any conclusions we have to check every ship that has returned here. We know that some ships that were on the scene did not come back to Pearl, so we have

CHAPTER 48

to check them also. And we also need to contact local fishermen who might have been in those waters. That will take some time."

Realizing that Kathleen would fare better if she were busy, Captain High offered a suggestion. Looking directly at Kathleen he said, "Bill and I can take care of the stuff he's already mentioned, but I think there's something you could help with. I presume you've already checked the patients in your hospital thoroughly, but what about the other medical facilities on the Island, like Wheeler, Hickam, and the civilian hospitals as well. Maybe he got shipped to one of them by mistake. Maybe he's unconscious or unable to talk. It's worth checking!"

"Yes," Kathleen replied, "Good idea."

"And I'll get on our end of this first thing in the morning." Bill chimed in, "If we haven't found him in two days, can we meet here again–same time, same place?"

Kathleen nodded her silent agreement.

"Okay, now let's get some chow!" Bill said smiling. He and the Captain headed for the buffet table. Kathleen remained seated, waving the other two to go ahead with a wan smile. She simply had no appetite.

On the way back to the VOQ, the Captain added one more task for Bill, "I want you to go to the Navy Morgue. Look at every dead body that was picked up out there–American and Japanese both. God forbid, they might have got Hiro mixed up with some of them!"

Bill just swallowed and said, "Yes, sir."

Two days later, the three met again to exchange information. Bill had personally canvassed all of the returning ships and–though he didn't mention it to Kathleen–the Navy Morgue. Nothing. Captain High had sent priority messages to other PacFlt ships that had been anywhere near the *Yorktown* sinking. They had replied in the negative. And Kathleen had checked every non-Naval medical facility on the Island. None reported having any wounded naval personnel, much less survivors of the *Yorktown*.

THE DOOLITTLE IRONY

They talked about next steps. Bill volunteered to speak to other Yorktown survivors who were still on base, not yet reassigned. Kathleen said she would talk to survivors still in the hospital. Captain High said he would talk to some of the senior officers both in Hawaii and Washington.

This time they agreed to keep each other informed of anything new by phone, but would not meet again for another week.

Bill and the Captain ate. Kathleen did not.

After leaving Kathleen, Bill expressed concern about her, "I'm afraid she's losing hope, Skipper."

"Well, frankly Bill, I'm beginning to lose hope myself," the Captain replied dejectedly, "We've checked just about every logical place. Nothing! The chances of us finding him at this point are slim-to-none. And that's not all the bad news. The Navy will probably soon classify Hiro as Missing in Action and notify his parents. His father is in frail health. News like that could kill him."

"It won't do Kathleen any good either," Bill opined gloomily. "Will she be notified?"

"No, she's not his legal wife. Official communications are restricted to the next of kin. At least his pay will continue."

◈ ◈ ◈

Just three days later Bill got a call from the Captain, "Come see me, ASAP."

ASAP expands to "As Soon As Possible." A literal reading of the phrase might suggest, "See me whenever your schedule permits." That is not the Navy meaning. In the Navy, ASAP means NOW!

Bill wasted no time. He knocked firmly on the Captain's door and was greeted with a worried sounding, "C'mon in Bill." The Captain was holding an 8x10 manila envelope that he had already opened.

"Sit down. No, first pour yourself a drink then sit down."

Fearing that it was news of Hiro's death, Bill simply asked, "What's up, Skipper?"

The Captain grimaced and began a long rant, "Do you remember a month or so back we had sort of a rough patch with Hiro?

CHAPTER 48

He had figured out that you and I were not here because of saintly motives. We were not getting him a Navy commission and bringing his girl friend to Hawaii merely to thank him on behalf of a grateful nation. No, he had come to realize that we were here merely to shut him up about what he had done in the Doolittle Raid. He had figured out that if word of that ever got out about him saving the Raid, it would embarrass the politicians back in Washington. They said they were interning Japanese-Americans because they couldn't be trusted to defend the country. But then along comes a young Japanese-American man who risked his life first to provide the Japanese misleading information about Pearl Harbor, and then give them other misleading information about Doolittle's Raid. The public would ask, "Why are you locking up Japanese-Americans? They are on our side."

Bill wondered why the Captain was telling him all this. He already knew it. Bill thought it might be some sort of cathartic exercise for the Captain. He was venting all this spleen about suppressing Hiro's story because he felt guilty for having been a part of it.

The Captain slowed down, but he was not done. "Anyway, you remember that Hiro rebelled and said that he had given his story in full detail to some friend of his who had already left Hawaii for Mexico. Hiro had told him to give the story to the Mexican press if Hiro was thrown in jail or made a prisoner of war."

"Yes sir," Hiro said hoping the Captain would get to the point, "I remember all that."

"Well, today I got this in the mail. Here, I'll let you read it for yourself." Bill took the letter and read:

> *Captain High:*
>
> *I apologize. I perpetrated a ruse at your expense. Do you remember the somewhat tense meeting we had when I accused you of deliberately suppressing the story about my role in the Doolittle Raid? Do you remember also that I said I had given a sealed envelope to Captain Tanaka, a friend who was captain of a ship en route to Mexico, and in that envelope was a detailed account of my story which*

THE DOOLITTLE IRONY

he would give to the Mexican press if something happened to me? Well, that was only partly true. I did give him an envelope, but there was no story inside. There was just this letter of apology to you which I asked him to mail when he got to Mexico.

I want you to know that I would NEVER do anything to harm the United States. It is my home. It is my family's home. It is where Kathleen and I want to spend our lives. I think Japanese immigrants decided long ago that, while certain Americans resent us and have passed laws against us, we would simply endure their abuse knowing that in the future the second and third generation Japanese-Americans would become educated. They would rise to positions of responsibility and influence. All America would come to accept and admire them.

I guess that's how I've come to accept the suppression of my story. I don't blame you personally. I think you are one of the good guys. But if the powers-that-be in America will not tolerate a Japanese-American being a hero today, then I am willing to wait. In the course of events, I am confident that America will change its mind about Japanese-Americans. We will become just plain Americans. Maybe then my story will become known.

Thank you and Bill for being my friends.

Hiro

Bill was moved by the letter, and he knew that Captain High had been also. They were both quiet for awhile, and then the Captain broke the silence, "I guess Hiro will never know whether or not his story becomes known. He's gone, died while defending the country that rejected him. It makes me feel like crap!"

"You're not alone there, Skipper."

CHAPTER 48

Another silence ensued.

Bill finally asked, "Where do we go from here?"

"I guess we go back to Washington, Bill, the Captain replied. "Hiro's story is gone. You and I are the only ones who know about it and no one would ever believe us. I think official Washington can breathe easy."

"Yes," Bill agreed, "There doesn't seem to be any loose ends. Everyone here at Pearl seems to have bought the idea that he was a spy. Joe Rochefort loves that idea. He told me he was going with it, whether or not it's true. Said it was the perfect cover story to keep his outfit secret. Anybody asks where the Navy got its advance information on Midway, he'll just say it came from some mysterious spy ring, about which he has no information. That will keep prying eyes away from Wypo."

The Captain acknowledged Rochefort's shrewdness with a "Hmmmf!" but noted, "I worry about Kathleen," the Captain said, "If it hadn't been for us she wouldn't be out here. She'd be home with her parents. But I guess she'll get through this. Lord knows there are lots of other widows and fiancées that have to, and there will be lots more before this war is over."

"When do you think we can leave, Skipper?"

There's a hop out tomorrow that we can probably get on if I use Admiral King's name."

"Then we'd better have one last dinner with Kathleen. I'll call her–1700 again. I'm not looking forward to it."

'No,' the Captain agreed, "Me neither."

Kathleen listened calmly to Captain High as he outlined the situation as he saw it, and the decision about going back to Washington D.C.

Her response was neither tearful nor distraught. She remained composed with only a small quaver in her voice, "Thank you, Captain, for your assessment. It's rather what I expected. I agree that our searches have not been productive, and offer little prospect of becoming so. I suppose reasonable minds would conclude that Hiro should be classified as 'missing in action.' Then, if no additional

THE DOOLITTLE IRONY

information is developed, a year later he'll be classified as 'killed in action' and his parents will receive a $10,000 insurance payment."

Bill and the Captain exchanged glances. They hadn't expected that Kathleen would know about such matters.

Kathleen went on, "I say that because this afternoon I received a telegram from Avaron, Hiro's younger sister. She told me that the Navy Department notified Hiro's parents that he is missing in action. They didn't understand so the Camp Commandant came to see them to explain. Avaron said he was very sympathetic, but Hiro's parents became quite upset when he explained about how in one year Hiro would be considered killed in action. The word 'killed' upset them. Avaron is very worried about Hiro's father."

Bill and Captain High just sat there, depleted, having no words that could bring hope to such despair. There was a long silence.

The Captain finally spoke, "Kathleen, though Bill and I have to go back to the States, I don't want you to think that we're dropping you and Hiro's family. I will stop at the camp where Hiro's parents are. I'll tell them about their brave son, and I'll talk to the Camp Commander too. He sounds like a person who might help. Incidentally, if it's alright with you, I'd like to stop by and see your parents and tell them about what a brave daughter they have."

That brought a tear to Kathleen's eyes and she lowered her head. Bill touched her shoulder to comfort her, but she straightened and composed herself. "I have an announcement of my own to make," she said, "Like you, I have had to conclude that Hiro is probably dead. I won't lose hope, but I must go on. I know that what I do here in the hospital is important. These young men need care badly. Some are burned terribly, others have missing limbs or broken spirits. I want to continue helping them, but I can't stay here. Even though I've been here only a month, there are many memories. I cry every time I see the Officer's Club and remember the engagement party. I'd like to get away."

Bill and Captain High said nothing, waiting for her to continue.

"I spoke to our Chief Nurse. She told me they need nurses aboard the *Solace*, the hospital ship that was stationed here until recently. Last March they sent it to the South Pacific. It's in Tongatapu now. She said that duty there is hard. It's hot, the hours are long, and

CHAPTER 48

life aboard is confining. She thought if I volunteered to do a tour there, the Navy would give me my choice for a next duty station. I've already decided to ask for Sun Valley, Idaho, where the Navy is opening a convalescent center. It's not far from Minidoka, the camp where Hiro's parents will be sent. I'll be able to help them."

Both Captain High and Bill were stunned. This was the girl they worried would become hysterical when they told her they had to go back to the States. And instead here she was, with plans for a brave new future.

Bill looked at her with admiration, "Kathleen, I'm impressed—and I know that Hiro would be too. You seem like you've got it all in hand."

"No, I don't, Bill, nowhere near. But I'll manage somehow. I want to thank you two. You did so much for Hiro, and you did so much for me. I hope we can stay in touch. I'd like to see you both again in the future."

Recognizing that this amazing young lady was giving them permission to go, Bill and Captain High stood and both hugged her tightly. They were all three choked with emotion.

"Good night, Kathleen," the Captain said from the door, "And good luck."

Bill did not trust himself to say anything. He was too close to tears. He just waved and smiled

Kathleen waved back.

⊕ ⊕ ⊕

"Bill," the Captain said as they walked away, "I'm going back to the Q and get drunk. Want to come along?"

"What time do we have to leave tomorrow, Skipper?"

"Late flight. 1700 show, 1800 go."

"I should go back to my room and get packed, but maybe I'll have one drink with you. Or maybe two."

When they reached Captain High's room, Bill flopped on the extra chair and his host broke out a bottle of gin. "How about gin and tonic?" he asked.

THE DOOLITTLE IRONY

"Sure," Bill replied, "That's as good as anything to get drunk on."

The drinks were extra large and extra potent. Neither Bill nor the Captain talked. There was nothing more to say.

That's when the phone rang. "Yeah, High here," the Captain answered curtly. Tonight he felt no need for telephone courtesies.

"Captain, this is Joe Rochefort,"

"Oh, hi Joe, you must have heard I'm leaving."

"Actually, no, I didn't. I'm calling you on another matter. Do you remember that you passed me the task of minding Hiro?"

"Sure, Joe," the Captain replied, wondering what would prompt such a question.

"And you remember you said if anything came up just to tell you and you'd take care of it?"

Again, the Captain replied, "Sure."

Well, I think you better go out to the Main Gate. I just got a call from the Marine sentry. Says there's some raggedy Jap out there who claims he's an ensign in the Navy. He gave him my name as his boss."

Rochefort paused, and then added, "I'm not sure what this is all about, but I thought you would want to check it out personally."

The Captain said nothing. His heart had skipped a beat and he determinedly put foolish thoughts out of his mind.

"Thanks Joe. I'll do that," and he hung up.

"Grab your cover, Bill, we have to go down to the Main Gate." He moved quickly out the door and through the lobby of the VOQ with Bill in close pursuit. As they covered the few blocks to the Gate the Captains pace grew more rapid until he broke into a full run. Bill wondered what in heaven's name had got into him. They burst into the Master at Arms office and the duty watch looked up, startled at their sudden entrance.

"We're here to see the Japanese man," the Captain announced quickly. With that, Bill's forehead furrowed and he looked unbelievingly at the Captain.

"He's in there," the sentry said, pointing to a door behind him.

Not waiting for permission, the Captain burst past the sentry and through the door.

CHAPTER 48

There he was. "GODDAMMIT, HIRO, GODDAMMIT! Is that really you?"

Hiro was startled at the outburst. "It's really me, Captain. Hi, Bill. I'm sorry to have been gone so long. I guess you're mad."

"MAD? What to hell are you talking about?" the Captain asked in a slightly higher octave than normal, incredulous at such a question.

There were no hugs, no tearful demonstrations. The tension of the past week had seemingly drained Bill and the Captain of such emotion. Now there was just disbelief that this was actually happening.

"Hiro," Bill said deliberately, "We have indeed wondered where you were. Maybe it would help me and the Captain both if you would explain." He sat down, "You go ahead. We'll just listen."

The Captain was grateful that Bill's request gave him a chance to regain his composure. He too sat down.

Looking contrite, Hiro began, "Bill, you remember we were on the hangar deck of the *Yorktown* when we saw those torpedoes coming right at us. Then the destroyer blew up and more torpedoes hit the *Yorktown*. When they did the whole ship shook and I went overboard. I remembered what you told me about swimming away from the ship to avoid getting sucked under when it went down. I swam like crazy … and then nothing. Next thing I knew I was looking up at the sky from the deck of a fishing boat. The fishermen gave me water and a few bites of food. At first they thought I was a Japanese survivor and tried to talk to me in Japanese. When I replied in English, they were really surprised. I learned they are Japanese-Americans too, and live right here in Oahu. They used to fish along the islands west of Hawaii. They called them the Leeward Islands and they run out past French Frigate Shoals all the way to Midway. They told me they fished for bottom fish like Opakapaka–that's hard for me to say."

"Yes, Hiro, It's hard for all us Mainlanders to say," Bill said quickly, hoping to avoid Hiro getting off on a tangent.

"When the war started, the Navy said they couldn't fish there anymore. But they didn't want to give up on that fish whose name I can't say. So now they sail out after dark and stay for a week or two

THE DOOLITTLE IRONY

in a cave on some volcanic island. They clean and salt the fish there and then sell them at the fish market in Honolulu. They found me just as one of their trips began so I had to wait a week while they fished before we came back. They were very nice. When they left me in Honolulu they even loaned me money to get the train out here."

"Goddammit," the Captain said in astonishment and just sat there looking at Hiro. "You have got to be the luckiest man alive! C'mon, we'll get you over to the hospital. You've got some ugly cuts there and I can tell you with certainty that you need a bath. You smell like those fish you can't pronounce."

Ten minutes later the three of them were in the Marine sentry's jeep headed back onto Base. The sentry had objected to the Captain's commandeering his vehicle, but Marine lance corporals hardly ever win arguments with Navy Captains.

They turned left onto Hospital Drive, passed the screened porch that fronted the building, and then left again into the Emergency Room entrance. Hiro looked worried.

"Captain, Kathleen might be working. I'll get her in trouble if I show up in the middle of her shift."

"Yeah, you might," the Captain agreed, "But before you meet Kathleen, we need to make you presentable." The Captain looked over at the orderly on duty in the Emergency Room. "We got a guy who needs medical attention," he said, "Where do you want him?"

"Over there in bed seven, sir. I'll try to find a doctor. There's a basin in there you can use to clean him up."

"Great," the Captain said, "And while you're at it, would you try to find a nurse named Kathleen Kelly? Tell her there's someone here that wants to see her."

"Sure thing, sir. I saw Kathleen just a bit ago up on the second deck."

Five minutes later Kathleen entered the Emergency Room looking prim and proper in her starched White uniform. "Oh, hi Captain," she said with some surprise, and then noticing Bill across the room she waved. "I was told there is someone here that wants to see me. What can I do for you gentlemen?"

"Actually it's not Bill and I that want to see you, Kathleen. We brought a patient for you. He's in Bed 7."

CHAPTER 48

She looked a bit puzzled but stepped over and parted the curtain around bed seven. She screamed! Loudly!

It scared Hiro. He backed up a pace and said, "I'm sorry Kathleen, I told Captain High that I shouldn't come in the middle of your shift."

"*HIRO IS THAT REALLY YOU?*"

"Yes, it's me. Why is everybody so surprised?"

By then Kathleen had crossed the few paces and grabbed him in her arms.

"Kathleen, for god's sakes, I'm naked. I was washing myself."

Kathleen didn't care. She embraced him as though he would somehow disappear, then broke into uncontrollable sobs as the emotions of the past week broke through. Hiro muttered consoling words but to little effect. She finally recovered her composure enough to speak, looked up, and tearfully asked, "Hiro, where have you been? Are you OK? Are you wounded? How long have you been back?"

A young doctor appeared at the curtain and looked at the two young people embraced alongside the bed, Hiro still naked. He reflected a second then said facetiously, "Well, Kathleen, this appears to be just the sort of therapy that would work on most of our patients! Good work. But for now, why don't you let me examine him in a more conventional way."

Kathleen blushed bright red and uttered, "Oh, yes, of course Doctor Muir, I'm sorry about this."

"Don't apologize, Kathleen, I think I know the story. Just wait outside while I give this guy a once over."

As Kathleen pulled the curtains around Bed 7, Captain High said quietly to her, "Kathleen, Bill and I should leave. Hiro will explain everything about his absence, and you two deserve some time alone together. So I'm going to call the Chief of Nurses and ask that you be excused for the rest of your shift. I'm sure she will understand. Besides, after this you wouldn't be able to concentrate on your duties anyway."

⊕   ⊕   ⊕

THE DOOLITTLE IRONY

As they walked back toward the VOQ, both Bill's and the Captain's step was a little lighter. "Talk about fairy tale endings, Skipper. Hiro goes into the Pacific twice, should have drowned both times, but was pulled out in the most unlikely ways, and is now rejoined with his Princess Bride."

"Yeah, I agree," the Captain replied, "Maybe it's fate's way of making up for his family being tossed into the internment camp."

"Well, if there's ever a time when we can tell this story, Hollywood is going to love it. Exotic setting, beautiful girl, danger, romance. It's all there!"

"You could write a book, Bill. Probably get rich!"

"Not a bad idea Skipper. I'll remember that in the future, but for now let's go back to your room and finish those gin and tonics we started earlier. This time we can drink to success."

The following day, Bill and the Captain were having lunch at the Mess. A number of officers they had worked with had learned they were leaving and stopped by to say goodbye. Several jokingly asked that Captain High extend their best wishes to "Ernie," a facetious reference to Admiral King.

Joe Rochefort stopped and said, "So I was right last night, huh?" and sat down at the table without benefit of invitation.

"Yes, you were, Joe," Captain High replied, "I thought I caught a hint of something in your voice, but I didn't dare think it was true. Incidentally, you can forget that little task about minding Hiro."

"I thought you might tell me that, Captain," and then he went on vaguely, "Still, it kinda makes you mad, doesn't it? I'd like to see some of those Washington twits come out and do what Hiro has done. It might change their minds!" Rochefort didn't try to be any more explicit. He knew the Captain had understood his message. "In

CHAPTER 48

fact, Captain, Hiro was in the office this morning and told me about everything that happened. I told him that going back aboard the *Yorktown* was a damn fool thing to do, but also a damn brave thing. I'm thinking about putting him in for a medal of some kind!"

Just as Roquefort left, Hiro and Kathleen came in smilingly. Both were in proper uniform and both had apparently been to work that morning. "Well," the Captain observed, "You both look fresh and well rested. Frankly, I'm surprised."

"And I'm amazed!" Bill added emphatically.

"Actually," Hiro said, "We were up all night. If we look OK this morning it's probably because we have so much to be thankful for. We talked about everything that you both did last week. I sure am sorry for all the trouble I caused."

"Sorry?" Bill repeated, "Hell, you're a hero. Commander Rochefort will probably get you a medal." Bill shifted his gaze slyly toward the Captain hoping to see some sign that he intended to put Bill in for a medal also. Nothing!

Hiro continued, "You're leaving in just a few hours so Kathleen and I wanted to share with you what our plans are." He and Kathleen sat and began their report, "I'll go first," Hiro announced, "For the time being I am going to stay here at Wypo if Commander Rochefort will have me. I think I can make a contribution, and I feel like it's my duty. After a while, I presume the Navy will have its own plans for me and I will go wherever they send me." He looked over at Kathleen.

Taking that as her signal to talk, Kathleen began, "Well, now that Hiro's back, I'm going to delay my plans to volunteer for duty on the *Solace*. We think that Hiro will probably get orders within a few months, and that's when I'll ask for a transfer. We both realize we have to delay our marriage either until the Navy changes its mind about married nurses or the war ends. Either way, we're looking at a long separation. We don't like that but it's what many couples have to accept today."

Then, in afterthought, Kathleen raised her hand to signal she hadn't quite finished. "We do want to ask that you both go ahead with your plans to visit both my family and Hiro's. They would both appreciate that so very much."

THE DOOLITTLE IRONY

"Sure, I'm looking forward to it," the Captain said sincerely. "In fact," the Captain added, "I've been thinking of just what I'm going to tell your parents, Hiro. I think I have quite a story which, incidentally, I will share with Admiral King as well."

The Captain paused to gather his thoughts. "As I see it, Hiro risked his life at least three times in the Service of America: once to alter a document that may have played a part in Japan's failure to sink our carriers at Pearl Harbor; a second time to alter a contact report that Halsey's carriers had long range bombers on board, thereby allowing Doolittle to surprise Japanese defenses; and a third time helping to salvage the *Yorktown*. In two of those incidents he ended up in the Pacific and probably should have drowned. So very briefly, my story is that Hiro is a hero."

Then, sarcastically, Hiro piped up with, "But we can't tell anyone because it would embarrass the same people who imprisoned my family!"

"True," the Captain admitted, nodding his head matter-of-factly, "But I don't plan to bring that up with your family. And I plan to tell Kathleen's parents that they have raised a brave, caring and responsible daughter who they should be quite proud of."

"Well," Kathleen said with a blush, "Whatever you do, tell them we love them and miss them, and please, ask them to write to us about everything that's happening–even if it takes more than one page!"

"And I volunteer to make certain Stanley Polasky likewise gets a full report," Bill added.

The Captain nodded approvingly and announced, "I hate to cut this off, but Bill and I had best be on our way. It's getting late and we have to be out at the Pan Am Seaway in Pearl City for the flight back to San Francisco. I have a jeep coming by for us at 1500."

"Then I guess this is goodbye," Kathleen said sadly.

"Not goodbye," Bill quickly inserted, "We'll see one another again so no need for get all gooey."

Kathleen smiled, understanding men's aversion to sentimentality. Nevertheless she stood, came around the table and hugged both him and the Captain.

CHAPTER 48

Hiro shook hands with both men warmly. He even gave Bill a brotherly hug.

"C'mon, Bill," the Captain said, "We only have about 45 minutes before our wheels arrive."

The plane loaded promptly at 1715 and by 1800 was taxiing out to the Middle Loch takeoff waterway. Every seat was taken but the Captain's rank entitled him to a window seat, with Bill alongside him. The big Boeing 314 aircraft lumbered down the waterway, gained speed, and reluctantly lurched into the air. As it gained altitude, Bill and the Captain watched Waikiki and Diamond Head drift by on the port side, a picture postcard.

Bill was pensive. "Skipper, seriously, what did we accomplish out here?" He had to speak loudly over the roar of the four Wright R-2600 engines.

"Good question, Bill, probably one that Admiral King is going to ask. Let's think about it. First, we did suppress the story about a young Nisei saving the Doolittle Raid. We're not sure that was a worthy goal, but that's what we were sent here to do, and we did it. We may even have got the young Nisei in question to accept the internment without too much rancor. He doesn't like it but I'd guess he might say, "OK, we Japanese-Americans will take this one for the team, but watch out because we're coming on strong."

"Well said, Skipper," Bill said, "That's probably just what Hiro would say."

"Second, we did express this nation's gratitude to the young Nisei by getting him together with his sweetheart. He was grateful for that and, if the two ever get married and have sons, maybe we'll have a couple namesakes."

"And third, we managed to recruit two very capable young ensigns for the U.S. Navy, both of whom have already proven their worth as Naval Officers."

"Yes sir, those are positive results," Bill agreed, "But the downside is that we didn't get Hiro's family out of Camp Harmony. In fact, by suppressing Hiro's story, we might have kept them there longer."

THE DOOLITTLE IRONY

"That whole racial thing is way above our pay grade, Bill. Not much we can do about reforming society. Maybe over time America will get smarter about that. Immigrants from other countries have overcome similar obstacles."

"Do you think we'll ever see Hiro and Kathleen again, Skipper?"

"The odds are against it, Bill. Too bad. I like them."

"Yeah, me too," Bill added wistfully, "I'm really looking forward to meeting their families."

◈ ◈ ◈

Fifteen hours and 2,110 miles later the plane set down in San Francisco Bay. It was about 0830 local as the plane taxied toward its Treasure Island Terminal in the shadow of the Bay Bridge. The pilot turned into Clipper Cove and nestled against the long pier that was used to load and unload passengers. They emerged from the plane awkwardly, stiff from having had to sit for such a long time. The sun had still not burned off the morning mist and there was a chill in the air despite this being summer. Captain High and Bill had slept fitfully through the night hours and were still trying to wake up as they walked down the long wooden pier. That's when they saw a young ensign waiting with a sign that read "CAPT HIGH" in large letters.

"Mmmmf," the Captain grunted, "This does not look good." He was right.

The ensign stepped forward and said, "Sir, I'm Ensign Scott from NAS Alameda," pointing across the Bay, "My Commanding Officer has asked me to provide you two messages and ask that you read them immediately. Here is the first." The Captain glanced at Bill, winced and opened it. Inside was a set of orders written in the usual argot of BUPERS, indecipherable except for the part that read, "REPORT ASAP TO SWPA MELBORNE AS SENIOR NAVAL LIAISON TO SUPREME COMMANDER SOUTHWEST PACIFIC AREA."

The Captain sighed, and the ensign took that as a sign to hand him the second envelope. It was double wrapped with multi-colored stripes along the edges of the interior envelope. The Captain's brow furrowed as he began to read:

CHAPTER 48

Top Secret/Sensitive/Eyes Only

Back Channel from CNO

To CAPT High, USN, In Transit

Good work on Doolittle flap. No blowback evident here. Molehill did not become mountain.

Next need you ASAP as my personal eyes and ears in court of His Highness Douglas MacArthur, Supreme Commander Southwest Pacific Area. He daily reports in glorious detail how he is personally winning the war. Would like your back channel personal perspective on that. Also need you to encourage SWAPA to weigh in on resource distribution debate back here in DC. Gist is that General Marshall wants to put Pacific on "Strategic Defensive," i.e., assign it only 30% of national resources while rest goes to support war in European Theater. I argue that it was Tokyo that attacked Pearl Harbor, not Berlin. Underlying whole controversy is the oversimplified perception that Europe is the Army's war and Pacific is the Navy's. Would be helpful if MacArthur were to remind Marshal that Army has significant skin in Pacific also.

I hope this reaches you before you leave Pearl.

No, you cannot take your protégé with you. Put him on next plane. Useful work awaits him here.

Warm Regards

Ernest King,

Chief of Naval Operations

The ensign waited until Captain High had read both documents and then said, "Sir, I've been directed to offer whatever assis-

THE DOOLITTLE IRONY

tance NAS Alameda can provide. I have the duty driver waiting out on the Avenue of the Palms to take you directly to Fairfield-Suisun Air Base. I'll collect your gear and put it in the trunk. You're assigned to an Army Transport Command resupply flight that leaves in about four hours. It should take you all the way to Brisbane, but it's going to be a long flight. It goes via Hawaii, Palmyra, Canton, Fiji, New Caledonia, and finally Brisbane–about 7,000 miles."

The Captain handed both documents to Bill to read, waited until he had finished, then resignedly said, "I guess this throws my plans to visit Kathleen and Hiro's families into a cocked hat, Bill. On my stopover in Hawaii, I'll try to phone them both and explain, but I won't have much time." Then with regret he added, "I guess you have to get back to D.C. right away, so you won't be able to visit the families either. I guess you'll just have to write letters."

"Sure, sir, I'll do that. And with your permission, I'll also write to Stanley."

"Good, I'm sure you'll say all the right things," the Captain replied as the two began the walk to the car, "And I have one other special request. Would you please visit my family when you get back to Washington. Tell them that we did some good out in Hawaii, and now I have to go to Brisbane and do some more good. Most important, tell them not to worry. They don't put old farts like me out where they actually have to fight. My biggest danger will be having a ton of paperwork fall on me."

They had reached the car and stood looking out over the Bay while the ensign loaded Captain High's two suitcases in the car's trunk. From their vantage point they could see San Francisco's northern waterfront from the Bay Bridge to the recently completed Golden Gate Bridge. Quite impressive! Ironically, a large sign had been erected nearby on which a heroic likeness of Brigadier General Jimmy Doolittle appeared with a B-25 in the background and a caption exhorting Americans to buy war bonds. The Captain and Bill looked at the sign and then at one another. Both smiled sardonically. They shared a secret that few others would ever know.

"Well Skipper, I guess I won't be seeing you for awhile." Bill said, trying hard to avoid sentimentality. "Be sure to give Dugout

CHAPTER 48

Doug my very best and I will in turn convey your very best to your wife and daughters."

"Yes, please do. I'll miss them–but they know about family separation. If you ever get married, you'll learn about it too."

"Me? Married? I don't think so, sir," Bill chuckled, "I'm a lost cause."

"We'll see. Remember that old saw: 'Women are born with more romantic sense than a man will develop in a life time.' When one of them decides you're 'the one,' you're a goner."

"Well, if that ever happens, I'll name the first boy after you sir."

"Thanks, Bill," Captain High said, "It's been great working with you. I know you'll go far. Oh, and I should have mentioned, I did put you in for a Navy Cross for going back aboard the *Yorktown*."

Bill was genuinely surprised, "A Navy Cross? Really? Thank you very much, sir," and saluted smartly.

The Captain returned the salute and got in the car. There were no hugs or tears. That would not have been manly. But as the car drove away both men had to choke back their emotions, realizing that the chances of ever seeing one another again were very small indeed. It would be a long, dangerous war.

CHAPTER 49

75 YEARS LATER

Caitlin stared down at her smart phone, the latest model from Apple. Her Dad had given it to her as a present last June when she graduated from the University of Pittsburgh. He presented it with the hope that she would use it to stay in touch with her family back home in Sewickly, a small town north of Pittsburgh along the Allegheny River. After all, she was going off to Washington, D.C., a big, impersonal city where who knows what might befall her.

Caitlin had indeed found the city to be big, at least by Sewickly standards. But she had been fortunate to find through her college friends a row house where she now lived with four other girls. It was actually rather comfortable, although the rent was an astronomical $1,000 per month. Her friends consoled her that the rent was not <u>that</u> high for Washington, D.C. and, after all, it was downtown, close to many of the exciting after-hours spots. Her new job with a firm on "K" Street paid $50,000 per year, and she rationalized that the rent was only about one quarter of her salary. Yes, she remembered there would be additional costs for taxes, transportation, food, entertainment, etc., but she would manage somehow. And if she did run into trouble, she knew she could depend on Dad to rescue her.

So Caitlin had met most of the physical issues in her new life in D.C., but she had made little progress on the personal ones. The exciting night spots that her friends had touted turned out to fall

CHAPTER 49

in one of two categories: (1) pleasant but too expensive or, (2) dark and depressingly tawdry. Caitlin rarely drank anything alcoholic, and had never been very social. At Pitt she had thought of sororities as somewhat frivolous. She dated only infrequently and considered the young men she did date as immature. But now she was in the big city and daily saw a bevy of well dressed young men walking briskly by, seemingly in a rush, apparently doing something important. Somewhere among them, she thought, must be a man I would like to spend time with, whose interests are like mine, and who would like a somewhat introverted, studious girl like me. Like most young, unattached people her age, Caitlin was lonely. She needed a mate.

But finding prospective mates was not easy. She didn't really like the idea of meeting one in a bar–Mom would never approve. Her workplace was no more promising, being populated mostly by balding, middle-aged men. Churches had become anachronisms for most young people, especially here in Washington. So Caitlin had resorted to something that most of her friends had already used for years: an online dating service. Some of the girls had warned that such services produced only "weirdos," men who lied about their age, marital status and earning power. Some of the girls had had to fend off a few excessively amorous men who thought the purchase of a dinner entitled them to spend the night. Others had had problems with disappointed suitors seeking to "get even" by calling them at midnight or even posting cruel lies about them online.

But others had suggested she could avoid those pitfalls by using a newer style of dating service that "puts the woman in charge." It enabled a woman to keep her identity secret until she was satisfied that the man in prospect was suitable. Like most dating services, it started with its members–both men and women–providing a photo and describing themselves: gender, age, interests, occupations, aspirations, etc. That information, except for the women's identity and contact data, was then put on a list and sent electronically to all members. Both men and women could review the list and determine if they were interested in dating any of those who appeared. Usually members did this on a smart phone. A picture and description of each member would appear. If unacceptable, one could eliminate them with a "swipe left." Those that looked promising one could "swipe right." If both a man and woman did a swipe right on one another, the system would set up an email exchange between them using a neutral email address, thus protecting the woman's identity. If after a few exchanges the woman thought the man a possibility, she could give him her phone number and the process of getting to know one another could proceed to more frequent email exchanges. If that worked out, a meeting for coffee might follow where the two could size up one another up in person. If that likewise proved satisfactory, a first date might ensue, with the understanding that each would pay his or her own way.

In the past few months since Caitlin had joined this dating service, she had tried that process probably a dozen times. Most she had terminated at the telephone phase. She had gone out on only one date, which she had not repeated because the young man indicated he was not interested in a long term relationship. That was a show stopper for Caitlin. She didn't visualize marriage in her near future–she wanted to start a career first–but somewhere down the line she wanted a family, children, the whole corny package just like Mom and Dad. She probably would not be a stay-at-home mom, but she would make sure that her children were never neglected.

Tonight she was going to meet another young man, this one an officer in the Navy. He had been a definite "swipe right." He seemed sincere, and he didn't seem to be hiding anything. She wasn't happy about him being in the Navy, knowing that service life was not conducive to family life: too much separation, high divorce rates, frequent moves, new schools and neighborhoods, etc. But he had sounded like a nice person on the phone and, after all, she didn't have anything else to do. So here she was at the appointed meeting place, Starbucks on the edge of Farragut Square. She had arrived a few minutes early because it was so close to her office. She ordered a simple coffee-of-the day–the *barista* drinks were too expensive for her tiny budget. It was now 5:35, five minutes past the appointed time. She reminded herself that he had to come all the way from the Pentagon via Metro. Still, being late on the first date was not a good sign.

That's when he stepped through the door. He was in a blue Navy uniform and her first thought was, "Oh, my. He IS handsome in that uniform!" He spotted her immediately and came right to the

CHAPTER 49

table. Caitlin stood and regarded him: tall, trim, a pleasant smile, she involuntarily thought, "Wow!"

He held out his hand to greet her and said with a friendly grin, "Hi, I'm Bill Russo, sorry I'm late."

"Oh, that's alright, five minutes hardly qualifies as late. Besides, you had to travel a long distance. I should have met you half way."

"No, no," he protested, "I actually enjoy coming over to the District. It's refreshing to see people who don't wear badges."

"Oh, you mean everybody in the Pentagon has to wear a badge?"

"Yes," Bill nodded with amusement, "At least one badge. I have three."

Caitlin smiled and said, "I should introduce myself. I'm Caitlin Jarvis."

"I'm very pleased to meet you, Caitlin. Can I get you anything to drink?"

"No thank you, Bill," she replied, using his first name, "I've got something, but go ahead and get yourself something. I'll save your seat."

Bill threaded his way through the crowd, placed his order, and turned back toward the table. She noticed that he had bought a simple coffee-of-the-day. Maybe he has the same financial problems I have, she thought. I'll have to remember that.

"Thanks for seeing me," he said as he sat down, "I know that many of the ladies have problems about service men."

"Oh, I really never thought about that," she lied, and then immediately felt guilty for having done so. "Actually I know very little about the military. I don't even know what those stripes on your sleeve mean?"

"Oh, that's my rank. I'm a Lieutenant Junior Grade."

"So next you'll be a Lieutenant Senior Grade?"

"Well, yes but we don't call it that. It's just Lieutenant. No Senior Grade."

"Oh, I see," Caitlin said, but again she did not. "What do the ribbons on your chest signify?"

"Well, actually, they don't signify much. I haven't been in the Navy long enough to have earned any ribbons worth talking about. I graduated from the Naval Academy last year. I was sent to Pensacola for flight training but that didn't work out because of an eye problem. So they asked me what I would like to do and I decided on intelligence. It's what some of my relatives did, so I thought I'd give it a try."

"Intelligence? You mean like double-oh seven? Do you kill people?"

"No, I haven't killed anyone all week," Bill smiled and then glanced at Caitlin to see if she had taken his remark seriously. She had not, but in the process he noticed that her eyes were a very pretty shade of blue. "No, intelligence in the Navy is pretty technical," he continued, "It involves things like satellites, electronic surveillance, and aerial photography. The idea is to figure out what your enemy is doing."

"Oh, I see." Again, she did not.

"What about you?" Bill asked, "What do you do for a living?"

"I work for a think tank," Caitlin continued, "It deals with legislative matters involving public health policy. I'm kind of junior analyst–like an analyst junior grade," she said pointing to the stripes on his sleeve.

He smiled, acknowledging the comparison. "Does that mean that next you'll be a senior analyst?"

"*Touche*," she said smiling, then in a more serious tone, "No, not in my case. I'm going back to graduate school this fall to work on a Masters and possibly then a Ph.D."

"Great!" Bill said enthusiastically, "I've thought about graduate school myself. I'm hoping that the Navy will send me. I think I'd like electrical engineering."

"No kidding? My dad's an electrical engineer. He used to work for Westinghouse but had to retire early because of a cutback."

"Westinghouse? That's an important name in engineering. The Navy has done a lot of business with them. What did your Dad do?"

"I'm not really sure. He never talked about it much, but he wore a badge like you say everybody in the Pentagon does, so maybe that means he was involved in some of your Navy work."

They exchanged small talk for a while longer, and then Bill suggested that Starbucks was very noisy and asked if Caitlin would like to find a quieter spot. She surprised herself by agreeing without hesi-

CHAPTER 49

tation. They crossed K Street into Farragut Square, a small park with seating areas.

"Very good choice, Lieutenant Junior Grade Russo," Caitlin smiled as they sat on one of the benches away from the traffic, "You must know the city quite well."

Bill smiled, "Actually, I have to admit that before I came I checked Google maps and found this place–just in case."

"That's nice." Caitlin replied, pleased with his answer, "I thought you might have brought other girls here."

Bill laughed, "Caitlin, I am not much of a lady's man. Most find me kind of boring."

"Well, I think you're doing just fine," Caitlin blurted, surprised that she had actually been so forward.

They sat in the unseasonably warm afternoon and talked of matters that two young people would on such occasions: their home towns, their parents, their siblings, and other safe topics. No politics. No religion. No past romances. They were quite comfortable with one another and without them noticing it, the early November light began to fail.

Bill glanced at his watch and suddenly blurted, "Caitlin, I'm sorry. I didn't realize what time it is. Are you hungry? Would you like to get something to eat?"

"Yes, I would," Caitlin replied, but then remembering he had only ordered coffee in Starbucks, she added, "There's a McDonalds just a few blocks away."

They walked leisurely down the street. He did not take her hand, thinking she would think that excessively personal. She would not have. In fact, it occurred to her if he did, she would not pull away.

McDonalds was not very busy and the two found a table in the corner. He insisted on paying–despite the dating service's rule to the contrary–and she insisted on ordering from the Dollar Menu: cheeseburgers, fries, and cokes. Not very nutritious but for a first date it was just right.

Their conversation wondered to distant relatives. "Where's your family from originally," Bill asked.

"Well, my great grandfather was Japanese? Does it show?"

THE DOOLITTLE IRONY

"Mmm, maybe your cheekbones are a little high," Bill kidded, "in a nice way of course! But no, I would never have guessed if you hadn't told me. I think it's kind of neat. How is it that your great grandfather was Japanese?"

"He wasn't actually a Japanese national. He was Japanese-American. Like you, he was a naval officer but unlike you," she said with mock admonishment, "He had a few ribbons worth talking about. He served in the Pacific during the Second World War and was awarded the Navy Cross twice."

"Wow," Bill responded, "I'm impressed! They don't hand those things out for nothing. But wait, I can't quite match TWO, but MY great grandfather got ONE Navy Cross. It was for something he did during the Battle of Midway."

Caitlin knitted her eyebrows trying to remember the family's stories she had heard about the matter. "I was never very clear on the details,' she said, "And I don't know much about WWII, but 'Midway' rings a bell. Did you say it was a naval battle?"

"Yes, it was probably the most significant naval battle of the whole war."

"And your great grandfather was there and mine might have been also. That's an amazing coincidence! We should look into it. I'll call my Dad and get more details."

Recognizing it as a reason to see Caitlin again, Bill said, "Good idea. I'll do the same–and then maybe we can compare notes."

Caitlin smiled–a perfect reason to see Bill a second time. The evening was working out just as she had hoped. "Great. Sounds like we're going to have a lot to discuss, so let's do it Saturday. That gives us three days to do our homework. And I've got just the place to do it: the reading room at the Library of Congress. It's beautiful and I have privileges there through my job."

"Sounds good! What time?"

Caitlin reflected. She framed her answer not so much on the research at hand, but on the opportunities it offered to have lunch or dinner with Bill. "Let's make it 10:00 AM," she suggested, "That way if we really do come across some interesting stuff, we'll have the afternoon as well."

CHAPTER 49

"Good idea," Bill said with enthusiasm, then glancing at his watch he added, "But I've kept you too long. It's almost 9:00. Can walk you home?"

"That's very kind of you, Bill, but I have another suggestion," Caitlin said, "You have a much longer trip ahead of you than I, so why don't I walk you to the Metro Station. It's still quite early and my house is only about twenty minutes away. I feel quite safe."

Bill seemed a bit reluctant to accept that solution but Caitlin stood, grabbed his arm and guided him out the door of McDonalds. "Don't worry. I'll be safe," she said, "You're as bad as my father! Besides, your Metro Station is on my way home."

Bill resigned himself to the matter and the two walked close beside one another to the McPherson Square Metro Station. This time Caitlin made sure her hand and his touched, and when he took it she squeezed his reassuringly, looked up at him, and smiled. At the station Caitlin said, "Thanks for a really great evening, Bill. I'm looking forward to Saturday. Who knows, maybe our great grandfathers knew one another."

"Yes, good, "Bill said nervously. She could tell he was trying to decide whether to kiss her. He didn't, and she thought that his shyness was all the more charming. Bill disappeared down the escalator and Caitlin began her walk home through the chill night air. Bill was a really nice guy, she reflected, but of course she didn't really know him, and he was a military person, so best not to be too excited about tonight. But she was nevertheless. It had been an very nice evening.

Saturday morning was cold. Caitlin would have preferred to walk from her row house in the Shaw neighborhood down to the Congressional Library across the street from the Capitol Building, but given the weather she opted for the Metro. She lived near the Green Line and it was only a few stops to the Archives Station at the base of Capitol Hill. She smiled to herself when at the top of the escalator she looked over and saw the Navy Memorial. "Appropriate!" she thought. Caitlin walked the few blocks up to First Avenue where the Library was located. She was early so she was surprised to see Bill waiting at the entrance.

"I thought I better be on time today," Bill explained with a smile.

"And well you should, Lieutenant," she replied with an impish grin. "Have you been here before Bill? It's a beautiful building."

She led him past the inevitable security guard and magnetometer, through the Great Hall, and into the Main Reading Room. She thought it quite spectacular. It was a large circular space situated directly under the building's dome. The ceiling arched to five stories and ornate colonnades were spaced around its periphery. In the center was a circular desk where the librarians sat, and around them were rows of desks arranged in concentric circles. The effect was inspiring, like entering a Gothic Cathedral. Caitlin had occasionally wondered if its architect had intended that. Maybe he thought that lofty Congressmen would occupy this room, doing their own research on pending legislation. That was certainly not the case in this era. Minions like Caitlin now did it for them and the Reading Room had become principally an architectural site for tourists to admire.

Caitlin resumed her lecture. "I come here usually not to find books, but to talk to the librarians about some obscure subject. They seem to know where to find information about anything. Notice that they're practically all women? There's a good reason for that. Remember at home when you couldn't find something, who did you ask? Not your Dad. He was hopeless, but Mom seemed to know where everything was. Same situation here. Women simply make better librarians."

She stopped and caught her breath, "But I'm running on like a tour guide. Let's go downstairs and get a table where we can work. It's not open to the public but like I mentioned before, my job entitles me to 'stack privileges.' That means I can wander about the shelves where the paper books are stored. They have a few work tables there where we can work without disturbing others."

Bill followed her down the steps and sat at the table she selected. "The last few days have been a learning experience for me, Caitlin. I learned my great grandfather and I have a lot in common. He went

CHAPTER 49

to the Naval Academy, just like me. And he was an intelligence officer, just like me."

"Sounds like your's is a Navy family."

"Well, almost," he corrected, "Three of the last four generation's were Navy."

"Oh, my," Caitlin interjected, "Who was the black sheep?"

"That was my grandfather. He was a 60's beatnik–but then he got married, rejoined the middle class, and went to law school!"

"Oh, my," Caitlin observed, "What a turnaround!"

"Well, it wasn't a total turnaround. For example, he didn't really approve of his son–my father–going to the Naval Academy, but it was free and because he did a lot of *pro bono* work he was short of money. So my father went, and then I went, and here I am." He held up his hand. "Wait, I'm getting off track. We're here to talk about our great grandfathers. So let me tell you what I've learned."

"My pencil is poised and I'm ready to take notes," Caitlin teased.

"I've learned he was a pretty neat guy." Bill emptied the contents of the large manila envelope he was carrying onto the table. "These are some letters and newspaper items my mother has saved. Based on this one press piece," he said, separating it out from the others. "It appeared in his hometown newspaper early in the War. He was apparently some sort of an intelligence aide to a Captain on the staff of the CNO–that's Chief of Naval Operations, the guy who runs the Navy. Anyway, he and this Captain spent some time in Hawaii during the first six months of the War. No one seems to have any information about exactly what they were doing there, but just before the Battle of Midway, my great grandfather–who incidentally was also name Bill–volunteered to join the crew of an aircraft carrier, the *Yorktown*. It had been badly damaged in another battle and before it could fight at Midway it needed a lot of repairs, new aircraft, and new crewmen. With much struggle, they managed to get it all together and sailed into the Battle of Midway with my great grandfather aboard. The Japanese attacked and badly damaged the *Yorktown*–so badly that the ship's captain ordered everybody to abandon ship. They did, but the ship didn't sink. The next morning there it was, listing to port but still afloat. Its captain decided to board it again and try to tow it back to Pearl. He asked for volunteers and

THE DOOLITTLE IRONY

again, my great grandfather raised his hand. But only a few hours after they got back on board, the ship was struck again by torpedoes and a second 'abandon ship' order was issued. This time the ship did sink, but the Navy recognized the courage of those who went back on board with a Navy Cross."

While Bill was talking, Caitlin had taken out her own package of materials. "That's a good start, Bill," she said holding her own package aloft, "These are letters that my mother inherited from her mother," Caitlin said and started shuffling thru them. "Here's one from 1942. That's about the time of the Midway Battle. Oh look at this, Bill, we may have hit on something! It indicates my great grandmother was in Hawaii working as a nurse at the time. I guess she was a Navy Nurse because it's the return address lists 'Ensign' Kelly. She must have just joined the Navy because she says she couldn't figure out what time 1800 was without counting on her fingers." Caitlin paused and interjected wryly, "I'd have that trouble too." Then she continued, "She mentions my great grandfather. He was apparently in Hawaii then also. Maybe that's where they met. She seems very happy. Oh wait, here's another letter dated just a week later. She talks of an engagement party that's to be held for her and Hiro. Engagement? After only a week on the Island? Wow, that must have been a whirlwind courtship!"

"They must have met before," Bill ventured. Then, looking at another letter, he asked, "What was the name of the town where she was raised? Was it Crawford, Washington? I got a letter here that my great grandfather sent to my great grandfather that mentions that name. He apparently had met a guy in Hawaii who knew a girl in Crawford, Washington. The guy proposed to her on one of those one-way phone conversations where you had to say 'over.' It was apparently hilarious, but it worked. She accepted."

Then Bill's brow furrowed and he looked across the table at Caitlin, "Wait. Didn't I just hear you say Hiro? That's the name of the guy that proposed on the phone."

"Yes, that was my great grandfather's name. Hiro, Hiro Yamada. So they did know one another! Wow, what a coincidence."

Bill nodded, "I should say! Seventy-five years later and here we are reading their mail. Let's keep going. Maybe we can find out more."

CHAPTER 49

"Here's one that mentions a Captain High. I'll bet that he's the guy your father worked for, Bill," Caitlin said, "Anyway my great grandmother thought he was pretty neat. She says he paid for their engagement party."

She paused, "You know, this just doesn't fit. Great grandmother didn't get married to Hiro until 1945. That's two and a half years later. That seems like an unusually long engagement, even for wartime."

Another pause and then, "Oh, and Bill, here's something really interesting. My great grandfather was a spy! Here my great grandmother talks about how everyone at the engagement party made sly references to it. Hiro has never told her about it but she thinks that explains his long absence after they graduated."

"*They graduated?*" Bill repeated, "Sounds like they went to school together."

"Maybe," Caitlin speculated, "I know that he graduated from the University of Washington. Maybe she did too. Let's check it out."

She moved to a computer console, entered a user name and password and said, "Let's see what the mighty-and-all-knowing Library of Congress knows about it." Her fingers moved nimbly across the keyboard, "Yes, here's the graduation list for 1941 and sure enough, there's my great grandfather, Hiro Yamada, listed in the School of Engineering. Now for the School of Nursing, yes, there she is, Kathleen Kelly. So they were college sweethearts!"

"Yeah, it looks that way, Caitlin," Bill observed, "But they must have been a controversial couple: Irish and Japanese, White and Yellow, not so good. Back then Japanese were treated like dirt. It wasn't long after this that they were herded off to internment camps. Do you know about that?"

"Yes, my parents made me read all about it when I was in elementary school, but this brings it home. You know, Bill, it's sad to think that Hiro and Kathleen suffered because of that. Today being Asian is considered cool. I mean if you're Asian people think you probably went to Yale or Harvard, or you're a concert pianist or something like that."

"Times change," Bill asserted, "like being gay. Twenty years ago it was a no-no. Today they're trendy. Who's to say what's right or wrong. Kind of makes you wonder what things we consider unacceptable today will be quite acceptable tomorrow."

THE DOOLITTLE IRONY

"Wait," Caitlin pleaded, "That whole subject is way too heavy for a Saturday morning. Let's get back on track. The question I want to answer is why was it so long–two and a half years–between Hiro and Kathleen's engagement and their marriage. I wonder if they lived together during that period."

"Lived together? Caitlin this was 1942. People didn't just 'live together.' That was a definite no-no."

"Yes, I can understand that. No birth control pills. But I wonder if they didn't have a few weekends when they threw caution to the winds. Two and a half years is a long time for an engaged couple to wait. Sex is a powerful drive."

Bill looked over at Caitlin sitting with her long legs crossed and her breasts pressing against her blouse, "Yeah, I agree with that," he replied weakly.

Not entirely oblivious of the significance of Bill's remark, Caitlin returned to the subject at hand, "So we've established that Hiro and Kathleen were classmates, he proposed on the overseas phone, she joined him in Hawaii, and two and a half years later they were married."

"Yes," Bill responded, "And we've also established that your great grandfather and mine knew one another in Hawaii."

"Bill," Caitlin exclaimed holding up a letter, "Here's something more on that. Kathleen is describing the engagement party to her mother, and she adds that Hiro volunteered to go aboard the Yorktown, just like your great grandfather did. They were both intelligence officers, so maybe they went together."

Bill nodded agreement, "Yes that would seem likely."

Caitlin continued, "Then Kathleen goes on to say that Hiro volunteered to serve on the *Yorktown* just to prove that Japanese-Americans are as patriotic as White Americans. He's apparently quite obsessed with making that point."

Again, Bill nodded agreement and then added a suggestion, "You know, Caitlin, we have quite a few letters, press clippings and whatever. It might be more orderly if we sorted them chronologically into a single pile. I'm afraid if we continue to read them randomly, we might miss something."

CHAPTER 49

"Good idea, Lieutenant Junior Grade," Caitlin said with mock gratitude, "I'm pleased to see that the Navy has instilled orderly, military ways in its young officers."

"No smart ass remarks, please," Bill retorted dryly.

The sorting took about 10 minutes, and when they finished they had a single sheaf of items. "OK," Bill said, "Now let's both go through them together, one-by-one." And so they started.

Bill was first. "Here's one where Kathleen describes to her mother that Hiro is apparently missing in action. Bill returned from the *Yorktown* sinking and told her that he and Hiro had become separated during the battle, but he said he was confident Hiro would show up. Kathleen could tell, however, that he really thought Hiro was dead. She's distraught."

Caitlin read the next. "It's another letter she wrote to her mother just a week later. She's been meeting with Bill and his boss. They've looked everywhere they could think of but Bill is nowhere to be found. The War Department sent a telegram to Hiro's mother saying that he is missing in action. If it turns out he is dead, Kathleen would like to return home, but now she's a Navy Nurse and has to see out the war. She's thinking about transferring to a hospital ship, just to get away from all her memories of Hiro in Honolulu."

"But there's a happy ending to this episode," Bill announced holding the next letter aloft, "In this letter, also to her mother, she writes in huge letters across one whole page, 'HE'S ALIVE!' She tells her Mom that now she will be able to see Hiro every day, even though they cannot marry. Oh, and get this. Kathleen adds in parentheses, 'Don't worry Mom. We're not doing anything bad.' Can you believe that? Then she adds sadly that Bill and Captain High had to leave. She's become quite fond of them and fears she will never see them again."

"Oh look, Bill," Caitlin said holding up the next letter. "Here's one from your father. I see his name is also Bill. "Was every male child in your family named Bill? Are you like George Forman's family?" she asked trying to be facetious. She looked up from the letter to see his reaction. Blank face. "Actually, our family's the same way," she admitted, "But we did add a little variation. In every generation there's been at least one daughter named 'Kathleen' or some version of it: Catherine, Kate, and now me, Caitlin."

THE DOOLITTLE IRONY

Bill looked a bit impatient.

"OK, I digress," Caitlin admitted, "Let's get back to it." She re-focused on the letter, "Anyway the letter's dated a few weeks after he and Captain High left Hawaii. Oh, wait, it looks like the Captain was sent to Australia at the last minute. Your great grandfather apologizes to Hiro and Kathleen for not being able to visit their families. He says he will write to them. In fact, here is one of his letters," Caitlin continued, "It's to Kathleen's parents in Crawford. He goes on about how strong and brave their daughter is, and he reassures them that she is safe. He also praises Hiro, and says that he will make a good husband and take good care of their daughter."

"OK," Bill said, continuing with the next letter, "Now this one is from Hiro's sister, Avaron, to Kathleen. She thanks Kathleen for her letter and says that the telegram from the War Department that Hiro was missing in action terrified her parents. Papa-san is not well and the shock was almost too much for him. But then the family received a personal telegram from Captain High reporting that Hiro turned up safe, and Papa-san rallied just as soon as he heard. She says that if Kathleen knows Captain High to thank him for his kindness."

"This letter skips ahead to late September 1942," Caitlin announced, "It's pretty grim. Natsuko writes to Kathleen that her family has been moved from Camp Harmony to a new place at Minidoka, Idaho. She says it's a huge camp that holds about 10,000 people. It's in the high desert, flat, dusty, and windblown. The whole camp is enclosed by barbed wire with machine gun towers every few hundred feet—and the guns point inward! It consists of numerous barracks-like structures, built of clapboard siding and tarpaper roofs. The family's quarters are small—hardly 15 feet wide and 30 feet long—and the dust blows right through the cracks between the wall and floor boards. She says it gets into the food, into their clothing and into other unmentionable places. She ends on a wry note. She says, 'At least they don't call it some phony name like Camp Harmony. It's The Minidoka War Relocation Center.'"

Bill smiled, "I think I would have liked Natsuko."

"Yes, me too," Caitlin said, and then observed sadly, "You know, I feel a little like a voyeur, Bill. These people are all now dead but here we are peeking into their lives, sharing a time with them that's more

CHAPTER 49

than 75 years past. I choke up a bit when I read some of this. Maybe it's the genetic connection."

Bill nodded, "Yeah, maybe. Talking of genetics, it's a little sobering to think that if some of these events had gone just a little differently, you or I may not be here at all."

"Yes, that IS sobering," Caitlin agreed emphatically, "So before we go completely bonkers, let's get back to the letters."

"OK. I guess I'm next," Bill conceded, "I like this one. It's from Captain High to his wife, dated November. He writes that Bill—my great grandfather—is a responsible, honorable young man and the Captain's wife should not worry about him dating their older daughter. I guess when Bill went back to Washington he visited Captain High's family and started dating my great-grandmother. Isn't it kind of funny, Caitlin, parents then had the same concerns as parents do today. Everything changes but nothing changes!"

Caitlin reflected on that but chose not to philosophize. She went back to the task at hand, "Here is the first letter we have that's dated 1943." she announced, "It's from Kathleen to her mother. She relates that for the last six months she and Hiro have been very happy with one another. They both worked long hours but could still find time to spend together. But now that has ended. Hiro has now received orders to Washington. His boss, a Commander Rochefort, has apparently taken Hiro under his wing and wants him to become a cryptanalyst. He's arranged a transfer so he can work under a woman named Driscoll back in OP-20G, whatever that is. I guess she is an expert."

"Wow, I'm impressed," Bill said, "Your great grandfather traveled in elite circles. Joe Rochefort and Agnes Meyer Driscoll are legends in Naval Intelligence."

Bill waved a letter in the air, "Here's another one from Hiro's family to Kathleen dated March 1943. This one is from Avaron and she talks of a guy named Stanley. He's apparently been quite kind to them… sent blankets which Avaron said the family desperately needed because the winter is so cold… also sent rice and canned fish. She says the family was ecstatic that Mama was again able to cook rice. Even Papa felt better because of it."

Caitlin was next. "Here's a letter from Kathleen to her parents dated August of '43. She reports that Hiro has been sent to

THE DOOLITTLE IRONY

Washington temporarily, and from there will go on to an assignment on an aircraft carrier. She doesn't expect to see him for a long time, so she has volunteered and been accepted for duty aboard the *USS Solace*, a Navy hospital ship. She's flying to join the ship in New Zealand and expects it to sail around the South Pacific treating servicemen wounded in the island campaigns there."

Bill took his turn. "This next letter is from Hiro to Kathleen. He reports that he has completed his 60 days temporary duty with Agnes Meyer Driscoll. He says she is really bright and taught him a lot about cryptanalysis, but he doubts that he will specialize in the field. He thinks it's too cerebral for him. He'd prefer to get away from a desk. He also reports he is now aboard his new ship. He won't say its name because of security–loose lips sink ships–but he does say he'll be back in the Pacific soon."

"Hmm," mused Caitlin as she moved to the computer, "I'm checking the Navy records now." A few taps on the key board followed. "It looks like it was the *USS Bunker Hill*. It was launched in December and commissioned in May, then assigned to the Pacific. That's probably the one."

"Look at this," Bill said glancing at the next envelop, "It's an official letter from Stanley's Draft Board. They say they cannot re-classify him from 2-B (Deferred, occupation essential to War effort) to Classification 1-A (Available, fit for military service). It goes on to say that, 'Your wish to join the Marines is laudable, but the 2-B classification not only exempts registrants from being drafted, it prohibits them from serving on active military duty.' I guess Stanley was trying to volunteer for combat but his job was too important. I wonder what he did?"

"OK, it's my turn again," Caitlin said moving back to their worktable, "Here's another one from the Captain to his wife. He's pleased to note that she has come to the same assessment of Bill Russo as he had, i.e., he is a fine young man. He also mentions that he is glad Bill has been promoted to Lieutenant Commander and is being assigned to the CINCPACFLT intelligence staff in Honolulu. With any luck the Captain thinks he may get to see him back there."

Bill looked across the table at Caitlin and said, "I hate to read this next one. It's dated May 1944 and in it Avaron advises Stanley

CHAPTER 49

that Papa-san has died. She says that in Japanese families a funeral is traditionally arranged by the eldest son, but Hiro is gone so would Stanley please take his place? Avaron explains that Papa will be cremated, in keeping with both Shinto and Buddhist customs. The family will not tell Hiro or Kathleen because they don't want to worry them." Bill paused, and then added sadly, "Life sure has been brutal to the Yamada family!"

"Wait, here's another one from Avaron, this time it's to Kathleen," Bill said, "I might as well read it too. Avaron does not mention Papa's death, but she reports that she is leaving the Camp to attend college in the East. Apparently a number of young Nisei in camp are going to school on the East Coast and the government is actually encouraging it. She's going to attend Stanley's *alma mater*, the University of Pittsburgh, and stay with some of his relatives there. That's really good news for Avaron but I wonder if Natsuko and her mother will be OK, especially since Papa died. Maybe we'll learn more about that in later letters."

The next letter was rather lengthy so Caitlin read only the highlights. "This one is pretty emotional,' she said, "From Kathleen to her mother. She starts by noting that it's June 1944 and her tour aboard the *Solace* is almost over. In August she will have a year on board. The work has been exhausting both physically and emotionally. She has seen men in great pain, with arms or legs missing, some burned beyond recognition, some having lost their senses staring blankly into space. She wishes she had never seen such horror, but now that she has she feels duty bound to provide the wounded the very best care she can supply.

"But then she shifts gears and gets to an incident that just occurred. The *Solace* is anchored just off Saipan, taking aboard some of the seriously wounded from the fighting on the Island. Japanese artillery shells are landing only 100 yards away and Kathleen is bandaging a young man who she notices is in a sailor's uniform. He tells her he's from the *Bunker Hill*, which she has learned is the aircraft carrier Hiro was assigned to. He tells her that it was hit by not one but two Kamikazes. Kathleen asks if the young man knows Lieutenant Junior Grade (I guess he must have been promoted) Hiro Yamada. 'Oh, you mean the Jap guy? Yeah, I know who he is but I don't know

THE DOOLITTLE IRONY

him.' Kathleen asks, "Was he hurt in the attack?' 'I don't think so,' the sailor replied, 'most everybody hurt was above decks. He would have been below.' Kathleen is relieved but angry as well. She hasn't seen her fiancée in a year, and then finds out that he is only a short distance away, aboard a ship that some suicidal Jap is trying to sink. 'Where is the sense to it all?' she asks."

Bill had listened closely to Caitlin's recap of the letter. "I'm no psychiatrist," he admits, "But it sounds to me like your great grandmother is really tired, suffering from post traumatic stress syndrome. She needs rest."

"Yes, I certainly agree," Caitlin responded, "So at the risk of getting our readings a little out of order, let me skip ahead to this one from her dated September '44. She tells her mother and father that she is safely back in Pearl Harbor, assigned to the Base Hospital. When she left the Island for the *Solace*, she did so to escape memories of Hiro. But since then she's seen so much of the War's horrors that those same memories seem sweet by comparison. Besides there's always the possibility that his ship will get back to Pearl and she'll get to see him. So she's decided to stay on there until the Navy reassigns her or the War ends. She adds that she has been promoted, a fact for which she is glad because now she won't have to call Hiro 'sir.' She draws in a little smiley face after that and signs the letter, 'Your loving daughter, LTjg Kathleen Kelly.' Sounds like she's doing much better."

"Oh, here's one from my side of the family," Bill announces, "It's from Captain High's wife to the Captain and she reports that their daughter's courtship with my great grandfather has been a whirlwind. The two now want to get married before Bill has to ship out to Honolulu. She's worried that the two are being impetuous. Wartime marriages do not have a good track record. She asks the Captain to write to both his daughter and my great grandfather and counsel them to be patient."

"Here's a press item dated October 1944," Caitlin says, "It's an editorial expressing optimism about the progress of the War. Paris has been liberated, Guam re-taken, and the Philippines invaded. There's even some cautious speculation that the War in Europe could be over by Christmas. Well, we know that that didn't work out."

CHAPTER 49

Bill held up the next letter. "Here's one from Kathleen to her parents dated November 1944, and it's really good news. 'Mom, Dad,' she writes, 'I have so much good news. First, I'M GETTING MARRIED! The Navy has decided to allow its nurses to marry other Navy personnel beginning in January–previously we could marry Army or Air Corps men but not Navy. (Weird!) It's a concession to their retention problems–can't keep enough Navy Nurses on duty. PLUS–and I can hardly believe this–Hiro is going to arrive back in Hawaii later this month. His ship has to go back to the States for repairs and his Intelligence Element will be temporarily assigned to CINCPACFLT headquarters. And here's another piece of good news: Bill Russo, our dear Navy friend who I thought we might never see again, is here on the Island also. He and Hiro will be working together while Hiro's here. We've already set 1 January 1945 as the date, and Bill will be our Best Man. How I wish you two were here."

"That really is good news!' Kathleen observed, "And here's some more. It's dated October '44. Avaron tells Kathleen about her new life on the East Coast. She wants to be a nurse, just like Kathleen, so she's enrolled in the University of Pittsburgh School Of Nursing. She lives in a suburb of Pittsburgh named Wilmerding. It's a factory town where they make air brakes. She says the entire area is very smoky. Some days the sun doesn't burn through until 10 o'clock. But she thinks the people are wonderful. They don't mind that she's Japanese. She says one man remarked, 'Japanese? So what? I'm a kraut–*the other enemy!* Besides, here in Wilmerding we got 'em all–hunkies, dagoes, mickies, Johnny Bulls–and now we got a nip. We all get along, and you will too.' Avaron says she works as a waitress at a diner named *Speedy's* and commutes to the University on a street car. She also adds that her chemistry class is very hard!"

That hasn't changed," Caitlin observed, "I almost flubbed Chem 101."

"Okay, Caitlin,' Bill announced, "Here's one you'll like. It's Caitlin describing her wedding. She is ecstatic. First, she says a surprise guest arrived, Captain High. He's being assigned to Admiral Mitscher's staff and will board the *Bunker Hill* when it returns here from Bremerton. 'And MY surprise was,' she writes, 'That you, Dad, had asked him to take his place and give the bride away. When he told me that I cried on his shoulder and hugged him just like he was you!' Then she goes on to describe the wedding. The Chaplain said a Nuptial Mass in the Base Chapel which she reports was beautiful. When the Priest asked 'Who giveth this woman …' Captain High said, 'I do on behalf of her father and mother.' Her matron of honor was the Chief of Nurses at Pearl whom Kathleen has known since her last tour there. As Best Man Bill was resplendent in his dress whites, and she's sending a picture of him to his fiancée back in Washington."

"So," Caitlin interjected, "That means he did not get married but did get engaged. That was the right move! I expect Captain High and his wife approved."

"Kathleen continues," Bill says, "'There must have been a hundred people present. We walked out the door of the Chapel under crossed swords and a hail of rice. People congratulated us and took pictures. There was even an official photographer there. He said the Navy wants to publish our photo as the first wedding under the new regulation permitting Navy Nurses to marry. Then, 'Kathleen continues, 'We had a lavish reception at the Officers' Club and–can you believe this?–we spent our honeymoon at the Royal Hawaiian Hotel compliments of Captain High. (He said he had a credit there from last time.) It was all so wonderful, Mom and Dad. The only things missing were you two."

"After all that good news Kathleen adds a few sobering notes," Bill continues, "She reports that Bill is leaving for Guam soon because Nimitz is moving his command there as an advance Base. In addition, both Hiro and Captain High will embark on the *Bunker Hill* in a few weeks to operate in the Western Pacific. Kathleen says she will worry about their safety."

"Here's an important one," Caitlin says pointing to the letter in her hand, "It's from Natsuko to Hiro, dated January 1945. She tells him that all Japanese families are being released from internment. They've been given no official explanation but some of the friendly guards have told them it's because of a Supreme Court decision, plus the fact that Japan is no longer a threat to the West Coast. Hiro's family will be given train transportation back to Seattle and Stanley is going to meet them. He's kept the house in repair and paid the taxes on their farm. Other families have lost their farms because the gov-

CHAPTER 49

ernment seized them when no one paid the taxes. She suggests that Hiro send a letter to Stanley thanking him for his many kindnesses over the last two-and-a-half years. She adds that the family will be fine and he should not worry."

Then with a big smile Caitlin adds, "And here's a really great letter from Kathleen to her parents. SHE'S PREGNANT! The doctor confirmed it. She's written Hiro but doesn't know yet whether he's received the news. She says if it's a boy she doesn't know whether they'll name it after Stanley, Bill, or Captain High. She adds facetiously that she has never learned Captain High's first name so maybe they'll just call it 'sir'"

"Well," Bill says changing the mood, "Here is a press clipping dated March 1945 which indicates perhaps not all is well. It reads, 'LOCAL JAPANESE MAN KILLED PROTECTING HIS HOUSE FROM DEMONSTRATORS. Mr. Akahito Tanaka was killed yesterday when violence flared outside his home in Crawford, Washington. Anti-Japanese demonstrators led by Mr. Fritz Imhoff had gathered on Mr. Tanaka's lawn and were erecting a sign that read *Japs go back to Japan*. Mr. Tanaka tried to stop them but one of the demonstrators hit him behind the ear with the post they were using to mount the sign. Fritz Imhoff later told reporters, "It was Tanaka's fault. He should not have interfered with American citizens attempting to exercise their rights of free speech." Crawford Chief of Police Kelly said that no arrests have yet been made. Although a number of bystanders saw the attack on Mr. Tanaka, none of them would identify the assailant."

"Uh-huh!" Caitlin exclaimed, "Here's another press clipping dated just a few days later. Fritz Imhoff was found outside his house semi-conscious with both arms broken. Stanley Polasky, who was reported to have had previous encounters with anti-Japanese demonstrators, was initially taken into custody. He was subsequently released when Imhoff refused to place charges."

"OK Stanley, you're my guy!" Bill erupted, thrusting his fist in the air, "Too bad you didn't break his legs too."

"Here's yet a third press item," Caitlin announced, "This one is ominous. 'BUNKER HILL HIT BY JAP SUICIDE BOMBERS On the morning of 11 May 1945, while supporting the invasion of Okinawa, USS *Bunker Hill* was struck and severely damaged by two Japanese *kamikaze* planes. Details have not yet been released by the War Department, other than to confirm that there were casualties. The ship remains afloat and continues to conduct air operations against the Japanese military on Okinawa."

"Attached to that is the very telegram that Kathleen received just a few days later. It's terrible. I don't think I can read it aloud, Bill. Here, you do it."

Bill took the flimsy paper, with ribbons of ticker tape pasted on it, yellowed with age, "It's addressed to LTjg Kathleen Yamada, Pearl Harbor Naval Station. It reads, '*The Navy Department deeply regrets to inform you that your husband, LTjg Hiro Yamada, was killed in action in the performance of his duty and in the service of his country. The Department extends to you its sincerest sympathy in your great loss. On account of existing conditions the body if recovered cannot be returned at present. If further details are received you will be informed. To prevent possible aid to our enemy, please do not divulge the name of his ship or station. Rear Admiral Jacobs, Chief of Naval Personnel.*'"

Bill looked across the table at Caitlin. Tears were streaming down her cheeks and she was trying to suppress a sob. Spontaneously, he reached over and took her hand. Like Caitlin, Bill was moved by the tragic news in the telegram. The two just sat there together, in silence, waiting to recover their composure.

Caitlin spoke first, "Bill, I don't know whether I can continue with this. I thought we were just going to do some family history but now I feel like I've been pulled 75 years into the past and I'm sharing my great grandmother's tragedy. I'm really caught up in this."

"Yeah, me too," Bill agreed, "But I want to continue and see how this all plays out. There are only two more items. Let's finish."

"Okay, but you do the reading. I'll just listen."

Bill nodded and gingerly picked up the next letter and began, "About a month has passed since the telegram arrived advising of Hiro's death, and Kathleen writes, '*Dear Mom and Dad, I was visited by Bill Russo a few days ago. He had promised to get whatever details he could on the Kamikaze attack and he came by to report them to me. He explained that two aircraft hit the carrier, the second just a minute or so after the first. Hundreds of men were killed, hundreds more were*

CHAPTER 49

wounded, and some are still missing. Bill talked to an officer who was there. He said that said he saw Hiro and Captain High having coffee in the wardroom just before the Kamikazes hit. When they struck the flight deck the avgas fuel they were carrying splashed across the deck and its vapors were sucked into the ship's ventilation system and blown into the ship's interior, including the wardroom. Then the vapors detonated like a bomb. The bodies of the men it killed were badly burned and unrecognizable. They had to be buried at sea. Hiro and Captain High were among them. Bill said their deaths would have been instantaneous. They would not have suffered.'

Bill could see tears welling up in Caitlin's eyes, so he hurried on, "This next part of the letter is not quite so intense. She reports that she will arrive back in Seattle on Friday, 1 June. Stanley has agreed to meet her at the airport and drive her back to Crawford. She adds that she is desperate to see her parents again and asks them if she can remain home until the baby comes."

"Oh my god," Caitlin laughs, "She asks her own parents if she can she stay with them? I can't imagine them allowing her to stay anywhere else!"

"There's only one more letter from Caitlin," Bill announced, "It's to Bill Russo and I'll read it aloud.

'Dear Bill, I was so pleased to hear about the birth of your first son–and was not at all surprised to learn you named him Bill. It's family tradition! On that subject, I should apologize to you for NOT naming our son Bill. After all, we did promise. But under the circumstances, I know you'll forgive me for having called him Hiro.

Let's see, there is so much to bring you up to date on since we parted in Hawaii three years ago. Hiro is healthy and bright. His two grandmothers spoil him rotten! But I fear for his future here in this area. There are many Whites who continue to despise the Japanese, even though the war is over. Many of the Nisei who lived in our community and who went to Minidoka have left for the Midwest and the East. Even Hiro's mother and sister are considering a move to the Pittsburgh area to join Avaron, who is about to graduate from college there.

"As for me personally, I remain unmarried and uninterested in getting re-married anytime soon. I think my parents rather thought that Stanley and I would get together, but that type of relationship never *developed between us. We remain dear friends and he adores little Hiro. He dates a girl in his office and I would not be surprised if someday they marry. I am employed as a nurse in the Veteran's Hospital in Seattle. It's a long commute but the bus ride reminds me of Hiro. It's the same bus we used to take to the University of Washington when we were students there. I take my job quite seriously. I believe veteran's health care is a sacred obligation that this country bears toward those men and women who have given so much of their lives to keeping us all free.*

"After hours I devote my time to another cause, one that Hiro cherished: making this country understand how unjust and cruel its internment of Japanese-Americans was. Right now I'm collecting photos and personal accounts from the people who suffered through it. I want to publish those and thereby document the matter for history so in that future America can't simply sweep the internment under the rug and forget it ever happened. I want America to recognize how egregiously the internment departed from the ideals we usually hold sacred. I want it to apologize and pay reparations to the Japanese-Americans who suffered through it. But I'm ranting on. Please tell your wife that someday I hope to meet her and your new son, Bill. Tell her also that I think she's a very lucky woman. Love, Kathleen'"

So that's it, Caitlin," Bill announced, "That is our last letter and, I think a fitting end to our historical research for the day."

"I feel drained, Bill. When we started, these people were just distant relatives. Now I feel as though I know them personally and shared some of their travail. God, they were strong. I really admire them."

"Caitlin," Bill interjected, "Do you realize how late it is? We were here right through lunch and never noticed the time. I'm famished. Let's go get something to eat–but this time not McDonalds. I know a place where we can have a nice meal then sit and talk."

They did just that. They noted that there had been no happy ending for so many of their great grandparents' generation. Widows had to endure lonely lives, raising fatherless children. The wounded were forced to continue as well as they could, impaired, often forgotten, and frequently suffering premature deaths. Those veterans who did undergo combat were left to deal with their post traumatic stress by themselves, and managed their anxieties by simply not talking

CHAPTER 49

about them. America as a whole had been fundamentally altered as the needs of the war accelerated social change to an unhealthy level. Massive population shifts had been necessary to provide labor for wartime industry, and they brought social turmoil to many parts of the country. Gender roles had changed as women left the home to work in factories. Racial tensions were exacerbated as young black soldiers who had fought for "freedom" returned to their still-segregated homes in the South. The ultimate irony was that all their sacrifice was seemingly for naught as tensions with Russia developed into a Cold War that would last through almost the rest of the century.

"You know, Caitlin," Bill commented when the discussion came to a pause, "These are pretty heavy matters for a Sunday evening. We sound more like a class on 20th Century history!"

So the discussion turned to personal matters. They talked of the events, now 75 years past, they had uncovered that day. Were they complete and accurate? Probably not. For example, Bill was skeptical of the story about Hiro going to Japan. Surely, he reasoned, no responsible firm would send a brand new employee to Japan when that country was obviously on the brink of war with the United States. So perhaps he was sent by the U.S. as a spy, under the cover of being a junior engineer. But if that were true, some investigative journalist or historian would almost certainly have uncovered the matter by now and written a bestselling book about it.

Caitlin agreed, and wondered about how Hiro had mysteriously wound up in Hawaii. What had he done before getting there, while he was in Japan? Bill remembered that this was the period during which the Japanese Imperial Navy was rampaging across the Western Pacific, about the time of the Doolittle Raid on Tokyo. He also remembered learning at Annapolis that naval historians still wondered how Doolittle could have achieved surprise considering the Task Force had been sighted by a Japanese picket boat and reported to Japanese Naval Headquarters. But neither Bill nor Caitlin could see how that could possibly have anything to do with Hiro. It would have required a series of events too improbable to even consider. Probably the Japanese just screwed up, just like maybe the engineering firm that sent Hiro to Tokyo screwed up. Caitlin and Bill agreed they simply had no answer and probably never would.

THE DOOLITTLE IRONY

They did, however, note that it was remarkable that they–both progeny of principles in the story–would encounter one another more than 75 years later. Yes, they agreed, it was a highly coincidental, but nothing more. The idea that some inexplicable force had reached through a 75-year time warp and moved them toward one another was a matter for quaint myth, not young adults of the scientifically enlightened 21st Century. Nevertheless, during their talk Caitlin did look across the table and conclude that Bill was indeed "the one." And when Bill walked her back to her row house and caringly kissed her goodnight, he sensed there was something fateful about it. And he remembered his father's counsel, "Women are born with more romantic sense than men develop in a life time. So when you meet 'the one,' just relax and she'll take care of the rest."

EPILOGUE

It took decades for America to come to grips with just how egregious the Internment had been. In 1976 President Gerald Ford admitted it had been a "national mistake." In 1980, Congress appointed the Commission on Wartime Relocation and Internment of Civilians. In February 1983 that Commission issued a report stating that President Roosevelt had had political and racial motives in directing the internment, that its imposition had been influenced by "war hysteria," and that there had been neither military necessity nor valid intelligence to justify it. That same year President Reagan signed the Civil Liberties Act to compensate those Americans of Japanese descent who had been interned. The legislation offered a formal apology and paid $20,000 as recompense to internees or their heirs. It was inadequate reparation for the enormous harm they had suffered, but it was America's material acknowledgement of guilt. In 1992 President H. W. Bush issued this statement: *No nation can fully understand itself or find its place in the world if it does not look with clear eyes at all the glories and disgraces of its past. We in the United States acknowledge such an injustice in our history. The internment of Americans of Japanese ancestry was a great injustice, and it will never be repeated.*

To their credit, Japanese-Americans of that era rose above their tormentors and remained true to the United States, their adopted country. They did not rebel against internment: they cooperated. Over 30,000 of their young men served with distinction in America's military service. Many became intelligence linguists and translators in the Pacific. In Europe they comprised almost all of the 442nd

EPILOGUE

Regimental Combat Team that fought in Italy, one of the most highly decorated combat units in American military history with six Presidential Unit Citations, 21 Medals of Honor, and almost 9,500 purple hearts. As much as any other element of American society, the Japanese-Americans of that day merit the title, "The Greatest Generation."

More than seventy-five years later, America is still beset with immigration problems. People from the Middle East, Africa, the Caribbean, Latin America, and elsewhere are coming to America in numbers that critics see as a threat to America's cultural, political, and economic fabric. Managing that onslaught will test the wisdom of U.S. policymakers. The Japanese-American internment should serve as a cautionary tale for them.

BIBLIOGRAPHY

The Battle of Midway, Thomas C. Hone, editor, U.S. Naval Institute Press, Annapolis, MD

Doolittle After Action Report, War Department, Headquarters of the Army Air Forces, Washington, D.C. https://www.ibiblio.org/hyperwar/AAF/rep/Doolittle/Report.html

Klayton K S Chun, *The Doolittle Raid 1942, America's First Strike Back at Japan,* Osprey Publishing eBook(PDF) 9781846036774

Steven George Bustin, *Humble Heroes, How the USS Nashville CL 43 fought WWII,* Copyright 2007, eISBN: 1-4196-5884-0

The Doolittle Raid, The History and Legacy of the first American Attack on Tokyo during WWII–Charles Rivers Editors, 2015, ASIN: B00RQYLOCQ

I Could Never Be So Lucky Again, an Autobiography by Gen. James H. "Jimmy" Doolittle, with Carol V. Glines, Bantam Books, 1991 eISBN: 978-0-307-42832-5

BIBLIOGRAPHY

Samuel Eliot Morison, *The Two Ocean War: A Short History of the United States Navy in the Second World*, Naval Institute Press, Annapolis, MD, 1963

Winston Groom, *1942: the Year that Tried Men's Souls*, Grove Press, New York

Eliot Carlson, *Joe Rochefort's War: The Odyssey of the Codebreaker Who Outwitted Yamamoto at Midway*, Naval Institute Press, Annapolis MD

James M. Scott, *Target Tokyo, James Doolittle and the Raid that Avenged Pearl Harbor*, W.W. Norton & Company, New York

Richard Reeves, Infamy: The Shocking Story of the Japanese American Internment in World War II, Harry Holt and Company, New York

Alistair Cooke, *The American Home Front 1941-1942*, Grove Press, 2007, ISBN 0802143326

Mary Matsuda Gruenwald, *Looking Like the Enemy: My Story of Imprisonment in Japanese-American Internment Camps*, 2005, Newsage Press, Troutdale, OR

Theresa Lorella, *Japanese Roses; a Novel of the Japanese-American Internment*, ISBN-13: 978-1484849798, 2013

Mary Brockway, *The Willows of Sky Pass*, Wings ePress, Inc. 2013, ISBN 978-1-61309-133-3

David Guterson, *Snow Falling on Cedars*, Haughton, Mifflin, Harcourt, 1994, ISBN 0-15-100443-9

Lightning Source UK Ltd.
Milton Keynes UK
UKHW020126261119
354216UK00014B/290/P